TESSA OF HUNDRFELD

TESSA OF HUNDRFELD

A.L. HEARD

Tessa of Hundrfeld

Front Cover Art by Eva I. / IsThisEva
Map by Saumya Singh @Saumyasvision/Inkarnate
Manuscript Formatting by Hermit Prints

ISBN: 979-8-9911881-4-2 (ebook edition)
ISBN: 979-8-9911881-5-9 (Paperback edition)

Contents

Part Two

Part Three

The Royal Family of Hjorrfold

King Alvis & Queen Ingegerd

- Havardr
- Stigandr
- Ragnhild
- Randel

The House of Hundrfeld

Lord Ingolf & Lady Gudridr

- Reidun & Trond
  - Egil
- Sindri
  - Tessa

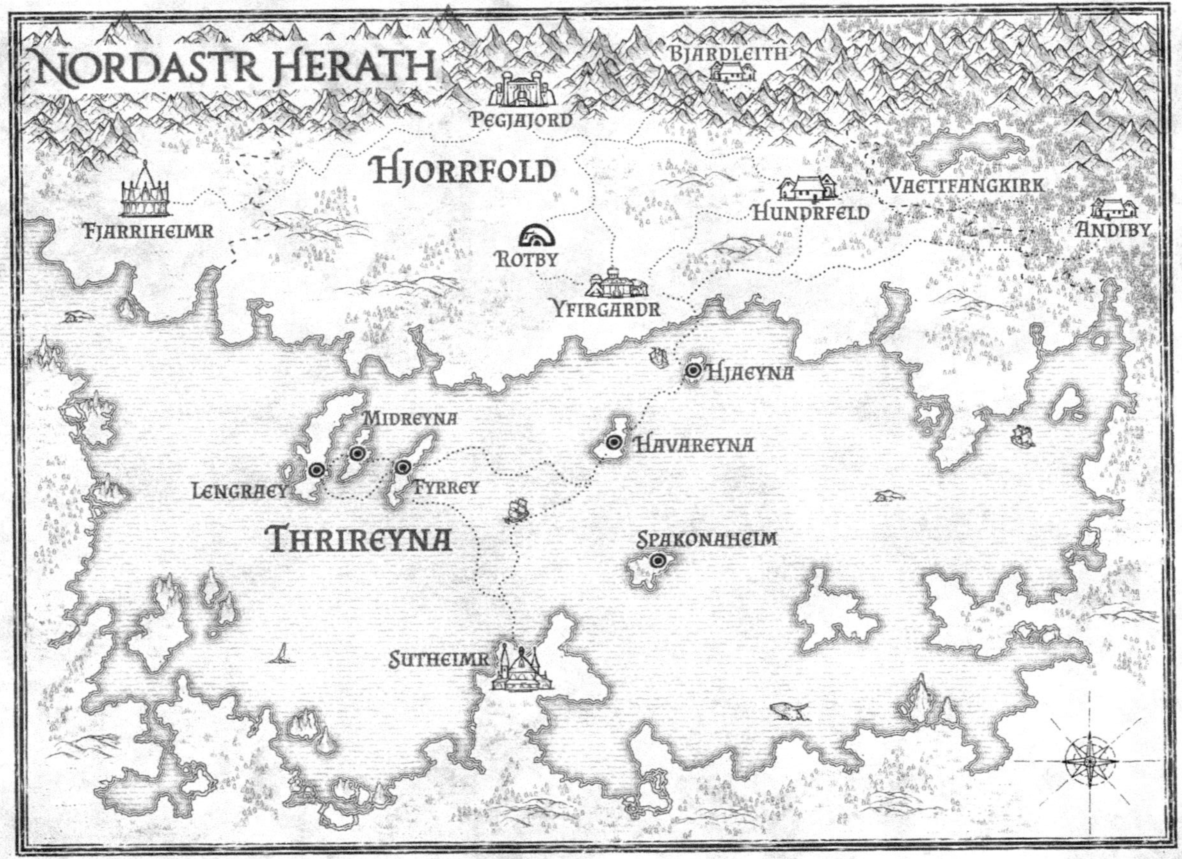
NORDASTR HERATH
BJARDLEITH
PEGJAJORD
HJORRFOLD
FJARRIHEIMR
ROTBY
YFIRGARDR
HUNDRFELD
VAETTFANGKIRK
ANDIBY
HJAEYNA
MIDREYNA
HAVAREYNA
LENGRAEY
FYRREY
THRIREYNA
SPAKONAHEIM
SUTHEIMR

Prologue

From The Book of Ormrdreyri

Tove bears five children, all to die in battle, but their deaths bring more in glory than their lives would bring in coin.

Bo marries the woman of his dreams, to the ruin of his family.

Njal's marriage in a full moon will end in poverty; but in a new moon, the marriage will be prosperous.

Knud's life will be as long as his hair.

Thyra will fail in all raids sailing east.

The edge of a sword is sharper when not dripping in mead, but still sharp nonetheless.

Alvis will succumb to the will of his family: first his wife, then his sons, and lastly his would-be daughter.

A loyal dog will safeguard the child until called to court, but even loyal dogs have fangs.

Havardr will only be the strongest when he's the only brother left, but if he kills them it will only weaken him.

Stigandr wanders north and south and east but will not find his way home again until he goes west.

The Queen's death marks the beginning; the prince's death the end.

The gate works both ways: it protects Hjorrfold's people inside it, but also its enemies outside. It should not be lightly broken and cannot be unbroken.

There will be a warrior prince, born in a winter three seasons long; his birth heralds spring. He must be careful to keep his eye for conquest turned outward lest war follows him back home.

A queen born of shadows will rule all she can reach, a king of equal measure at her side. United, they are less dangerous than apart.

The neglected prince is most dangerous when left to his own devices: a tight leash must be kept on him.

An endless war with no beginning and no end, destruction unimaginable, can only be stopped by a dead man.

Five hundred years after the founding, a great weapon will be born on the witch island. Only the true heir can hope to wield it, though they must know when to strike.

The greatest queen of Hjorrfold will be skjaldmaer like her foreaunt. The greatest skjaldmaer will always be of royal blood, always escorted by their family to the marshes.

Spakonaheim will be due south of the capital on the fifth moon of the following years: 479, 499, 500, 512, 525, 529.

If a son of the crown steps foot on Spakonaheim, it will bring ruin to the worlds.

One brotherly feud will end with another brother's.

A warrior of royal blood will bind his neighbors to his will; a mage of royal blood will rule them.

The royal family must keep their family tree well-pruned or see their own ruin.

When the shackles are broken and the magic flows freely, the shield maidens will fight once more to undo their great mother's betrayal.

When enough blood is spilled, there will be peace in the lands of Hjorrfold.

Part One

I

Havardr

497–500

HAVARDR WAS NO scholar, as his tutors could well attest to. He learned what was required and no more. When the hour glass emptied to mark the end of his lessons, he was out of his seat before the last grain of sand settled; his studies left forgotten so he could find his sword.

The one exception was when he found the book.

His father's library was tucked away on the third floor of the castle, near the rooms where Havardr and his siblings were forced to work with their tutors and where the visiting mages worked. The library was the largest room in the castle, save the Great hall, and it was covered with books from floor to ceiling, a grand waste of space, and it stunk of books and dust. Havardr only went when he was well and truly fed up with his studies, because no one save the royal family was permitted and he could feign some intellectual pursuit or the other when locked inside.

On one such day, when he was only eleven and whiling away a gray-skyed afternoon, he discovered the book by accident. He'd been stacking gold coins on the edge of a chair, bargaining with himself that he could stay here so long as the coins didn't tumble to the ground, when they inevitably fell. As he bent down to collect them, he noticed the tome in an abandoned corner of a bookshelf, pushed so far back one could hardly see it. It was the golden words on the spine that drew his attention, brighter than his coins even under the layer of dust that obscured the runes.

"Ormrdreyri," he read aloud, saying each syllable one at a time as he decoded the runes. The book was thicker and heavier than any he'd ever seen. Havardr doubted many besides himself could lift it; that was how he knew it was important.

Knowing nothing else, he stole it away to his room that night. He couldn't very well be caught with it, so he waited until most of the keep had gone to sleep and the mages and tutors were long gone before he returned for his prize and locked his bedroom door behind him. People would notice if Havardr, the prince who scorned reading, was suddenly engrossed in a book. He couldn't afford their curiosity. The secrets hidden inside would be for him alone.

It was a book of prophecy, and those prophecies would be his.

Only the most ancient of books and inscriptions used the runic language—mage and witch gibberish, the old language of his long-dead forefathers. Havardr could read runes, but poorly. He'd been forced to learn the rudiments, just as he'd had to learn some magic rites: necessities for any future king.

"*If* you become king," his father always said scornfully. "It is a privilege to be earned, not one handed down on a whim." King Alvis had had a second son after Havardr, then a daughter and another son, as if he couldn't be sure to get a reasonable heir without so many options.

Havardr would ensure that the kingdom needed none but him. It was his birthright as the eldest, and a warrior besides. He would sit on the throne of Hjorrfold, or none would, and the prophecies would make sure of it.

It took him many long hours to make any progress translating the runes. He thought it would be the work of a few days, but the weeks dragged on. He spent many late nights by candlelight, piecing together the clues hidden in the runes, and only after several moons did he realize he'd wasted his time: he was reading prophecies about centuries long passed and people long dead. In anger, he crumbled up the parchment with his scribbled translations and nearly threw it in the fire... until he saw the opportunity it presented.

Carefully, he smoothed out the pages and checked the histories to confirm the words safeguarded there. They were true, almost every prophecy, and for the few that weren't, it helped him hone his translations as he learned what he was doing wrong. As he worked line by line, he grew confident he was one of the best runic readers in all of Hjorrfold, though no one would ever know it.

He jumped ahead in the book. Again and again, dozens of pages at a time, until he recognized more and more of the names and events. His great-great uncle who had died without an heir after suffering a magical ailment. His great-grandmother, who had built the stables outside of Yfirgardr. His grandparents, who had disappeared on a raid to the far lands (and, according to the prophecies, had died most painful deaths). At last, nearly three-quarters of the way through the book, he saw hints of his parents, of himself and his siblings, and he concentrated on these entries with renewed fervor.

The witches who'd recorded these words hadn't been as discerning as Havardr would've liked: pages upon pages contained nothing but meaningless notes on peasants and the movement of stars. Eventually, he'd whittled it down to the relevant parts and put all his efforts into extracting as much knowledge as he could.

It was the only time in the whole of his life that he neglected his training, too weary during the day to care much about his sparring matches. His brother and his sister bested him more often than not, despite being so much younger than him.

"You've lost your edge," his brother Stigandr taunted after he'd disarmed Havardr. Again. The runt wasn't destined for the blade—he was marked to be a mage and only trained in warcraft by the same rule that forced Havardr to learn some rudimentary magic, so that they might be knowledgeable kings when the time came—but he'd beaten Havardr six matches in a row. Magical trickery or not, Havardr shouldn't ever lose to him.

The boy wasn't even ten, and Havardr was nearly a man grown. He'd have to do better so no one got suspicious. Next time he'd slam Stigandr into the dust and wipe that smug look from his face.

"Must be," Havardr agreed, though he knew in truth he was gaining an edge. He would endure his little brother's insolence because it wouldn't matter in the end. He was certain he'd read about Stigandr's death already, and it would be well before his own.

A full three years after he'd found the book, his nights spent unlocking its secrets and how best to wield them, it was time to act. If what he read was true, had little time to waste: it was already the 500th year, and he could not afford to let the last few months slip away or he'd lose his best chance with it. With a final push, he wrote down everything that might be relevant and, at last, he was done.

First, he burned the book.

Then, he summoned Sindri of Hundrfeld.

Hundrfeld's keep was among the first that had sworn fealty to Yfirgardr, so long ago they were nearly as noble as Havardr's own family from how many marriages and alliances the two families had struck. Sindri was of an age with him, and by virtue of their shared nobility, they had spent many years together as Sindri trained at court each spring. They had sparred together, hunted together, and when they'd grown the first tufts of a beard at the cusp of manhood, they'd raided together. They were good friends, closer than Havardr was with his blood siblings, and he knew he could trust Sindri.

"Let's sail together," Havardr said when Sindri arrived. Sindri was as tan as ever, his hair blonder even than Havardr's from the sun and his eyes a dark gray like a winter storm. He was lean and lithe and handsome, his only fault was the crooked nose he'd earned on his first raid; he'd never let anyone get the better of him after that.

"Of course, brother." He grinned wide, always easy smiles when it was the two of them. "Where to?"

Sindri was always up for an adventure.

"A raid on the islands," he said. That was all he could offer while they were still at Yfirgardr. The city was crowded, and the keep's walls had ears; he didn't dare say more where someone might overhear. Particularly his parents or his siblings, who would surely put a stop to his plans. They'd think him reckless and conniving; he couldn't disagree with the latter.

"The islands?" Sandri's eyes brightened. He'd never seen the sea until he'd come to Yfirgardr, and he'd fallen in love with it the first time he set foot on a dreki, though he couldn't swim or sail worth a damn.

"Aye. My father's gifted me a dreki of my own for my name day." It was a small ship that could barely hold the crew necessary to sail it. No doubt his father had chosen such a vessel so that Havardr couldn't go too far and thus couldn't cause too much trouble. Unfortunate, because he had quite far to go on this trip, but for the best: it was crucial they had as few men with them as possible.

It'd be less suspicious when they didn't make it back.

"Your own dreki." Sindri whistled. "A kingly gift indeed."

Havardr preened at this. Sindri knew Havardr craved the throne and knew how much he deserved it. All the glory he'd won, all the plunder he'd brought home; Stigandr, with his books and his magic, could never lead a raid.

It was easier than he'd hoped to convince his father to let them sail; it was his mother who protested.

Queen Ingegerd was in many ways a reflection of her eldest son. With long, sandy locks and a stern expression that Havardr recognized all too well from his looking glass, she looked more regal on the throne than his father despite her lowly birth. She clutched her handful of bones and runes and other talismans, then threw them on the stone floor before the dais, their clattering echoing throughout the Great Hall. Though Havardr was closer to the casting than her, he could barely make out the symbols and wondered how she could read their secrets from her gilded chair.

"The omens are bad," she said, turning to her husband and ignoring her son. She often ignored Havardr and his sister Ragnhild, the two children who'd been given to the sword. As a mage, she looked down on them, he was certain, and favored Stigandr and the baby Randel, the two boys she'd be allowed to teach in her own ways.

If only their father, a warrior like him, would show the same favoritism, but he preferred to be seen as 'fair.'

"Do the omens say the boy will die?" Alvis asked his wife, with less scorn than Havardr would've liked, but enough to show he didn't believe her nonsense.

"He might wish he had," Queen Ingegerd said darkly. "But no, he will sail and he will return, but this will reap nothing good."

Good for whom? Havardr wondered. She was right that he would do a great deal that would turn out poorly for those opposed to him, and her reading made him only more sure he was on the right course.

"But nothing bad?" Havardr prodded.

His mother finally cast her gaze on him. Her eyes were a dark blue that reminded him of the sea on a summer's day: beautiful and unwelcoming.

"The omens are bad," she repeated haughtily. "He should stay in Yfirgardr until the season's end." Her eyes flickered to the talismans. "Until the year's end would be best."

Havardr balked at this, but before he could protest, his father intervened on his behalf. "Wife, I value your council as always, but I see no harm in this. It doesn't seem to pertain to the matter we recently discussed..." He paused, giving Ingegerd a cryptic look. She nodded; he continued. "So I say we let the boy go. You say no harm will come to him, so allow him this trip with his friend. If any ill comes of it, then he will learn to heed the omens as he should."

She arched an eyebrow at him, as if asking, '*And if no ill comes of it?*' She didn't protest, though she eyed Sindri warily, and Havardr wondered at that. She'd been curt to Sindri of late, a change that had happened not long after Randel was born. Havardr never challenged her on it because he didn't care about his mother's moods (or her omens, so new in comparison to the prophecies he'd found).

With his father's blessing, he arranged the trip and set sail.

Due south, straight to Spakonaheim.

2

Ingegerd

501

QUEEN INGEGERD TUNED out the petitioners pleading for justice and traced the compass on her neck as she thought. Her husband, the ever-revered and esteemed King Alvis, would all too happily deal out verdicts to the line of peasants who'd come to the throne for arbitration. She only attended in case he was stumped or if someone requested a reading, then she would cast their lots and interpret the omens. None here today would ask, though; those who believed sought her council in private, away from the Great Hall and its king.

It wasn't that they didn't respect her or her abilities. There was a power in prophecy that demanded secrecy. It was better suited to the quiet seclusion of the queen's sitting room, not the watchful, greedy crowd that sought the king.

The Great Hall was, indeed, the largest hall she'd ever seen. The ceilings towered some fifty feet over them, lined with torches so high they needed to be lit by magic. Columns lined each side, leading guests from the tall wooden doors directly to the dais where her and her husband's thrones sat, raised so they might see over the heads of those who visited. A hundred, perhaps two, might crowd inside, though she'd never seen such numbers.

Ingegerd spared a glance at her husband, his brow furrowed in concentration as he listened to the farmer before him prattle on about goats or beets or some such nonsense. She knew he cared for it no more than she did, but he put on a good show for the people. She'd give him that.

Theirs wasn't a love match by any means, and over the years she'd grown to resent her husband and his ego. He himself had a healthy respect for magic wielders, but his councilors and nobles didn't, and that attitude had pervaded the people. Oh, the common folk believed in the power and utility of magic. Ask any parent whose child ailed, and they would beg for a healer's magic, yet there was no prestige in being the wielder of those remedies.

The nobles were coldly polite to her, their queen, but mistrustful of the mages at court. As if magic wasn't holding the entire kingdom together. It was woven into the land itself, a radiance she'd felt when she first left her home of Andiby and crossed the border into Hjorrfold. It had surprised her how deeply rooted the magic here was, when there were so few mages compared to Andiby. Decades she'd lived in Yfirgardr and still it could leave her breathless how strongly the magic clung to this place.

And yet, magic craft had fallen out of fashion among the nobles here centuries ago, so they couldn't understand how she clung to it so tightly. Did they think half the royal children were given to magic without reason? The only common magic in Hjorrfold was the small magic used by peasants and servants. If not for the royal family, there would be none of the mages and witches who frequented court; they would seek patronage and respect in other lands.

They scoff and doubt, but magic like mine keeps death from overtaking this kingdom . . .

But Alvis, for all his faults, knew this. All the rulers of Hjorrfold respected the magic of the land, the blessing and the curse of maintaining the balance of blade and mage. It was why Alvis had personally come to her people to seek their strongest daughter for marriage. And she'd gone willingly, accepted his hand in exchange for her people's continued independence. No tithes or tributes paid, no danger of raids or skirmishes, but access to Hjorrfold's vast well of magic.

Though Alvis didn't know that last condition. Smart as he was and as much as he knew about his magical responsibilities as king, it would require a more nuanced understanding of blood magic to realize how thoroughly his kingdom was bound to its royal house. In truth, the magic was beyond Ingegerd's grasp, too bound to her husband's bloodline for her to access, but she understood enough: if her people's blood sat on the throne, her people could draw from Hjorrfold's magic.

Though perhaps the people of Andiby were no longer hers to claim.

She moved her fingers from the grooved edges of the compass to its surface, letting her nails catch on the nearly invisible markings along the gold surface. Unfortunately, it only held the power to show her the way back home, not the way forward. It would never be of much use to her now that she was permanently installed in Yfirgardr. She knew in her bones she would never leave this city again. She didn't mind: her work was here, in the castle walls.

The large wooden door that separated the Great Hall from the private areas of the keep opened, and the room fell silent as her son entered, flanked on both sides by members of the city guard. Curious, Ingegerd stopped fidgeting with her compass and sat up straighter.

Havardr was up to something. Her son, full of youthful bravado, wasn't subtle. He was, however, very determined. She needn't ever wonder what his aim was. He'd made it very clear when his brother was born that he meant himself to be king. Only seven, and he couldn't handle competition.

So while she didn't know what had spurred Havardr on his mysterious raid with his boyhood friend a year ago, she knew he did it because he felt it would aid him in his quest to become king. She hadn't wanted him to go, not because she cared which of her children would next wear the crown, but because she neither trusted her eldest son nor liked the omens she'd seen before the trip.

That Havardr and Sindri had come back alone, the rest of the crew dead, should have vindicated her concerns. The deaths of a few raiders from humble backgrounds had stirred little interest at court. So long as the two noble youths had returned alive, then no one had noticed the loss of the other men.

Ingegerd had noticed, as she'd noticed the haunted look on Sindri's face when they'd returned. As she'd noticed he'd left immediately and hadn't returned to Yfirgardr in the months since.

"I request leave to travel to Hundrfeld," Havardr said. "For a hunting trip."

A formality. He'd never been denied a trip within the realms of Hjorrfold, and certainly not to see Sindri. Despite Ingegerd's dislike for the youth and his damned dogs, there was no politic way to end the friendship: they were both of high blood, the same age, and in love with the blade. They'd fight and raid together until the day one of them died of it, she was certain.

"Of course," Alvis said, somewhat irritably. This request could have easily been made in private, yet Havardr was before them with a full crowd in attendance. He did this often, no doubt trying to make his presence known among the people of Yfirgardr. What a delight it would be for them to have seen not only the king and queen, but the prince, too!

He, of course, wore his best cloak—black wolf fur trimmed with white hare—and had styled his blond hair with an iron band engraved with battle scenes from his forefathers. It wasn't a crown, but from a distance, it looked like a royal diadem. That, combined with his confident, regal bearing, gave the look of an heir apparent.

It was insolent, and neither king nor queen appreciated the small ways he attempted to usurp authority.

Ingegerd didn't envy her other children the difficulty they'd have managing him should he not become king. He wasn't one to give up power without a fight.

"Aren't you going to check the omens?" Havardr looked at her defiantly. Inwardly, she sighed. The more he tried to seem kingly, the haughtier he appeared. It was embarrassing that she'd produced such a son.

There was no need to check the omens. Any danger Hundrfeld posed was years away, and it wouldn't come from Sindri. The boy looked at Havardr like he'd hung the moon. He'd die for Havardr and his honor long before he allowed him harm. At least right now, he would. Should either marry…

It didn't matter. That was a consideration for another time, and she wouldn't check the star charts for such childish reasons.

"Are you worried?" she asked sweetly, matching his insolence step for step. "I didn't think a prince of this household would be concerned about traveling within his own kingdom such a short distance."

Instantly, his expression soured into a scowl. "I'm not concerned—"

"Or perhaps you worry whatever beast you mean to hunt will best you?"

His face darkened to an angry red. "Of course not—"

"Then I needn't check the signs. We agree, there is no danger. No catastrophe to circumvent in this friendly visit and ordinary hunt. I shouldn't wish to delay your trip when there is no greater danger than a spooked horse. Please pass on our well wishes to Sindri and his family, and we await your return."

The court seemed to hold its breath. They didn't understand what was going on, but only a fool would miss the tension between mother and son. All eyes turned to Alvis. Would he disagree with his wife? What would it mean if he did?

He didn't disagree. He rarely did in public, and he wouldn't after the last time she'd cast omens for Havardr and they'd both ignored her.

"Be well, my son," was all Alvis said, dismissing him with a look and turning his attention to the next petitioners.

If Ingegerd at all cared about the petitioners, she would've missed it. She'd have looked away from her son as he left and not caught the way he smirked to himself, looking quite satisfied as he walked briskly out the way he'd come. While it might appear to those present that he'd been humbled by the exchange with his parents, his satisfaction showed he hadn't been cowed at all.

Ingegerd felt, strangely, that she had fallen into some trap of his. Had he not wanted her to look at the omens? Was he planning something on this trip that he didn't want foretold? Was there more to this hunt?

She picked up her compass and worried it in her hands. Ignorant to the world around her, she thought and thought and thought, recounting every prophecy she knew and all the signs she ever read. She tried to discern if there was any real danger in allowing this trip. By the time all the visitors had left and the Great Hall's doors closed, she truly couldn't see any harm in it. Whatever Havardr thought he'd won today, she'd let him have the victory. It was meaningless in the grand scheme of things, and Ingegerd had much larger fates to unravel.

3
Trond

501

TROND WASN'T PLEASED when his brother had returned home with a babe in his arms. Oh, he was pleased that his brother was taking responsibility for the girl he'd sired with some maiden he'd never even bothered to mention, but Trond wasn't pleased that the situation had arisen at all. It was so unlike Sindri, a youth who had never so much as hinted at a lover.

But then again, Trond's brother was never so reckless as he was when with the king's son.

It didn't bode well that this mysterious girl-child had appeared in Hundrfeld not long after Sindri had answered Havardr's summons. Trond had met the eldest prince but a handful of times, and had never much cared for him. He had some admirable qualities for a warrior—fearless and brazen among them—but none would suit him well on the throne. Havardr and Sindri were thick as thieves, having been forced upon each other so often at an impressionable age. If Sindri were to have an affair with anyone, Trond would have guessed Havardr.

It had been no surprise that Sindri left when Havardr beckoned, and less still when the two had gone to gallivant across the sea to raid and pillage as all young men thought was their right. Trond supposed the little one was the result of some drunken tryst that Havardr had encouraged, and again he was proud that his brother knew enough about the woman to inquire after her when he returned to Yfirgardr.

Yet Trond had been speechless when his brother, still a child himself, came into the hall at Hundrfeld with the small bundle held protectively to his chest.

"She's mine to care for," Sindri had said, stone-faced and miserable as he handed over the girl for his brother and lord to judge. "I must."

"Aye," Trond agreed. He swallowed thickly as he took in the sleeping girl, knowing their steady lives at Hundrfeld were forever changed. "You must."

The girl was a quiet thing, fair skinned but dark in everything else—eyes as dark as a moonless night and wisps of raven-black hair. She barely cried even when she was hungry. Her nursemaid said she was the easiest baby she'd ever cared for, but warned the calm babies were more troublesome as they grew.

"Her father was the same," Trond grumbled. He remembered well his younger brother's wild toddler years, though the baby resembled her father in no other way, excepting this possible similar disposition. And Sindri's dogs loved the little bundle, sniffling and licking and nuzzling whenever they could. Always a favorable sign, when the dogs took to a baby.

After her second moon in the keep, they did the ceremony to name her as part of the family. Tessa of Hundrfeld. A strange name, but Sindri was insistent.

"Her mother picked it," was all he said with an urgency that made Trond hesitant to press. He suspected the poor lass had died in childbirth, a devastation Trond understood all too well.

Whatever unease Trond had felt when Sindri had first presented Tessa was soon replaced with the joy of having a child back in their ancestral home.

And then that unease returned tenfold when his brother left a few months later, again at Havardr's summons.

"You leave again so soon?" Trond wouldn't deny his brother's request—he didn't have the heart to deny his brother anything, in truth, not if it would do him no harm—but the whole business reeked. What could Havardr want with Sindri so soon? More raiding? The boys were barely sixteen and had been lucky thus far. Trond hated that so much glory was placed upon sailing and pillaging, when it was more difficult to rule well.

"It's just a boar hunt," Sindri said with wide, pleading eyes. He looked just like their mother, hickory-gray eyes and a mess of tawny hair that framed his usually cheerful face; he was somber now, and it worried him. Trond dreaded when Tessa grew old enough to wield such power over him, a look and pout enough to break his will, and knew it was inevitable that his niece would hold even more. “I’ll be back within a fortnight.”

He never came back.

The cold, lifeless body that was carried into the hall a week later was not his brother. It was the shell that had held his soul, less luminous now than Trond ever thought possible.

“How did he die?” Trond asked the men who’d brought him home. He couldn’t look away from the prone figure, no matter how much it broke his heart. These were the last few minutes where he had some semblance of a brother left to him.

“Boar tusk,” one said. “It gouged him and he bled to death before the prince could carry him to a healer.”

The roan-coated dog at Trond’s heel growled, and the man flinched back. He was wise to: the bitch would mangle him within minutes if Trond let her, but Trond didn’t punish messengers for the deeds of their unworthy masters.

Two more stepped forward. One offered him the tusks, the other the hide, both bowing deeply after they laid them at his feet. Gifts from the absent prince.

Trond was no great hunter, but he knew the difference between a wound caused by a dagger and a boar, and it was insulting that the young prince thought otherwise. Or perhaps the git knew Trond couldn’t challenge him on the boldfaced lie, not without bringing the matter to the king. As just as Alvis was, it was difficult to believe there’d be any true justice brought against his eldest son. Not when the only proof he’d ever have was a corpse that would rot before he brought it to Yfirgardr.

Trond built the pyre himself. He cut the trees and chopped the wood and piled each piece, one by one, in the low field outside Hundrfeld. They’d built the keep in the only flat patch for miles, a valley between the rocky plains suitable for a large keep and the grounds they needed to raise their dogs. They’d trained litter after litter of pups here, and foolishly Trond had thought Sindri might teach his daughter the same in this very spot.

“Worst mistake of my life,” he said to the shell that once was his brother. He laid the boar hide over him and sniffled to see Sindri disappear. “Should never have let you go on that hunt."

Trond held his orphaned niece so she could see the fire as it burned late into the night. Thank the spirits she wouldn't remember it, and damn them for not giving Tessa her father long enough to remember him.

Havardr arrived a few moons after Sindri's death. Convenient that he'd missed the funeral, though Trond dared not do more than hint at the slight. It was for the best, anyway; Trond had learned to master his grief since then.

"I've come to see the girl," Havardr said after the barest nod to courtesy was given. When Trond didn't move—he in fact did the opposite, his muscles tightening in a rigid refusal to allow this man anywhere near his niece—the prince put on a sympathetic smile. "She's the child of my dearest friend. I mourn him like a brother, and would like to pay my respects to his daughter."

Unfortunately, Trond couldn't refuse him. Not without risking his neck. What would happen to his vassals and his household and to Tessa if he were dead? There were no other heirs, none but the little girl, who was years and years away from being ready to lead.

The nursemaid brought Tessa out, flowers braided into her hair to make her more 'presentable' to her prince. She toddled about the great hall, trailed by pups not much older than her. They formed a protective bubble around her, which soothed Trond somewhat; should Havardr get too close, they would defend her. He didn't, though. He was content to watch from afar as she babbled to the dogs.

"Bring her over," Havardr said, and the nursemaid obliged. She held Tessa up for Havardr's inspection, gaze downcast and arms trembling. Havardr leaned down to meet Tessa's eye, and the girl was too young to know she stared death in the face; she stared right back. "She's healthy?"

"Aye," Trond said. He wanted to throw Havardr out of his halls. Would have, if it wouldn't risk a war.

"Strong," Havardr said approvingly when he poked her and she grabbed his finger. He never said her name, not once during that whole visit. Didn't say Sindri's either, for that matter.

"Aye," Trond said again.

"She'll be my ward." He stared down at the baby with covetous desire, like a dragon looking upon its hoard.

Trond clenched his hands into fists. He nodded toward the nursemaid. She looked as shaken up as Trond felt and was all too happy to scurry away with her charge. Back upstairs in the safety of the private quarters were not even Havardr would dare go uninvited. Only once they were out of earshot did Trond address his prince.

"She's no one's ward. She's my niece. A daughter of Hundrfeld. What need does she have of a protector when she has one already?"

Havardr shrugged. "Royal patronage can hardly harm her, can it? She'll want for nothing. The least I can do for my friend's daughter."

The least you could do is leave us alone, Trond spat in his head. *You've already done the worst to us.*

But as much as Trond wanted to tell off the little shit, this boy who stood before him and presumed he could give orders and take whatever he wanted, Trond knew better. By all accounts, Havardr's interest was a fickle thing. While he had the focus and discipline to master the blade, he'd never been able to turn that zeal toward anything else. It was a generous offer, one made in earnest, but he was a young man. He would send them some gold and ask after her now and then, but Havardr didn't want the responsibility of an actual ward.

Better to appease him until he lost interest in Tessa. A quiet baby was easy to fawn over, after all, but once she was an obstinate, shrieking toddler, Havardr would change his tune.

So Trond made the second worst mistake of his life: he allowed Havardr his claim.

4
Tessa

507

THE DOGS SKITTERED about, agitated from being kept indoors. They normally had free rein of the castle and the grounds, but an early snowfall had forced most of the household to stay in the keep. For a week now, they'd lived off the stores and spent most of their days in the great hall. There were stories and contests to keep them entertained, and Tessa found she enjoyed being snowed in. It made the world smaller, more comfortable.

But the storms had brought them only a temporary reprieve from the outside world: even with the snow deep and the winds strong, the servants were sent to dig out the courtyard so they could open the gates for the Ondljosbod. Even Tessa helped, though she was but a child. She took up a small shovel and made a small trench for her dogs, space for them to run and play while everyone worked and worked.

One night, there was a faint glimmer in the sky during the evening games, and all the children rushed to the windows to see it. Despite being the future mistress of Hundrfeld, she had to elbow and push among them until she finally got to the front. Pressed against the wall, she rose onto her tiptoes, her nose resting on the windowsill as she looked, looked, *looked*—

"Oh!" Tessa cried with excitement and pointed. There'd been a brief, greenish-blue flicker that crossed the sky, just above the hills to the east. All the children shouted in delight, hopping up and down as they made wishes and sent prayers to their ancestors.

Later, as her uncle tucked her into bed, she clasped his hand in both of hers. "Can I come this time?" she begged. The lights only appeared in the very dead of winter, when it was too cold for the very young or the very old to go out and see them. Tessa was only seven and had been denied the chance to go every winter. This was the first time she dared even ask.

Her uncle smiled, putting his other hand over hers and winking. "I think you can," he said, and she could barely sleep at all that night nor sit still the whole of the next day.

With the outside world suitably opened back up to them, there was a flurry of activity as the keep prepared for the Ondljosbod.

Tessa went down to help in the kitchens. They would spend the day preparing food for the festival, while those who could read and write made the banners. The food was all the favorites of the dead they missed; the banners would list their names and deeds, praise for the good they'd done in life. The two would be used to coax the dead from Draugrheimer, the land of the dead, so that they might dance across the sky.

Tessa's old nursemaid helped her make the sweetened nuts and dried fruits her father had loved, and they giggled as they snuck bites. The kitchen was alive with joy, because everyone was so happy for the chance to be close to their lost loved ones again. Tessa had never known her father—not that she could remember, anyway—and she wished for nothing more than to catch sight of him. She wanted him to see her, to know she was alive and well and missed him.

"Can you miss someone you never knew?" she whispered to her nursemaid as they rolled the dough for rolls.

She'd leaned in and tapped Tessa on the nose. "Of course, little one. Your heart can long for many things, even things it's never had."

They dressed warmly for the trek. The entire household was buzzing with anticipation. What a happy day!

They set out together as the sun began its descent, keeping the warm food beneath their cloaks. The eldest in each family was charged with carrying the banners, and they whipped in the wind, sounding like shrieks; it gave Tessa goosebumps. If the lights were the spirits of the dead, was this their voices?

They walked and walked in a long line like a snake, winding out of the keep and north, then east along the trees until they reached some hills. They scattered then, each family finding their own place.

Trond guided Tessa away from the others, to the tallest hill. The sun had nearly set, dusk casting the world in beautiful shades of pink and purple. When they reached the top, he fell into the snow and let her sit on his lap. They faced north and waited in silence.

Night fell. The stars twinkled. Still, they waited.

It began slowly. A shimmer of light, green or blue or white, dancing across the sky so quickly, you'd blink and miss it. But they came more and more often until gradually the lights filled the entire sky. Tessa sat there, breathless, humbled by the beauty of the Ondljosbod.

Her first.

"The lights show how thin the barrier between worlds is," her uncle whispered, and she startled to hear a sound besides the wind and the banners. "If the dead can come back, even as light, it shows they are never as far away as they might seem. We're all together, all the time; when we are bound by love, no separation is permanent."

Tessa nodded. She didn't understand, but she knew she would. Someday.

She took out the bundle of food, still warm from being pressed against her body. They nibbled at it as they watched the lights. They seemed to grow brighter, seemed to take up more and more of the sky until there was nothing else left but the dancing spirits, but she knew there were places where they couldn't see the lights. It made her heart ache, that not everyone could see such a thing.

"Which one's my father?" she asked as loudly as she dared. She worried she had been too quiet, because Trond didn't answer at first, but eventually he did.

"All of them," he said. "None of them. When we die, we have no more body to tie us together. Imagine how hard it must be to keep all your thoughts in one place when you can be everywhere all at once."

She turned to watch him watch the sky, and was shocked to realize he had tears in his eyes. She'd never seen a grown-up cry, and it fascinated her. "Why are you sad, Uncle?" She reached up and brushed away his tears with her mittened hand. "I thought this was a happy time."

"It may sound strange, but you can be happy and sad at the same time." When she gave him an appalled look, he laughed. "I mean it. I am so very happy to be brought close to my family again, and to share this with you, but I am so very sad to remember all the people I've lost."

That sobered Tessa. She had no father (no mother, either, but no one spoke of her and it was hard enough to miss a father she didn't know, never mind a mother who didn't seem to exist), and she knew her father was Trond's brother…but Trond must've had his own parents, right? And he was much older than her, so perhaps he'd lost friends, too. She wiggled in his lap so she could read the banners behind them.

Sindri. Reidun. Egil. Ingolf. Gudridr.

How careless she'd been not to look at them before.

Trond caught her gaze and pointed to the largest banner. "Sindri, my brother. You know that name, yes?" He waited for her to nod. He swallowed thickly, then continued to point to each name. "Ingolf and Gudridr, my parents. You'll have heard their names, I expect. Your grandparents were good people, and I am proud to be their son. They would have spoiled you worse than I do." He tickled her through the thick furs and she giggled. He was much grimmer when he continued, tracing the final names with his fingers. "Reidun was my wife. Egil, my son."

"You were married?" she blurted out. "You had a son?"

Why hadn't she heard this before?

"Aye," he said. Tessa had little experience with sadness and none at all with devastation, but she recognized it now. And she understood why her uncle had never spoken of them before: it hurt him too much. "They died before you were born, I'm afraid. My son took a single breath in all his life, and my wife took her last right after."

This Tessa understood. Childbearing was the most dangerous thing a woman could do, or so the women in the keep said. Tessa herself had known two women and three babes who'd died from it, and knew that the strongest witches were the midwives. They were few and in great demand, but even with the very best in attendance, a birth could always go wrong.

Sometimes magic wasn't enough.

Tessa hoped she never had children: the risk seemed too great.

"I wish I'd known them," she said. She loved her uncle dearly, but she knew her father's death had hurt him; now she knew that other losses plagued him, this other family she could've had but had lost before ever knowing them.

"Me too, little pup."

Watching the great dance of lights, Tessa tried to imagine them: her grandparents, her father, her aunt, and her cousin. They'd all be together, of that she was sure, and would be overjoyed to see her at her first Ondljosbod.

"How did my grandparents die?" she asked. She hated that she'd never asked before.

"Old age," Trond said with pride. Dying of old age showed one's prosperity, and for a noble family, it showed they'd kept the peace in their lands. There was honor in many deaths, but this was a rare feat.

"And"—she faltered slightly, having never dared ask this before—"my father?"

Trond sighed. She'd thought he'd stiffen at the question, but instead she felt his whole body go lax in defeat. "He was killed."

It was Tessa who went rigid. She hadn't imagined her father's death, but she realized she'd never thought it violent. "How?" A pause as she considered, and then more darkly she asked, "Who?"

"A boar. Or a man."

She imagined a man like her uncle. Saw him in her mind's eye, saw him on a hunt against a boar. It could happen to anyone, even the best hunter. Boar were huge, dangerous, unpredictable creatures.

...but men were more dangerous.

There was one man in particular, a man who visited every year in the name of her father. A man that her uncle glared at and whose name Trond refused to speak even when he was in Hundrfeld with them. She'd never seen her uncle treat anyone with such contempt, yet his respect was required, because this man was the king's son.

Whatever a king was. Whyever that mattered.

"Havardr," she whispered. She took his silence as confirmation and seethed.

Her father's murderer, invading their home and forcing her uncle to relive this insult year after year. "Why haven't you challenged him?"

If you were wronged, you could challenge the other party to a contest. Archery or axe-throwing, a race of some sort or perhaps a test of endurance. The will of the world would help the just party overcome the unjust one, and that would be that: everyone would know you'd done wrong, or they would know you'd done none. The people who worked the lands near Hundrfeld would sometimes come to Trond for judgement in these matters: theft, land disputes, and yes, even murder.

Her uncle believed in Havardr's guilt, even if a boar had perhaps dealt the actual blow…so why had he not challenged him?

"You are too young to understand," he said gently, "but there is no contest against him that I could win. He is the king's eldest son. There's no proof, and I'm an old, lonely man. I wasn't on that hunt. I saw nothing, I know nothing, and I am nothing to these people." He spoke practically but bitterly; he'd reasoned this out many times before, no doubt always coming to the same conclusion: there was nothing to be done but mourn and move on.

"But he'll be king," Tessa protested. If it mattered that he was the king's son, then being the king must matter now. "How can such a man be king?"

"The king has other children," Trond said vaguely. "We can always hope one of them is more worthy." He rubbed a soothing circle on her back, one she could barely feel through the layers of fur. "That's not what Ondljosbod is about, little pup. We aren't here to be upset about what cannot be undone. We come to celebrate what was. So stop hogging the nuts and let me tell you about the time my brother cheated me at a race around the keep…"

Hours later, when she could barely keep her eyes open and her sides were sore from laughing, she realized her uncle was right: celebrating was a much pleasanter way to spend the festival nights…but the flame of her rage had been lit, and it wouldn't be so easily extinguished.

5
Trond

509

THE GHOST OF his brother haunted Trond, but Tessa's light shone through the darkness of his grief. She looked less and less like him as she grew into her features—her hair and eyes too dark, her complexion too fair, her expression too contemplative—but there was something of his spark inside her. Sometimes Trond had trouble seeing any of his brother in her at all, then she'd smile mischievously and laugh without a care in the world, and for a moment, Sindri was alive once more.

A shame she'd never known her father. She would've been the most spoiled child in all of Hjorrfold, if only the prince had any decency. Trond would simply have to do his best to make up for the losses the young girl had already been dealt by being a doting and attentive uncle.

But as she grew, it wasn't merely the ways she did or didn't remind him of Sindri that struck Trond: it was her strength.

Tessa was unnaturally strong. Though good-natured and not prone to tantrums, she'd broken many of her toys over the years. Dolls and clay horses and wooden swords weren't safe, all eventually brought to him by small hands and misty eyes. Always with a whimper of, "I didn't mean to."

Yet Trond didn't know just how strong she was until he took her hunting.

It was her ninth winter, well past due for a proper hunt. She'd snared smaller prey around the keep: birds and rabbits, mostly, though once she'd been delighted to catch a lemming. But she was old enough and skilled enough to try her hand at larger game. He'd taught her how to use a bow the summer prior, and she'd been begging for a chance to use it outside of her target practice. The snow made prey easy to track, so they waited until the first snowfalls had blanketed the land.

"Could we find a bear?" Tessa asked as he tied her quiver over her leather cloak.

"They'll be sleeping, little pup." All the better; bears in Hundrfeld grew twice as large as they did in the mountains, with so much game to feed upon. They were rare, though, with no natural caves to offer them shelter.

"Then what will it be?" Her bottom lip quivered. "Not hares. I've already caught loads in snares."

"Not hares," he agreed. He paused, letting the anticipation grow. "We'll be hunting elk."

Elk seemed the perfect introduction, safe because of the distance, but sufficiently interesting because of their size. They were also traditionally the first big game any youth on the cusp of adulthood would hunt, though Tessa was too young yet to kill one on her own. Good practice, though, and exciting to see that future milestone draw a little nearer.

Tessa's eyes went wide, and she clapped her hands in delight. "Elk! Elk! Elk! We'll be hunting elk!" she singsonged.

They set out just the two of them. No servants, no dogs, just uncle and niece out to claim tribute from the wilderness they governed, with much fanfare from those in the keep. They were each armed with bows and knives; Tessa's cloak and boots were so big she looked about to fall over as she waded into the snow. But she handled herself well, as careful and surefooted as any hunter twice her age.

They found tracks in the woods a few miles from the keep, and Trond delighted in his niece's excitement. She dutifully listened as he explained how to follow the clues the elk had left behind, and soon he let her lead the hunt. It was his fault, letting her get so far ahead, but when she crossed a frozen stream, he heard her wordless call. When he followed her gaze, he saw the elk at the top of the nearest hill, nosing at the snow for hidden greens.

"Your bow," he said calmly. "Take aim and—"

And she was off, nocking her bow and loosing an arrow before he'd understood what was happening. "Tessa!" he yelled in warning, but she never slowed down even to shoot.

The arrow flew, and it seemed she ran nearly as fast. The shot was true and hit the creature in the neck, though not deeply enough to kill. It reared and then bolted, cresting the hill and disappearing from sight. To his horror, Tessa threw aside her bow, drew her hunting knife, and disappeared after it. His throat tightened in panic. This was no small creature like the elk found further south by the coast. This was a mammoth of a beast, the tips of its antlers reaching a good two men high. It could trample Trond if it had a mind to; it could run Tessa over without breaking its stride.

"Tessa!" he called hoarsely as he scrambled up the hill behind her. He didn't know whether to ready his bow or his blade, or to keep his hands free so he could grab Tessa and run if need be. "Tessa!"

He scrambled up with his hands on the ground to steady himself and keep from sliding back down. When he reached the peak, he saw the blood splattered across the snow and—

Nothing. Below was a line of trees and the telltale signs of little feet following bigger hooves. He followed, terrified of what he'd find. His heart beat in terror, remembering his wife's last moments and the death of his son. *Not again not again not again*, he prayed, not caring what spirits listened so long as they did.

Not far into the trees, he found Tessa and the elk. Tessa stood over the beast, its hot blood steaming in the air. Her hands were covered in it, though not much else. Her cloak was clean, and it made the sight more harrowing.

Trond approached slowly, as though Tessa were the wounded animal in need of comfort. "Little pup," he said calmly, "did you finish your hunt?"

The corner of her lips twitched. She was proud—as any child would be, to have made their first kill and to have taken down such a wonderful creature as a prize—but she must have sensed his concern, because she didn't smile. So she merely nodded.

"With your bare hands?" he asked, though he knew the answer already.

Again she nodded, and a hint of her pride shone through in the way she lifted her chin.

He knelt in front of her and put his hands on her shoulders. "You did very well, my heart. You are very strong and fast and brave. I'm very proud of you."

She soaked in his praise, then frowned and looked down at the dead beast. Her hand went to her belt, her hunting knife sheathed once more, before she turned her puzzled expression back to Trond. "Did I do something wrong?" she asked.

"No," he said instantly. She truly hadn't. It was a hunt, the elk their prey, and she'd killed it with brutal efficiency. The wrongness wasn't in *her* or what she'd done: it was how others would use it. "You'll soon be the best hunter of all Hundrfeld. I was much older when I killed my first elk all by myself. Your father was a better hunter than I, and he was twelve, I think, when he managed it."

Her dark eyes went wide, as they always did when he mentioned Sindri. He wished he could give her the gift of a mother's memory as well.

Normally, that would be the end of it. She was still so young, too young to be drawn into the court politics and schemes that had gotten her father killed. But she'd killed her first elk, and by the oldest laws that made her a woman. Nine years old, but an adult in the eyes of some. So much growing left to do, so much left to learn…but perhaps she was ready to learn this one truth.

"You did nothing wrong," he repeated. "But I fear they'll come for you when they realize how much you're capable of. And depending on who comes, I don't know if I'll be able to stop them."

He thought of the prince, who had yet to grow bored with his annual visits to Hundrfeld. It always had the air of a quartermaster inspecting the stores, dispassionate and transactional in a way that made Trond feel dirty for allowing it. Havardr stayed as little as was polite, dining with them two nights and leaving the third morning at first light. He made sure Hundrfeld's treasury was well supplied and offered to send tutors from court; he never seemed offended when Trond refused the latter. Trond's pride could barely accept the gold, but he felt it was owed to them as recompense for Sindri.

Havardr's interest was already unnerving, and she had nothing to offer. What would he do if he got wind of this hunt? If he thought he could use Tessa as a weapon, he would get his claws in her and never let go.

But instead of fear darkening her expression, it brightened in understanding. "King's son." She said the title as if it were a curse, and Trond realized he had perhaps been too open with his disdain. Then, very seriously, she said, "I won't let him know. I won't let anyone know, Uncle."

It broke his heart how well she understood the danger.

They dragged the elk back to the keep, then had it sent to the kitchens. "We celebrate my niece's first hunt!" he said, lifting her up onto his shoulders. "Tonight we feast!"

It would've pained him to lie outright and take all the credit for the kill, but the household was happy to assume everything but the truth: Tessa had helped, as expected, but Trond had done the real work of tracking and killing the beast. They doted on Tessa and congratulated her on her success, and for her part, Tessa never bragged she'd done it alone. A quiet child, no one thought it strange when she didn't elaborate on her adventure.

All of Hundrfeld rejoiced in their little heiress's achievement, and Trond allowed himself to enjoy it, too. There was no harm done, after all, when only two in the entire world knew the truth and both had agreed upon secrecy.

The only lasting reminder was the head: he had it mounted and hung above his chair in the great hall. A good reminder to both Tessa and himself of what she was capable of... and the importance of hiding in plain sight.

6
Stigandr

510

STIGANDR WATCHED HIS brother from his bedroom window. His room was on the northwestern corner of the castle in a stone tower that had once served as a lookout before it'd been made into living quarters. He can trace the whole history of the keep from this vantage point: the dark wood of the Great Hall, the uneven stonework of the wall, and the mismatched stonework for each latter addition to the castle. This window also gave him the best view of the main courtyard where the soldiers trained and a more distant look at the sea; on the other side of the curved room, there were small windows through which he could see the mountains out north on a clear day.

He loved his room in the tower. Despite the keep resting high on a hill and the city ofYfirgardr cascading down the slope, none could see as far and clearly as him. He felt he could see all ofYfirgardr from here...and today it afforded him a chance to spy on his brother.

Havardr and he had been close as young boys, but his older brother had become less interested in Stigandr as they'd grown older. Stigandr had felt the loss acutely at first—when he was seven, it was a hard blow to lose his best friend—but had grown to understand it. His brother valued two things above all: warriors, and his position as heir to the throne. Stigandr only got in the way of both.

The children of Hjorrfold were set on one of two paths: the blade or magic. While many noble households employed tutors of both for their children, once they reached their tenth year, it was time to pick a single path. It was thought that you could never truly excel in either if you tried to master both. Indeed, there were many infamous examples that proved the point, most of whom came from his own family line. There were prophecies that warned of a warrior mage who would conquer the land and sea, but all who'd tried had died painfully at the hands of more skilled fighters or more powerful mages.

Stigandr had been destined to be a mage since before he took his first breath, but he could wield a knife better than most. As a boy, he'd enjoyed his turns on the training pitch as he squared off against the other children. There were times he'd wished to be a warrior like Havardr, though his fate had been sealed the moment Havardr had been given his first sword years before Stigandr was born. By tradition, there were an even number of royal children with an even split among them between mages and warriors.

Havardr, warrior.

Stigandr, mage.

Ragnhild, warrior.

Randel, mage.

There would be no more after Randel. His mother had said many times she'd more than done her duty to Hjorrfold, and if she had a fifth child, she'd be obligated to have a sixth. Randel had been a trying pregnancy for her, and if it weren't for her own vast stores of magic, she likely would've died in childbirth.

But that shouldn't have mattered, their difference in studies. Havardr had never minded, except that he was glad he didn't have to learn much magic.

It was his bone-headed desire to become the next king of Hjorrfold that made him distrust Stigandr. In his mind, Stigandr was his competition, not his brother or friend. Stigandr (and to a lesser extent, Ragnhild and Randel) was the benchmark he always had to surpass. Whatever acknowledgement Stigandr achieved for his spellwork, Havardr sought twice as much notoriety on the sea. A waste of his efforts, honestly: Stigandr had no interest in being king.

He would do it if his father chose him, and he would do it well. He was in many ways better suited for the throne—at least by his judgment—than Havardr. He was more level-headed, had spent more time in the Great Hall when petitioners came to seek justice from the king, had attended meetings with the Council at his father's request, and was far more learned in history, politics, geography... pretty much everything that didn't involve a weapon.

Stigandr also didn't possess Havardr's single-minded determination to make Hjorrfold the greatest kingdom ever seen. It already was, by most accounts, but to his brother, it wasn't enough. He'd hinted often that he wished to expand their borders and conquer everything the sea touched.

Stigandr didn't know why. Havardr's favorite thing in all the world was raiding the coastal islands outside of Hjorrfold's domain. If Hjorrfold possessed everything, who would be left to pillage?

Havardr's second favorite thing in all the world was visiting with his friends across the noble houses to challenge them to duels, eat their best food, drink their best mead, and do whatever else he did when out of sight of their family. Perhaps that would occupy Havardr's time when he'd conquered all the world: imposing upon other's hospitality and avoiding any actual governance.

He visited Sindri most of all, going every year without fail. Sindri used to come to Yfirgardr, but had stopped some years ago after a boar hunt. Havardr offered no explanation, though to be fair, no one had ever asked for one. Stigandr assumed Sindri had been injured in the hunt and was embarrassed by the scars or limp it had left him with.

A shame, really. Stigandr liked Sindri. He made Havardr nicer.

That was where Havardr went now. Always alone, always gone for a week or more, always returning with a spark in his eyes. Stigandr envied him that, he supposed. A friendship with someone outside of the city walls. How novel.

"Stigandr."

He turned at the sound of his father's voice. If it had been someone else, he might've been embarrassed to be caught spying on his brother. Their father knew well how fraught the brothers' relationship had become and judged neither for it.

"Are you ready?" Alvis asked. His father wore a perpetual scowl that made him look more dignified with his long beard and bear cloak. His hair had long ago gone gray, but his eyes were still the bright green of the royal line, the perfect mirror of Stigandr's.

Stigandr spared one last look out the window—his brother had mounted his horse and was heading down the hill to the city gate—before facing his father again. "Of course," he said and pushed away from his perch. There was nothing more to see, anyway.

His father led him down the stairs and through the smaller back hallway that snaked below the private areas of the castle, windowless and torch-lit. Whatever lesson King Alvis had in store, it wasn't one he wanted people to know about. The whole thing was intriguing: yesterday, he'd called Stigandr to his personal study in the late hours of the evening when few were still awake and ordered Stigandr to secrecy about their planned meeting. Even his mother wasn't to know, which was all the more curious. Not because it was unlike his father—Alvis was a reticent man by nature—but it was strange to find himself in the inner circle for once. Stranger still that his mother was outside of it.

They reached a wooden door, so plain and boring that Stigandr had never paid it any mind before. His father bent forward and dug out an equally uninteresting key from a mat, one edge stuck beneath the door. "Close it behind you," he said gruffly as he stepped inside the door, opening it only enough to slip inside.

Instead of a room, there was a set of jagged stone stairs that led down about fifty feet before curving to the right. It was so different from the smooth, sleek walls and floors elsewhere in the keep that Stigandr toed at the grooved ground. These steps must be carved right into the hillside itself, and poorly at that. Stigandr did as he was told, making sure the door clicked shut. By the time he'd turned back around, his father had lit a torch and was already disappearing out of sight, lighting more torches as he went.

Stigandr followed. The path was silent and oppressive as they walked ever downward, spiraling always to the right. Round and down, round and down, Stigandr lost track of how long it'd been. For several long minutes, neither of them spoke, so long that Stigandr's mind wandered. What was this place, hidden deep beneath the city?

Eventually, silvery writing appeared on the dark stone, a mix of ancient runes and strange symbols he didn't recognize on the ever-curving walls.

"This spellwork is ancient," Alvis said as they continued their descent. The hill upon which Yfirgardr sat was tall, and it felt as though they were walking to the very bottom of it. The air felt heavy and thick, the stone walls pressing in tightly around them. It was like a tomb.

It probably was a tomb, actually.

"I'm no stranger to ancient magic," Stigandr said dismissively. His father, the great king, had made his fame from pillaging farther east than any before him. Like Havardr, Alvis wielded little to no magic. Stigandr had in fact never seen his father cast even the most basic of spells, though he knew Alvis *must* have. There were rites and duties that fell upon the kings and queens of Hjorrfold that he must surely carry out. And how ancient could that spellwork be, really? The keep was five hundred years old, yes, but that was only old in the world of men, not magic. The spells his mother taught him were far older, as old as the earth itself.

Alvis stopped short. He rounded on Stigandr in the cramped space, the torch casting his face in an eerie glow that made every line of fury more pronounced. "Do not think yourself above this, boy. What I show you today is what the very foundation of Yfirgardr stands upon, what allows Hjorrfold to exist at all. If you neglect your duties, it might all crumble down around you."

Stigandr's heart skipped a beat. "Does that mean I'm to be king?"

Alvis merely rolled his eyes. "I've made no decision. You're all too young. It's too early to know what mettle you're made of." He turned to continue down the winding staircase. "I'll teach it to whoever takes the throne, if I think you won't serve your people by doing the rites yourself. Don't think you're not replaceable."

Such a loving father he had.

When they finally reached the end, the narrow corridor suddenly gave way to a room with a tall ceiling that stretched wide above them. The space was taller than the Great Hall, though bare of any furniture or columns or windows, only the rough stone walls as they curved up to form a dome about them. There was no need for torches here: the entire room, huge as it was, was covered in the same markings as the stairs, the faint glow illuminating the whole breadth of the space better than any fire could. Stigandr whistled in fascination as he spun around and took it in. This much magic would have taken ages to cast, would require a lot of maintenance, and must have a powerful effect.

"Even your mother has never been to this place." Alvis said it with no small amount of pride. It was rare indeed that he could claim stronger magic than Queen Ingegerd. "She might've heard tell of it in Andiby, but this place is only for our bloodline. The wards would've killed her before she'd made it this far."

"It is impressive," he conceded, because it was. "What's it for?" What purpose could have required so much time and magic?

"Protection."

When he didn't elaborate, Stigandr didn't press. If that wasn't part of today's lesson, there was nothing he could do to wheedle it out of him.

"And what's our role in it?" he asked instead. "How do we keep the magic intact?"

At this, his father grinned in that same way Havardr did before a fight. He walked to the farthest end of the room, where a small, cave-like opening led into darkness. It was barely big enough for a man to fit through, which was perhaps why Stigandr hadn't noticed this dark spot before. He walked towards it with curiosity and had to kneel to look into the yawning blackness. There were no glowing symbols carved around it, but there were painted markings. He stepped closer and traced them gently, his fingers barely making contact. A list of names, some of which he recognized.

"There rest all your ancestors who have served Yfirgardr," his father said. He held out the torch to cast just enough light to see through the opening. There were rows and rows of shelves lined with urns and gilded boxes.

"So it is a tomb," Stigandr said. Such things weren't common among their people. Pyres and burial at sea were the norm. The burial mounds of Fjarriheimr were well known—the closest thing to a tomb on this side of the sea—but few traveled to that kingdom and fewer still could recall the names or deeds of the men and women buried there. Tombs were an idea, not a real thing. Not in Hjorrfold.

Yet here was one, beneath his own home.

"This is no mere tomb." Though Alvis didn't raise his voice, it echoed off the walls and cast his annoyance back at Stigandr.

Stigandr cocked an eyebrow. He didn't need to ask for his father to get the message: *then what* is *it?*

"This isn't only the dust and bones of your forefathers," his father said. "That isn't enough. Magic like this requires blood. My blood. Your blood. Any of our line will do." Then he walked away from the dark crevice to the center of the large chamber. There was an indentation in the ground, a shallow divot like a bowl where the stone was rubbed smooth. There was a circle of warding around it, then another around that, and another and another as they streamed outward to cover the whole of the floor, then the walls, all the way to the tips of the vaulted ceiling.

"How much blood?" Stigandr asked, suddenly feeling the weight of the years. The keep was very old, and there had been many kings and queens of Yfirgardr since then. How much of themselves had they poured out for the sake of this land and its people?

"Scared to bleed?" His father drew a knife and gripped the blade in his hand, drawing it down in a swift motion. He held out his clenched fist over the ground, squeezing out the blood and watching it fall, drip by drip. As each drip landed, there was a pulse in the wards, a silvery flutter that raced outward, upward, a glow that became fainter and fainter the farther it traveled, but was unmistakably brighter with each drop.

"Not much at all, then," Stigandr said, more to himself than his father. "How often?"

"Depends on how much you give." Alvis sheathed his knife and wrapped his hand in a handkerchief. Would he ask a healer for a remedy or salve, or would he let it heal on its own? "A few drops every moon will do, but it cannot wait a year. There will be too many cracks in the spellwork. Short of splitting your throat, there might be no way to repair it properly."

Because all the people who know this magic are dead, Stigandr assumed. He crouched down to inspect the warding more closely. While the names painted in the tomb were in familiar runic letters, these symbols were foreign to him. There were pieces here and there he'd seen during his studies, albeit in different forms, but it was mostly incomprehensible to him. If they didn't continue their offerings or if a quake shook the earth and damaged this place, they would be well and truly fucked.

"What do they protect us from?" he asked, hoping for a clue to help him piece it all together.

"There are evil spirits in the world," his father said coldly, motioning at Stigandr's shoulder and then his own. Every royal child born in Yfirgardr was given a mark on their tenth year, the one that marked them as part of the family and that offered protection. Most families with magic in them had such traditions, though sometimes it was a ritual or a hair clipping offered to the spirits or perhaps an enchanted token.

The mark he understood. It was a rite of passage for their family, and while he wasn't sure it did much of anything, it certainly did no harm.

This place, though... Stigandr thought this was all a lot of trouble for the vague threat of 'evil spirits.' There was more to this, other secrets his father wasn't yet willing to share, something that would explain the space around them hundreds of feet below the castle.

But he conceded the line of questioning. Pushing his father for more had never done him any favors.

Stigandr stood up and dusted off his hands. "Are there any other rites that go along with the bloodletting?"

Alvis hesitated. "No," he lied, and wasn't it terrible that he did such a poor job of it? Though Stigandr suspected only he and his mother knew Alvis well enough to see it. "Let's head back. That's all for today."

Stigandr lingered in the chamber. This little excursion had been equally intriguing and disappointing. Every show of good faith his father made always seemed to be coupled with distrust. Alvis *had* shown him this place, but he'd explained so little of it. Perhaps it was enough that he could make his own inquiries—

As Alvis rounded the first bend in the stairwell, taking the torch with him, the room dimmed. The sigils on the walls twinkled like stars in a clear night sky. Beautiful... and eerie, since these constellations were not the familiar ones he's known all his life. He shivered, then rushed after his father. Part of him hoped to never come down here again, though he knew he would likely have no choice in the matter.

7
Havardr

513

By the time the girl was thirteen, she hadn't reached her potential yet, so Havardr decided to act.

Hundrfeld had been the perfect place to keep her because of their reclusive nature. After Trond had lost his wife and unborn child, he'd all but shut the doors on visitors to Hundrfeld and travelled nowhere outside his own lands. Over a decade after their deaths, he was still mourning their loss and that of his brother, so was loath to share the girl, since she was the only family he had left, and so no news of her had traveled farther than the towns that flew Hundrfeld's crest. The problem was just that, though: Trond saw the girl as family.

There was no neglect in her studies or training. She could write passably well and seemed knowledgeable enough. Her footwork on the training pitch was sound, and her skills with a blade were undeniable. She was accomplished as any noble's daughter.

Havardr wasn't looking for just any nobleman's daughter. He needed a weapon. In that regard, she was lacking. Like an uncut gem, she merely required the proper work to make her truly shine. He'd decided what needed to be done on his journey to Hundrfeld, and thought how best to deliver the blow as he dismounted in the courtyard in front of the keep. It was very near where he'd first met Sindri when they were introduced as boys. For a traitorous moment, he wondered if Sindri's room had been left undisturbed since he'd last seen it, or if they'd perhaps repurposed it for the girl. He shook his head to dispel the thought and focus on the task at hand.

He entered the great hall just as Trond did, appearing in the far doorway that led up to the family's rooms. He strode in wearing a heavy cloak that had no place in the warmth of summer, and his shoulder-length hair rested by the chain that bound it. He'd once been a fair blond like his brother, so fair that it had taken years to tell the locks had gone the same silver as his eyes. As usual when he saw Havardr, his expression soured.

"Havardr," he said curtly, with no deference in his voice and never a title to match Havardr's rank. Havardr allowed the impudence only because he knew he had gained far more from their strained dealings than Trond ever could.

"I'm sending her to Vaettfangkirk," he announced. They hadn't yet gone through the niceties of small talk, so he cut right to the point.

Havardr hated small talk. He suspected Trond did as well.

Trond froze at his words. He looked like he was made of ice, and he sounded like it when he asked, "Tessa? To Vaettfangkirk?"

"My sister trained there for five years," Havardr assured him. Vaettfangkirk trained women in the skills necessary for warcraft, and though they typically took in girls who'd been abandoned by their families or orphaned by the very battles they would train for, it was an acceptable place to send daughters from highborn houses as well. Why, should Havardr ever have a daughter, he would escort her there himself.

He'd read as much in the book.

"Five years?" Trond repeated numbly, his shock palpable. He staggered backward and his legs hit his great seat. He didn't sit down, though; he strode forward and down the steps until he stood in front of Havardr. Havardr was used to being the tallest man in any room, but Trond was level with him. It made Havardr feel small, but he dismissed the unease. Perhaps they were equal in height, but not in blood. "No," Trond said firmly. "She won't go."

Havardr couldn't help it: he laughed. He thought for a moment Trond might hit him, and though he craved seeing if he could best the older man in a fight, there was nothing to be gained from it. He still needed Trond, if only for a little longer.

"And why not?" Havardr asked. "The girl enjoys fighting, does she not? And she's quite skilled. Five years with the very best women warriors in all the lands—what more could any girl wish for? Why, if I'd been a girl, I would've begged for such an opportunity."

Even as a man, he'd begrudged his sister's going. The honor of training there had given her status he'd had to work for through raids and battles, not merely by attending a school. No matter. It'd worked out in his favor, hadn't it? Five years away from court would've ruined him.

"She'll be a woman grown when she's done!"

"All the better!" What a nuisance, raising a teenager. Havardr was doing them both a favor. "She'll be able to come and stay at the capital, where I can see she has the best opportunities to prove herself among the warriors in Hjorrfold. Honestly, I can't see why we're even discussing the matter."

"You come into my halls," Trond growled. "You, the man who killed my brother, and now you wish to steal away my niece as well?"

That stung like a blow. It was Havardr's turn to step back, though he caught himself before he went too far. Trond was right, of course, but he wasn't supposed to *know*. And if he knew about the hunt, he damned well should have had the decency not to bring it up. If he felt he'd been done wrong, he should challenge Havardr to a contest so that they could put it behind them. To keep it secret and use it as a weapon made Havardr feel cheated of his chance to wash the blood away.

"I'm not taking her," Havardr said, pushing down his resentment. Trond was a reasonable man; he could be persuaded if Havardr could calmly explain why this was the right choice. "She would be with the skjaldmaer, the best shield maidens in all the lands." When he saw that did little to move him, he added, "*I* wouldn't even be there. I needn't escort her, either. You could have the honor. And my offer for her to come to court is to give the ability to carve out her place in the world. She won't be a girl forever, and as a woman she'll want every advantage possible to do whatever she'd like. Let me pave this path for her."

Trond's shoulders were still rigid, and his hands were clenched. Havardr was thankful there were no dogs in the hall today, for they'd surely sense their master's fury and be snarling at him for causing it.

Havardr hesitated for a moment, wondering how to deal the final blow. A threat would guarantee compliance, but it would make the road ahead much rougher than it needed to be. No, then. He'd have to exert pressure elsewhere.

"This is what Sindri would've wanted," he said. And then before Trond, red-faced and mouth open to protest, could get a word in, he added, "Perhaps we should ask her if it's what *she* wants."

That did it. With a satisfying click, Trond's jaw snapped shut. It was his right as her uncle to deny anything Havardr demanded (though not his as a bannerman of Hjorrfold, but Havardr knew not to push his luck there—Trond was sworn to the king, and for the moment that was still his father, and the last thing he wanted to do was involve his father), but Trond saw himself as honorable. Perhaps he could convince himself to ignore his brother's wishes or argue that this wasn't what Sindri wanted for his daughter, but he wouldn't deny his niece if she wished to go.

And he might not have asked her at all, but now that Havardr had suggested it, his honor would compel him to.

"Very well," Trond conceded. "We'll ask Tessa what she wants."

They summoned her into the hall, with Trond in his great seat and Havardr forced to stand to his right. It was bad enough when he had to do this at his own home, giving deference to his father and mother, but that was to a king and queen. Trond was his bannerman. When Havardr was king, he'd make sure all lords yielded their seats to him if he was in attendance.

But it was of no real consequence today: this hall was a small thing in comparison to the Great Hall of Yfirgardr. It was half so tall and perhaps a third as wide, though a good length. *To give the dogs room to run*, Sindri had once explained to him. Granted, there were more windows, translucent ones laid into the thatch roof and making the room glow with sunlight. But there wasn't even a dais for Trond's wooden chair, the arms and feet ending in dog's paws and a howling head carved along the back, so that he had to look up at anyone who approached. In that respect, Havardr preferred to stand so he could tower over them all.

The girl came in, taller than he'd remembered. Nearly as tall as a woman grown, she would likely still grow and be of a height with most men. Her hair was long and dark as the midnight sky, kept long and unbound, as most unmarried maidens did. She resembled Sindri very little (though Havardr supposed he'd be more surprised if she *had* resembled him), but the halls of Hundrfeld suited her well. She wore a plain dress trimmed with fur and a gold necklace with the Hundrfeld crest, mostly hidden in the long strands of hair draped over her shoulders, only appearing when it caught the light. She moved with easy confidence, as if she didn't have a fear in the world.

She stopped a few feet away from them, nodding to her uncle and then cocking her head at Havardr with a cool gaze. Her look was assessing and reminded him of an opponent on the training pitch more than a young girl receiving a visitor. Not all was lost, then. She had the right instincts. Once they'd been honed, she'd be a valuable weapon indeed.

"The king's son wants you to train at Vaettfangkirk for five years," Trond said without preamble. "Would you like to go?"

Havardr watched her carefully to gauge her reaction and plan his arguments accordingly. But her face remained a mask of indifference as her attention left Havardr and turned fully to Trond.

"Am I going?" she asked, tone neutral.

Trond gritted his teeth. "If you'd like to."

She nodded. "Should I go?"

At this, Havardr was ready to interject. It wouldn't be hard for him to sound convincing. It *was* the best place for any young woman to train if she wished to be a great warrior, and there were no worthy tutors in Hundrfeld to train her. If she wanted any sort of renown, her choices were the blade and marriage; she was useless to him if she chose the latter. But Trond spoke first, and he spoke honestly.

"You would learn more there than I could hope to teach you," Trond admitted. It looked like it pained him a great deal, a good example of why Havardr didn't hold the truth so tightly that it could strangle him. "It is a great honor to learn from the skjaldmaer of Vaettfangkirk."

Again, she nodded. Her eyes flicked to Havardr before she asked, "Why does he want me to go?"

Her refusal to speak to him was amusing. She owed her life, her position, everything to him, but she was more interested in her uncle's opinion than what a future king could offer her. In that way, she was still very much a child; she'd learn to respect him properly sooner or later, and until then, he chose to be amused by these tiny rebellions.

"He says your father would've wanted it." Trond sighed heavily. "He is likely correct. Sindri would've wanted any child of his to become the great warrior he dreamed of being himself."

"And you, Uncle? Do you want me to go?"

"If I could have you by my side at Hundrfeld the rest of my days, I would make it so. But you're barely a child anymore, and I won't be the one to stand in the way of your heart's desire. If you wish to be a great fighter and go to court to raid with the finest warriors of Hjorrfold, this path will help you achieve that dream."

She pursed her lips. He wondered if she'd make an impetuous, youthful decision or if she'd need time to consider. Havardr supposed he could spare a few weeks here while he waited—

Abruptly, she turned to him. "You'll continue to send gold to Hundrfeld," she said. Before today, she had rarely spoken to him directly, and he was surprised not only by the demand, but by the vehemence behind it.

"If you wish," he said easily, and offered an indulgent smile. What was gold compared to a throne?

"And she'll come home every autumn," Trond added.

At this, Havardr whirled around to glare at him. This was too much. "By tradition, they stay until—"

"Most stay because they have no families," Trond said. His demeanor had changed, and he addressed Havardr as if *he* were the child here and not the girl. "That's why they're there. It's not unheard of for the wealthy girls to come back home to celebrate the harvest and the year's spoils."

Unfortunately, that was true. Havardr ground his teeth as he thought of how best to argue. It wasn't the time to begrudge them their impudence, but it grated on his nerves. The audacity! They thought this was a negotiation when, in actuality, it was an order he'd been kind enough to mask.

Trond pressed his advantage. "Tessa will come home each autumn, so she continues the rest of her education before she goes to Yfirgardr." A pause. "*If* she wishes to go to Yfirgardr."

So be it. Havardr could work with this. They'd more or less agreed to what he wanted, and if they thought they were getting something in the bargain, their compliance was guaranteed.

"Very well." Havardr bowed slightly to them and gave a wry smile. "I'm glad we're in agreement. Let's break bread and drink some mead to toast the occasion."

Yes, he was deliberately taking Trond's role as host. After their backtalk and attempts to undermine him, he felt due some pettiness.

"Let's," Trond agreed.

The meal was pleasant, at least for Havardr. There was an undercurrent of tension that Havardr normally ignored, but tonight found thoroughly enjoyable. He allowed himself a small, satisfied smile as he watched them. Though they might've thought they'd won, he could hear the hint of melancholy as the table discussed the girl's impending departure.

The gold would continue to flow to Hundrfeld, a gilded leash binding the people of Hundrfeld all the more to Havardr. Sooner or later, Trond would realize he'd sold his niece's future for a few chests of gold; Havardr would enjoy the day he and the girl realized their mistake.

8
Alvis

515

"I'M NOT SURE what we should do about Randel," Alvis said. He settled into the ornate chair behind his large desk, a silk cushion helping ease the pain in his lower back. His private study was filled with few decorations and even fewer luxuries, but the cushion was one of them. Though he supposed the costly furniture might count as well; there would be no map as fine or detailed in all of Hjorrfold as the one currently laid out on the long, high table that filled most of the space.

Ingegerd didn't stir from her place over the table. She'd spread out her bones and trinkets across the map, rolling them over and over to see how they clustered. Although Alvis had seen firsthand his wife's skill and the truth she could read from the signs, it looked like utter foolishness to watch her in action. It also made it much more difficult to pick out the true seers from the frauds: any fool could toss about knucklebones and pretend to see the future.

When it was clear she wouldn't answer, he continued. At times like this, he found she was sometimes listening and even meditating on his words while she worked.

"Stigandr sent word that his talks in Bjardleith are going well. I'm skeptical, but I'm pleased to hear he's still alive, at least."

No response.

"Ragnhild still refuses to speak to me, but she's not so far in her travels yet that she can go without notice. A caravan arrived yesterday that had seen her crossing the Isthmus. I fear each time, it'll be the last we hear of her."

Ingegerd let out a heavy breath through her nose, scooped up all her tokens and shook them in her hands. They clanged, the sound of bone on metal on stone grating his nerves, before she opened her palms. She stared at the pieces as she let them fall one by one back onto the map.

"Ingegerd—"

She growled in frustration and slammed a fist on the map. The very expensive and one-of-a-kind map that had been in the royal family since the founding of Yfirgardr itself, added to over the centuries. A few pieces shook. She placed her hands on the table and leaned forward to meet his eye. "There is no change. The three-headed hound still comes, the skjaldmaer still looms over your death, and the cracks in Draugrheimr grow. Everything we do, yet the fates continue to work against us."

He very much doubted there were cracks in Draugrheimr, the land of the dead. No spirits or ghosts haunted the land or their people, and he couldn't imagine such a thing. But Ingegerd believed in this end of worlds, and there was no amount of reason that would make her give it up. He suspected, if anything, it was more metaphorical than literal.

And her assertion that there'd been 'no change' wasn't completely true. They'd prevented raids on their towns nearest the mountains. They'd ended a plague before it had spread from the small village where it'd sprung up. When the long winter of Havardr's birth was coming, they'd been able to prevent mass starvation with their careful planning. They had done a great deal of good for Hjorrfold together, but in this one respect they'd failed, and she was increasingly unable to see past it.

"There's nothing we cannot overcome together," Alvis said with conviction. He believed it wholeheartedly, and he hoped his belief would rub off on her. "Now, Randel—"

She waved a hand like the question was beneath her. "We needn't do anything. Randel's a boy, long removed from any trouble."

What she meant was that he lacked ambition. He was well-suited to his position as youngest child, with no interest in any responsibility and enjoying the privileges of indulging in his hobbies. Alvis was inclined to agree that

Randel posed no danger. But if they were to speak of threats and ambition...

"And Havardr?" It was strange to him that Ingegerd didn't worry about their eldest, the one most intent on the throne. Alvis thought him not the best suited for that kind of power, but he was young yet and could be crafted into an acceptable king...if he would be patient enough to learn. *That* was Alvis' concern.

Not Ingegerd's, though. She scoffed at his worry, as she often did.

"Magic kills me, and a woman kills you. Havardr seeks legitimacy more than anything else. He won't work against us, because it goes against his interests. None of the things that threaten Hjorrfold are within his capabilities." She taped a finger on Yfirgardr, the nail dyed black from the inks she used in her spellwork. He remembered when he first met her, days before their wedding; her nails had been a faint bluish-gray then. "The danger isn't from within."

His wife hadn't always been so paranoid. When they married, she quietly fulfilled her queenly duties. She sat with him in court. She listened to the Council and gave her advice when sought, but mostly she told the fortunes of the people of Yfirgardr, especially the women. It was only after she'd born Randel and nearly died birthing him that her demeanor had changed. She said she'd come so close to death, she'd seen into the great expanse of the future and been shaken by what lay ahead.

She'd become obsessed with prophecies. She *needed* to uncover the truth of the future, and set her not inconsiderable talents to trying to prevent the cursed future she foresaw. It had sometimes split her in two: the mother who prided herself in Stigandr's abilities and wished to see him excel, and the queen who feared a green-eyed mage who would destroy Hjorrfold itself. Sending him away had been Alvis' idea, his suggestion to help his wife overcome the stranglehold her fear had on her. She could love her favorite child from afar, safe from the possibilities she saw in the stars.

Alvis was more pragmatic in his approach: she had seen the manner of his death, and he would do all that he could to prevent his bloody end.

"Then what do you suggest we do?" he huffed. It hadn't been his intention to discuss anything other than state business when he'd asked her to come to his study, but then again, as far as Ingegerd was concerned, there was no state business more important than this. Without his noticing, she'd maneuvered them from talks of grain supply and islands to target come raiding season to her concerns that their whole family was doomed.

The green-eyed mage will unleash the three-headed dog, devourer of this world and all others…

A skjaldmaer settles a debt and deals the king a bloody end…

Prophecy was by no means an exact art. The future could be seen in any number of ways, from card readings to star charts, palm reading and dreams, interpreting signs in nature or reading the casting of tokens. Ingegerd preferred the latter, though there seemed to be no limit to where she would go to divine the secrets of the future.

When she'd first started prattling on about what she'd foreseen, he'd ignored her. But she'd predicted enough destruction that he'd be a fool to ignore her. When she spoke of the future, he listened. They'd killed many men and women, hoping to avert the impending crisis. They'd sent away two of their own children, yet still she cast and read the same devastation awaiting them.

"There is nothing to be done now." She took the purple velvet pouch she used to hold her tokens and scooped them up. "There is no immediate danger. We are safe for now, and we should take advantage of these moments of peace to increase our treasury and our food stores. Train new soldiers and find more mages seeking patronage. The court of Yfirgardr must remain a beacon to those skilled enough to safeguard us when the hound appears."

She gave these orders as though it weren't what he had done his whole life. He'd inherited the throne at twenty-three, unwed and without siblings. His younger brother had died as a boy, and his parents had never been able to replace the lost mage of the family. Alvis had done well managing the kingdom, but he knew he needed magic blood to undo this tragedy. When they'd married, Ingegerd had been rather shy; now she was lecturing him as though he hadn't been raised to rule.

"When the dog makes itself known," he said, unable to hide the condescension in his tone, "what will we do?"

If she noticed his tone, she ignored it. She tightened the strings of the pouch, and it disappeared into the folds of her dress. He wondered if she ever took it off her person. It'd been many years since they'd shared a bed, so he didn't know how his wife conducted herself in the privacy of her chambers.

"Kill them, of course," she said. "As soon as they arrive at court, as soon as they make a move against us, as soon as we *know*, we cut off each head and leave the body to rot."

"Of course," he said, amused. His wife had never killed anyone before—though he supposed she'd ordered her fair share of deaths—yet she spoke of it so breezily. Easy when it was words and not deeds. "And who among us is powerful enough to kill this world devourer?"

Here she hesitated. "We have many here who would defend us, but I suspect it will be Havardr who will have to deal the killing blow."

Ah. So the real reason she wouldn't send him away or set him with an impossible task like the others. Randel would be her back-up, then. She would train him as needed, but she would rely on Havardr. Warrior against warrior, as it'd always been.

If only Havardr knew his mother had such faith in him. The two had never seen eye to eye, not after Stigandr was born. Havardr saw the time she spent teaching Stigandr, time that she never deigned to spend on Havardr, and grew resentful. Not that she had much to teach a fighter, but such realities meant little to a small boy who felt he'd lost his mother.

"Let's hope we can prevent the dog from ever rearing its heads," he said.

He didn't like to think what would happen if they couldn't stop it, this great hound his wife so feared. All that they'd done, only for it to come to nothing...he could justify it all if they succeeded; he'd never forgive himself if they didn't.

9
Tessa

516

TESSA SWUNG HER sword in an arc to hit the practice targets, spun to avoid the blow aimed at her, and then froze so she could regain her footing. She was balanced on a log above a pit of mud, a half-dozen other logs within jumping distance should she need them. So far today, her clothes were still clean. She doubted it would last much longer: the skjaldmaer of Vaettfangkirk took excellence as a personal attack.

The skjaldmaer were shieldmaidens of the highest caliber. The best warriors in any land, Hjorrfold or beyond, and all women. It was no easy thing to complete the training—a fact that Tessa hadn't properly considered when she'd agreed to attend—but it wasn't until she was enclosed within their marsh-bound school that she'd learned that the only way the skjaldmaer knew how to achieve mastery was through failure. There was always some weakness to find, exploit, and systematically beat out of her.

Bergunn, one of the elder skjaldmaer who oversaw Tessa's training, tsked in the back of her throat. She stood at the edge of the mud with her arms clasped behind her back, glaring at Tessa as if she were as bad as the muck.

"Again. That was sloppy."

As far as Tessa could tell, it had been perfect. But she'd learned years ago not to argue. She bit her tongue—literally, since it was the only way to stop herself from snapping at the old bitch—and got ready for the next round. New ghostly apparitions materialized and lashed out at her; she swung the sword with practiced ease to hit them all, barely needing to move on her perch this time. It was easy enough, except that she'd been at this for hours. Her stomach was empty, her back was oozing sweat, and her muscles were sore from the effort.

Excellent though she might be, Tessa couldn't keep at this forever; sooner or later, she'd give Bergunn exactly what she wanted.

Tessa had also learned not to complain. These physical annoyances were deemed distractions, and her inability to ignore them signified they would get her killed on the battlefield. She supposed that might be true...if it were hundreds of years ago when Hundrfeld might have to defend itself from an attack in the dead of night. Since the only battles she was likely to face were ones where she was the aggressor, raiding some nameless village at the edges of Hjorrfold's reach, she didn't think her death in battle was as imminent as the skjaldmaer seemed to think.

"No," Bergunn croaked in frustration. "You swing too wildly. You must be more precise, more purposeful with your movements. You'll throw yourself off balance or leave yourself open to counterattacks."

It was the hardest task yet, not rolling her eyes. The *real* problem was the thin sword. Tessa hated the thing because it was too light, too dainty. Give her a war hammer or battleaxe, something with some heft to it. She was strong, and she preferred a weapon to match. Why parry and dance with an opponent when she could beat them into submission?

But her mastery of the heavier weapons had come early in her training, and she was rarely allowed to use them anymore. She'd been too good at them, so the skjaldmaer had no comments to give, no rebukes or suggestions, and so they'd banned her from skills where she truly excelled.

It was the closest to a compliment she'd ever received here.

"Again." Bergunn clapped her hands, and the drill started over.

Tessa lasted another hour before she cracked, tired of the poor excuses for why she wasn't good enough. She'd done it well every time, and if she was any worse now than at the start of the day, it was because she was exhausted. But they weren't here to practice sword work, not really.

They were here to break her.

"When will you start listening?" Bergunn scoffed. "It is a wonder you've made any improvement at all in the three years you've been here."

If she weren't so tired, so hungry, so sore, then she might've been able to keep her mouth shut. But she was, and she couldn't any longer.

"When will you start watching?" Tessa snapped. "No one here can do it better than me, and we both know it. You step on the log and show me yourself, if you think you—"

The answering blow was no surprise, but it took her with such force that she nearly toppled over into the mud. She winced when she realized she hadn't: if she'd fallen, her humiliation might've spared her worse. But bravado and skill were never an acceptable combination in the eyes of the skjaldmaer.

Tessa dodged the second stone, blocked the third with her blade, kicked away the fourth, and succumbed as the fifth connected with her temple. She fell backward and landed hard. Mud splattered everywhere, got in her mouth and over her eyes, but her concern was the next rock. She sucked in a ragged breath and brought her hands up to protect her head.

Once the rocks stopped, there was a brief respite before Bergunn followed her into the sludge. Next came the thud of a rod. As much as they knew about fighting and weapons, Tessa didn't think any of the old bats could fight anymore. If Bergunn or another skjaldmaer had come at her fairly, she'd stand a chance, so of course they didn't. Their weapon of choice was magically imbued rods that sent ice-cold jolts of pain through her. They employed these rods with brutal efficiency whenever they felt Tessa's effort or attitude was lacking.

Which was often.

She gasped at the first strike, but caught herself before the next. She didn't count them. Counting only made it worse, gave the illusion that it would end. *Last time it was only fifteen. If I can only endure fifteen, it'll be over*...but then it wasn't fifteen, it was twenty, and the last five were worse than the first fifteen had been. It was never the same, not in number or brutality, and putting words to it wouldn't make it end any sooner. So she merely braced herself and tried not to hope for anything at all.

Pain was something she hadn't known until Vaettfangkirk.

Tessa had been hurt before, of course. Bruises and scrapes when she'd fallen while riding, if a practice sword had hit her too hard, or the time a bear had scratched her leg right through her cloak. She hadn't known at the time that they were pale imitations of true pain, but she'd learned quickly how little she'd known.

When they realized she was hard to hurt, they'd hit her harder.

Finally, mercifully, the blows stopped. The pain didn't, but the sharpness of it took on a duller edge as the cold settled in. She waited one, two breaths to be sure it was truly over before she rolled onto her back and stared up at the night-darkened sky. It'd been morning when they'd started.

"You let yourself get hit in the head," Bergunn scolded. She was wiping mud off her rod. Although she held no remorse for beating Tessa again, at least she looked tired. "You were always going to be hit. You can't dodge them all. You should have taken the rock to the back to protect your head. As strong and talented as you are, you still have much to learn."

Tessa couldn't muster the energy to groan. Unfortunately, Bergunn was right, though there were probably better ways to teach the lesson than throwing rocks at a child's head. She knew she'd lived a sheltered life in her uncle's keep, but such treatment was unheard of in Hundrfeld. If such a case made it to Trond's halls, it wouldn't be tolerated.

The thought of her uncle made her heart ache. Trond would be furious if he knew about any of this. He wouldn't have allowed her to come at all, much less return year after year. If he saw even a day of her life here, he'd risk the war he dreaded to bring her home. Hundrfeld's safety for one girl.

That was reason enough for her to stay quiet. She could endure to keep her people free from Havardr. But it wasn't the only reason. As miserable as Vaettfangkirk was, there was a method to their brutality. Tessa wanted to become whatever they were shaping her into. Cut away all the weakness so there was nothing left but a warrior that couldn't be bullied or coerced like Trond was. As much as she loved and respected her uncle, part of her couldn't forgive that he'd never tried to avenge her father's death.

So she would let the skjaldmaer do their work so that one day she could.

But there was much yet to learn, including learning to hold her tongue. That might be the most necessary to learn for her plan to work, for she didn't aim so low as Havardr's death. No, she would obliterate him.

"Go to the infirmary when you can walk," Bergunn said, her voice already distant as she walked away. "And find yourself a meal."

"Yes, Bergunn," she croaked, though no answer was expected.

Despite her years of beatings, Tessa didn't have a mark to show for them. There was but a single mage who lived in Vaettfangkirk, and she employed that magic to two ends: making the enchanted weapons and apparitions for training, and healing every trace of injury after said training. Tessa's skin was smoother than it'd been when she arrived, laced with phantom scars only she could see or feel.

Aside from warcraft, they taught meditation of a sort. If the beatings didn't sufficiently cow Tessa, she was forced to stand for hours. Sometimes it was in the snow or the rain, but often as not, it was in the halls of the Vaettfangkirk, alone and forgotten. Not so forgotten that she could sneak away to her room—she'd tried that once, and suffered a great deal for the presumption—but left to stew in her own misery. In the unending hours, when her body would grow numb and she'd yearn desperately for home, her mind was free to escape this awful place.

While she wasn't standing this time, it was much the same. She would lie here, waiting until her body had mended itself enough for her to walk again, and until then, she could let go of the physical world and lose her consciousness to the void. There, she walked among the stars and felt like one with the aether. She could be anywhere at all, any Tessa she wished to be. Any Tessa would do...so long as she wasn't the one on her back in the mud.

10

Ove

496–517

OVE HAD NEVER dreamed of being a warrior. Noble as that calling was, even as a small boy, he had looked forward to a life of farming the land his family had been gifted by the royal family some hundred-sixty years ago. A hard but quiet sort of life.

He'd grown up in Rotby, a homestead a day's ride from the capital where several families lived together. They worked the land and hunted the small patches of forest and gladly paid their tribute to King Alvis, for none of them needed to worry about anything more dangerous than a bear or a storm. Their home hadn't known a raid since Ove's great-grandfather's boyhood, and even then, the queen had sent warriors to defend them as they rebuilt. They'd been three families then. Now they were seven, some with four generations living together.

Ove had no aspirations to leave home. With nearly one hundred living among the squat homes, it had been a busy, full life. He'd never even been interested in traveling to Yfirgardr—he'd seen the big city on the hill once or twice from a distance and thought it grand but unwelcoming. Ove's little brother Halle never thought so. He spoke of the city with longing and snuck away whenever he could to gaze upon it.

It was clear from a young age that Halle wouldn't be content in Rotby. While the other children played their games where they chased the goats or hid among the bluffs and climbed the scraggly trees, Halle fashioned branches into swords and dueled with the wheat. When he announced at fifteen that he wished to join the king's raiders, it surprised no one. By no means did he want to send his brother away, but Ove wouldn't deny Halle the chance to live out his dream.

Their family scrimped and saved what coins they could spare, and while their mother made him clothes for the journey, all the children of Rotby had helped him practice with spear and knife. They had no swords or shields—what use did they have for such extravagances?—but they did the best they could with what they had. The entire homestead thought Halle looked a proper warrior when they saw him off.

And he did well. He didn't visit home but once, though he sent them furs and spices and fruits, accompanied by letters in his sloppy, inexperienced hand. It was one of the few things Rotby could boast of: they all could read and write. Never had they been so glad for it as when Halle's letters arrived.

I met the king's son. He's big as an ox and very good with a blade.

I returned from my first raid. We pillaged an island a week's journey by dreki. I don't much like to sail but the sunset is beautiful on the water.

They have given me a new bed in the barracks in my own room. It's a very high honor.

The prince has chosen me for a raid with him and another noble. I hope for a lot of plunder to send to you with my love and thoughts.

Their father read each letter out to everyone in Rotby, all of them so proud. His success felt like their success, their little Halle forging a way for himself in the big city.

They went through four harvests without Halle, working the stingy land and minding their goats. Two of Ove's four sisters wed. A new family moved to Rotby, and they helped build them a home. They joined another homestead to hunt a dire bear that had killed two horses, and they ate its meat for a month. There was a winter with only one snowstorm, and they celebrated the mild weather with a feast. Ove ignored his parents' pestering that he should settle down and start having children of his own, because how could he marry anyone from Rotby when they all felt like family? And there were enough distractions—broken carriage wheels and fences to mend and goats to shear and fields to till—that he could escape their meddling. All was well.

Until the day a man on horseback arrived with a chest of gold and a letter from the prince himself, commending Halle for his bravery and skill. He'd died on a raid and his remains commended to the spirits of Draugrheimr, and in honor of his service to Hjorrfold, the prince was extending an invitation to any of Halle's siblings to take his place among the city guard at Yfirgardr. None of them wished to go, devastated that they'd lost Halle twice now and unwilling to lose their home as well.

It was late when the messenger had arrived, and despite their grief, the family had invited the man to rest with them before returning to the keep. Ove watched him, this man who'd sat at the same tables as his brother and breathed the same air and lived, if not the same life, a parallel one. He envied this stranger, who might not even have known Halle but might have. In the years Halle had been gone, there were people in his life who'd known the man he'd become, a man Ove would now never get to meet.

Come morning, Ove took the letter, left the gold, and went with the messenger. The only thing worse than Halle dying was his dream dying with him. Ove would just have to carry it on for him.

The city was oppressive. So big, so loud, so *heavy* in the way it overwhelmed his senses. He stared at the messenger's feet as they trudged up the great hill to the keep, scarcely breathing for even the air seemed to crowd his lungs.

When they arrived at the keep, they gave Ove his brother's bed. There was nothing else to give him.

"We'd give you his armor and his sword," they told him, "but he died at sea."

They led him to the room on the second floor of the barracks, small but tidy and not too hot, despite the heat of summer. A good room, he supposed as he sat on the bed. It offered a safe haven from the city, at least, and he was glad not to have to share for the first time in his life. It had never bothered him to sleep in the loft with the rest of his family, but he wanted some shield to protect himself from these strangers. Even if that shield was only a curtain hanging at the entrance to his room.

He tried to imagine his brother here and found he couldn't. Could barely remember what Halle looked or sounded like. He traced the bedding, recognizing it as the blanket their mother had made for Halle when he'd first left

Rotby. A piece of home, a bridge connecting the brothers once more. For the last time.

Ove put his face in his hands and wept.

Then he found the nearest tavern and drank until he could forget.

Ove wasn't well-suited to the life of a warrior, not at first, so they started him in the castle guard. He was used to knowing everyone; here he knew no one. He was used to the tasks of a hunter and a farmer; he had no notion of a warrior's life. The games they'd made up to help Halle were a joke, children playing at battle, as he soon learned. His training was brutal because he had so much ground to make up, and every night, the dual ache of his body and his heart plagued him. The mead helped numb it, but only a little.

But slowly he grew accustomed to this new way of things. He was strong and used to hard labor, yet still he put on muscle. He walked differently. Dressed and wore his hair differently. Spoke differently (or, rather, spoke much less). Pieces of him changed as Yfirgardr forged him into a weapon, and he wondered how different Halle had been at the end. If Ove would've recognized him.

Despite all the changes, the routine of this life suited him, and he was so homesick that he threw himself into it. The only way to keep himself from feeling the pain of what he'd lost was being too tired or too drunk to notice. Both states made it easier for him to follow orders, because if he was following orders, he didn't have to think. He became a good fighter, not because he wanted or tried to, but simply because the rest of him had been whittled away.

He'd come to serve in the city guard, but he got so good with a sword and an axe that the raiders took notice of him. One of the older, established raiders named Hakon invited him on a raid. His brother, Ove knew, had gone on many raids and would have thrilled at such attention; Ove accepted.

There was enough mead on the dreki to keep him in his cups for the voyage there. He was drunk when he jumped onto the sandy beach and pulled his sword, so drunk he'd forgotten his shield. But the feel of his blade sliding into someone's belly, that memory would never leave him. It was a fight for his life after that, and he had little time for thought, but he distinctly remembered asking himself, *Is this the life Halle wanted so badly?* When they'd finished hauling their plunder onto the dreki, Ove was raw. He couldn't stop shaking, and it wasn't until Hakon handed him a flagon and he drank it all down that he could master himself enough to help row.

Suddenly, the mead wasn't just to forget his brother but to numb the other moments haunting him.

"You did well," Hakon praised when they returned to Yfirgardr. He clasped Ove's shoulder and shook him a little. "Very well indeed for a first raid. You'll be on my crew for the next one?"

And he was. The next raid and the next. Other raiders invited him, and he accepted them all. Because that was all he could offer Halle: glory through Ove's sword.

Ove lived in that fog for several years, and when he came out of it, he was surprised to find himself an officer. They'd offered him a bigger, finer room, which he declined. The newer guards balked at this, but the older ones, the ones who'd been there before him, nodded in understanding. The room was the same as he'd first found it, though now he had his own sword and armor, a shield with many marks of battle etched on it, and his own scars as proof of a dozen raids he couldn't fully remember. Oh, he knew the feel of battle well enough, but the memories all blurred together.

All the days seemed interchangeable, whether he was patrolling the castle or out at sea. In all his years in Yfirgardr, there was only one moment that stood out to him and broke through the fog of his despair.

It was one night in the Great Hall celebrating the year's end. The guards and raiders were in foul moods—cold weather and winter storms meant they were months away from the raiding season and no one wanted wall duty in the snow—and not even the food and music could cheer them. So it was Prince Havardr, the best of the raiders, who took it upon himself to cheer them.

Ove was by no means a small man, but Havardr was taller and broader. He had long sandy hair like the queen and a tidy beard like the king, and those hauntingly green eyes all the royal bloodline bore. His voice boomed over the noise in the Great Hall as he called everyone over and produced a set of dice, much to everyone's delight. And he drank and gambled with them well into the night, never complaining when he lost and generously giving away his earnings when he won.

When the prince sat out one game, he sat at the only empty bench: right next to Ove. Ove tried not to stare at him—the prince was just a man, same as him, after all—but he couldn't help it. Havardr had a presence that drew the eye and demanded attention.

Havardr noticed Ove's staring, turned to him and smiled. "You're a good raider," he said, putting an arm around Ove's shoulders. His cheeks were flushed from drink and his words slurred. Havardr had a reputation for always being ready for battle, but Ove doubted he was ready then. Oh, he would kill anyone foolish enough to attack him, but it wouldn't be clean or skillful as he did it. "You'll come with me in the spring."

"Thank you," Ove said, his throat tight. "Sir," he added belatedly, though he knew not if that was the right way to address a prince.

Havardr didn't seem offended. "There's much glory to be had at sea. And riches. You'll have enough gold to buy anything you'd like soon enough."

Ove nodded. And then, because he was very drunk, he found himself saying, "I don't do it for the gold, my lord. Or the glory."

"You don't?" Havardr raised an eyebrow and looked at him more carefully. "What else is there to fight for?"

"My brother was a raider." Foolishly, he thought perhaps the prince would remember him, so he added, "Halle. He died on a raid"—his heart clenched as he tried to count the years and found he didn't know—"years ago."

"Halle," Havardr repeated, his expression blank. But then he smiled, a charming and princely smile at that. "I remember him. Same red hair as you and as quick with a sword as you. Died with honor." He patted Ove hard on the back before standing up. "I think it's my turn again. Wish me luck, eh?"

Ove left the Great Hall. Halle, despite having the same big ears and wide forehead, hadn't much resembled Ove. While Ove did have fiery red hair that made him stand out more than his size, Halle's hair had been a glossy black. He could forgive Havardr for having forgotten, though. There were so many men and women in the barracks, it would be impossible for a man such as him to remember them all by name. And it'd been so very long ago. But the sting of Havardr's indifference, his careless forgetting of the most important person in Ove's life, it forced him to go back to his room and remind himself that Halle had lived, he had mattered, and he'd been *here*.

Because if Halle didn't matter, then Ove's life was for nothing.

II

Alvis

517

"FATHER."

Alvis looked up from the ledger and sighed. While he didn't enjoy the tedium of checking the treasury, he would prefer it to whatever nonsense his son was about to pester him with. Perhaps Alvis should find an empty keep on the edges of Hjorrfold for him, so that Havardr could find some small amount of lordship to distract him. Maybe if he saw how dull rule truly was, he wouldn't be so eager for the crown.

"Havardr," Alvis said calmly. He put the ledger down and folded his hands atop it. "To what do I owe the pleasure of your company today?"

"I've been thinking about the future."

"The future?" Alvis asked skeptically. "And what exactly about the future interests you?"

Havardr sat across from him in the larger of three seats at Alvis' wide desk, the one typically reserved for Ingegerd. "I wish to make sure Hjorrfold's interests are secure," he said nonchalantly. "With Stigandr and Ragnhild missing—"

"They are not missing," Alvis interrupted, irritated as much with his son as his wife. This was the man they'd created by not setting him stricter limits. At first, it'd seemed trivial to let him have his way—what was wrong with a prince who wished to raid and hunt?—but the older Havardr grew, the less appealing a king he seemed. He grasped and grasped with no care for what he claimed. If only Alvis didn't have more pressing matters requiring his attention, he could've brought the boy to heel years ago. "They are completing tasks I have set for them."

"They *seem* missing," Havardr said. His smile was roguish, the one he thought was subtle but was as obvious as him walking up with his battle axe drawn. "Gone for years and no one knows where or why…"

"*You* don't know," Alvis snapped. "And you envy the distinction they'll gain if they return successful. Yet you have never sought any similar task, nor would you gladly accept any I might give you. You only wish to set sail and plunder weaker lands, using this to aggrandize yourself in small, measured increments on these short trips instead of taking the time necessary to do these duties I have entrusted to your brother and your sister. Why do you complain as though being in Yfirgardr isn't exactly what you want?"

Havardr looked taken aback by this assessment, though he could hardly protest: it was true, every word of it. Havardr wanted the love of the people, and he used his skill in battle to bring back riches that he gladly bestowed upon them. And most importantly, he knew that being present was half the battle. A man they could see, who might appear on walks through the city or in the castle courtyard, was far more powerful to them than a distant prince or princess they could barely remember.

"I'm the only one here," Havardr said, though his confidence was shaken. There was a wobble in his voice that had first appeared when Stigandr was born and he'd realized his seat on the throne was no guarantee. Several decades later and he hadn't quite shaken it.

"You are *not* the only one here. There's always Randel."

Alvis regretted it the moment he said it. It was an empty threat, as they both knew. A great deal would have to go wrong for his youngest to become king. He'd blame Ingegerd for coddling the boy, but she'd coddled Stigandr too, and he'd risen above it to become a promising young man. Though this promise was what had forced him to send Stigandr into the mountains on a fool's errand; perhaps in the end, it would work out best for Randel that he'd never attracted anyone's notice.

Havardr grinned. "Yes, there's Randel. A boy. I'm a man grown, with years upon years of dedication to this land and its people. How much gold have I added to our coffers?" He gestured to the ledger. "Father, be reasonable. This isn't about my pride or desires alone. I'm being practical. There are secrets you told Stigandr, are there not? Ones necessary for the kings of Hjorrfold to know, yet you have told them to a son who has been gone for so long I doubt anyone in Yfirgardr would even recognize him should he come home tomorrow."

"You're not the king." Alvis gritted his teeth. Though he bristled at his son's presumption, Havardr had a point. Only he and Stigandr knew of the wards and how to work them. He could tell Randel, but there was quite frankly no difference between telling Randel and Havardr: Randel was a pushover, and would yield to his eldest brother with even the mildest pressure. Havardr might be brash and grate on Alvis' nerves, but he was competent when he set his mind to a task.

Perhaps it would be best to tell Havardr a little of the wards. There was nothing wrong with having a backup. He wouldn't teach Havardr all the rites—doing so when he hadn't chosen an heir was only encouraging Havardr to be underhanded in gaining an edge over his siblings—but enough that he wouldn't be in the dark should the worst come to pass.

Yes, Alvis decided. He could appease Havardr with this so that he would be satisfied and stop pestering Alvis for things that did not yet belong to him.

"Very well," he said and stood up so he wouldn't have to see Havardr's triumphant look. He gestured for Havardr to follow and didn't look back to make sure he was.

"What's this?" Havardr asked when they stopped outside the door.

Alvis bent down. The key to the bowels of the castle was simple, plain, and poorly hidden. It lay under a mat outside the very door it opened, only enough discouragement to keep an honest man out. Alvis didn't kid himself that most men in Yfirgardr were honest, but those who weren't would likely not find much interest in an unremarkable door in the unused part of the castle.

And the few foolish enough to investigate, all would end up dead for their efforts.

All but Havardr. He was just the right mix of dishonest and curious to have opened the door, and his blood would keep him alive. Upon further reflection, it was best that Alvis showed it to him so that he didn't muck things up on his own.

"This," Alvis said, holding up the key, "leads to the oldest protection Hjorrfold has. Only those of our blood can pay the price necessary to keep us safe. Whoever takes my place as king or queen will have this responsibility for the whole of their life, and the responsibility of passing it on to their children, or to nieces and nephews who can carry on our burden. You understand?"

Havardr nodded, reaching out for the key. Alvis allowed him to take it and open the door, even let him lead the way down the winding staircase once they'd lit a torch. At the bottom, Alvis was unsurprised yet disappointed when Havardr investigated with no sign of reverence. Stigandr had feigned aloofness, but his interest and respect had been impossible to hide. He'd understood the weight of where they were and what they did.

If only that bloody prophecy hadn't made me send him away, Alvis thought. *If only his mother weren't so paranoid...*

Alvis explained the wards and the blood price that must be paid. He didn't bother with the intricacies of it—if he died unexpectedly, he hoped that how little Havardr knew would force him to seek out Stigandr—but enough Havardr enough that it should satisfy him.

"And this is the greatest secret in all of Hjorrfold, isn't it?" Havardr asked, finally with a bit of wonder in his voice as he knelt down to touch the divot where blood was spilled.

"It is," he lied, because if Havardr thought this was all there was, he wouldn't pester Alvis or Ingegerd for more. He laid a hand on the stone wall, the silver glow of the wards like an old friend. The years of machinations to avert doom, the sordid history that necessitated this chamber and its blood price, these were concerns he would pass on only on his deathbed. "This is the most—"

The blow hit him square in the back of the head, knocking the words out of him so quickly he had no idea if he'd said them or simply lost them. He fell to his knees and had to brace himself so he wouldn't crash onto the ground.

"Wh—?" He didn't finish the question, instead looking up to meet the cold gaze of his son. There was no need to ask: his foolish, greedy son would ruin it all. "Don't," he warned with as much authority as he could muster. Not a plea—even now, with his thoughts muddy, he knew this wasn't how he died.

Havardr was no skjaldmaer. Whatever he had planned, this wouldn't kill Alvis.

But as Havardr aimed a kick to his head, Alvis wondered if perhaps this might be worse.

12

Havardr

517

HAVARDR HADN'T *PLANNED* on attacking his father. There'd been no plan, aside from making his demand. After years of waiting for his parents to announce an heir or for his wayward siblings to return, it was time to act. Whatever his father shared (or didn't share) would guide how he proceeded.

How could Havardr know his father would give him the last secret to being king?

As his father explained the wards, Havardr realized how easy it would be to maintain them. He could do it himself. He didn't need his father at all. If he could remove Alvis from the picture, make him disappear long enough to legitimize his own rule, announce his death after he'd secured power...the idea had come so quickly, he didn't have time to think it through. He knew he could do it, that this was his best chance, and he'd taken it.

So he'd knocked out his father, ensuring his path to the throne with two swift blows.

When he saw his father bleeding onto the stones from his wound, Havardr's heart lurched. He didn't *regret* his actions per se, but he didn't want to *murder* Alvis. This wasn't some idiot on a raid foolish enough to get in his way. This was his father, the king of Hjorrfold.

What if Havardr still needed him?

He checked Alvis' pulse—steady though somewhat weak. Good. This was salvageable.

The trek back up the stairs was longer than he remembered. He left the torch in the hallway and closed the door behind him. He had the key tucked away, and he saw no need to lock the door: he himself had walked past it a hundred times and never noticed it. Speed was more important at the moment.

It wasn't far from the private quarters to the small infirmary tucked between the Great Hall and kitchens. There were only a couple of apprentices when he arrived, and he gave them a look that had them fleeing before he'd even gone two steps through the door. He was by no means skilled with magic or potions, but there were some tricks every soldier at sea needed. Tinctures for wounds, of course, and the draughts to fight seasickness. But there was one he'd been taught by an old warrior ages ago, a man who credited this potion with saving his life.

Havardr found and mixed the herbs with inexpert hands, saying the rudimentary enchantment that brought out the right properties in the drink. This potion could instill a magical sleep, slowing down the passage of time for the sleeper. It was used in battle when a comrade was gravely injured: they could administer the draught so they didn't bleed to death, then travel to a healer of adequate skill to save them. So long as you continued to administer the drink, the sleeper would remain frozen in that moment, never getting better but never getting worse, either.

It was perfect. He could keep his father alive just in case, but have him out of the way while Havardr established his own rule. Once he was recognized as king, then he could kill his father... or keep using his blood for the wards. Perhaps no future heirs of Hjorrfold need ever spill blood again. All Havardr had to do was come up with an appropriate lie for his father's disappearance—a trip that he never returned from, but to where?

Wherever Stigandr or Ragnhild went. Yes, that would do. They couldn't complete whatever task he'd given them, so Alvis had gone to rescue them. Havardr could sully his siblings' reputations while showing himself as the reliable one who was fit to be king.

This has all worked out extremely well, he thought as he lifted his father's head and forced down the drink. Alvis' skin glowed faintly as the magic worked its way through his body, the light stronger at the back of his head as it sealed the wound. Hmm, that might make it tricky later. Havardr would have to wait until the magic had almost worn off, then get more blood before administering the next batch. If he—

"Havardr?"

His head snapped around. His mother stood at the bottom of the steps, a swirl of fire dancing around her hand instead of a torch.

Oh. He'd forgotten about his mother.

"What's the meaning of this?" she asked, her gaze moving between him and his father's prone body, the blood on the floor and the potion in Havardr's hands. "What is this place?"

"There was an accident," Havardr said. Could he convince his mother to go along with his plan? Unlikely.

"An accident?" Her eyes looked glassy, like she couldn't understand. She looked around as though she expected there to be someone else hidden in the darkness, but there was no one. She took a step into the chamber, then another. "He can't die *here*..."

Every step she took felt like a noose being tied more tightly around his neck. If she took Alvis upstairs, everything was ruined. They'd find healers. He'd wake up and reveal what Havardr had done. They'd banish him, or worse. It was over for him. It was only a matter of time.

"Mother," he pleaded, just as she staggered. The light in her hand flickered, then went out as she dropped to her knees. "Mother?"

"What's happening?" she wheezed. She looked at her hand, magic trying to fizzle to life, but no new light took shape.

Havardr went to her, his father forgotten. He placed a hand on her back, helpless. "I don't know," he admitted.

Both of her hands went to her throat as she gasped, looking up at him in confusion and then fear. "Magic?"

Havardr looked at the wards surrounding them. He felt nothing, but he knew those attuned to magic might feel the literal weight of it. So much ancient magic...was it possible it could hurt a mage?

His mother's breathing had slowed. She rested her full weight against him, and when she met his gaze, it was full of shocked anger. "What have you done?"

she whispered. "You've doomed us all!"

Then she went limp in his arms. Dead, staring up at him with unseeing eyes. All those years of bending over her tokens to read omens, and she'd never seen this coming. It was almost an accomplishment to have bested her, though he hadn't even been trying. That might've been the only reason it worked.

What *had* he done? More importantly, what would he do now?

One missing parent he could've used to his advantage. Both? It was too sudden and suited his interests too well. Even those who supported his claim to the throne would find it suspicious. People would know. No one would challenge him outright, but they would know and they wouldn't accept him as king.

No matter how he presented it, it made him the villain. If he had at least challenged his father and beaten him in combat, then that would've been something. He had no excuses for his mother, and no means to justify killing them so sneakily: there was no honor to be found in his parents' deaths.

The only comfort was that his siblings weren't in Hjorrfold. They'd tear him apart for this, their own feelings about their parents be damned. In fact, when they heard, they might come back from wherever they were hiding. He could best either of them in a fight, but it would only further ruin his reputation to kill more of his family. He didn't want a coup; he wanted a throne. A legitimate throne that no one would question. He didn't want to spend the rest of his life looking over his shoulder for a dagger.

Randel. Randel was still in Yfirgardr.

It was an errant thought. Another loose thread he'd have to handle, except Randel wasn't a threat. He never had been, the foolish boy uninterested in anything but his own amusement and ease. Like Stigandr, he was skilled at illusions. Unlike Stigandr, he did as Havardr said.

Slowly, very slowly, a plan came together. Havardr carried his mother to the top of the stairs and left her body there—he'd have to wait until darkness came to move her again—then went to find Randel. This would take some convincing…

13
Ove

517

IT WAS WHEN the queen died that Ove truly came back to himself and decided to let his brother go. With all that grief around him as the city mourned, it pulled him out of his own. As the citizens of Hjorrfold crowded the streets outside the keep to watch the smoke from her pyre, Ove stood among them. He wept with them, but for someone else.

There was a line to travel from the city gate, up the long hill to the keep, and through the courtyard to watch the dead queen as she burned, her body melting away to let her spirit free. Ove fell into step with the procession, waiting his turn. Many had little tokens in their hands—small wooden carvings of the queen, parchment with prayers, ribbons marked with her name—that they threw onto the fire when they were close enough. Ove held his own token deep in his pocket.

The king and his eldest son Havardr sat high on the wall of the keep, watching the pyre in the courtyard and the long parade of visitors. The king sat with a dead look on his face, eyes puffy enough that Ove could make out the signs of his tears even from the ground. The prince sat quiet and proud, his face unmarred by signs of grief. There were empty seats on the ramparts for the missing royals: the second eldest son and the princess, both absent for some years now in the far lands; the youngest prince, too distraught to attend the funeral; and, of course, for the queen herself.

Ove had seen the queen in the Great Hall several times, though she'd rarely cast her gaze his way. A few times, her vivid blue eyes had lingered on him, and he would shudder. She had a way of seeing through a man, and he didn't want to know what she saw in him. There was nothing recognizable about her when he got close enough to the pyre. The fire had been raging for hours, and there was only the vaguest hint of a human-shape left.

He took the threadbare piece of cloth from his pocket. It had been Halle's swaddling blanket many, many moons ago. He hadn't known their mother had kept it until after Halle had left; he'd found her with it in her apron pocket one day, and she'd confessed she couldn't bear to part with it once he'd left. She'd sent it to Ove not long after he'd arrived in Yfirgardr. He understood now that some things needed to be let go.

"Rest well, my lady queen." He tossed the cloth onto the flames, tears in his eyes as it sparked and turned to ash. "Rest well, little brother."

He lingered with the other guards and raiders in the courtyard until the fire went out. A few of the healers and kitchen servants came in then, poking through the ashes to collect some in little jars and pots. Ove found it ghoulish to gather the ashes and keep them. In Rotby, they left them on the pyre and let the wind take them, letting the dead decide where they'd like to rest. But the queen was from another land. This might be the way of her people: her ashes kept or perhaps spread somewhere, or maybe even used for some magical purpose that Ove couldn't hope to guess at or understand.

There had been nothing left of poor Halle to burn. His body commended to the waves, forced to rest at the bottom of the sea…

Ove sniffled and turned away from the pyre. He went straight to his room, and he promised both the queen and his brother that he would never drink another drop of mead again. He would live, and he would be present while he did it. If the world was cruel enough to take away good men like Halle and powerful queens like Lady Ingegerd, then it would do what it would with a man like Ove: he'd wasted enough time in grief.

It was time to live.

THE DAY AFTER the funeral, black flags of mourning hung from the keep walls, and the gate was closed. The flags flapped in the wind, harsher than usual this time of year, and served as a warning to the city: no business would be done in the castle, so no petitioners or tradesmen should bother to make the long journey up the hill.

The whole castle was summoned into the Great Hall at noon. There were no strangers among them: it was the warriors from the barracks, the nobles who sat on the Council, and the men and women who served the royal family. Ove knew all the other guards, of course, but also many of the stewards and maids and cooks, and some healers who had helped cure his hangovers and bruises over the years.

The only ones who might be considered strangers were those on the dais. Prince Havardr stood next to the king, who sat heavily on his throne. The queen's chair was empty, of course, as was the spot next to her chair where Prince Randel should be. The boy was only ten and had been so distressed by his mother's death that he hadn't been seen since, barricaded in his room to cry in peace. Ove was all too familiar with grief's power to steal one's will to live; he was glad no one had forced the poor lad to attend... whatever this was.

"My people," the king said, his voice sounding thinner than usual. It barely carried through the hall, and a hush fell over them so that they might better hear. "My heart is broken at the loss of my queen. I no longer feel up to bearing the weight of Hjorrfold alone after so long having a partner. I intend to go to Pegjajord with Randel to mourn and to recover in spirit before I can take up the burden of kingship once more."

If they hadn't already been silent, the announcement would've shut them all up. There were several dropped jaws around him, and some guards eyed each other nervously.

Pegjajord was a mountain sanctuary tucked between the mountains north of Yfirgardr. Not technically in Hjorrfold's territory, though not so far out of it as to belong to anyone else. Those who visited took a vow of silence, gave up their worldly claims, and dedicated themselves to meditation and prayer; as long as they were within the walls of Pegjajord, they were suppliants. Such a vow required them to stay several months, though it wasn't uncommon for people to stay for years, and in rare instances, for the rest of their lives.

There was also a tithe for those who went, a dedication of gold or food or other goods that helped keep the sanctuary running. While many went there to mourn the loss of loved ones, it was only those who could afford to do so. People like Ove had no hope of being accepted within the tall stone walls, or of seeing the stained glass or hearing the hundreds of bells chime. It was a place only for the wealthy; the rest of them had to take the blows life dealt them and move on, or die themselves.

How very nice to give up your responsibilities for a few years, Ove thought bitterly. *And know it'll all be waiting for you when you're ready, taken care of by someone else.*

The silence stretched on until one Councilor coughed and asked, "How long does His Majesty plan to stay?"

"However long necessary," the king said tiredly. His eyes sagged and his whole body drooped, as though holding itself together was too much to ask. "Havardr will be in charge until I return. With the Council to guide him, of course. Listen to him as you would me. Follow him as you would me. Hjorrfold is in capable hands."

Again, there were concerned looks shared at this announcement, but this time they were accompanied by whispers, all amounting to some variation of, *Is Havardr the king now?*

Alvis pushed himself up from the throne, and a boy discreetly handed him a cane. "I must rest before the journey. We leave at dawn." And then he hobbled out, the sound of his uneven steps echoing around them. Alvis was by no means a young man, but he seemed to have aged several decades overnight. The door clicked shut behind him—the last time many of them might see their king—and all eyes turned to Havardr.

Havardr stepped to the front of the dais, as confident and regal as ever. Normally he wore a finer version of a warrior's tunic, but today he wore a silken black tunic and several gold necklaces glittering faintly with jewels. He bore no cloak, which only accentuated the thick muscles of his arms. He'd been grim-faced during the funeral—the only sign he wasn't untouched by the family's tragedy—but Havardr had never been close to the queen. The queen didn't support the city guard or her eldest son's constant raiding, which had gained her no small amount of disapproval among the city's warriors.

For his part, Ove had never minded her words, no matter how harsh. If the king and prince had listened to her caution, perhaps Halle would've never been killed on that raid. He'd be here, safe in Yfirgardr, with no duties more dangerous than breaking up fights at the taverns and preventing squabbling farmers from fighting in the Great Hall.

"My people," Havardr said, the same words his father had used but resounding with authority. His voice filled the hall and drowned out the whispers. "It is with a heavy heart that I take this burden while my father and brother mourn our loss. Rest easy, for Hjorrfold will see few changes with my father's departure. We will continue to be strong. A beacon of light as we protect our lands and continue to prosper."

The Council nodded approvingly. They seemed less perturbed by this change than the rest of them, though Ove wondered if it was because they were better at masking their feelings. They filed out one by one, offering words to Havardr as they exited. Staking their claims for power through the new head of the city, no doubt, and plotting when best to set their own agendas before him. They might think the young prince was an easier target than his mother and father before him, but Ove found that unlikely. Havardr would allow himself to be used only so far as it suited him: he might be new to governance, but he knew how to lead on a battlefield. They would not find Havardr easy to control.

Havardr sent most of the staff away next, so they might return to their duties. A few of the guards, the ones most loyal to the king, were selected to accompany the wagon to Pegjajord and to wait there at the foot of the mountain. They would protect the stronghold and safeguard the king's return. The men and women puffed up their chests in pride at being hand-selected for this assignment, but Ove was grateful not to be among them. It sounded boring, to do nothing but wait on the whim of an old man. There wasn't even a city there to offer distraction, no chance of raids to make his heart thunder in his chest.

They left for the barracks to collect their personal effects and prepare for the trip. Ove didn't see a single person he'd miss in that lot, and was glad to see them go. They weren't ones who'd be useful in a fight. They trained and polished their armor and fought for the best patrols in the quieter parts of the city or in the keep. Didn't like to get their boots dirty, those ones. He almost laughed. They didn't know what life was like out on the land or at sea.

Soon, the Great Hall held only Ove and the other raiders, the ones who went where they were told and didn't protest. The ones who trained like their life depended on it, because it often did.

"I said not much would change," Havardr said, his voice lower though it still carried, "but there is one change I think necessary. I want to expand Hjorrfold's borders. These lands that we raid again and again. Why do we risk our lives taking what should be given freely in tribute? Instead of going each season, we need only go once and take their lands by force. I have spoken with my father about this, and he has agreed this is the time to try."

"We fight for glory, sir," one woman near the back said, far enough away that she could hope to hide in anonymity. "No more raids means no more glory."

Havardr nodded. "There is no finer glory to be won than by the sword," he agreed. "But what honor is there in beating the same islands and the same villages again and again? There are many lands in the sea and beyond. We've been so worried about what's on our doorstep that we're too scared to go past it. We take the islands, then we can go farther and farther. There is a whole sea at our doorstep, with untold riches that could be ours should we but have the desire to take it.

"There is still plenty of glory to be had in conquest, and this is a project not just for us but for our children and our children's children. The greatest mistake the rulers of Hjorrfold ever made was to stop when so many other people could benefit from our prosperity. Think of it! All the lands you could say you conquered! If you wish for glory, I can think of none higher than that!"

There was a startled silence before they broke out into cheers. Ove was among them, not because he cared for his own honor, but he knew it would be exactly what Halle would've wanted: glory and riches for their family in this new age of conquest.

"For Hjorrfold!" they called again and again. "For glory and Hjorrfold!"

14
Tessa
518

VAETTFANGKIRK WAS HOUSED in a marsh surrounded by thin, reedy trees. The air was so humid, Tessa felt like she was swimming. It was so wet and uncomfortable compared to Hundrfeld, with its mild winters and milder summers; another reason she wouldn't miss this place when she left.

Tessa stood with Bergunn and two other skjaldmaer at the edge of the marsh, still within the protection of the trees. The familiar sounds of the encampment drifted towards them—the goats that gave them their milk, the clatter of weapons from girls' training, the clatter of a blacksmith's hammer on the anvil. It might've filled her with a sense of loss to leave this place for good, but Tessa held no fond memories of this place: her time here had been lonely and painful.

Despite the evidence of their presence, in all her years here, Tessa had never met another trainee. It had only been her and the older skjaldmaer who had served as her instructors, all similarly grim-faced, silver-haired women whose fighting days were long behind them. She hadn't even been allowed the company of her dogs, trapped day after day in a lonely cycle that felt more like an exile than education.

She'd woken at dawn to pack her things. She had few, but she'd taken her time. A satchel filled with clothing, the weapons she'd forged herself or been gifted, and two day's supply of food. They always gave her food for the journey, no matter how often she reminded them that Hundrfeld wasn't far and that her uncle's people would provide for her.

"We don't trust men," was all they'd say as they packed the bags and forced them into her arms.

Today, she couldn't help but agree. There were men approaching on horseback, but they didn't carry the banners of Hundrfeld and no dogs trotted after them. Whoever they were, they weren't her people.

"The king's men," Bergunn said, then spat on the ground. Her disgust mirrored Tessa's own, though how Bergun recognized they were from Yfirgardr she didn't know. "Why do they come for you?"

Tessa didn't know what quarrel the skjaldmaer had with Yfirgardr, but in this one thing they agreed: fuck the house of Alvis.

"I don't know," Tessa said. She had expected to go to the capital and play the part of Havardr's pawn, a role she would begrudgingly endure as long as needed. If she wanted to ruin the man who'd ruined her father, she would have to get close. He would have to trust her, and she would have to learn how best to undo him. Then she would deal the killing blow and ruin everything he'd wished to build at the expense of her and her family.

He'd never see it coming.

She couldn't help a smirk; she quashed it immediately.

"You wish to go with them?" Bergunn asked. She glanced sidelong at Tessa, and her raised eyebrow made it clear she'd seen Tessa's indulgent smile.

Tessa shrugged, amused by the protective note in the older woman's voice. Where was that protectiveness when she'd been the one beating Tessa bloody? "I won't have much choice."

Bergunn humphed. "Always a choice. They daren't step foot in the marsh. You can stay as long as you'd like. You're a fine enough fighter. We'd find a place for you."

"High praise," Tessa grumbled. Unfortunately, it was the highest possible here. She could think of no worse fate than being condemned to Vaettfangkirk for the rest of her life and shuddered. Whatever lay before her in Yfirgardr, she'd go gladly if it meant escape from this wretched place. "They'd wait me out. I won't stay here, trapped like a fox in her den."

"You're no fox, girl." The men had reached the edges of Vaettfangkirk's land

and lingered there. Bergunn glared contemptuously at them, as though she'd love nothing more than for them to trespass and learn how the skjaldmaer welcomed unwanted visitors.

"Aye," Tessa said as she bent to retrieve her bags. She knew better than to expect an escort; not once had a skjaldmaer set foot past the shade of these trees. "I'm a hound." She took her first step forward, only to stop short when Bergunn put a hand on her shoulder. Tessa didn't know Bergunn's hands were capable of such a gentle touch.

"You'll always have a place here," Bergunn said, rooted to the spot. "All the daughters of Vaettfangkirk may call this place home... unless they shed blood for Yfirgardr."

Tessa hesitated. She wouldn't ask—she was too stubborn to let her curiosity show—so her silence would be the only invitation she'd give Bergunn to explain herself.

"What you do, whatever you came here for, it's not our business," she said. "But there's one thing we cannot abide here. You may serve yourself, your family, or whoever else you'd like, so long as it isn't in the name of Yfirgardr or its kings and queens. Vaettfangkirk must remain neutral in all things. It's how we've survived this long."

Tessa looked over her shoulder and quirked an eyebrow, but Bergunn had let go of her arm. The older woman turned around and walked away; the others were already gone. Tessa watched until Bergunn too had disappeared and she was alone. A lonely skjaldmaer, walking away from her sisters and right to the men they hated.

That's all right, she thought as she continued her walk. *I hate them too.*

And you're no true sisters of mine.

The men relaxed when they spotted her. A tall one with ridiculously polished metal armor hailed her. "Lady Tessa of Hjorr—"

"Hundrfeld," she corrected. There stood a white mare that she assumed was her mount, so she went to it and slung her bag of food over its back, then fastened her weapons to the saddle. The satchel, packed full and heavy, she dropped at the men's feet. She wasn't above managing her own things, but these men had the look of city guards, and she resented their presence enough to make things difficult for them.

"Of course," the man said. "Lady Tessa of Hundrfeld." He nodded to the satchel and after some hesitation, one of the men went to lift it. She enjoyed that he balked at the weight she had carried so easily.

"I take it you're from Yfirgardr," she said. One unexpectedly useful skill she'd learned from the skjaldmaer: hiding her disdain. Best to practice now with these men before she arrived at the city and had to perform for Havardr.

"Yes, m'lady," the first man said with a curt bow. "We're here to escort you to the castle. Prince Havardr sends his regrets that he wasn't able to accompany you himself, but he's been quite busy ever since he's taken over for his parents."

She'd heard all about Queen Ingegerd's mysterious death and King Alvis' retreat from the capital last year. Trond had had much to say about it when she'd last been home, none of it good. Her uncle had never much liked Havardr and was prone to speaking ill of him . . . though given her own experiences with the man, Tessa agreed the circumstances were rather suspicious. Not suspicious enough to accuse him of matricide, so she'd keep her thoughts to herself.

Besides, she should be thankful Havardr was so occupied. It had saved her from his presence when she was last in Hundrfeld and had spared her of it now.

They rode that first day with little conversation. Tessa kept her eyes on the horizon, giving no indication she sought their conversation. They took a hint and said little, even amongst themselves. They kept her squarely in the middle of the group. She was never in the lead, never able to stray far behind, never more than a few strides away. She toyed with making a run for it. It would be stupid to even attempt it—she had nowhere to run but Hundrfeld, and she wouldn't bring Havardr back there if she could help it—but it pleased her to imagine a daring escape. She made a game of it, picturing for one full morning what she would do if she fled and traveled north to the mountains, and then in the afternoon if she instead stayed and fought them first.

There's only eight of them, she thought. *None with a bow, and none so large as Havardr . . .*

At night, when they made a pathetic little camp and bickered over who took on which chore, she sat at the edge of the firelight with her back to them. She stared up at the stars, wishing for the lights of the Ondljosbod. But she saw only stars and constellations obscured by the moon's light, and she was as lonely as she'd ever been at Vaettfangkirk. Lonelier, even.

Toward the end of the second day, she knew they were close to Hundrfeld. She'd hunted these lands as a girl. She knew them better than she knew her own reflection. But as the hours passed, their party ignored every path that would take them to the keep. At first she thought they were simply unfamiliar with the area and were taking a longer, clearer road marked by the wagon wheels of traders, but when they passed even the main road to Hundrfeld, she pulled her horse short and waited for the men to do the same.

"Is there a problem, m'lady?" one of the guards asked. The one with the shiny armor (she'd seen him polishing it the night before like a fool). He looked the same as the others, though his horse had a better saddle and he'd successfully avoided the chores like collecting firewood or cooking. The leader, she assumed, as much as a group this small had need of one.

"My home is only a few miles that way." She nodded north, never taking her eyes off him. "This is the last road that leads there. I thought perhaps you didn't know the way."

He stiffened slightly at her words. "My lady," he said apologetically, and she bristled. "Our orders are to take you straight to Yfirgardr. We're not able to make any detours."

She'd not bothered learning these men's names because she honestly hadn't cared, and now she regretted not putting in that simple effort; it was hard to appeal to someone when you couldn't properly address them.

"It'll take no more than an hour of our time," she insisted. "It's just over that ridge. Once we're atop it, you'll see the walls." She'd made this journey every year for five years. She'd lived on these lands her whole life. She ached down to her bones with longing to break into a gallop and run home. They could follow her, and she would go with them when she was done. How much harm could it really do?

A lot, unfortunately. Her preference for Hundrfeld would be used against her, she knew. If she displeased Havardr, he would soon learn that the best way to strike at her was through Trond and Hundrfeld. She had no illusions that her every word and action on this trip would be reported to Havardr. She couldn't afford to make a scene.

"We can deliver a message," the guard offered. He snapped his fingers, and a man stepped forward. He was tall and pale with ruddy hair, and while he hadn't sat comfortably on his horse, he stepped easily across the uneven ground. Used to the plains, then.

"I need parchment," she said. He seemed to think he was doing her a favor, but she couldn't keep the ice from her tone.

They gave her supplies, and she puzzled over what she could write. She was conscious of the eyes on her as well as her lack of wax and a seal. So she wrote, and then as she handed the red-haired man her letter said aloud, "Tell my uncle I'm well and travel to Yfirgardr as planned. No need for him to visit. I don't want to trouble him, but if you could be so good as to bring my dogs—"

Here she was interrupted by the first guard. "There are no dogs allowed in the city."

She stared at him dumbly. She'd had dogs all her life, as did all the people of Hundrfeld. Even on her rare visits to other keeps, the nobles had their own dogs she would play with and sneak food under the table. A place with no dogs? She'd allowed it of Vaettfangkirk, because it was a place without men and so was already strange and exclusionary. But a city? She couldn't imagine such a place.

"Why?" she asked, unsure if she seemed stupid in her shock or if they could sense her scorn. No wonder her people thought so little of the capital.

The guard shrugged. "Queen's law. No dogs allowed within the city walls. Haven't been any for near on two decades now."

Ah, that would explain why she'd never heard of the law. The people of Hundrfeld had long memories and wouldn't be ones to forget this slight, whether aimed at them or not, but they weren't prone to gossip. This asinine decree had been so long ago, they would've let it move from their lips to their hearts, where it would rest until undone.

She wondered if this bizarre decree had at all contributed to Trond's dislike for the royal family. It certainly wouldn't have helped.

Two decades... was my father still alive? What would he have thought of it?

Tessa shook her head. There was little point in wondering. She'd never known

Sindri and could begin to guess what he might've thought about anything at all.

"Isn't the queen dead?" she asked. Surely such a foolish thing could be undone. It was hard enough to give up a visit home when it was within reach, but her dogs too? It was the one thing she'd been looking forward to about Yfirgardr, that her new jailor would be more lenient than her former.

His mouth became a thin line, lips white and nearly disappearing.

Right. He'd probably known the queen. She wasn't some distant figure to him, more an idea than a person. He'd have been required to bow to her, to swear loyalty to her, to carry out her wishes. It was a misstep to have spoken so callously of her death.

The red-haired guard saved her by taking the parchment and inclining his head. "I'll deliver it, m'lady." He tucked it into his belt and turned to the head guard. "No need to wait for me. I'll meet you in the city." And he'd ridden off before anyone could protest. Tessa took the hint and nudged her horse on as well, before the guard could comment on her lack of respect for the late queen.

She didn't bother speaking again for the rest of their journey. Four days without a word.

15
Havardr
518

HAVARDR SAT ON his father's throne in the Great Hall. It suited him well, this high seat of polished black stone. He could see everything, hear everyone, and, most importantly, they could all see and hear him. This was a king's seat, and he was a king in all but name.

He'd waited a few moons after his mother's death to use the throne, opting instead to stand whenever he was in the Great Hall, but as people got used to seeing him there on the dais without his parents, he grew bolder. By now, the people of Yfirgardr were used to his rule. It was only when people visited from distant keeps that they seemed surprised to see him so openly taking his father's seat, though they said nothing. They all accepted his place, and in another year or so, perhaps he could announce his father's death at Pegjajord. Randel could even return for the coronation. They were the only two left in the family, after all, and Randel had earned some consideration.

Everything was coming together perfectly. Better than he could've hoped. His parents had gotten rid of Stigandr and Ragnhild for him (and if they hadn't returned yet, he doubted they ever would), Randel's compliance was guaranteed, and his mother had removed herself through that misstep in the ward tomb. With no obstacles in the city, he'd turned his plans outward and began to conquer in earnest.

After giving a proper fortnight to mourn his mother, Havardr had set out with fifteen dreki across the sea. Between three moons, they'd taken a few islands that bordered the seas they'd claimed ages ago. Havardr had raided there countless times, the coast as familiar to him as the shores by Yfirgardr, but instead of taking all they could carry, this time they'd stayed. They'd forced everyone to bend their knees and bow to him. In their broken attempts at Hjorrfold's language, they'd pledged their allegiance. Some had even looked relieved as they traded one craven moment of surrender for future peace.

It disgusted him how easily they gave in.

Despite their cowardice, he'd made the most of it. The people mattered little; it was the land he wanted. Havardr had renamed the first in his own honor, and he delighted whenever anyone spoke of Havareyna. He hoped the people were learning their new language well so they could properly express their gratitude should he ever return to that island to see its progress.

Today, though, a very different piece of his plan was coming to fruition.

At midday, as expected, there was the noise of horses arriving in the courtyard. The main doors to the Great Hall had been thrown open that morning to allow in petitioners from the city, and they now cleared a path to make room for a party of guards. Havardr sat up straighter and held the arms of the throne a little tighter in anticipation.

The girl was certainly no longer the wiry creature he'd last seen in Hundrfeld a few years ago. She was tall—as tall as the men escorting her—and carried herself with a warrior's confidence. She might be the one surrounded by armed men, but she showed no fear or concern. Her hair was as dark as a raven, plaited on her left side to keep it from her eyes, while other braids fell over her shoulders. Her clothing was plain, worn leather designed for ease of movement with no ornaments. Even her belt had nothing but a small bronze buckle, unlikely to have any decoration or crest on it. She'd come straight from Vaettfangkirk, then, as ordered; she was still dressed like a fledgling skjaldmaer.

Unlike most guests upon their first visit into the Great Hall, she kept her eyes fixed ahead. She didn't marvel at the high ceilings, or take in the crowds of people, or study the carvings on the columns and walls. She looked Havardr dead in the eye as she approached, barely even blinking and her gaze never wavering.

Havardr held back a grin. This was much more promising than the shy, meek girl who'd hidden behind her uncle. *This* was a warrior.

His great weapon, ready at last.

When they reached the edge of the dais, the men with her took a knee and bowed deeply to him; she didn't.

"Tessa of Vaettfangkirk," she said, her voice even and low, yet it carried across the hall. A good voice for battle. He saw the way the people looked at this strange girl with bated breath, keen to know more and devouring every word. "At your service, Prince Havardr." Then she inclined her head slightly.

Havardr smirked. A warrior she might be…but still a noble's daughter. Proud and too self-important. No matter. A little haughtiness would do well at court. It would help align the two of them in the people's eyes. Soon they wouldn't see *her* at all: they'd look at her and see Havardr.

"Come now…" He stood and reached out his hands, stepping down the five wide steps to stand before her. "We don't stand on ceremony among family." He relished her shocked expression as he pulled her in for a hug. She remained stiff, and it was hard not to chuckle. So long as she didn't resist him, he could ignore her insolence.

"Family?" she repeated when he released her. She took a step back and nearly bumped into the soldier still kneeling behind her.

"You are my ward, are you not?" Then he turned his attention to the crowd and held a hand aloft. "This is the daughter of my dearest friend, Sindri of Hundrfeld. Her father has died"—he paused long enough to let this surprise sink in and to enjoy Tessa's discomfort at their shock—"and I have brought her here so that she might become a raider and a warrior like her father. She will be treated with every courtesy you would give my brothers and sister. Welcome, Tessa of Yfirgardr!"

Applause spread through the hall like a wave. He turned back to her, hoping to enjoy more of her shock. Her face was smooth and neutral once more as she accepted the cheers. Serene, unmoved, disinterested. So very unlike Sindri, though he was barely her father. If only she'd looked or acted more like him, then perhaps Havardr would think of her as a person more than an instrument. She didn't, though, and with her coldness seemed almost inhuman. She could still be made of stone, truly, for how distant she carried herself.

It was easier this way. He'd been attached to his first axe, and he'd sulked for nearly two moons after it broke. No point in getting attached.

He embraced her once more, earning more approval from the crowds, and dismissed her escort. With an arm around her shoulder, he led her out of the hall and to the king's study nearby. Bookshelves lined two of the walls, and he'd had them cleared of his father's books. They were now lined with weapons and trophies from his conquests, the rest bare in anticipation of future ones. Once the door was closed and they were safe from prying eyes, he guided her to a chair and sat near her.

"You're finally here," he said, leaning back and appraising her once more. Muscular, fit, and tan, exactly as Ragnhild had been when she'd returned from Vaettfangkirk. Ragnhild had been a talented fighter when she'd left Yfirgardr and a monstrously good one when she'd returned; he'd have to put Tessa through her paces to make sure she was just as promising. He had a feeling she'd be better, though.

"I am," she agreed. "What exactly am I here for?"

"To become a great warrior like your father, as I said. A shame he died so young. He would've been out there at sea, helping me conquer islands..." He felt a slight pang of loss whenever he thought of Sindri, even all these years later. He really had hoped to do this together. Alas, it wasn't meant to be. So, as he always did when his mind wandered to his long dead friend, he simply forced himself to think of anything else. "Have you heard about that? That I've conquered some islands? The men and women who fight with me have grown rich in plunder and honors."

Tessa blinked and stared dumbly at him. "I've been at Vaettfangkirk," she reminded him. "I've heard nothing of anything."

Unbothered by her curtness, Havardr leapt to his feet and gestured for her to follow him. There was a great map of Nordastr Herath spread out across the other end of the table, showing Hjorrfold and its neighbors, the sea, and what merchants had told them of the southern continent. Tiny ships marked the farthest edges of Hjorrfold's expansion. The map itself was colored to show the previous boundaries—at some point he would need to find a mage to add in the new boundaries—and he pointed out the areas where it had already grown.

"This island was the first, then we took little ones to the west…the south has so much empty sea, we haven't gone far that way. There's this trio of islands here"—he tapped them with his knuckle, one by one—"is where I'd like to go next."

She took in the map and his words without the faintest sign of interest, and again she reminded him of a statue. "And you wish me to help you do this?"

"Of course!" he said warmly. His excitement would catch eventually, he was sure. What warrior wouldn't wish for such an opportunity? "That's why we learn warcraft, isn't it? To use it on those less skilled. The age of plundering the same tired villages again and again is over. It's a waste of our time and resources. We look to grow. We show our skill by conquering those less capable and adding them to Hjorrfold, where they can contribute safely without fear of raiding."

"Ah." She traced the map with her eyes once more before looking up at him. "And I will be rewarded for my contributions with gold?"

At last, some interest.

"And honor," he added. "And glory. They'll sing our names for generations."

"Generations," she repeated hollowly. Her gaze flickered to the map again. "This is a lot of land…it would take years to even visit it all, never mind conquer it." She looked at him then, with a question lurking beneath the surface. He wasn't sure what it was, but he thought he knew the answer.

"Years," he agreed. "If it were easy and quick, it wouldn't be worth doing."

"No, I suppose not." She crossed her arms over her chest and stared at him. "All right then. When do we begin?"

Havardr grinned. *Finally*.

16
Ove
518

Ove arrived at Yfirgardr a half day behind the escort, and he rushed to make it that close. If the wrong sort were paying attention, they might figure out he'd spent a full day at Hundrfeld with Lord Trond. Ove had no wish to draw suspicion on himself or the items he'd been tasked to deliver to the young lady. But he'd made up the lost time as best he could; hopefully, no one would think anything of it.

As he passed through the castle gates, the other guards welcomed him, told him to take care of his horse and report to duty when he was ready.

"I have a letter for the lady," he said, affecting bored annoyance.

This guard, some older fellow from a farmstead even smaller than Ove's, wasn't part of the escort that had brought the lady to Yfirgardr. He echoed Ove's annoyance when he said, "Best do that first, then. Nobles hate to be kept waiting."

Ove wasn't sure where they'd put the lady, so when he got in the keep, he asked among the guards and staff. The place was a maze, especially to someone who only knew the outer rooms meant for the public. When he'd first been given castle duty, he'd gotten lost several times. He'd never known a building could have so many rooms. He understood the layout now, after years of pacing the halls and escorting drunk Councilors back to their rooms.

"Lady Tessa?" The guard crossed her arms over her chest and shook her head. "Best go to the prince first. He's made it clear she's not to be disturbed without his orders."

Is she a guest or a prisoner? he wanted to ask, but the barb would be lost on her. She was doing her duty; he wouldn't be able to fulfill his until he'd seen Prince Havardr.

He went to the large, kingly study near the Great Hall, filled with shelves and the largest desk he'd ever seen: bigger than his bed and carved from a single piece of wood. There stood Prince Havardr, looking out the high window to the courtyard. How long had he been standing there, watching? Had he seen Ove arrive?

Had he been counting the minutes, waiting for Ove to arrive?

"You went to Hundrfeld to deliver a letter," Havardr said. In such a small space, his voice boomed like waves in a storm. It was a good voice for battle and grand halls and giving orders at sea. It wasn't a voice for small, delicate spaces, though it suited the prince perfectly. Despite his high birth, he also seemed unfit for dainty things. Still the largest man Ove had ever met, he dominated any space he occupied.

And his eyes... that eerie green. Ove didn't think he'd ever seen that green anywhere else, except in the royal family. Even in his drunken fog, meeting the prince's steely green gaze during raids had always made Ove shiver.

He worked hard not to shiver now.

"Yes, sire. I delivered the letter to the lady's uncle and brought her one in return." He held it out, the unsealed parchment with a lord's perfect handwriting. It'd been the easiest thing Ove had ever read.

Havardr walked over and snatched it, eyes flickering across the page. Ove had been there when Lord Trond had written it. Now he watched the prince's lips move as he silently went through the short missive once, twice, a third time in rapid succession.

Hope you are well, niece. Good luck to you in Yfirgardr. You are the pride of Hundrfeld and will be missed.

So brief and to the point, Ove would think the man heartless if he hadn't seen Trond's eyes full of tears as he wrote it, heard the strain in his voice as he'd given his real message to Ove.

Havardr folded it back up and handed it to him. "And you read the letter she gave him?"

"Yes, sire."

They'd been given orders, after all, to read any message uncle and niece tried to share with each other. Ove was one of the few in their party who could read, which was partly why he'd volunteered. Mostly he'd pitied her, so close to home but so far. He'd read the girl's letter to her uncle as soon as he was safely over the ridge and out of sight. Her blocky handwriting wasn't nearly so nice as her uncle's, but it too had been short and without the ornamentation nobles employed to hide their true intentions. It hadn't been sealed, barely even folded, as though she'd expected his perfidy and made it easier for him so he wouldn't have to burden his conscience.

"She said she was heading directly to Yfirgardr and not to expect her."

He raised an eyebrow. "That's all?"

"That's all," Ove said. He was glad that he had no need to lie. He'd never been good at it.

Havardr accepted this with a nod and moved on. "How did she seem on the journey? I want to make sure she'll be content during her time here, so if she was unhappy or upset…"

Here it was trickier. He didn't want to reveal the whole truth, though he couldn't contradict the other guards who'd been with her. Honesty was best, but dismissive of her obvious disdain for the situation.

"She seemed annoyed not to stop in Hundrfeld when we passed it, but she didn't protest. You've seen their letters. I don't think they're sentimental, her and her uncle. Practical. She's a warrior. Like you, sire. She'll do fine once she knows Yfirgardr and gets put to work. Doesn't seem like one who'll get restless. But the others could tell you more. I spent very little of the trip with her."

"Hmm." Havardr's brow furrowed in thought. "They had much the same opinion. Quiet, practical, and in need of activity. Not one to talk." Then he focused his attention back on Ove. "What else did he give her?"

There'd been no hope of sneaking it by him, so Ove handed over the bag. "I already looked inside," he assured the prince as Havardr took it and inspected the contents. "A belt, a dagger, and a necklace. Family heirlooms, I think. They have dogs on them."

The prince seemed uninterested in all but the dagger, which he looked at with unfocused eyes. Trond had said it had belonged to the girl's father, though Ove didn't know much of Hundrfeld or their lords. He and most of the guard hadn't known Tessa existed until they'd been sent to retrieve her, though that could be said of almost any lord or lady who didn't reside at court. Even Trond was a name Ove had rarely heard, so much so he couldn't be sure he *had* heard it or only thought he had. But Trond had said this significantly, and the prince's reaction was certainly... *unusual.*

He put the bag, forgotten, on the edge of the desk and pulled the dagger from its sheath. His look was distant, as though he weren't in the keep at all but in some old battle long ago. With one hand, he tested the edge and tip of the blade. "Still sharp," he said with a smile, and sheathed it again. "Anything else?"

"There are some pastries and a flask of wine, but those were from the servants and not her uncle."

"Then you may deliver them to her. Tell me her reaction." He gathered the bag's contents and handed it back to Ove, who inwardly winced. He would have another private audience with the prince, then. One was more than he'd ever aspired to, and it'd been enough that he never wished for the distinction again. Even when they'd raided together or at that one winter feast, he'd never thought Havardr had truly noticed him.

"Yes, sire," he said and bowed as low as he could, clutching the bag to his chest. He'd gotten off easy; he worried it was only a matter of time before he had to choose between his prince and this strange girl. In spite of his many years serving the king, he was certain he'd pick the girl.

A servant led him to Lady Tessa's rooms in the back, northernmost part of the keep, then scampered away, leaving Ove to knock and introduce himself.

"M'lady," he said once the door was opened, and he bowed slightly. "I'm Ove and I—"

"The soldier they sent to Hundrfeld." She stepped aside to give him entry, and he was so startled she'd remembered him he didn't stop to think if this was a smart idea. He simply went inside and stood there while she closed the door behind him.

The room was large and had extravagant furnishings: tapestries in blue and gold, sheer curtains made of lace, and a porcelain tea set laid out on an impossibly narrow table under the window. The bed was large and covered not with furs but with a soft down blanket embroidered with animals like geese and rabbits. It was a room fit for a princess, yet here was a girl with dark hair done in a warrior's plaits and in clothing more suited for the training pitch than a court. In fact, the only evidence of personality in the room was in one corner, where weapons were laid out among the oil, wool, and flint needed to maintain them.

"Well?" she prompted, and he handed her first the letter, then the bag. She read the words as silent and still as a statue, impassive and stoic. She read it but once before she walked to the fire and cast it in. "Anything else?"

Ove hesitated. Until this moment, he'd merely withheld information from the prince. Information he could still deliver. If he did as Trond had bidden him, it could be used against him as much as it could them.

"He said..." Ove took a breath to calm his nerves. This was worse than storming a beach on a raid. "He said he'd come for you, if you wished. Send word and he'll be at the gates of Yfirgardr to do what he must."

It would mean war, most likely. He'd seen it in Trond's face. The question was, *why* would it mean war? Why would a prince take a lord's niece and refuse to return her if asked? What was so important about this girl? Ladies like her were only brought to the capital for one of three reasons: to marry into the royal family; to serve on the Council; or to serve as warriors or mages. Trond had seemed worried it was the former, though Ove doubted it. Havardr was married to the sword. Besides, it was obvious to anyone with eyes that the girl would make a fine warrior. Any skjaldmaer would be a welcome addition.

Tessa seemed unsurprised by this message, and none too pleased by it. "He knows better than that," she grumbled. "This is a matter of patience, not brashness."

"He also gave me these..." Ove reached into his own pocket and pulled out a handful of coins. If he'd been caught with them, he'd say it was a lord being generous to a messenger. But he'd been instructed to give them to her, so he did. They were all marked with the hound crest of Hundrfeld, but of different sizes and metals. More than a dozen, though he didn't know how much they were worth; he was too used to the bronze coins of the city that made up most of his pay or the gold he won for himself if he sailed to raid.

She took them and sorted them on her palm, a small smile appearing at the very edge of her mouth. She closed her hand around them and, serious once more, she said, "Thank you, Ove. It might seem a small thing you've done delivering this, but I truly appreciate it." She paused and added, "Even if you read our letters, and even if you told Havardr or his men everything you told me, and even if you report back to them after you leave here. Do what you must, and know that I thank you all the same."

"I—" He blushed and had no idea what to say.

Thankfully, Tessa required no answer. She secreted away the coins and replaced them with silver ones marked with the castle. She offered them as if they were worthless to her, though she understood they meant something to him.

He lingered, enchanted by this girl. Everyone else like her—the prince, the king, the other nobles and Council members who resided in the city—expected loyalty and punished when it lacked. Tessa and her uncle assumed it wasn't attainable to them, didn't fault Ove for being unable or unwilling to provide it, and rewarded him regardless for the small service he'd done for them.

So young and so different...he worried she wouldn't survive at court. She was meant for wilder, freer places than this. Like him, honestly. But they'd both been forced into a life they wouldn't have chosen for themselves, here in Yfirgardr, at the beck and call of those who used them as pawns more than knew them as people.

Twice he'd sailed on the same dreki as Havardr, yet he hadn't learned Ove's name; five minutes with this girl, and she'd taken care to learn it.

"Is there anything else I might do for you?" he asked, mostly to delay his departure.

"I'm a ward of the prince," she said mildly, though there was fire in her eyes. "What more could I need?"

17
Ove

518

OVE HAD BEEN given a day of leave as reward for his part in escorting Tessa from Vaettfangkirk, so he slept in as a rare treat before making his way out of the barracks. He'd missed any chance at breakfast, and he tried to judge by the sun how long it would be until lunch was served at midday, when he stepped out into the courtyard to a large crowd.

When you entered the climbed the high hill of Yfirgardr and entered the keep, there was a narrow, cobblestone path that ran from the gate right to the Great Hall on the left side of the castle and the barracks to the right; the farthest end led into the armory and other storage rooms Ove had never paid much attention to. The rest of the courtyard was covered in sand and lined with benches and racks of equipment. The training pitch was where new guards were trained and seasoned fighters showed off their skill in sparring matches. It'd been some time since Prince Havardr had lifted his axe for anything but battle, but nearly any day of the year, there were men and women dueling.

While the Great Hall was home to all the visitors to Yfirgardr, the courtyard belonged to the guards and raiders who lived in the city. Even those who didn't have a room in the barracks were able to visit and practice or simply talk to the other warriors. It was the true heart of Hjorrfold, and there was Tessa in the middle of it.

Today the gate to the castle was closed, barring the way for anyone seeking an audience with the prince, and it appeared the whole barracks had emptied to see their new guest fight. It looked like the nobles on the Council were there as well, standing on the steps into the Great Hall to have a better view over the cluster of men and women on the training pitch. Even the windows of the castle were crowded with faces, servants trying to steal a glimpse of their new guest.

Ove couldn't blame them. Skjaldmaer were supposed to be the best fighters in the land, though they rarely left their marshy home. The last to enter the city had been Ragnhild, and she'd left four years ago; there were a great many who'd joined the guard since then who'd never had the pleasure of seeing a shield maiden in action. Having seen Ragnhild in her prime, Ove was curious to see how Tessa compared, and it was this curiosity that had him forcing his way closer to the center.

Havardr stood at the edge of the training pitch, arms crossed over his chest as he watched. Tessa and a few other men and women were going through a drill to practice footwork while swinging a weapon through a series of defensive arcs. All of them moved with a smooth efficiency that spoke to years and years of training. Yet Tessa looked better. There was a fluidity and ease to her movements, like this was all second nature to her. While others had their brows knit in concentration to make sure they placed each foot in the proper spot, she looked…bored. There was a vacant look in her eyes, as though her mind was elsewhere while her body performed.

When the practice ended, the others were exhausted, shoulders slumped and feet heavy as they found space on the long benches to drink water and rest. Tessa walked with them, a faint sheen of sweat on her brow, but no more tired than if she'd walked the mile up from the city gates.

"Well done," Havardr said, looking pleased. "Tomorrow we'll have you sparring—"

"Tomorrow?" She frowned at him. Ove noted that while she looked up at him, the inches difference in their height seemed to matter very little to her.

He raised his eyebrows and put his hands on his hips, appraising her with the first hint of disdain he'd ever shown for her. "Will you not be rested by morning?"

Tessa mimicked his posture perfectly, right down to the scorn in her voice.

The only difference was that he wore a tunic made of silk trimmed with gold embroidery, and she wore a warrior's tunic of dark linen speckled with dust from the training pitch.

"I didn't realize we were done today. It's been what..." She glanced up at the sun. "Two hours? I've never had such a light day of training since I was a child, and I thought the noble warriors of Yfirgardr had more in them than drills."

Havardr went red in embarrassed fury, and Ove worried for her. He'd seen Havardr strike insolent raiders, both at sea and in the city, and it wouldn't do well to have a girl challenging him in front of most of the barracks. Ove could feel the tension among his comrades, the men and women nearest him unable to look away, rapt with what they might see. But to his great surprise, Havardr threw his head back and laughed.

"Come now, Sister!" He threw an arm around her shoulder in an overly friendly gesture that made the girl squirm. She allowed it, but just barely, though Havardr seemed not to notice. "You must give them some credit. Not all of us have been fortunate enough to train with the skjaldmaer. I forgot how Ragnhild came back from Vaettfangkirk. Strong as an ox but with the energy of a foal."

The crowd relaxed. They all breathed out together, some laughing shakily with their prince. Ove was still worried; he knew Tessa was trapped, though it'd be hard to explain how such a girl could ever be forced into anything she didn't want, and wondered if Havardr would lash out at her behind closed doors. He wasn't particularly known for his temper, but few things triggered his anger more than being questioned. Ove knew men like him didn't take kindly to being so publicly cut down by those they felt inferior. Perhaps her status as his 'sister' might save her from the worst of it.

"So shall we spar then, Brother?" she asked, an edge to her voice like naked steel.

"Alas, my days of sparring are long gone. I save my energy for the battlefield. That'll come soon enough, and then you shall see how well I wield a blade. You're welcome to stay in the courtyard and continue drills with the guards. If they wish for some informal matches against you, then by all means, but the real bouts will be tomorrow, as I said. I have my best and fiercest ready to face you for the pleasure of the Council."

He bowed slightly to the nobles behind him, and they preened in approval of the attention.

Tessa looked as if her time had been wasted, but she graciously didn't say as much. Though she might as well have: it was so plain on her face, Ove swore it couldn't be clearer if she'd spoken aloud.

Havardr left with the Council, important men and women off to do important business. Ove didn't doubt it was a difficult thing, planning a war. There were soldiers to coordinate and rations to gather and dreki. So much had to be done before the first battle was ever fought. It was why Ove had never led a raid, despite his experience in battle: he didn't have the head to plot it out. He was glad all he had to do was gather his own weapons and armor, then attack in whatever direction they pointed.

When they were gone, there was a general sense of uncertainty. Should they return to their duties? But Tessa shrugged, went back to the center of the training pitch and began another sequence of forms. She moved with the determination of someone who didn't care if she was alone or not.

"May as well," Ove said. He went to the rack and pulled off a practice sword, one of the heaviest wooden ones that made wielding a real sword like slicing a hot knife through butter. He took up position to her left and joined in with a routine more familiar to him than the one she was working through. Although she gave no indication of seeing him, her posture was less rigid and her expression softer.

Others soon followed, each bearing their preferred weapon. There were dozens of them on the training pitch at any moment, with no two people doing the same drills. When they got tired, they rested and watched the others. There was a sense of camaraderie that Ove had rarely experienced sober, and a lightness in the air that never came with practice.

They trained frequently and rigorously at Yfirgardr, but it was too harsh to be enjoyable. The officers—himself among them, especially when he'd craved respite from the real world by any means, especially exhaustion—worked them hard, because if they were masters of battle at home, when their bellies were full and they were well-rested, then they might still be competent when they were fighting for their lives. It was mind-numbing, grueling work.

This was neither. This was, dare he say, fun. There was laughter, both on the pitch and from the sidelines, where people watched their friends and rivals. They heckled each other good-naturedly, or cheered in approval when someone mastered a new form. It lifted Ove's spirits, because he knew in his heart this was the world his brother had craved: a brotherhood of the best fighters in Hjorrfold, and him among them.

The sun swept across the sky, and they kept at it. Soon it was disappearing behind the western walls of the castle, and highlighted the edges of the Great Hall in dusky hues. They were slowing down, all of them but one.

Tessa never took a break, not even for water. The only sign she'd been at it for hours was the sweat on her tunic. But she must have noticed the rest of them slowing down, unable to keep up with her unending supply of youthful energy, because she abruptly stopped and joined them on the benches.

"You fight well," someone said. "Better than Ragnhild."

"High praise," she demurred. She wasn't even out of breath! "You all are worthy warriors yourselves. I look forward to battle at your side."

This earned wide grins from many. They all looked happier and younger than they had in months. Even their victories taking the small islands hadn't produced so many cheerful faces.

"Would you care for a duel, m'lady?" Ove offered. Her face lit up, and he winced as he backtracked. "Alas, I'm beat. I wouldn't be an equal opponent for you on the best of days, but I'm an old man. I can't keep up with a skjaldmaer."

"Old man," she scoffed. Her lips curled into a wisp of a smile. "You couldn't be much older than Havardr?" Her voice lilted slightly at the end, making it just enough a question that he could choose whether to answer.

"I've seen thirty-eight years," he said after a moment.

"Younger than my uncle, then. Not so old," she teased, then faced the crowd. "Your fellow here offers me a duel and then declines to fight it himself. I would gladly face anyone here, should you be up for it."

Men and women both, officers and new recruits, all of them held a spark in their eyes. Whether they wanted to fight her or wished to see someone else do it, Ove couldn't say. He wished he'd said something earlier, when he'd had the energy. He might've been able to last a few minutes at the start of the day, but now he wasn't sure he'd make it past the first blow. There were some murmurs among the crowd as people encouraged friends to accept the challenge. Eventually, a young man with long brown hair pulled tight stepped forward.

"I'll fight you, my lady," he said with far more enunciation than Ove had ever mustered in his life, all compacted into five words.

Ove didn't know the lad well, because he was some lesser noble's son who'd come to spend his few years at court to gain notoriety before he returned home, never to return. He was a lanky sort that looked older than he was from a distance but would never pass for a man up close with his sparse beard and the baby fat in his cheeks. A good sort, though. Kind to the servants, which was more than could be said for other noble sons and daughters who'd spent their time in the castle, raiding alongside their prince while it was convenient and going home when they'd had their fill.

He wasn't particularly strong, but he'd impressed a lot of the officers with how agile he was. He was a talented, technical sort of fighter. Not their best by a long shot, but he wouldn't disgrace himself by stepping forward.

"I thank you...?"

"Sixten," he said.

"I thank you, Sixten." Tessa bowed her head as she accepted. "Name your weapon."

"Long sword," he said and raised the wooden one in his hands.

Tessa looked surprised by his choice, but didn't comment. She walked to the rack, and Ove held out a wooden longsword for her.

"I confess," she whispered to him as she laid her hands on the sword but didn't yet take it, "I have not dueled another person in some time. What are the rules?"

"Another *person*? Do you fight with chickens and cows in Vaettfangkirk?" Then, realizing what he'd said, he flushed and blurted, "I'm sorry, m'lady. That was rude of me—"

She waved a hand dismissively and took the sword from him. "You could hardly know. Here it seems there's no magic at all, much like in Hundrfeld."

Her features softened briefly as she mentioned her home, and he ached for her the way he ached for himself when he thought of his brother. "It's all a lot more straightforward like this, I imagine. No, at Vaettfangkirk, the skjaldmaer conjured up creatures of shadow to fight against."

Ove shuddered. It sounded like the things of nightmares. He gulped and asked, "And what were the rules when you fought these shadows?"

"Last as long as you can before you get knocked out." She said it as if it were obvious. She must've read some of the shock in his expression, because she added, "You can't outlast a shadow, no matter how good you are."

"No, I suppose not," he conceded. It didn't seem possible to tire her out. If she'd trained against monsters, he supposed she'd more than earned her stamina. "The rules are nearly as simple here. Fight until you win."

"How does one win?"

"You knock out your opponent or have him yield. If it goes on too long, we might end it and settle it based on who struck the other more." He shrugged. "Usually someone yields."

"That doesn't sound too bad." She winked at him and turned around, marching to meet Sixten on the pitch with the sword slung over her left shoulder. It was heavier even than the sword Ove had used earlier—most of the younger recruits had difficulty with the two-handed weapons because of this—yet she carried it like it weighed nothing at all.

Both took their positions ten paces from each other and raised their weapons. For Sixten, he looked more comfortable with it as he lifted the sword into a standard starting hold. Tessa, likely a traditionalist in her training like many of them were, wouldn't have practiced much with a long sword. In fact, she seemed to test the weight and her hold on it even as she lifted it to mirror Sixten.

The longsword wasn't common among their people. It was a powerful weapon but unwieldy, worse even than the giant battle axe Havardr preferred. It came to Hjorrfold through trade with the southern half of the sea, a land so distant that only merchants ever saw it in person. For the rest of them, it was a mythical land that only existed in the strange objects brought from there. The first items to appear always seemed to be practical ones, like the spades and plows his family had used based on designs from the south. Next were the armor and weapons, like the longsword and the strange plumed helmets that many of the wealthier families liked in spite of being terribly impractical. Finally came arts and luxuries, though Ove hardly knew of either.

In all honesty, he considered the longsword a luxury. In battle, it offered reach, but required more space than was often available when they broke land and charged ashore. Ove always kept well away from them in battle to avoid their errant strikes. But in the courtyard with a wide patch of space hemmed in by spectators, there was a great deal of room; ideal conditions for this type of match.

Sixten bowed prettily, like he would to Havardr. "May luck find you," he said as he straightened. It was the standard start to any formal bout; once repeated by your opponent, the match began.

All heads turned to Tessa.

"Luck is made," she said instead and advanced.

They fought with quick efficiency. You had to balance keeping a defensive posture while trying to find a weakness where you could rush in and attack. Parry, rebalance, strike, defend. Sixten was indeed swifter and more confident with his chosen weapon, and it showed, all muscle memory. Tessa didn't fumble the way most would with an unfamiliar weapon, but she'd lost the sleek lines she'd had during the earlier drills. She matched him step for step, blow for blow, but there was a slight crease in her brow, like she was concentrating hard.

They moved back and forth, though mostly with Tessa retreating and Sixten pursuing. He could win this sparring match, they all saw it, but he could never corner her. He needed to make his move quickly. Ove felt it in his gut, a knot of anticipation. Sixten's advantage was his experience, and it dwindled the longer they fought. He could see it, Tessa's calculating look, an expert of one craft about to learn another.

And he saw the exact moment she mastered this one.

One second she was defending, letting Sixten lead and merely reacting; the next, she twirled out of his reach. With the longsword held behind her (with one hand!), she blocked his blow and set herself up for an attack on his own unguarded back. He stumbled away just in time with only the tip of his sword repelling her blow. She never gave him the chance to regain his footing: immediately she pressed the advantage. She swung in a wild flurry of attacks. Left swipe, right, left, overhand, over and over Sixten was forced to retreat and defend from the barrage of blows. He stumbled once and Ove held his breath, but Tessa's arm twitched as she redirected her next swing to miss him. Once he had regained his footing, she began again.

"She isn't even tired," someone near him said in awe.

"It seems not," Ove agreed. Not even a little. If anything, she looked more focused and engaged than she had all day. Like she'd been going through the motions before, and now she'd been set free, allowed to be herself.

It was beautiful...and terrifying. This wasn't a weapon she was familiar with, yet she wielded it better than Ove did his own sword that had kept him alive for some eighteen years now. Ove was certain that not a man or woman here stood a chance against her in single combat. He wondered if even Havardr, the best among them all, could beat her in a fair fight.

Not that the prince fought fairly. He was strong and skilled enough, and experience favored him in most battles, but he wasn't above trickery. He'd kick dirt in your face, grab you by the hair, knee you in the balls, whatever it took to win. Most wouldn't even think of doing some things he'd seen Havardr do.

A loud *whack!* pulled him back to the moment. Sixten was on his knees, one hand still on the hilt of his sword while the other braced against the wooden blade. Tessa had brought her sword down on his, and it was a wonder it hadn't broken. She kept pressing down—Sixten's arms were shaking under the strain—and said, "Yield."

The boy, too stubborn or stupid to know when he was beaten, said nothing. He stayed there on the ground, knees in the sand and losing the battle inch by inch.

The courtyard was silent, as if they all held their breaths and were waiting between heartbeats.

Tessa eased off her sword. Sixten rolled away.

Again, she allowed him to recompose himself before attacking. Ove thought that generous and knew, instinctively, that there wouldn't be a third time.

As they continued, it seemed more even. Sixten could keep up with her and even got a few swipes in (though they were easily defended). Sixten, poor boy, bit his lips as he tried valiantly to stay in the fight. The recovery emboldened him, as though it had been his skill and not her mercy that had saved him. Ove couldn't remember Sixten ever joining on a raid (were they even called raids anymore, if the point was conquest?) in his year since coming to court. That was probably why he didn't sense the trap until it was sprung.

Bored or simply out of patience for someone so below her skill, Tessa feinted a downward strike. When Sixten moved to block it, she instead flipped her sword around, dodged his blade, and hit him square in the head with the butt of her sword. He cried out in pain. He reached for his nose with one hand, the other not strong enough to keep his sword up. The tip fell to the ground and lodged itself in the sand. That was when it happened.

Tessa stepped back. She readied her sword. She stepped forward. Thrust. Too hard. Too fast.

She hadn't realized the boy was helpless. She'd never had a real fight against a real living creature, he was certain. She fought ghosts and wisps and bad dreams, not creatures of flesh and blood. She didn't understand, didn't realize she'd already defeated him with the hit to the head.

The blow would have knocked the wind out of anyone wearing armor. Even made of wood, it would've dented the metal. Shades above help anyone wearing leather armor; it would bruise something awful.

Sixten wore neither metal nor leather.

He had on his fine linen tunic and a golden chain, given to him instead of earned. The tip of the sword broke his skin with a sickening tear. Blood spurted as the blade continued to skewer the boy.

His hand fell from his nose, eyes glassy. Then he fell to his knees before collapsing sideways, dead before he'd hit the ground.

While all eyes were on Sixten, Ove cast his gaze to Tessa.

She stood there, looking down at Sixten with an expression of complete shock. She was frozen, stuck in the moment she'd taken her first life. He knew then that she hadn't meant to. Worse, she hadn't even considered it a possibility. She was as blindsided as the rest of them; she didn't know what it was to fight with mortals like them.

She recovered before everyone else, though. She dropped beside him, lifting his limp head with one hand while the other scrambled at his neck for a pulse.

"Is there a healer?" she demanded of the crowd. "Fetch a witch!"

Her words shocked the life back into them. The crowd shuffled awkwardly on their feet and wouldn't look at her. There was no accusation, no anger, just a collective sense of shame and loss.

"Well?" she demanded, her voice rising in frustration. "Go!"

It was Ove who stepped forward. She knew him, if only a little; he would bear the responsibility of breaking the news to her. He walked to her side, around the body, and sat with her in the dirt.

He put a hand on her shoulder like one might calm a startled horse. "There are no witches or mages in Yfirgardr."

She reared back as if slapped. "What? But the queen—"

"Is dead," Ove said. "The other princes are gone. The magic folk left. No one to sponsor them. There's no honor to be gained when a man blind to magic sits on the throne." Ove swallowed. "Besides, there are no healers in all of Hjorrfold who can help him now."

Tessa's head snapped back to the boy in her arms. There was blood soaking his tunic, though none on her yet. His pale blue eyes stared blankly at the orange and pink sky. Ove turned away, so that his brother wouldn't be the one staring back at him.

"Come," he soothed. He stood and gently pulled her away; she came willingly, which he was glad of. He wouldn't have been able to force her. "They'll take care of him." He motioned to the others and hoped they would.

He led her inside the keep through the barracks to avoid the Great Hall and the Council room and the king's study and all the places Havardr might be. He knew the way to her room and took the longest, most secluded way there. She couldn't be seen like this and certainly couldn't face the prince until she'd had time to recover.

"I killed him," she said dumbly once they were in the cool shade of the keep. "I didn't mean to. I didn't—I thought—"

" 'twas an accident," he said. "These things happen."

They walked a few more paces before she asked quietly, “Do they happen often?”

Ove wished he were a better liar. “No. I’m afraid they don’t.”

They didn’t speak again.

18
Tessa

518

TESSA WAS SUMMONED to the Great Hall and went with something akin to dread. She didn't fear Havardr, but what she'd done in the courtyard had left her feeling empty. There would be consequences—there *should* be consequences—and she wasn't ready to face them.

In Vaettfangkirk, there'd been no other people for her to fight. There'd been no danger to anyone but herself, and she'd been healed so completely every time that she'd taken for granted how dangerous even a sparring match could be. She'd been so foolish, not thinking it through. She should've knocked that boy out the first chance she'd gotten. Better a head injury than death.

That poor, stupid boy. So determined to prove his worth. He should've yielded—

"It doesn't matter," she told herself. She stood before the small polished mirror hanging above a washbasin. She'd tried rinsing away her guilt with cold water, then tried spotting the murderess within her reflection, and found neither effective. "He's dead either way."

As she was led from her room to the Great Hall, her anxiety only grew. It wasn't until she stepped forward to meet Havardr that she realized what she really dreaded: not Havardr and his judgement, but knowing Trond would find out, and she wouldn't be the one to tell him. Her shame would make it to Hundrfeld before she ever did, and she would have to live knowing she bore his disappointment without ever getting the chance to hear his comfort.

"Step forward, Sister," Havardr said, voice booming. The Great Hall was nearly empty, no doubt a rarity, since Havardr seemed to thrive on the attention of vast hordes of watchers. How fortunate, she supposed, that few ears would hear him rebuke her. It was some of the officers who'd been overseeing the training, as well as some Council members; the former stood stiffly, waiting for their own chastisement, while the latter were stone-faced in displeasure.

Not in sadness, she noted. There were no dark morning clothes or clipped beards.

"Brother," she said once she'd reached the dais. She stood a few feet back from it, with her hands clasped behind her back, and inclined her head slightly in the appearance of deference. No matter the circumstances, she refused to bow to the man who'd killed her father. She kept her mind's eye on the knife at her belt. Just in case.

"I hear there was an accident in the courtyard," he said. His tone was scrupulous, his expression unreadable. "Tell me about it."

"I was dueling with the noble boy. Sixten, he said. Longswords. During the match, I ran him through with my sword." Her own voice was flat, devoid of the regret she felt; she knew that as prince, Havardr had a duty to the people of Hjorrfold under his protection. As a warrior, well…she'd only heard rumors, but she doubted he would care if that were his only role. But he had a front to put on, especially with the king gone, and couldn't afford to ignore a death in his own courtyard.

"You killed one of my bannerman's sons?" he asked sternly.

She held his gaze as she answered. "Yes."

It was only because she was so close that she saw it, the crook in his lips of a barely contained smile and the gleam in his eyes. He was pleased. He was glad his new weapon could skewer some poor boy with a practice sword, because he meant to turn her on his actual enemies.

Enemies, she scoffed. *That's too intimate a term for them. The people he means to conquer and slaughter are merely in his way…*

"You will go to Sixten's family and make amends. Take a token from your house. A dagger or a belt, perhaps, would do."

Cast off your former allegiances so that you are only mine. He might as well have declared it before the entire court.

"Yes, Brother." While she hated calling him that, it was better than 'sire' or 'prince.' She would do what she could to prevent anyone from calling him 'king.'

Havardr nodded in approval, then cast his attention to the Council. They looked mollified—someone from her station rarely did penance, and a personal trip there added to her degradation. He then turned to the officers, the men and women whose esteem he'd long ago won and in whose eyes he could do no wrong, and asked, "Would one of you escort Lady Tessa to Hjaeyna to complete this task?"

They hesitated, and she cursed silently. Any strides she'd made to win them over, she'd already lost. Oh, they might still appreciate her skill and her stamina, but they wouldn't want to degrade themselves by participating in an act of atonement. Guilty by association. She wouldn't force anyone to go with her. This was her mistake, and hers alone.

But before she could say as much, a man stepped forward. Ove. The red-headed guard who'd gone to Hundrfeld. The one who'd given her the heirlooms she would need to give up. The one who'd first joined her on the training pitch.

The one who looked nothing like her uncle, but reminded her fiercely of him.

"I will take the lady," he offered, bowing deeply to Havardr as he said it. When he rose, he said, "It's my fault, sire. I was the fool who suggested a duel, and more so for not properly overseeing it. The boy's death is my fault as much as hers, and I owe the family my regrets."

Havardr cocked an eyebrow. "Did you strike the killing blow?"

Ove shook his head.

"Did you encourage the boy to fight?"

"No, sire."

He pulled at a loose strand in his tunic. "Then you have no apologies to make. The boy made his own decision, ill-advised as it was. But I accept your offer to take my sister. There are dreki already waiting at the shore: take ten men to row and set out tomorrow."

"Tomorrow?" Ove asked, then bit his tongue and cast his head downward.

"Apologies, sire."

Havardr ignored his impertinence. "We're to sail to Thrireyna by week's end. I don't want to delay this conquest, not after so much work has been done in preparation. You will have a day, then the rest of us will join you at sea and head west." He stomped his foot, then raised a hand. "It is done. Go prepare."

Tessa paused only a moment, long enough to remember she was no longer in Hundrfeld and didn't quite understand this place despite how familiar it might seem, then turned on her heel and left. She had no wish to be in Havardr's company more than necessary. He'd let her go, so she went.

She might not have looked back at all, but she turned her head towards Ove and nodded once, the smallest movement, in thanks. An ally, however unexpected, wasn't something she could afford to lose.

IT TOOK NO more than an hour to ready herself for the journey. She hadn't yet gotten the chance to fully unpack her meager possessions, and most wouldn't follow her on this voyage. She needed two tunics and two pairs of breeches—one to wear, one to wash—and her armor. Of the weapons she'd brought, none was ready for battle; she'd find something in the armory that suited her. That left only the task of finding an appropriate offering for the lords of Hjaeyna, wherever that was.

The belt her uncle had gifted her was a thing of beauty, made of black leather with a silver buckle bearing a hound crest so wide it would reach above her navel when she wore it. There was room for a sword on the left, a dagger on the right, and both top and bottom were trimmed with fur. Without asking, she knew it was to commemorate her time at Vaettfangkirk. Though she'd never held it until this moment, it was too precious to give away.

The dagger was her father's. She recognized the metal sheath and its dog howling at the moon on a snowy hill. It was difficult to value a man she'd never met, but she hoped to stab this dagger through Havardr's heart. Fair payment for the heartbreak he'd brought to Trond.

She set these items aside and looked at the gold necklace with its small pendant, simple but lovely. A polished locket set in a thick golden circle. A gift from the first king of Hjorrfold to the first lady of Hundrfeld, when she had first sworn him fealty, ages and ages ago. It had stayed in her family as a token of their loyalty and was hers by rights.

Tessa held no loyalty to Havardr, and little to Hjorrfold. She would do what was best for Hundrfeld and her people, and would strive for as little collateral damage as possible. Trond respected their legacy, but even he wouldn't claim any ties to the royal family besides those necessary for peace. He would understand her choice.

Her mind made up, she wrapped the necklace in a silken kerchief and tucked it into a pouch on her belt. This was the thing she could bear to lose, though she dared not show what she'd kept. Not yet. She hid the belt and the dagger deep in a chest, buried beneath her clothes, and locked it.

SHE WOKE BEFORE dawn and went down to the gates, walking around the edges of the courtyard to avoid the training pitch. The place was eerie, so quiet and empty compared to how it'd been but a day before. She kept her back to the training pitch and waited. The guards on duty kept a respectful distance (or was it fearful?), and she ate the bread and figs she'd nicked from the kitchen.

Alone as she was on her perch against the keep's wall, she was aware that her solitude was only an illusion. There were so many people, not just in the city, but in the castle. It put her on edge. Made her feel like she was always being watched. If not for the errand that had led to her escape, she'd be happy to be free of this place for at least a moon, perhaps two.

Ove arrived as the sky lightened with the first rays of sunlight. As he walked towards her, she appraised him anew. She hadn't expected to see so much of him in Yfirgardr, or she would've paid more attention when they'd first met. He had a kindly manner about him, though she could see the calluses on his hands and the scars on his arms; he'd had a tough life. His ruddy hair was short, as was his beard. His eyes were the same light gray as Trond's, and when he smiled at the sight of her and waved, she felt homesick.

"You beat me here," he said and bowed to her. Not as deeply as he'd bowed to Havardr yesterday, but she noted he did it at all, and with no audience at that.

"I would prefer to get this over with," she admitted. "I don't like this hanging over me."

His face grew serious, his earlier lightness gone. "Aye. It's hard the first time."

"It gets easier?" She knew it did. It must, for people to keep raiding and pillaging.

"It does," he admitted. "And in the heat of it, it's far too easy. Let's head to the shore then, shall we?"

The guards opened the gate only wide enough for them to pass through, then sealed it shut behind them. It was too early to receive visitors, and they were the only ones leaving.

"Where are the others?" she asked as they walked down the stone path that led from the keep to the city walls. It was early and still quiet, yet Yfirgardr was waking up: carts passed by, men and women opened their shop doors, children ran to wells to fetch water. They paid her and Ove little mind, as if they couldn't care less about two warriors from the castle.

It doesn't take much to be anonymous here, she thought.

"They're already at the ship," he said. "They went down last night to get things ready. They'll be waiting for us. I chose warriors I've fought with before. They'll give us no trouble."

Give me *no trouble,* she thought. She had killed one of their fellows, not Ove; she would need to watch her back. *What they must think of me…*

She truly didn't know. In Hundrfeld, a stranger would be shunned for killing one of their own, even by accident. They would have to be purified by a witch to be accepted back into the community, so it was often easier to leave and start anew elsewhere.

It didn't seem to be like that in Yfirgardr, though. There were certainly friendships among the guards and warriors, but not everyone had grown up here in the capital. From Ove's accent, it seemed doubtful he had. Even with so many people in the city, the barracks were overflowing; they must be from across Hjorrfold. It must be easier to accept fresh faces and let go of familiar ones. It wasn't Hundrfeld, where everyone knew everyone.

They passed through the city walls—here the gate was thrown wide open and looked like it hadn't been shut in years, the gap large enough that three wagons could enter side-by-side and the walls so high they towered above them all—and followed the road south to the coast. There were clusters of tents built in the shadows of the city wall, and men and women milled about the campfires. A few saw Ove and waved, and he always waved back.

The uneven stone road gave way to dirt soon enough, a path worn by thousands of feet passing over it but not paved for the ease of carts. There wasn't a proper harbor, just a flat beach made of sand and pebbles. Yfirgardr, despite being the center of Hjorrfold both literally and metaphorically, was not easily accessible to anyone but its people. Merchants would have to land elsewhere, in the ports farther east, and then travel by wagon inland. It must have been crucial to safeguard the city back when it was a lonely keep on a hill, and it had never outgrown that history.

Unfortunately, this meant they had to wade into the water to launch their dreki. Tessa and Ove threw their bags aboard before they helped the others, half their group on one side, half on the other, as they pushed and ran into the surf. Once the boat started to float and rush into the waves, they all jumped aboard. It was like mounting a horse that was already mid-stride, and it took Tessa three tries before she was able to hook her leg over the edge and climb on. She landed with a less than graceful plop, much to the amusement of the crew.

"Don't sail much, eh?" one older man with gray hair and grayer teeth asked.

"I'm from Hundrfeld," she said. "This is the first time I've been on a boat."

The old man spat over the edge. "It's all right. You'll get your sea legs soon enough. Everyone does eventually."

She wanted to ask what that meant but soon found out: the boat lurched over a wave. Tessa widened her stance so she wouldn't topple backwards. Less than a minute aboard, and she wasn't sure she much enjoyed being at sea.

The sail billowed and drove them southwest to Hjaeyna. Tessa stood at the bow of the boat where a dragon's head—the dreki that gave this type of boat its name—roared out at the crashing waves. It had ruby eyes that glistened in the sun. Before them was nothing but water, more water than she'd even imagined. She stood there, transfixed, as she imagined how far it spread, how deep it went, and what might lurk beneath.

Ove came by and offered her a flagon of water. "You can't drink it," he said, nodding to the sea. "Looks like any river or spring you'll have by Hundrfeld, I expect, but it's saltier than Bjarngrim's balls."

She grimaced. That was quite an image. Bjarngrim was the first king of Hjorrfold, the one who'd united all the lands and built the keep on Yfirgardr. The one who'd given her family the necklace she was about to offer Sixten's family. More legend than man, Tessa didn't know whether he deserved any reverence, but if he was like his descendants, perhaps not.

"I didn't know Bjarngrim's balls were salty," Tessa said. "Speaking from experience?"

He threw back his head and laughed, then clapped her on the shoulder. "Aye, lass. It's how I've lasted this long. Know how to make the right friends." He grinned at her with crooked teeth. He looked younger when he smiled.

She returned his smile and thanked him for the water. The rest of the crew kept their distance, though some of them did so out of necessity. Though the sail was doing most of the work, a few of them manned the rows of oars to make sure they didn't go too far off course.

"How do you know which way to go?" she asked. Her own travels had taken her few places: the hamlets and homesteads bound to Hundrfeld, the marshes of Vaettfangkirk, and now to Yfirgardr. To leave Hundrfeld, she'd taken the roads, but at home she'd known every hill, crag, forest, and river. Within fifty miles of Hundrfeld's keep, she could find her way home by sight alone. But there were no landmarks at sea, and no roads. Miles and miles of blue sky above blue water. Even the coast of Hjorrfold was barely visible anymore.

"By day, we use the sun. Rises in the east, sets in the west, same as on land, and we'd best know where we plan to go between."

"Maps," she said, feeling foolish. "There are maps of the sea."

He nodded. "And some of us have traveled enough that we know the islands and the best places to make land in Hjorrfold. I don't know that I could make a map myself or read one, but I know where I'm going because I've been there." He tapped his head. "I know which direction and about how long I should be sailing."

"So you know the way to Havardr's new islands? The ones he conquered?"

"Of course," he said. "Raided them a few times. Doubt I'll ever go there again now that they're part of Hjorrfold."

Strange that after the slaughter of being conquered, these people might find more peace than they'd had before.

"And these new islands? Thrireyna? Do you know them?"

At this, Ove shrugged. "Not really. I know they're west of anywhere I've ever been. Don't know that I'd ever find them on my own, but when we join the fleet, we'll sail together. Just a matter of following."

Tessa turned back to the sea. With a hand over her brow to shield her eyes, she looked up at the sun and wondered how you could travel on a cloudy day, or if you had to pick a direction and hope for the best.

"What do you do at night?" she asked.

"Use a compass." Ove reached beneath his tunic and pulled out a small stone circle with holes in it. "The constellations, the stars, they can point you in the right direction. Depending on the season, you hold up a different side of the compass. For summer, it's the archer." He pointed to a cluster of holes at the top where the stone met the leather strap. "You hold this up to the sky at night, align the archer with the holes, and that's north."

She reached out, and he let her hold it. The stone was dark gray and warm from having been against his skin. The holes clearly meant something to him, but if there were any patterns to them, she couldn't make them out.

"Will you teach me?" she asked and handed it back, scared of dropping it. The idea of being lost at sea was a worry that hadn't occurred to her until that moment. At least in Yfirgardr, she knew the way home even if she couldn't go there. She imagined it must be easy to get turned around, forever lost among the rolling waves.

"On the way west," he promised and tucked the compass away. "We'll be at Hjaeyna long before dark."

"Will we?" She scanned the horizon again. Nothing.

"Hjaeyna's the closest island to Yfirgardr. The first added to Hjorrfold, I'd imagine. There's a lighthouse there. A big stone tower where they light a beacon each night. It helps keep ships from running aground in the dark and welcomes raiders home. Centuries ago, when these seas belonged to no one, it was also the first warning of incoming raids. They would light the beacon, and the fishermen of Yfirgardr would race back to shore."

"Surely it isn't that close—" She stopped short and climbed higher onto the bow. At the very edge of what she could see, there was something solid. The water sprayed and rolled, never sitting still, but that speck was unmoving. If a wave took it from view, a moment later it reappeared in the same spot. "It is close."

"Aye," Ove said somberly. He cleared his throat awkwardly. "Do you know what you'll say to them? When we deliver the body, I mean."

Sixten. The boy she'd helped wrap in linens. He rested in the small hold under the ship where it was dark and cold, or so she'd been told. Where he wouldn't rot as quickly and might still be recognizable to his family. She shuddered. What had her father looked like when he'd been brought to Hundrfeld, the body laid at Trond's feet?

"The truth," she said. "I'll tell them the truth."

THE LIGHTHOUSE CAME into view first. Taller than the castle towers at Yfirgardr, the column of stone glistened in the morning light. There was no smoke from the beacon, and Tessa wondered how far it might travel on a clear day. If the wind was favorable, would it carry the smoke all the way to Yfirgardr? It seemed impossible, but that was its entire purpose.

As they neared the island, they were welcomed by small boats of curious fishermen. Some waved and shouted, but many simply watched. It was clear these were lands unused to raiding: no one fled or sounded an alarm. They all went about their business once the dreki had passed, unconcerned with the armed men and women heading to their home.

Unlike Yfirgardr, there was a small dock. A single large ship bobbed in the water, bigger than the fishing boats they'd passed but smaller than their own modest craft and without the dragon mast. For the family's travel, no doubt, should they ever go to the mainland. As they neared the dock, a tall, lean woman appeared and threw them a rope.

"Welcome, travelers," she said. "What brings you?"

"Prince Havardr sends us," Ove replied, his hand on Tessa's shoulder to keep her quiet. "We wish to speak to your lord and lady at once."

"Is there danger?" the woman asked, her gaze sweeping first across the crew and then out to sea. She seemed unconcerned.

"No," was all Ove said.

"Well," she said, pulling Tessa onto the dock and then gesturing for Ove to follow. "Best take you, then."

The longhouse was low but long. The squat building had a moss-covered roof and was made of sun-bleached wood that reflected the light. She doubted there was a single staircase in the place, though perhaps a ladder to an attic loft or storage hold, but no true second floor. When they entered, there was one large-ish hall that could fit twenty, lined with doors that must lead directly to the family's rooms. There was a narrow doorway with no door that smelled of meat and sugar, likely leading to the kitchen and servants' quarters. It was small enough that it could fit comfortably inside Hundrfeld's keep, but too large to be confused for a peasant's home.

A lord and lady sat at the far end of the hall, the lady with embroidery draped across her knees and the man with a pipe that blew the darkest smoke Tessa had ever seen. Like Trond's great seat, theirs lay flat on the ground with no dais lifting them, though unlike Trond, no dogs flanked them. They smiled good-naturedly as she approached. She thought she saw some of Sixten in the lady.

"I bring you ill tidings of your son," Tessa said, cutting right to the quick. She saw no reason to dance about her true purpose, and she knew in their place she would appreciate forthrightness. "I am Tessa of Hundrfeld"—she took a knee and bowed low, her right arm over her chest so her palm lay above her heart—"and I have killed Sixten."

The woman gasped, a strangled sound that was more shock than pain; that would come later. When Tessa looked back up, the man was grim-faced. If he were surprised, she couldn't say, but he seemed suddenly tired, as if he'd aged a hundred years in one instant. He pushed up from his chair and motioned for her to stand; she did.

"Walk with me," he said, then left the hall without waiting to see if she'd follow; she did. They left through a large door at the rear of the hall to a stone walkway that led around the back of the longhouse. Only after they'd walked some distance did he continue: "Tell me what you've done, Tessa of Hundrfeld."

She told him. About her arrival in Yfirgardr and the training. About Sixten's offer to spar, his choice of weapon, and her foolishness in allowing him to continue when he was obviously outmatched.

"I should've forced him to yield sooner. I could have."

His father shook his head. "It might've saved his life, but he would've felt the failure too acutely. A young man's decision, to pick his honor over his life. He would've never forgiven you if you'd stopped him." He gave her a sidelong glance. "A skjaldmaer…aye, he would've liked the challenge and not thought it through."

Tessa wanted to argue that the responsibility and shame lay with her and not his son, but she saw the firm line of his jaw clenched tight. There was no hope of convincing him. Instead, she pulled out the necklace and offered it to him.

"A token of my apology. It has been in the hands of Hundrfeld for centuries, the reward for our sworn fealty to Hjorrfold. It's the best I can offer. Our past for your future."

Sixten's father didn't reach out to take the necklace, and when he opened his mouth to refuse, Tessa pressed on.

"Your son could act no differently than he did, as you say," she said. She took his hand and placed the necklace in it, closing both her hands over his fist. "Nor can I. This is all I can give, though I know it does nothing to ease your pain. There is nothing that can undo losing your family."

But if Havardr had even attempted to make things right…even if he'd killed my father in cold blood like Trond suspects, it would've shown he thought our loss mattered. Some consideration, some regret, it must count for something.

Reluctantly, he accepted it. Tessa felt as though a huge burden had been lifted from her shoulders, like she had been trapped under a boulder all her life until that moment and was finally free.

"I bear you no ill will," he said as if by rote, though she could see he meant it. The man was old, older than her uncle, yet his son had been so young. "He was my youngest. My last. The older two died in raids... I was a fool to let him leave, but he had his heart set on following his brother and sister..."

And now he has, went unsaid.

Emotion overcame him, and the words stopped altogether. There were no tears, though. He held onto that small dignity still, waiting to shatter when he was alone.

"I—"

"You and your crew may stay the night," he interrupted, voice firmer than it'd been before. His fist was so tightly clenched around the necklace, his knuckles were bone white, and she worried he'd cut himself on the pendant. "You'll be shown every courtesy as a guest of our humble home. We'll have rooms for you. And food. Forgive me and my wife, though, if we don't join you."

She thought of the way Trond had always scowled when he'd heard of Havardr visiting. "On behalf of my companions, I thank you. Your hospitality is most generous... but I will stay on the ship."

A look of relief washed over his features, like she'd eased a concern of his he perhaps wasn't aware of until it was gone. He didn't protest, so she knew she'd acted rightly.

"Would you like us to carry the body up from the dock, or—?"

"I will do it," he said quickly. "I'll retrieve him."

Tessa lingered behind the longhouse, enjoying the salty air that the breeze carried to her. She didn't want to disturb the household, so when the kitchen servants came out to ready wood for a pyre, she made herself scarce. The island wasn't large, but it was large enough to afford her the space to wander without being in anyone's way. A few of the fishermen saw her as they returned to their small homes; she took that as her own cue to return to the dreki.

She saw Ove sitting on a log at the edge of the dock. He jumped to his feet as soon as he saw her, worry creasing his brow. "Are you all right?"

"Me?" she asked. She motioned for him to sit back down, and she took the spot next to him. The wood was still warm from the sun.

"It's no easy thing, what you did. Especially if you're really sorry for it. You left with that lord and didn't come back, not even when they came for Sixten. Everyone else went to the house for lunch, and still no sign of you."

How strange to have someone worrying about her. She'd never encountered such a thing outside of Hundrfeld and hadn't expected it.

"I didn't want to interfere," she admitted. "If someone had killed my uncle, even by accident, I wouldn't want to see them if I didn't have to."

Again she thought of Havardr, imposing himself again and again.

And she thought of how very much she wanted to kill him, though she couldn't yet. Every time he smiled at her or praised her or acted like he didn't know or care she hated him, it all grated on her. She would do no such thing to Sixten's family if she could help it.

"You're a good lass. If you plan to stay out here—"

"I do. And if you mean to offer me company, don't bother." She kicked the sand, finer than any she'd seen before. She was enchanted by how solid it seemed until you touched it and it flew into pieces. It reminded her of the shades at Vaettfangkirk, but like a harmless cousin. "This'll be your last chance for a while to sleep under a roof and have a hot meal. Hear there's not much of that when you're at sea."

Or at war.

Ove was quiet before grunting, "If it pleases you, I'll go." He lingered, giving her the chance to change her mind; when she didn't, he pushed up again and started towards the path to the longhouse. "Send for me if you get too lonesome," he called over his shoulder.

Thankfully, he hadn't put up much of a fight. Tessa wasn't in the right state to argue, or to be sociable, for that matter. There were always so many *people* around, and soon they'd be cooped up on that boat together for weeks and weeks…

Funny thing, her wanting time to herself. She'd been so alone in Vaettfangkirk that she'd been about ready to talk to the trees or the grass out of loneliness. Now she almost missed her small room and the silence that came every night after she was free of the other skjaldmaer. She missed nothing else about it, only that she'd been allowed to be herself in those quiet hours before her next day of torment. There was no performing or hiding, no need to be anyone but Tessa, even if Tessa was a miserable girl who missed her home.

"I will go home someday," she promised the sea. "I will go home and sit in my uncle's seat and make sure the people of Hundrfeld are safe. I will, I will, I will..."

19
Havardr

518

There were twenty-three dreki sailing west, the largest and swiftest ships in Hjorrfold. Havardr personally owned fifteen of them (or his father did, which these days was no significant distinction), and the rest were offered freely by bannermen and rich merchants hoping to ingratiate themselves with the crown. It had worked, and should they remind Havardr of their generosity whenever they asked for a favor, he would return it in kind.

Each dreki held some thirty men, so there were nearly seven hundred warriors in total. It had taken months after his call for conquest to gather so many, and more had come after they'd taken the first few islands. They continued to trickle in at a steady pace, and he'd commissioned several more ships to be built, including a great longboat big enough for eighty men.

The boats, admittedly, were more straightforward than the people. A dreki that could float was fit to sail; a man or woman in armor wasn't necessarily fit to fight. Many would-be warriors had flocked to Yfirgardr at the promise of riches and glory. While many had proven to be battle ready, others had needed extensive training. More annoyingly, many needed weapons and armor, and he'd spent more from the treasury outfitting them than he'd gained in tribute and plunder so far.

Seven hundred soldiers in battle was a great thing, except that it was no simple task to feed and house them all. The barracks in Yfirgardr held 150 comfortably, though his master-at-arms had squeezed in fifty more. The rest were throughout the city itself, filling every inn, tavern, and wayhouse. Those who couldn't fit—and there were a great many—made do with tents outside the city walls. No issue when the weather was fair and the days long, but he would have to do something for them come winter. He prayed for a long summer and autumn, so he needn't worry about it for a while yet. The last thing he wanted was to send them home and risk them not returning the next spring.

The logistics of war were unexpectedly troublesome. It was so unlike raiding. Havardr said he wanted to go pillage, anyone who wished to come was free to do so, and they were sailing within a few days. This required a great deal of organizing and planning. The work was tedious, and Havardr didn't have a mind for it. He managed it all out of sheer necessity—Hjorrfold had no experienced warmasters to do the work for him—and there were times he missed Stigandr. Stigandr would've been very good at this work, far better than Havardr ever could be, and then he could focus on the actual fighting while his brother handled the boring matters.

But there was no more Stigandr. He'd made sure of it.

And at the moment, there was no Tessa. He'd been pleased with her skill once he'd seen it firsthand in the courtyard. After seeing the dead boy's body that she'd killed, he'd been happier still. To do that with a blunted wooden sword...she was strong indeed. She was worth a dozen men at least, and because he'd publicly bound her honor to his by claiming her a sister, every kill she made would be in his name. They would be the two best warriors, she and he, and he would build his empire on their prowess.

They set sail for Thrireyna at dawn on a warm day, carried out to sea by a steady breeze. Once offshore, they turned south instead of west: they would need to give Tessa time to catch up.

He'd given her a small dreki, and it would be difficult for them to maintain the same pace as the rest of the fleet. It was, in some ways, a test to see how she would fare with the odds stacked against her, and in others, it was a punishment for the delay. It wasn't because she'd killed that boy, though he was glad he had that as an excuse. He didn't care about some dead noble's son he'd never heard of, except that he'd had to account for her excursion to Hjaeyna before they could make for open waters.

Though in retrospect, it could've been worse. He was glad it'd happened when it did, with only the common guards and warriors watching. It would've been a lot harder to smooth over if it'd been during the exhibition matches he'd planned for the Council, though ideally she would've killed someone with no family at all. Much easier when no reparations needed to be made.

When they arrived within sight of Hjaeyna, there was happily no reason to delay at all: Tessa's ship was at sea with a flag raised to show they were ready.

"Blow the horn," Havardr ordered.

The horn sounded, a long sharp note followed by two shorter ones. A pause, then it was repeated. Ten times it would ring, to make sure everyone heard. The nearest dreki took up their own horns and joined in until soon the waves themselves echoed with the message: *sail on*. The wind was in their favor, and the islands far. It would take a full week of constant travel to reach their destination, and he knew they'd have to stop along the way: for supplies, to make sure their previous conquests were still willing to bend the knee, and to keep everyone's spirits up.

Once they arrived at Fyrrey, the first island of the trio, he thought it would take them at least a fortnight to take it, given its size. Because of its location, it was absolutely crucial they do so quickly: if things took longer than expected and the weather turned, they'd have to live there instead of risking the journey back in winter when the sea was treacherous.

Not that he'd told anyone of this likelihood. Raiders were used to time at sea, but only as long as it took to get where they were going—a day or two for each village they raided, no more—and to sail back. There were no camps ashore, no frivolous stops to oversee conquered peoples, and no waiting out the weather before moving on. Conquering was not the same business as pillaging, and this campaign would be longer than the previous one. If his warriors had known that ahead of time, they might not have been so eager to enlist, but he was confident once they had their plunder in hand, they would be more than content.

"Who will claim the most kills?" his hornsman asked as Havardr took a seat behind him at the ship's stern. He preferred staying at the back of the ship so he could keep an eye on the crew. On days when they needed to row, it was easy to maintain order, because everyone was tired; when the wind carried them, as it did today, people got restless and could start trouble.

"Besides me?" Havardr took the dried meat offered to him and bit into it. He was stronger than any man had a right to be—a rare gift from his mother—and always earned himself the most kills and therefore the most honor.

The hornsman laughed. Havardr didn't remember his name and knew he should. This man had been by his side for months and months, conveying his orders to the other dreki. But Havardr didn't know his name, or hardly anyone else's. He lived and trained with these people, fought and bled with them, might even die with them one day, but he kept them from his heart. He'd learned with Sindri that true friendships could only be used against him.

"Of course, besides you," the hornsman chortled. "You fight like a dire bear. I wonder if you need the rest of us at all, though I suppose a thousand dogs can take down a bear."

Havardr grunted and continued to eat. He enjoyed the praise and the respect it showed, but constant flattery grated on him.

Unbothered by his silence, the man continued. "That Tessa girl. She might actually give you some competition. Not much experience, but plenty fast and strong. Young blood and all that."

"She'll do well," Havardr said. Or she had better. He wasn't sure what he'd do to her if she failed to live up to the prophecies. He'd sacrificed Sindri and a dozen men to get her, nevermind the years of waiting around for her to grow. If she proved unworthy…

"Oh, I have no doubt. The men, we make our wagers. Usually to see who will be second to you, but this time, most are interested in if she'll outdo you."

He refrained from rolling his eyes. That was why he tried to keep his raiders occupied, otherwise they made stupid bets amongst themselves and got angry when they lost. "And what do they say?"

"A little more than half think she'll kill more."

Havardr stiffened. He tried to remind himself that anything she did, she did in his name, but a direct competition between them undermined that unity. He had to remain first in the minds of his warriors; being second wasn't an option.

"A girl who's never been in a proper fight?" he said dismissively. "Not likely."

The hornsman, unable to take a hint, persisted. "A skjaldmaer, though. She killed that boy, and everyone saw how easy it was. I reckon she'll want to kill as many as she can to wash away the dishonor of that duel."

That gave him pause. There was truth in what he said, and any child raised by Trond would be over-worried about honor.

"I guess I'll have to try harder," he said with a lopsided grin he knew the men appreciated. He meant it, too.

TESSA'S DREKI KEPT up with the fleet, though only barely. When the air was still and the sails limp, it fell behind and sometimes would disappear behind the crest of the waves. When the wind picked up, though, she'd regain the lost ground. The smaller size made it more nimble and easier for even a slight breeze to help along.

He made sure she was at the back when they arrived at Fyrrey, determined to get a head start in battle. He needed her to fight so everyone would see her skill and so that they could make quick work of the poor savages, but he would not be outdone by a child.

As soon as his lookouts had spotted land through their spyglasses, he gave the order to hold. The horn blew, a series of five high-pitched blasts that sounded like gulls cawing. Since they were approaching from the east, they would wait until dusk could cover their arrival. By the time they hit shore, it would be night and most of the villagers would be asleep. He had his lookouts watch all day to confirm they were indeed nearing a settlement.

"Where there's smoke, there're people," one assured him. "We're too far out to tell how many, though. If we sailed a little closer—"

"No. Surprise helps us more than knowing how many. As long as they don't have a stone wall, we'll get the better of them."

If there was a stone wall, they were well and truly fucked. Havardr had heard of contraptions that could hurl stones and destroy buildings, but he'd never seen one himself and certainly wouldn't know how to direct their construction. There were mages who could wield such power, or so the tales said, but such things were more story than reality these days. Hjorrfold was a kingdom built on the sword, with magic relegated to household tasks: lighting torches, healing injuries, and keeping homes warm. To find a skilled enough mage to breach walls…

Stigandr and their mother were the most talented magic users in the kingdom (though Randel had ended up better than expected), and they wouldn't have been able to do it. Destructive magic was so uncommon in Hjorrfold, as good as banned for how few people studied it, that Havardr had never seen it at court. Stigandr probably would do something trickier, like disguise himself as a local and open the gate from the inside, or enchant someone to do it for him.

The best Havardr could do is surround the village and starve them out. There was no glory in that.

"There'd better not be any walls," Havardr growled. The lookouts nodded and swallowed, as if they had any control over the matter.

Once it was suitably dark, they snuffed their torches and began to move. They didn't dare use the horns, the signal instead given by waving a banner. There were just enough stars and moonlight to see. Hundreds of oars slipped into the water and drove them forward. They would be nothing but a dark blot on the horizon, if anyone saw anything at all.

Havardr stood with his battleaxe at the ready. It took over an hour to get to shore, the village indistinct but for some fires. Their view of those orange dots was mostly unobstructed, and Havardr grinned in pleased anticipation: no walls. Movement, though. Animals or guards, he knew not, but either made it trickier.

He felt the instant the dreki skimmed the ground and readied himself. Once it caught the sand and lurched as it got stuck, he jumped into the water and charged. His men—the fastest, strongest rowers in all Hjorrfold—abandoned their oars and followed him. The wooden frame of the boat had creaked loudly, louder than the surf, when it'd run aground, and their splashing had drawn attention. There were shadowy figures lurking near the beach, night-blind from their fires and helpless as Havardr reached the first of them.

He roared as he swung his axe, no longer caring for secrecy. It was time for battle, and he craved the thrill of bones breaking and blood spilling. He lived for these moments, when he felt more alive for each life he took. The first bodies hit the ground before he'd broken his stride, before anyone else could join the fray, and he rushed through the slippery sand to get closer to the village. There was shouting and the clang of a bell.

Good, he thought. He preferred when they put up a fight.

To raid, they traveled in small numbers, which in turn necessitated targeting smaller settlements. Bring thirty men to attack three hundred. But this island was larger than most, and so was this village. It stretched on and on. Whenever Havardr thought he'd reached an end, he'd round a building and see a line of buildings continuing into the night. There must've been a thousand living here.

The battle went on well after all twenty-three ships had landed. The veterans had been smart and helped surround the space, cutting off retreat and advancing to drive the terrified people towards the village center. Havardr was aware of their efforts, and though he approved, he preferred his own task of cutting down any man and woman who dared raise a weapon against him.

In a lull in fighting, he caught his breath. He was usually at the epicenter, because their enemies rightly thought if they could take him down, they could save themselves. But there was nothing near him but broken bodies, so he took off his helmet and wiped the blood and muck from his face with his arm. It must be over if he had this moment of respite, but as he surveyed the village, he found this wasn't the case.

The battle was still raging, but some distance away. He could hear battle cries and petrified pleas for mercy, the whoosh of spears flying and the clang of metal clashing.

He put on his helmet and stormed over.

Havardr had expected to come across a standstill between his warriors and the defending villagers. Battle lines drawn as they made a last-ditch effort to stave off their inevitable defeat, throwing everything they had, knowing there was no hope of freedom past this moment, this final chance.

That wasn't what he found.

He encountered a row of Hjorrfold warriors, marveling as Tessa deftly defeated each opponent as they came at her, often multiple fighters at once.

She disabled them one by one, killing only those who were properly armed and merely incapacitating the rest. She was like a ghost, the shadows embracing her like one of their own. Her inky hair disappeared like black mist, and there were three thick lines of ash drawn down her face to obscure her pale skin. Covered in soot, her armor blended with the darkness, transforming her into the likeness of a demon. When she turned his way, he saw what the villagers saw: a creature of the night come to claim them, an instrument of death who wouldn't stop until she'd taken them all.

For a heartbeat, he felt fear.

But she blinked and turned away, rushing back into battle with her sword raised and a screech like a banshee.

Havardr stood there, transfixed like everyone else. He didn't take action until a bulking man landed a sword strike across her arm. Blood flowed freely, and she adjusted her grip on her sword to account for the injury, but Havardr rushed in and took out the man's legs from behind with his axe. With a sickening squelch, the man's knees tore apart as steel met flesh, and he screamed in agony and fell at Tessa's feet. She watched him fall and looked up at Havardr, anger flashing through her black eyes.

"I had him," she said.

"You're welcome," he said pleasantly. He understood her annoyance—he'd flay anyone who dared interfere like that—but he enjoyed saving her. It served well to remind the onlookers who the true master here was.

"Thank you," she said. "Brother." She looked almost grateful. At least she remembered her place.

There was little left to do after that. Anyone with any spark of resistance in them lay dead or dying. The aftermath of the battle had ravaged the village: doors were smashed, homes were burning, and everywhere there were people weeping among the scattered bodies of their kinsmen. The scene was familiar: devastation and the acceptance of it. It looked like ruin and tasted like victory.

A woman with finer clothes than the rest sat next to a well, three dirty children clutching her skirts, all her mirror image. She looked haunted, though he admired the way she turned her nose up at him as he approached.

"Are you in charge?" he asked gently as he crouched nearby. Close enough that they couldn't escape if they tried to flee, but not so close that he could strike them. He'd learned this was the right distance to put people at ease.

"I am the chieftain's daughter," she said. He was relieved she understood him, though her accent was so garbled he had to strain to unspool each word. "For whatever that's worth."

Not as much as it was worth yesterday, he thought, though he was kind enough not to say it.

"You know this area well, then?" he asked.

She shuddered. "You're not here to raid."

His men and women were going through every building in this village, taking whatever valuables they could get their hands on. "Well, not *just* that."

"You take slaves?" she asked uneasily. She held the children tighter. A good mother, he noted. She'd claw his eyes out if he tried to take them.

"No," he assured her. Slavery was an ugly business, and in his mind, an unnecessary one. Why force people into servitude when you could simply bend them to your will instead? Those who followed willingly were far better subjects than those who always needed watching. "You are free to stay here, in your home, so long as you bow to Hjorrfold and its king."

"Hjorrfold," she sneered, then spat on the ground. "Fuck Hjorrfold and its king."

He smiled darkly at her. "King Alvis is my father."

The color drained from her face.

"We are fair in our rule," he continued. "We expect tribute, but you are otherwise free to live much as you did before."

"And you expect us to help you conquer our neighbors."

He shrugged. "Your help would be appreciated, but it isn't required. It's hard to betray your allies. I won't demand it from you, though you'd be rewarded for it. Your compliance and tribute are all that's required." Or he'd rip every family apart and scatter them across Hjorrfold. They wouldn't be slaves, but they would never see each other again and never make it back to their home. But he wouldn't threaten if he didn't have to.

She hesitated. "You will let us bury our dead and perform funeral rites. You will not take all our food. You will leave the holy treasures in our sanctuaries in the woods. You do these things, and I will help you with anything you ask."

Havardr considered. All were reasonable requests. As long as they were cooperative, he would've granted them anyway. "We will need some food," he said. "While we take the rest of the island. But we will leave you enough for winter." He put a fist over his heart and bowed his head—though he never took his eyes off her—to show his pledge.

Awkwardly, she mimicked him.

"I can't say I'm displeased by your decision," he said as he stood up, "but why are you so willing to sell out your fellows to strangers?"

"I hate you for what you've done to my people," she said, "but it's no different from what the bastards on the other side of the island have been doing to us for centuries. You just did it all at once. We're fishermen and weavers, and they come here to make us slaves. It's their turn to know what it's like to be on the wrong end of a spear."

The enemy of my enemy... the common language of us all.

"We'll return your kin," he promised. He could make an example of this village: compliance was rewarded. "I'll order my men and women to the beach so you can perform your rites. I will have guards patrol," he warned, then paused in consideration. "Do you have healers?"

She shook her head. "Our magic is in the earth."

He took his leave and gave orders to let the people bury their dead. They would make camp on the beach, and tomorrow he would seek that woman again. This was an excellent victory, but there was much to do. They would need to coordinate food, and he would grill her for all she knew of not only her neighbors here, but on the nearby islands. Ideally, he would get a map to help him plot out the rest of his campaign, something more detailed than the vague sketches given to him by merchants and the handful of raiders who'd made it this far.

The sun was just beginning to make itself known over the sea, promising a clear day. A good omen, and he didn't even need a mage to tell him that.

He found Tessa at her small dreki, standing in the surf. It was low tide, and she was inspecting the hull while rubbing saltwater into her wound and cleaning the soot off. Her crew was nowhere to be seen—no doubt they'd lingered in the village, looking for their share of the loot, and were now making camp to celebrate. Yet she was here with nothing but what she'd come with.

"You've done well," he said. He was glad not to have an audience to perform to. He could say what he meant without worrying about how others might perceive the encounter. "How did it feel?"

She froze at the sound of his voice, then shrugged and continued to clean herself. "It was nice not having to hold back, I suppose. I liked knowing exactly what the end was, instead of fighting and fighting until I was told to stop."

It reminded him a little of Ragnhild, who'd always seemed surprised when the day's training had ended and she could rest. They must work the girls hard at Vaettfangkirk, and it was well worth the effort.

Thinking of Ragnhild, his eyes went to Tessa's wounded arm. The cut wasn't as deep as he'd thought, though it glistened red with fresh blood. The salt would do it good, but she'd have to bind it soon.

"We have no mages or healers," he said, nodding at her arm. Useful though they were, he didn't want to give up a single seat to someone who couldn't fight. "There might be herbs in the village to help fight infection, but if you want to remove the scar, it'll take work to find someone skilled enough back home."

Ragnhild hadn't let a single mark stay on her body after Vaettfangkirk. She was very particular about it and would often seek the healers as soon as she left the training pitch. Her companion, some girl she'd trained with, was similarly insistent: every wound, no matter how small the scratch, needed to be washed away and could leave no lasting mark. Ragnhild had not been that way as a girl, often proud of the scrapes and bruises she'd earned climbing on the walls of the keep or in the trees on the road down to the city.

Havardr made this offer now to Tessa to show he understood the strange quirks of skjaldmaer. He would use her, as he used the chieftain's daughter, but he could make it worth her while.

But Tessa glanced down at the wound before firmly saying, "No. I'll keep it." There was a fierceness in her eyes he didn't understand, as if she was delighted to have some mark on her otherwise unblemished skin. When she looked at him, he had difficulty understanding her at all. Her eyes were like the surface of the sea at its deepest: dark and smooth, it appeared calm, but no one could guess what lurked beneath. It gave her a blank look, impossible to read.

No matter. He didn't need to understand her. So long as she did as she was told, that was more than sufficient.

"As you wish," he said. "I prefer my scars where they are as well. They show who we are, do they not?"

"Or remind us what we've survived," she said, and it was the closest to outright agreeing with him she'd ever come.

When Havardr turned his back, he walked away with a smile. He'd invested years in getting her ready, but he wouldn't go easy on her. If the prophecy was wrong, he wanted to know sooner than later.

It didn't seem wrong so far.

20

Ove

518

A FEW DAYS before they landed on Fyrrey, Ove found this was his favorite trip to sea yet. Perhaps it was because it was one of the few he wasn't drunk the whole time, but he thought it might have more to do with the company.

Ove took his turn at the oars, passing a water flagon to the man he replaced before settling in. They'd been without wind for two days—though still better than traveling against the wind—and it was hard work to keep up with the other dreki. They were a crew of fifteen where only ten could row at a time, trying to match the pace of larger ships that held thirty or more men and could have as many as twenty-six rowers. They were lucky that their smaller craft gave them the advantage of not having as much to carry, but it was exhausting. Prince Havardr's ship was but a speck in the distance. They had to rely on the other ships to know their path.

Ove rowed for hours. It was mind-numbing work, but sometimes they sang to pass the time. Over meals, they would tell stories. But the sun was directly above them, no clouds in sight to shield them, and the sea so still there wasn't the hint of a breeze to offer relief. They rowed in silence, too sweaty and tired to talk.

After his turn was up, Ove went to sit at the stern. When his arms no longer felt like jelly, he reached over the edge to bring up handfuls of water to wash away the sweat. The water was blissfully cool against his overheated skin. He dozed, shoulder to shoulder with another resting warrior.

When he awoke, he was alone at the back of the ship. The others were handing out rations and water to those still rowing. The sun was nearing the far horizon, and there was the flutter of wind at their backs. When Ove got up and stretched out the kinks in his back, he noticed Tessa at the oars. She'd been there all day, before and after him, and looked as though she hadn't rested at all.

He grabbed some dried fruits and a loaf of bread and sat beside her on the bench.

"You ever get tired?" he asked. "I can take over for you while you eat."

"I already tried," one of the younger raiders said, tone light. "Stronger than an ox, she is."

Tessa flashed them both a glare, though there was no venom behind it.

"We're falling behind. Are there no mages in Hjorrfold who could conjure a fair wind?" She didn't even sound out of breath, and her pace never faltered.

"There might be," Ove conceded. "Just not ones who would work for Havardr. He scared most of the mages and witches out after his mother died. No secret the prince doesn't care for 'em, though I wouldn't mind someone conquering a cloudy sky and full sails."

The others chimed in their agreement.

"Some of you use magic," she said after some consideration. "I see the way you light the torches or cook the fish."

"Small magic," the lookout said. She had the spyglass tucked in her belt. When she snapped her fingers, the tiniest glimmer of a flame sparked, then she waved her hand to put it out. "A lot of us learn it as kids. They don't in Hundrfeld?"

"People do," she said. "We had a witch in the castle, a midwife in the village, and I suspect there's a lot of small magic to be found. My uncle doesn't know any, and I never learned."

"Do you want to?"

Tessa huffed a laugh. "If we ever finish all this rowing, I might take you up on it. As is, my hands are full."

This earned a hearty laugh from everyone, even the others at their oars.

"You really Havardr's ward, then?" the lookout asked.

"So it seems,"Tessa muttered. Ove didn't think most of them heard her, and she gave a curt nod as well.

"Hmm," the woman hummed. "Bet it's a gift and a curse, all that attention from the prince."

"He goes through favorites rather quickly," a man at the oars just ahead of them added. His back and arm muscles strained to keep the pace, and his face contorted in determination as he continued. His voice wasn't nearly as even as Tessa's. "Honors and gold on 'em all, piles and piles of it, but that just means you get more dangerous jobs. Gets you killed sooner than later."

Ove wondered if this was what had happened to his brother: if he'd shone too brightly, too quickly, and it had gotten him in over his head before he was ready. Not that Ove knew the details of the raid that had killed his brother. It could've been an inexperienced captain or a storm. Or maybe it was simply his time. But what if he had been a favorite of the prince's? Havardr liked things risky—more wagered, more won, as he said—and he brought his favorites. The best way into Havardr's good graces was to do well in battle, but even the best of them only had so many raids in them.

Like this fleet. Sailing to the far edges of the world, not for a simple raid but a hundred raids' worth of battles. He remembered taking those other islands, how tiring it'd been to go from one battle to the next and the next with hardly any time to catch his breath in between. But as long as the prince was able to keep going, the rest of them had to as well.

Maybe they were lucky to find themselves at the tail end of the fleet: it might buy them an extra night of their lives.

"Am I a favorite, then?"Tessa asked. "Should I be worried?"

"Oh, you're a favorite," the lookout said. "But I don't think you've got much to worry about. Not unless they all ride dire wolves and have dragons protecting their villages and their skin's made of iron."

"Ha!" someone called. "That'd be a sight!"

After another half hour, Tessa finally yielded the oar to Ove. She didn't go far, taking the empty spot on the bench and eating the food he'd offered her earlier. She ate as if she'd never had a proper meal in her life. Like a famished dog, she went through double her rations and then a full flagon of water. When she stopped, it seemed more because she was conscious of their stares and not because she was sated. At this rate, she'd eat them out of supplies if this trip lasted them a day longer than expected. Though since she might single-handedly get them there, it seemed fair enough.

"First raid, eh?You excited or nervous?" Ove asked, measuring out his words with his strokes.

She hesitated, a good sign it was the latter. "It's still far enough off. I don't know how I'll feel when it happens." She rubbed her palms on her tunic. "You?"

"Before my first raid, I nearly threw up from nerves." He chuckled at her skeptical look. "It's true. Of course, I was also quite drunk. Might've been the mead, might've been the fear."

"Does it get really easier?" she asked quietly.

The boat was small, without even the semblance of privacy. On a larger dreki, there'd be no hiding how poorly she'd slept. They'd all given her the benefit of the doubt that the dark circles under her eyes were because it was her first time at sea; it seemed there was another cause entirely.

Ove weighed his words carefully. "It normally isn't like with Sixten. That was an accident. In the heat of battle, when it's your life or theirs, you don't even notice that you're killing. It won't hit you until later, and then you'll be too relieved to be alive to care much, bad as it sounds."

Tessa took this in without a word, her expression remaining placid. He hoped that this would help her put the mess with Sixten behind her. Not his words, necessarily, but this whole business on Thrireyna. Sixten was but one boy, and dozens of men and women were going to fall on her sword. In their line of work, you couldn't let yourself dwell on the lives you took, or you'd go mad. You'd hesitate, you'd hold back, and eventually it'd get you injured or killed. Too much heart and you shouldn't pick up a sword.

"This is what I was raised to do," she said. "My uncle taught me to hunt. The skjaldmaer taught me to fight. Havardr brought me to Yfirgardr to help him with his wars. If I fail, I'm as good as dead."

He swallowed thickly. Damn the others for their talk. Damn this voyage being too long. They'd say far more than they should before it ended, himself included, and it would only make Tessa more anxious.

"Take it like any match on the training pitch," he said. "One swing at a time. That's all we can do."

FOUR DAYS CAME and went, and the whole world seemed different.

Ove walked on unsteady feet from the broken village back to the shore. He was tired, bone-deep tired from the journey, the battle, and then the looting and celebrating that had followed. There'd been mead passed around, some foul-smelling swill they'd found in the village, but Ove had declined. Old habits died hard, but that was one he was happy to break: he was too old to drink away the sound of screams. So he'd slipped away from the revelry when it got too out of hand, hoping to collapse on the dreki and sleep, the rising sun be damned.

But then he saw a figure on the shore next to their boat.

It was Tessa, sitting on the sand where the waves just barely lapped at her toes. Gone was the soot she'd covered herself with—even to his eye, she'd looked like a monster when she'd leapt from the boat—but still wore her armor. Her sword stuck out of the sand behind her, cleaned of blood. She was leaning over her shoulder, and it wasn't until he got closer that he saw she was sewing shut a large gash.

He stopped short as he watched the needle going in and out, dragging a thread through her skin. She didn't flinch or cry out, and her hand was steady as an oak. When she finished, she bit through the extra thread and then poked at the wound to inspect her work.

"You know," Ove said as he sat beside her, "someone could've done that for you."

Tessa shrugged. "Everyone was busy. I needed it done."

"Are you going to join the festivities?" The sound of singing carried over the gentle crashing of waves.

"No."

They sat in silence.

"Your first raid," Ove said when the silence grew too heavy. "An excellent start. You did well. I hear your father was a good raider in his day."

Tessa's gaze was out to sea, so he couldn't be sure what emotion flickered through her. It looked like anger.

"So I hear," she said.

"I was sorry to hear he died," Ove went on hesitantly. He'd heard of Sindri of Hundrfeld, though he'd never met the man. A great friend of the prince, the two had gone on many raids together as boys. Sindri had disappeared ages ago, some time before Ove had arrived in Yfirgardr, but there'd been rumors about why. Injured, or his brother thought it too risky, or perhaps a falling out with the prince. It hadn't been until Tessa's arrival at Yfirgardr that the truth was revealed: he'd had a daughter and wanted to stay at home. A pity he'd died before the girl had come to court to show off her prowess. "He'd be proud of you."

Tessa scowled. "I have no idea what my father would think of all this. I didn't know the man at all."

"What do you mean?"

"He died when I was a year old. I don't remember him. All my life, he's just been a story they tell in Hundrfeld."

Ove's jaw dropped. The way the prince had talked...the Council had appeared as shocked by Sindri's death as Ove had been. How could he have died when Tessa was a baby? Someone would've heard about it.

And yet...

No one had known about Tessa. She'd arrived a stranger. Was Hundrfeld really so reclusive as this?

"My uncle says he went on a raid with Havardr," she said, the words tumbling out of her as though she didn't quite mean them to. "There were a dozen of them that went, and only he and my father returned. And when he came back to Hundrfeld, he had me with him."

Ove's blood ran cold. That would've been some eighteen years ago...when Halle had gone and never come back.

"I already had no mother, and then my father died a little after that. Killed on a hunt. I was sent to Vaettfangkirk, and as soon as I was done, Havardr sent you"—she nodded at him—"to collect me. I wasn't allowed to go home, as you know, so now I have no uncle, either."

"You have the prince's sponsorship," Ove said. "That's no small thing."

It was the wrong thing to say. He could tell as soon as he said it he'd upset her, but he wasn't sure why. He was reeling from all that she'd said, and the possible connection to his brother.

Halle, did you know this girl's father?

Does it matter if you did?

Was the timing merely a coincidence?

Yes, he decided. He was seeing something that wasn't there, hoping for a way to claim his part in her story. Or to see Halle alive once more in this extraordinary young woman. The dark hair, and she'd be about the age he was when he died. As if he could right the wrongs of his brother's life through hers.

Tessa pushed up from the sand and walked to the boat, patting its hull. The water sloshed around her knees. "I have a dreki," she said. "And a crew. *Those* are no small things."

"And the honor of victory," Ove said. "I had a brother who died on a raid. Many years ago. I…" He swallowed. "I wouldn't have come to Yfirgardr if not for that. And while I'd rather have my brother back than all the riches and honor I've earned since then…I like to think he'd appreciate every victory, because I fight in his name. It's not much, but it's all we can offer the dead."

Tessa looked up at the dragon's head as she considered. "There's much I'd like to do in my father's name. My uncle says I should worry about my own, but as you said… an offering to the dead." She turned back to him, her eyes so dark against the sea and sky. "So we will win and conquer, and I will dedicate each victory to my father and your brother and all the others lost too soon, until all the world mourns them as much as we do."

Ove was seldom afraid. He respected the sea's power and the possibility of death, but fear rarely gripped him. Hearing her promise and the intensity of it, the assurance that she knew she would do this terrible task no matter how long it took, it frightened him. Not for his own sake, but for hers. Ove's own journey with mourning had left him the shell of a man for over a decade. He'd taken lives to remind him of the one he'd lost.

Tessa wanted revenge, but how could you blame fate for a bad turn? Against whom, exactly, was this vengeance aimed?

When would she be satisfied that she'd done enough?

But just as he'd had to learn the hard way, these were things she'd have to work out on her own. She would be sated sooner or later. Hopefully, she wouldn't have lost her way too much to get there.

And spirits save those who stood in her way.

21
Stigandr
519

STIGANDR ACCEPTED THE wooden platter of cold meats when it was handed to him. He took a few pieces and passed it on, eating while trying to follow the conversation. The people of Bjardleith didn't speak the same language as Hjorrfold, and it'd taken him a while to get a grasp of it. He was nearly fluent—he'd never have survived this long if he weren't adept at it—but after a day of travel, then the hours it took to set up camp, and now after several shared glasses of mead, the words didn't come as easily as they usually did.

Bjardleith's people had kindly taken him in when he'd shown up at the edges of their lands four years ago. A good thing, too: he'd in no way been prepared for the constant chill in the air, or the treacherous mountain passes, or the deadly wildlife.

Or anything about this journey. He'd been given the very general mission of establishing positive relationships with the people here, but since Hjorrfold knew little of their mountain neighbors, it had been no simple task. The language difficulty hadn't occurred to him, though it should've; he'd been comprehensible only to those clans closest to Hjorrfold, but more than a few days into the mountains, he hadn't understood a single word anyone said. Add to that the different customs, and it'd been difficult to navigate simple tasks like asking for food and shelter.

Eventually, he'd been taken in by Drusilla and her people, and they'd had the patience to teach him everything he'd needed not only to survive, but to thrive here.

Take this tent, for instance. Stigandr had helped set up the wooden poles and built the fire. He'd laid the furs over the poles to keep in the heat, and he'd picked away the stones from the ground. And he would help take it all down when they moved on in a few days, bundling everything tightly for the journey until they'd reached the next place, wherever that might be.

He leaned back and took in the tent. When he'd first seen them, they hadn't looked like much. Wood and fur seemed inadequate for shelter in the harsh mountains. Everything in Yfirgardr was made of stone. Wood was too precious to waste on buildings. They needed it for ships and shields, and if you were very wealthy, you might have a chest or piece of furniture made from it. No, in Hjorrfold they were people of stone and brick, building to last.

In Bjardleith, they didn't build settlements to last. They traveled often, searching the mountains for fairer weather or new pastures for their herds. Staying in one place too long meant death, so they traveled lightly. Yet it was a comfortable arrangement. The tents were warm, and while Stigandr had never slept on the ground before, he couldn't deny he slept well on his pile of furs.

Furs from animals he'd hunted himself. Another novelty of this place: he needed to hunt. Not with spears or arrows like back home, but with magic. The people here didn't know the healing charms or illusion magic of Yfirgardr, they weren't skilled in prophecy like his mother, and they didn't use their skills to conjure creatures like in Vaettfangkirk. Those were talents unknown and uninteresting to them: they'd honed their magic craft for the hunt.

They'd taught him how to track not only with his senses, but with magic. They'd taught him draughts to keep away the cold, to hide his breath. They'd taught him the charms that allowed him to tiptoe over the snow, leaving not a single footprint behind or rock disturbed.

And he'd learned how to use his magic to kill.

In Bjardleith, they were skilled in using the elements to attack. They cast fire not only for the heat and light, but honed it like a blade and launched it right into the heart of a beast. They could do the same with ice and lightning, and with astounding accuracy. It wasn't quite battle magic—that ancient art all but forgotten in Hjorrfold—but it was close.

After they'd warmed up to him, they'd taught Stigandr this magic as well. While he could, technically, do everything they'd shown him, he was far more deadly with an actual weapon in hand. They thought him funny because he always brought a knife on hunts, and he laughed with them. He had many magical talents, but they weren't for killing.

His musings were interrupted when a woman entered the tent. Bundled from head to toe in furs, only her eyes were visible as she stomped and brushed away snow. When she took off her hat, Stigandr recognized her as one of Drusilla's distant cousins who rarely traveled with them. Even among nomads, she wasn't content to stay put: she moved between clans easily and often.

The crowd welcomed her, but she ignored them. She scanned the circle of men and women until her eyes landed on Stigandr. He went rigid as she walked over and knelt in front of him. That didn't bode well.

"I have news from Hjorrfold for you," she said, the *r* sound not rolling freely like it did when he said it.

He nodded. "I thank you"—he motioned from his heart to hers—"and gladly listen."

"Your mother is dead."

The people here often spoke without ornamentation, always blunt and to the point, but he was certain they overdid it when they talked to him. Like speaking to a child, they made it as simple as possible so that he could understand them. Normally, he appreciated it. Now he wished there'd been at least a little more said to dull the words before they hit him.

"Dead?" He went numb with shock. "How? When?" No need to ask why. There was reason enough, he was sure.

The woman held out her hands apologetically. "Many moons ago. Maybe a year or more? News travels slow from the lowlands, and most don't care, so it stops before it makes it this far. They say she died in her sleep. An illness, maybe."

Stigandr nodded and thanked her again. There was no point in asking more questions: that was all she knew, and she'd only taken care to know that much because she knew it would interest him. He was the only person from Hjorrfold on this mountain, or the next, or the next. It had felt freeing to be so far away from anyone who knew him and their expectations. Now he'd missed his mother's funeral; he finally saw the drawbacks. This was no secret mission. It was exile.

And this whole business was strange. His mother had seemed indestructible when he was a boy. She had believed with a stubborn assurance that she would outlive his father. Stigandr had believed it himself, though she'd shared none of her prophecies with him. That was an art she'd never been able to teach him, but she had so much other wisdom and magic to impart that he'd never felt the lack.

Maybe if she'd let him in, he could've helped her stop it. Or at least he wouldn't feel so blindsided.

For the first time in four years, he felt alone.

"What will you do?" Drusilla asked him. They were alone in her private tent, the one at the head of their temporary village. It looked much the same as the others, if not for the silver furs marking the doors. A pair of white wolves, killed by Drusilla herself, of course. Everyone else in the sleepy village was tucked away for the night, warmer than anyone had any right to be this high in the mountains.

Her lips curled around the edge of her pipe, the long one made of a giant cat tooth, longer than his arm and carved with all manner of mountain creatures he hadn't known existed until he'd seen them. A few he was still skeptical about, but after an enormous creature hunted them on his first trek up the big mountain, he'd adjusted his expectations.

"I don't know," he said, thinking it was true but then realizing it was a lie. "I think I'll have to go back."

"Why?" The harsh, rough sounds of her language used to make him think everyone was angry. He'd learned quickly to look at their eyes to tell how they really felt.

She handed him the pipe. Normally, he declined, but tonight he accepted it. He took a long puff and held it in his lungs, letting it strangle the air and rational thought out of him while he considered her question. From anyone else, it might've been an accusation or a challenge. He knew her well enough to know it was just curiosity. Slowly, he let out the smoke. He watched it dissolve before he answered.

"My brother will take advantage and try to become king."

"And this is bad?"

"Probably. He's only concerned about his legacy, not the people of Hjorrfold. He'll act in his own best interests and not care if it's in theirs."

"Probably? So maybe not?"

"I haven't been home in years. He might've changed." Imagining Havardr change was like imagining a river altering its course: it would take much work, and the river would resist the whole time. "Or maybe my father will choose my sister."

"And if it is just as you worry and your brother becomes king and the people suffer…this is your concern?"

He bit back his gut reaction that *yes, of course, it's my concern*. Bjardleith emphasized community and choice in a way that was almost uncomfortable. There was structure and there were leaders, but there was more input from the people. They couldn't be forced into submission: they had to agree to be led. No tyrant stood any hope among the mountain clans, because they'd be killed within a week.

Not that Havardr would be a tyrant, necessarily. He could be very charming, especially among other warriors. And he was liberal with his gold, which endeared him to peasants and nobles alike. But that was a Havardr who was trying to gain favor. A Havardr who already had the throne was less likely to worry about what people thought. He was single-minded to a fault, and wouldn't care who he hurt to get what he wanted, even if it was the people he'd sworn to protect. And they would endure it. Without an alternative laid before them, the men and women of Hjorrfold would endure his rule no matter how much they might hate it. If he had a crown upon his head, they would likely choose him over Stigandr or Ragnhild anyway, because it was easier to accept a bad king than to replace him.

But was it his concern? Did the family of his birth really bestow any true responsibility? It was rather presumptuous to think he knew what was good for Hjorrfold or its people, given how long he'd been away. Would they want him there? Why did he care when he had a comfortable life here? He could stay in the mountains, oblivious and with people who respected his leadership and gifts. He'd earned their trust and support already, a feat which he might never accomplish at home.

You were raised for the throne, a voice not unlike his father's whispered.

So was Havardr, he countered. *By the same parents. Why should I be any better at it?*

Stigandr didn't have his mother's gift for omens and prophecies…but he knew his brother. He'd seen the way their mother dismissed him and their father watched him warily. He remembered whispered conversations with his sister, where they both feared Havardr would do something reckless that couldn't be undone. Any bit of power he'd ever gotten, he'd never given it up.

Perhaps it needn't be his concern. He'd left. Whatever events had unfolded in his absence, he'd had no part in them and didn't know the circumstances. This might indeed be what Hjorrfold wanted.

But if it wasn't…that nagging doubt. His gut told him this was bad, very bad. And he was one of the few people who could stop it.

"It is my concern," he said with conviction. "This is the time to go. If I don't, and things go poorly, it'll be a lot harder for me to help."

Drusilla hummed around the pipe. She wouldn't stop him, he knew, or argue. She would ask her questions to understand and help him make sure that he understood, and he could almost love her for it. He wished he did love her, because then it might be easier to turn his back and stay. But as beautiful as she was, as strong and clever and wonderful, they had never been more than partners. Their alliance was too useful to risk with romantic feelings, and, thankfully, none had ever developed.

"When will you go?"

"Soon. Tomorrow, if you can spare me. It's a long trip." And dangerous. No one from Hjorrfold could make it this far into the mountains but him, and he would have to survive the trip back.

She inclined her head. "I'll send you a guide."

"I don't need one."

"You do. Even a capable man must learn to accept help."

He smiled, the only concession that she was right.

"How will you do it? Will you make yourself known as soon as you arrive? How will your brother react? Your father?"

"I don't know," he said in answer to all her questions. Clearly, much had changed since he'd left. He'd always assumed he would return home and announce his presence at the city gates, but that no longer seemed wise. "I think I'll need to lie low and see what's changed while I've been gone."

Drusilla nodded approvingly. "But be ready to kill your brother," she said with the same practicality she'd instruct a hunting party. "Don't throw your life away if you're not willing to take his. You are better off staying with us if you won't cross that line."

She spoke from experience: she'd wrestled control of this clan from her brothers-in-law, who hadn't been happy when her husband had died and she'd continued to lead without him. She'd killed every one of them when they wouldn't back down, and she'd do it again if necessary. Regret wasn't the way of Bjardleith.

"I don't—"

"He will kill you," she assured him. "From all you have told me, he'll kill you without a second thought. He'll only worry about how it'll make him look. Be ready to strike the blow yourself if necessary."

They spoke no more of it, instead smoking and talking and enjoying the last of each other's company. Stigandr would set out the next day, with Drusilla's parting words heavy on his mind. He loved the brother he'd known as a boy...but he dreaded to see what man he'd become.

Part Two

22
Tessa

520

Tessa lingered in her room, watching the shadows shift as the sun moved. She'd been summoned to the Great Hall, and while she would obey those summons, she refused to be at Havardr's beck and call. He might think himself king, but he wasn't. So she sat in the nice, cushioned chair in one corner and drummed her fingers against the armrest while she measured out the minutes.

They had returned three months ago from their conquest of Thrireyna, the trio of islands better known as Fyrrey, Midreyna, and Lengraey, respectively. It had taken the better part of eighteen months to do so to Havardr's satisfaction. They'd methodically spread from that first landing, killing and negotiating and beating resistance out of the people there one village at a time. Their progress had slowed on the second island when the weather turned frigid. Some of the land routes became impassable, and chunks of ice made the sea dangerous. The worst had been a blizzard that had trapped them in the tiny huts they'd stolen from a small tribe who'd heard of their coming and fled, though luckily they'd left behind most of their supplies.

She remembered Havardr's continuous contemptuous sneer when he'd found this out. *"They should've burned it all rather than let us have it."*

Given how necessary it'd been to their survival, she supposed he had a point.

But the thaw after that storm had been the beginning of the end: the men and women of Hjorrfold were fed up with being away from home, and wanted nothing more than to finish the job so they could leave.

All well and good when your home was a broad place like Hjorrfold and you were satisfied to be anywhere in it. Tessa's home was just a tiny piece of it, and it hadn't felt like a victory to return to Yfirgardr. Most of the warriors were satisfied, though, even the ones who lived in the tent village outside the walls. 'Civilization' they called it, though it seemed less comfortable than the huts they'd stayed in on those islands.

Tessa knew what this summons meant. Havardr had brought them home as promised, but he was by no means done conquering: there were still lands where the people didn't bow to his face and curse him behind his back. He was insatiable, and though she wasn't privy to meetings with the Council, she knew what he was planning. The only question was who was next.

She wondered if the warriors knew they were about to set out again. Would they have rushed home if they'd known how short their return would be? Tessa didn't mind, but hers was a unique position. She was motivated by revenge and wanted Havardr to gain all that he wished, so it would only devastate him more when she destroyed it. Those who could return to their families likely wouldn't want to set out so soon.

Though, like her, they might not have the choice.

When she'd ridden the line between impudence and absentmindedness, she set out for the Great Hall. She'd chosen a simple wool tunic, plain white except for purple embroidery at the hem, and her favorite brown breeches and boots. She had more regal outfits as befit her new station, all of which had been commissioned and completed for her while they were at war, but she didn't much care for them. Pretty as they were, they were dresses for a princess or a noble lady meant to be an ornament. She was a warrior and preferred to look the part.

She didn't want to look like Havardr, prancing about in velvet or silk laced in gold, weighed down by rings and necklaces. All his spoils and finery on display. The man even wore a golden dagger on his belt, as if that would do him any good in a fight. What did he mean to do, blind his opponent with reflected light?

A herald announced her arrival, and the Great Hall went silent as she stepped inside. She ignored all the curious onlookers—the nobles at court and the peasants seeking an audience and the servants doing their best to keep it all in order. They still found her an oddity, this warrior princess who'd seemingly sprung fully formed out of the air. She could feel their gazes, hear their whispers. She kept her eyes on the throne and its occupant; as his 'sister,' it was her right to look the king in the eye, and she did it every time.

Not that Havardr was the king.

"Sister," Havardr said with a wide grin and a loud voice that echoed off the walls and high-ceilings. It was a good voice, she had to admit. In battle, it carried over the screams and the clang of metal, and his voice had a regal air to it when it thundered in the hall.

"Brother," she said back. It was getting easier and easier to say it without snarling the word. She stopped at the bottom of the dais, her eyes never leaving his, even when she nodded to him. While she wished to make him speak first, she had to appear interested in his summons. "To what do I owe the pleasure?" she asked in her neutral, uninflected tone, the one that had finally rescued her from beatings at Vaettfangkirk. She'd spent a lot of time perfecting that tone, her general air of disinterest, and it had grown rusty from disuse while at war. War was a rough place for rough people, and if your tone was disrespectful, no one noticed.

While court was a different sort of battlefield, it was one where the veil of civility was essential. She was a servant of the king, after all; she had no interests of her own, and to indicate otherwise was dangerous. Worse to be impolite to the prince unprovoked; no one understood there had already been provocation.

"I have good news. We ride in a week's time to wage war on the Fjarriheimr and bring them the advantages of Hjorrfold's laws and wisdom." Then, for the nobles nearby, he added, "Their mines will make a great asset to our people, will they not?"

There was laughter. It was a clever idea to use the Council's greed to fuel his wars. There'd been the general feel of annoyance when Havardr returned. The islands were large, at least when you were marching across them in armor, but their wealth was in food: herbs, exotic vegetables, and this strange, small version of boar only as tall as one's knee and that were so tame, they would eat out of your hands and lived in pens within the villages. These were practical and necessary boons, but they didn't sparkle like the jewels around Havardr's throat.

Mines, though. There was good coin to be earned (and made) from mines. Metals or salt or precious stones... it didn't matter. All was more appealing to the wealthy nobles on the Council, who had mostly given up on honor through combat and preferred to let others do the dirty work of raiding and conquering. 'I own a mine' sounded much more impressive than 'I own a boar farm' to this lot.

"Yes, Brother," she said automatically. Tessa knew very little of the Fjarriheimr. She could find them on a map only by virtue of their being the end of the known world: they occupied the farthest stretch of land to the west, right at the edges where the maps ended. She supposed they might have mines in that area, though she knew none of the particulars. She didn't have a mind for trade beyond, not at this scale anyway, and her limited role within the court made it unnecessary. She was a blunt object, a weapon honed for one single purpose.

So while she had no idea how Fjarriheimr might fit into Hjorrfold, she knew how they fought. They were excellent archers with some of the best horses in all the lands. Because they were neighbors to a land known for pillaging, they had fortifications all along their eastern border and lookouts all along the coast. They were a large, single, organized land, not some collection of independent villages.

Despite how vast Hjorrfold was and the large swaths of land it possessed away from the sea, they were raiders: they fought with swords and heavier weapons like axes and war hammers, and they did it on foot. Oh, they could throw a spear and shoot arrows just fine, but those were hunting tools. The idea of fighting from horseback—a necessity if they went to war with Fjarriheimr—made Tessa anxious. It didn't play to their strengths. How hard was it to kill a horse? Could they contact Trond and get war dogs in time? There were dogs trained for taking down large game, so surely they could be turned against horses.

And they would need to gather their fastest horses and collect shields. Some shield work drills would be necessary, since the soldiers here were inexperienced with the threat of arrows being rained down upon them. She also suspected that more than half of the men and women in the barracks couldn't ride, and those that could were only passable. Not at speed, and certainly not with a weapon. Tessa had only marginal training on horseback, since the marshes weren't ideal conditions. She would need to talk to Ove and the other officers. She would need detailed maps of Fjarriheimr. Had scouts already been sent ahead? Would they have battle mages to contend against?

While her mind buzzed with dozens of questions and logistics, she nearly missed what Havardr said next.

"You will stay in Yfirgardr," he said, and though his voice was even, she could see in the gleam of his green eyes he knew how much this would hurt her, how much it would unbalance her.

And damn him, it worked.

"What?" she said in confusion and hated that she'd frowned before she could wash away any reaction at all. "But Brother, I—"

"I will lead the campaign myself," he continued, with that same glimmer of triumph in his expression. "You will stay behind to protect Hjorrfold. We cannot leave our home with no one to protect it, and someone must guide the Council on how best to rule while I am gone."

It's never stopped you before, leaving them to their own devices. She bit her tongue.

Havardr had gone again and again without caring what he left behind, so long as he brought back more than he'd taken with him. And what was this nonsense about needing someone to protect Yfirgardr? And this utter lie that she would guide the Council when she had barely even been in the Council's presence. He might call her pretty words like 'sister' and 'princess,' but there was no authority behind it.

Did Havardr not have a younger brother? Couldn't Randel be fetched from Pegjajord? Then he could stay instead of her, and she should be out there fighting. The boy was thirteen and had been allowed three years to mourn. Couldn't he pull his weight despite his pain like the rest of them?

Better yet, send for Alvis himself. Bring the true king home to rule as he once did.

There was no point in saying any of this. Havardr did as he pleased, and he did so in whatever way would best serve his purpose. It would be foolish to challenge him, especially when he was ostensibly doing her a great honor. There was nothing to be gained by publicly arguing the point, except the satisfaction of angering him.

Besides, she knew the real answer to her questions: she was doing too well. Her success in battle detracted from his. Even though Hjorrfold's warriors fought under his family's banner—an ugly crown with a lightning bolt through it, as unimaginative as Havardr himself—and swore their battle oaths to him, she knew the tales they told around the fire weren't about his victories, but hers. They appreciated her daring, her skill with a blade, her strength. She fought alongside them on the front lines, in the very thick of it, and never shied away from a challenge. The women had even started wearing black lines of soot into battle like she had, and she'd been forced to continue the fashion herself.

Havardr was a great fighter. The best she'd ever seen, and strong as a bear. But he was the prince. He was *supposed* to be that good. Tessa was one of them, or so the common folk felt. Noble birth or not, she didn't have the haughty accent of the Council and rarely dressed in the same finery. She was willing to wade through the muck with them and took less than her fair share of the plunder.

They liked her. And soon she would be the only one at court. She didn't know how, but she'd make this work to her advantage.

She had to.

"Of course," she said blandly and inclined her head. "I am at Hjorrfold's service, as always. I'll do my duty in Yfirgardr and maintain the peace while you fight for our glory."

"Good." He seemed equally pleased by her answer and how easily she'd capitulated.

The fool, thinking this a sign of her subservience. She was simply better at biding her time than he was. And when she found the time and manner with which to strike, he'd never see it coming.

23
Stigandr

520

It had taken time to say his farewells and leave Bjardleith. Though he'd wished to leave as soon as possible, Drusilla's people insisted on throwing him a feast. He could hardly refuse the honor—a true sign of his acceptance, since they feasted only for the equinox and the parting of good friends, whether in death or if they joined a new clan—so they dined and danced and smoked well into the night, out in the open where it was cold but so the spirits could bless them.

One by one, Stigandr was given gifts and gave his own when he could. This wasn't a land of riches, filled with jewels and precious metals. Their nomadic lifestyle made these types of trinkets undesirable, since they were often heavy and had no practical purpose. Warm cloaks and homespun clothing, decorative pipes and daggers, engraved tools and the like, that was what they craved. Stigandr had very little to give, as he was no skilled craftsman. He could hunt, though, and had furs and tools that he gave to those whom he knew best: the hunters, the other mages, and Drusilla's advisers.

Drusilla he saved for last.

"You saved my life, taking me in," he said in his own language. It was the only thing he'd been able to teach her, and this was the last time he could offer it to her.

"You save my life when you kill that assassin," she said, the consonants of his tongue sounding sharp on hers. "Life brings life." A saying among her people, though it didn't translate well. It'd taken him a while to understand the sentiment, since the idea of paying good fortune forward was so foreign to his people. It was always blood feuds that seemed to last, grudges instead of favors.

"I wish I had more to give you in thanks..." He reached into his tunic to pull out two scrolls, tightly bound so they would take up as little room as possible. "A map of Hjorrfold," he said and handed her the first. It was more than a map—it held notes on who she could and couldn't trust, should she ever find herself in his lands. The second was a letter that promised safe passage to Yfirgardr, though that was dependent upon showing it to the right people. "If you ever need to visit me."

Drusilla accepted both scrolls. She touched them to her forehead and nodded, then smiled widely. "I do not visit you. You visit me." She took off her necklace, a snowflake carved from a mountain goat's horn and fastened on a leather strap. It was a gift from her brother to mark her first hunt.

"I can't accept this," he said, switching back to her language. "You've had that your whole life—"

"Life brings life," she insisted. "And this will give you and your friends safe passage in Bjardleith if they need it."

He let out a breath through his nose. Knowing there was little point in protesting, he took the necklace and put it around his neck.

"What will I do without you looking out for me?" he asked.

"Hopefully not die. I like you, Stigandr. You do too good a thing. Your people are better with you alive. Better still, that you're returning to them."

He left at dawn as silently as he could. When he slipped out of Drusilla's tent, he made sure not to wake her, and as he roused his traveling companions. Drusilla had insisted on sending him with two guides, mostly for their own safety when they returned without him.

Stigandr used his newfound magic to lay a spell of stillness so they wouldn't make a sound. The mules' disgruntled sighs were muffled even to his ears. They walked in a line down the narrow path that led from this flat clearing in the mountains down the steep slope to the next, winding through rocks and snow. Stigandr had walked this path dozens of times over the years, yet each time it looked new. The sparse growth of ragged trees and falling rocks shifted the landscape in subtle ways, and avalanches in larger ones. It made the landscape of Pegjajord all the more beautiful for how fleeting it was.

Their journey took them to the lower parts of the mountain, where the passes were wider. There was more plant life as well, their progress marked by how much green they saw each day. He hadn't realized how much he'd missed the color until it was all around him; he felt more at home than he had in ages.

His guides left him in a small village made of stone. An actual fixed residence for its people, these weren't the nomads he was leaving behind but the hunters who traded with both Bjardleith and Hjorrfold, though they made it clear they cared for the politics of neither.

"We trade," one said sternly when Stigandr tried to ask about his mother's death. "You want gossip, go farther down the mountain."

He couldn't yet, though.

He'd entered Bjardleith and spent most of his time far to the east. The most direct path home, obviously, would be to leave the mountains and head straight to Yfirgardr over the rocky plains that lay between the mountains and the coast. If he were returning to his parents on the throne, he'd do so without hesitation; with his brother in charge...

The eastern lands belonged to Hundrfeld. While Lord Trond seemed by all accounts fair and level-headed, he was by those same accounts a man of honor. He was oath-bound to the throne, and if he felt Havardr was the new keeper of said oath, he might hand over Stigandr. Worse, Sindri was the heir to Hundrfeld after his brother. Although he hadn't been to court in ages, Sindri and Havardr were thick as thieves. If Havardr wanted Stigandr in chains, even if this were merely a drunken wish he'd shared with his boyhood friend, Sindri would do anything to make it happen.

Spirits, he'd been gone so long, Sindri might now be master of Hundrfeld outright.

The eastern plains weren't safe for him, and it was unlikely he'd hear anything but heavy praise for his brother and no truth at all.

He would instead travel through the lower mountain passes as far west as he could, then work his way to Yfirgardr through the farms and homesteads there. The nobles from those keeps raised more mages than the east, and so at the very least would be skeptical of Havardr's transition to power. They might also be more inclined to help their mage prince on his travels, since their shared magic might gain them favors should he sit on the throne instead of his brother.

It was not a straightforward journey. It would take a month just to go through the mountains safely, and possibly that long once he was in Hjorrfold. He would have to disguise himself, and of course stop along the way to find out what he could.

He waited until he'd left the mountains to transform himself. He found a quiet brook, using moonlight and smoke to work the magic. He reshaped his reflection: gone were his light brown hair and green eyes, his pale skin and clean-shaven face, his tall, slender frame. Instead, he wore a darker complexion with cropped hair lighter than his own, and brown eyes to muddy the green. He'd grow out a beard too, the only truth in his disguise. His features shifted, reshaping his nose and making his cheekbones more pronounced, his eyes wider and set farther apart. He hid beneath fake muscles and a paunch that suggested he enjoyed his mead more than he should, and when he stood and looked down at himself, he felt the illusion complete. No one would ever mistake him for a prince of Hjorrfold, and even someone who knew him would be unlikely to spot him beneath the disguise. He could travel freely without fear of recognition.

The last part was trickiest: he made a potion out of pebbles from the stream to make his voice gravelier. It sounded odd to his own ear as he tested it, his voice more like his father's than his own.

He'd returned his mule to Drusilla's people when they left him, so it was slow going as he walked the plains. It didn't bother him, though perhaps it should. The longer it took him to reach Yfirgardr, the harder it would be to undo Havardr's work. Still, he couldn't bring himself to rush: he'd missed this land, and he'd spent too much time at the slower pace of Bjardleith. He camped in little nooks between hills or occasionally in caves when he was fortunate enough to find one. He hunted small game, since he didn't want to waste the larger animals who were the livelihood of the people here. He fished in the rivers he crossed, though he had little to show for his efforts because of how terrible he was at it, even with magic.

It was over a week before he came across anyone else, and they welcomed him wholeheartedly into their home. They had a squat hut with a loft, and they were happy to share a meal with him around the fire. It was cozy, and so distinctly Hjorrfold that he felt truly at home as he ate real bread with warm butter and honey.

"What brings you out to these parts alone?" the matriarch of the family asked. She looked nearly eighty, but when she smiled, Stigandr caught a glimpse of the youthful beauty she'd once had.

"I was out in the mountains for years," he said. "My ma and pa died, and I didn't quite know what to do with myself, so I traveled."

"Those mountain folk are wild ones. Good with magic, though. Bet they taught you how to hunt. No one survives up there without being able to hunt." She held up her slice of bread and grinned at him. "Been a while since you had any, eh? No grain'll grow up there, I expect."

Stigandr laughed. "I didn't realize I missed it until this evening. I cannot thank you enough for your hospitality." He paused, wondering how best to proceed. "I've been gone for a while. Used to live near Yfirgardr. I hear things are changing in the capital. Is it worth going back that way? Is there any honest work there?"

"Always work for fighters," the oldest man said. He must be the son of the old woman—they had the same eyes, chin, and laugh. "You hear about the prince's wars?"

Stigandr shook his head. "Only heard the queen had died and that Prince Havardr was in charge while the king mourned."

"Aye, you have it right. The king and the wee prince went to Pegjajord and haven't been heard from since, at least not by us common folk."

"Never saw the king in my life," the old woman grumbled. "Except on the back of a gold coin, and I suspect he wasn't half so handsome in the flesh."

The family chuckled, and Stigandr joined them.

"And Havardr then needs more fighters?" Stigandr asked. "What for?"

The man shrugged. "Apparently, the largest kingdom in all the world ain't large enough. Never satisfied, men like that. Have everything but want more."

The rest of the family was quiet, and Stigandr couldn't tell if this was because they agreed or if they were embarrassed to speak so strongly in front of a stranger.

"The prince's always been a fighter himself," Stigandr said with a shrug. "No surprise he'd want to continue raiding even if he's in charge now."

The man shook his head adamantly. "This ain't no raiding. He's conquering. He's taking these people and adding 'em to Hjorrfold, making 'em bow to him and pay tribute like the rest of us. Now mind, I pay my share like everyone, knowing it's my price for safety should the mountain folk ever decide they're tired of rocks and snow."

Conquering? Stigandr's blood ran cold. Their father allowed this?

"You don't approve?" Stigandr prodded.

The man waved away the idea. "The prince can do as he pleases. Won't matter much to me and mine. I think it's greedy, is all. He bites off more than he can chew, and it'll be good people who suffer for it. There's a reason his pa and his pa's ma, and the rest of 'em never tried to take more than they already had."

Stigandr didn't disagree, so he didn't. Instead, he changed the topic, and instead they talked about the upcoming harvest and if the family planned to travel to the nearest keep to celebrate. It was a good night.

THE NEXT FEW people he encountered were less inclined to chat. They gave him directions and were willing to trade work for food and shelter, but they kept their opinions to themselves. He perceived a general sense of weariness with the doings of Yfirgardr, but that didn't mean approbation or condemnation. These people were so far removed from the court gossip, and even war would be troubled to find them here, securely placed between the mountains and the sea, hundreds of miles away from the nearest border.

It wasn't until he reached an actual road (in truth, it was barely a dirt path, but he was feeling generous) that he was able to find a village. The people there were friendly and delighted in his ignorance.

"The prince's been gone for years," one young woman said in a stage whisper that fooled no one. "Went off to grab a few islands, came home to get more soldiers. Went and grabbed himself some more islands, bigger ones at that, and came home to—" She paused here, waiting for the other women to chime in, and together they finished with a chorus of, "Get more soldiers!"

"So he goes back home," Stigandr pointed out. "He hasn't completely disappeared."

"If you spend more time away from home than you do at it, then you might as well be gone," she said. "This latest trip, we saw some of the men and women marching across the plains to join those who couldn't fit in the dreki. Thousands of 'em, can you imagine?"

"They haven't come back," another woman pointed out. "Gone almost a twelve-month and still out there."

"And by the sound of it, not likely to be back soon," a young man said conspiratorially. "This is a proper war against another kingdom with an army of their own. Not a bunch of savages hiding on islands."

"In over his head, some say," someone added. This was greeted by a chorus of hums in agreement.

"You don't approve?" Stigandr bit into an apple (apples! another treat he'd missed) and raised an eyebrow.

"Not our place to approve of a prince," the man said with a distinct air of disapproval.

Stigandr wasn't surprised that his brother might have difficulties. He was an excellent fighter, sailor, and raider; none of that seemed like it would be relevant in a prolonged war on land. War wasn't brute strength against brute strength, and at this scale, it wasn't as simple as taking a force by surprise. It was strategic. It was drawn out. It was complicated, and it required tact at negotiating terms.

Havardr hadn't even been good at negotiating playtime with their tutors as children, and he was a full ten years older than Stigandr.

"Is Prince Randel in charge, then?" he asked. There would need to be someone in Yfirgardr to oversee the Council. Even Havardr would realize the dangers of leaving them in charge for too long. He doubted Ragnhild had returned, and he doubted even more that she'd be inclined to help Havardr. Randel was so young. It'd be easy to bully him into whatever Havardr needed.

"That pipsqueak?" a man scoffed. "Hasn't been in court since the queen died. No, it's been Lady Tessa who's been keeping things together, and a fine job she's done." His shift from scorn to admiration was so quick that it gave Stigandr pause.

While his first instinct was to defend his little brother, they were likely correct in their assessment of his current worth. Randel was a mage who had lost his primary tutor—their mother—and Havardr wouldn't have been inclined to replace the loss with other mages. Their father would've been at a loss to do so, since he would have little understanding of Randel's talents or who might be a suitable instructor for him. Unfortunate, since Randel had always shown a lot of promise. Lots of raw potential…but very little interest in hard work.

So he pushed aside his meager defense of his brother and focused on what was likely the more important part.

"Who is Lady Tessa?" he asked. "Is she his sister?" Of course she wasn't, but he had to maintain the facade of ignorance (though it was becoming more and more apparent that it wasn't a facade at all).

"Too responsible to be one of Alvis's children, isn't she?" a woman barked, and they all hooted in laughter.

Stigandr tried not to be offended. She had a point, after all. Not a single one of the four of them was in the city, ruling their own people. Two who couldn't be bothered, one who'd disappeared, and one deemed incapable.

"She rules well, then?"

Lots of nods.

"She sees to everything herself, they say. The Council does less now than they did under Alvis, even."

"Used Havardr's wars to line their pockets off the work we do."

"Lets them have their little meetings, but she does what she thinks is best, not what they recommend. You know they collect grain from us every year, bushels of it! Say it's in case of famine, but Lady Tessa did an accounting of the amounts, and it wasn't enough to feed more than Yfirgardr! She made sure we'd all be safeguarded should the winter come and last longer than it should."

"They say she listens to everyone personally who comes for an audience."

"She has the Great Hall open every day to hear petitions! She's very fair."

On and on the praise went. It seemed like everyone had something to say about how amazing this Lady Tessa was. Better than the royal family who'd disappeared on them, despite oaths to protect the land and safeguard its people.

I'm here, he thought. *I'm here to make sure things are in order*.

That they were in order, at least by every account here, unsettled him.

"She sounds like a great lady," Stigandr conceded once he could get a word in. "Tessa. Strange name, that. Where does she hail from?"

"Hundrfeld," a woman said. "Bet they're mighty proud of their girl."

"Hundrfeld?" Stigandr repeated. A no-name girl from Hundrfeld? It made no sense. The only way it might've been believable was if she were—

"Aye," the woman said. "Daughter of Sindri. She's the heir to Hundrfeld."

"Sindri?" Stigandr couldn't contain his shock. He'd never heard of Sindri having a child, and he felt he should have, given how close he and Havardr were. Honestly, he'd thought Sindri's inclinations weren't for women at all, not with the way he looked at Havardr, though he supposed that'd never stopped anyone from marrying and having children to continue their line. "Has he come to Yfirgardr with his daughter? Or is he out west with Havardr?"

The woman looked absolutely delighted to share more gossip. "Sindri's dead." And before that new shock could settle, she went on: "Died shortly after the lady was born. Accident, sounds like."

Stigandr was glad he was already seated, because he would have hit the floor with that one.

Sindri was dead. He'd had a secret daughter. Havardr had visited Hundrfeld every year since that accident, but Sindri'd been dead that whole time...a secret child, now at court as Havardr's regent.

The thoughts whirled in his head as he tried to wheedle the truth out of them. There was just enough information to know this was dangerous, that this was a crucial piece of whatever Havardr had planned for Hjorrfold, but not enough for Stigandr to understand why or what or how.

As the night wore on, his companions grew bored with courtly concerns and turned to local ones. Whose son was courting whose daughter, how fortunate to have such a long summer, if they might catch glimpses of the Ondljosbod this winter. Stigandr let this conversation wash over him, basking in how familiar it was. He was home.

But home wasn't the same, either. Not with his family spread across the world, war on the horizon, and a stranger keeping the throne warm for them. In the pit of his stomach, he dreaded this Tessa of Hundrfeld and what might be necessary to get rid of her.

24
Tessa

521

Tessa worried she was constantly being watched by men and women loyal to Havardr, and for several moons that fear had kept her from roaming the castle. It took some time with the Council and with the common folk in the Great Hall to realize the truth: no one was loyal to Havardr.

They were loyal, in their way, she supposed, but to the throne. They'd blindly followed King Alvis until he'd sequestered himself away in the mountains. When Havardr took over, they'd followed his lead without question, because he sat in the king's chair. And once Havardr was out of sight and Tessa was the one on the dais, they'd bent their knees to her as willingly as the others.

It was a good thing for them that she was doing her best to be fair.

"How is the grain supply?" she asked. She had little experience with running a keep, never mind an entire kingdom, but she drew on what she remembered from Hundrfeld. Trond's highest concerns had always been food for the people under his protection and fighters capable enough to do the protecting. Everything else, be it riches or festivals or the like, it all came secondary to those two goals. Since she was already well acquainted with the forces of Hjorrfold, she assumed that meant food was her next priority.

"We are well stocked," a councilor assured her. Lord Birger, she believed. There were over twenty members, and sometimes their names and titles blurred together, especially because her mind was overfull of figures and sums. "We have enough to feed the city for the winter."

She nodded. A good start. "And the men and women who live in the lands around Yfirgardr?"

The councilor quirked his head. "What do you mean?"

"Do we have enough grain on hand to feed all those who live nearby and are more beholden to Yfirgardr than they are to lords and ladies in other keeps?"

"My lady." He seemed uncomfortable. "That isn't our concern—"

"Where does the grain come from?" She didn't actually know, but she suspected. "Do we buy it?"

Silence. She narrowed her eyes and glared around the table until another councilor cleared her throat (Tessa couldn't even attempt a name) and said, "Some of it, yes. The rest is given freely by the homesteads—"

"Given freely," she said, and let the words hang. "It's their tribute to the king, yes?" *Of course they hand it over freely, because otherwise it's their necks*... Tessa drummed her fingers on the table. Things weren't as they were in Hundrfeld, that was for certain. "They contribute for the benefits Hjorrfold provides, correct?" She waited for eager nods. "Well, I would assume that one such benefit would be food should there be a famine, plague, drought, or over-long winter. They no doubt have their own stores, as do many of the people within the walls of Yfirgardr...yet it is still our responsibility to make sure there is enough to feed them should the worst happen. That is what they swear fealty for, isn't it? They give up independence in these matters for the assurance that they will be taken care of. How can any lord or lady call themselves such if they aren't ready to fulfill their end of the bargain?"

More silence, more uncomfortable than before.

Tessa sighed and waved a hand. "I'm not interested in a debate on the purpose of monarchy. I ask because I feel it is my duty while I safeguard this city and its neighboring lands for my brother." Mostly true. She did none of it for Havardr, though, and would rather stab him in the eye than call him brother. She sent a silent prayer that fate would make it so.

"We don't have enough," another councilor said. A younger noble, one replacing his sickly grandmother. Lord...something with a C. Or was it G? Since he was less established, Tessa hoped that meant he was more open to change...or would follow her, if only to make a name for himself. She could work with either. "But we could acquire more food. We have perhaps two-thirds of the amount you request. It's too late in the season to demand more from our own people, but through the markets and trade, we should be able to increase our stores."

A straightforward answer. She appreciated that. "Very well. Please see that it's done. You may take the funds necessary from my personal holdings."

She added this last part to nip any dissent in the bud. She wasn't squandering the royal treasury on a whim, and she had plenty of her own coin. What was she going to do with it, anyway? It was hard enough getting anything to Hundrfeld without notice, leaving a rather large amount sitting somewhere in the bowels of the castle. She'd had to keep it because Havardr believed she was motivated by greed like he was, so she might as well put it to use.

"That is most generous, my lady." Several other councilors echoed this sentiment. "And if we do not use it all this winter…?"

She shrugged. "Then perhaps we'll collect less tribute from the farmers next year." Then, before they could stew on this scandalous notion much longer, she asked, "What other matters should we discuss?"

The councilors admittedly were less enthusiastic about her rule than most were. Aside from his commitment to conquering every land he'd ever heard of, Havardr had more or less given them the run of the kingdom. Oh, he'd held meetings with them and listened, but it seemed that he granted every proposal they made, so long as it didn't interfere with his own plans. When they learned Tessa was not so easily swayed, they were put off. It was a slow process, getting them to trust her.

They respected her. She wore a dagger everywhere she went and dressed in a warrior's tunic, and there'd been plenty of tales of her skill in battle. Admittedly, killing that poor boy had done wonders for her reputation, though she would just as soon give Sixten back his life as have the fear it'd earned her.

Trust was harder, though. They were wary of her, as well they should be. She was a stranger, the unknown daughter of a noble boy long dead. She was older now than her father had ever been, and few of the Council members cared for the reclusive keepers of Hundrfeld. But Tessa worked hard. She listened to them, took their advice before acting, and didn't play favorites. She was fair, or as fair as she could be, and they begrudgingly accepted this was the state of things.

Emboldened by her success with the Council, as soon as she was free, she went to the private wing of the castle. Normally she would be out on the training pitch with the guard, taking part in drills, but she wanted to try something she'd been putting off.

She wanted to see what the royal bedchambers looked like.

Tessa had been given a lavish room at the end of the northern corridor, where guest rooms were furnished for visiting nobles. Her room was a floor below where the royal family stayed in the increasingly rare event any were in Yfirgardr. Perhaps she should've been insulted by the placement—Havardr publicly called her sister, but privately treated her as something less—but she preferred it: it allowed her to retain her identity as a noble from Hundrfeld and kept her away from Havardr.

Despite her attempts to wheedle information about the other princes and princess, little was shared. Stigandr and Randel were mages, the elder off traveling and the younger mourning. Ragnhild had trained at Vaettfangkirk like Tessa had, though at a younger age and with no trips home until she'd completed the training; she too was off traveling. Strange that no one could even point in the direction they thought the middle two had gone. Ingegerd, a mage, was dead; her husband, formerly a warrior, was in mourning with the youngest child. Nothing of their personalities was shared with her, or at least little of substance. That strange loyalty to their royal family kept the Council and nobles from speaking ill of them, and their separation from the common folk meant the servants and guards could share little with her but rumors, though they shared eagerly enough.

So perhaps the only true way to get to know them was to visit their rooms. The rooms would be honest and unbiased, at least, and she could draw her own conclusions.

The king's chamber and queen's were connected by a small room between them. The shared room looked very much like the king's study by the Great Hall, though with less personality. The king's room was similarly grand, but uninteresting. It was piled high with scrolls and books coated in dust, but she got the impression of a man who only cared about kingship.

"I see where Havardr gets it," she mumbled as she closed the heavy door behind her. They might care for the crown in different ways, but clearly it was their dearest concern.

The queen's room was…not what she'd expected. Tessa had heard of the queen's devotion to prophecy, but since there were no soothsayers or mages in Hundrfeld, she had no idea what that meant. As soon as she stepped into the room, she was hit with the cloying smell of spices. Shelves upon shelves were lined with vials and dried plants and crystals and bones. The space was lived-in and cluttered in a way the king's room hadn't been. The king must've only used his room to sleep; this was the queen's refuge, the place where she relaxed and worked in equal measure.

The place where she'd died.

The bed hadn't been since after they'd last found her, some two years now. Tessa touched the very edge, noting the stiffness of the blankets. It felt like a tomb, heavy with decay and neglect. Her father's room in Hundrfeld had been tidied up and was aired out each spring so it didn't feel abandoned. No one had shown the queen such care, giving the room an oppressive feel. Relics lay everywhere, forgotten and ignored, and would continue to.

Havardr's room was the only one locked, and she found herself only mildly disappointed. He had his secrets like anyone else, but she didn't think them particularly deep. He was straightforward with what he wanted, and there was little hope of finding anything incriminating to use against him. He was a man immune to blackmail, as the people of Hjorrfold were unwilling to see their prince for what he truly was.

Ragnhild's room was messy, unexpected from a skjaldmaer. Order had been their way of life for years, and for Tessa, at least, sloppiness had been beaten out of her. Perhaps this was Ragnhild's rebellion when she returned home: clutter upon clutter. There were weapons, of course, mostly gilded daggers or jewel-encrusted swords. Pretty and useless, which was likely why she'd left them behind. Lots of clothing and jewelry, beautiful and embroidered and fine, fit for a princess. Tessa noted that the room seemed to have been occupied by two people: clothing for women of two different sizes, the enormous bed dipping on both sides instead of in the middle, and a table by the window still set for two. Strange that Ragnhild should have a lover that no one mentioned, though she had the impression Ragnhild wasn't of much interest to the people of Yfirgardr beyond her training at Vaettfangkirk. Ragnhild the woman, the actual person, might as well have not existed.

Tessa understood that all too well.

Randel's room was still a child's room. It reminded Tessa of her own room as a girl, filled with knickknacks and toys. He'd been only ten or so when he'd left, and she wondered at the boy who had a model of the constellations on his desk, a telescope at his window with a notebook charting the moon and stars, a stuffed jack rabbit on his bed... yet had been so destroyed by his mother's death he'd left it all behind. She had so few people in her life that she cared for, and only one she cared for deeply. If Trond died, would it ruin her like it did Randel? She thought not, though she suspected that was because of how he'd raised her: we honor the dead when we keep going. He'd honored her father by raising her; she'd honor him by returning to Hundrfeld as its master.

The last room was tucked away at the end of the hall, occupying the tower whose spire twisted so high above the city gates it was the first thing she'd seen of the Yfirgardr, a bold red banner that appeared when they crested a hill miles out. When she touched the iron handle, it shocked her. She jerked her hand away, not from pain but surprise. Stigandr was a mage. Had he enchanted his door so that no one but he could enter? But when she reached out to try again, nothing happened. The handle was warm to the touch, yes, but not unpleasantly so; she pushed inside.

The room was rounded with the curve of the tower. There was a window facing south with a view of the courtyard and another facing north to show the mountains. Like the queen's chambers, Stigandr's shelves were lined with crystals and herbs and other strange tools she assumed were for magic craft. Unlike the queen's chambers, the room didn't feel dark and musty. If she hadn't known Stigandr hadn't been seen in years, she'd have thought he'd been here that very day. It was like time had stood still here, the room holding its breath as it waited for its master's return.

There was also a large assortment of books, and Tessa read the titles as she walked along the shelves.

Runes and Ruin

Potions, Draughts, and Ointments

Illusion Craftwork

Conjuring and Command

Necromancy and Shadow Magick

Earth Magic: A History

On and on it went, scrolls packed among books among tomes. Curiosity piqued, she took one at random—*Protective Charms and their Counter Measures*—and unrolled the scroll. Her education at Hundrfeld had been primarily practical skills like hunting and fighting, but her uncle had insisted she be proficient at reading, writing, and numbers. While she might not enjoy reading, she thought herself good at it, yet she could barely understand a word on the parchment. To make matters worse, the edges of the scroll and between the lines were filled with notes written in a miniscule, precise hand. Words in the text were circled, underlined, or crossed out, with arrows drawn all about, leading from portions of the text to handwritten notes.

Tessa pulled another work from the shelf—this time a book written entirely in old runes—and saw the pages littered with the same meticulous notes. A third and a fourth confirmed that the owner of these books, likely Prince Stigandr, had not merely collected these books or even casually read them: he had studied them with great intensity. As she returned them to their proper place, she wasn't sure if she was more impressed or intimidated. Never once had she put so much effort into her studies, yet here was someone who had. And voluntarily at that, since she'd seen no such dedication in the other bedrooms.

"Being a mage must be hard work," she mumbled.

On a whim, she took one scroll and tucked it into her belt. It promised *Defensive Shields and Warding*, whatever that meant. Tessa was no mage, had never aspired to any magic at all, and held no illusions that she'd learn any magic from the weathered parchment or its notes. She did, however, hope to learn *something*. Whether it was how to counteract the defensive magic of others, or to improve her own reading, or simply to learn more about the lost prince, it would be worth her while to try.

On her way out, she pulled the door back into place and wondered why, of all the royal family, only one had drawn her interest.

25
Stigandr

521

STIGANDR KNEW HE was only a few hours from Yfirgardr when he set out from the inn, and his heart jolted slightly when he saw the castle appear in the distance. He rounded a bend between two sloping hills, and there it was: the castle on the hill and the tiers of the city below. His tower, and its weathered banner flapping in the wind.

After months of travel, Stigandr was home.

As he got nearer to the city itself, he saw the land around it pock-marked with new buildings: vast numbers of wagons and tents with campfires strewn among them, too many to count. The city seemed to have doubled in size, though he doubted this accounted for more than a few hundred inhabitants to the city's five thousand. It was a small, thriving town outside the city walls, and it seemed to be predominantly warriors, with a sprinkling of blacksmiths and merchants.

He credited his brother's war for it. Stigandr wondered where all these people had come from, and more importantly, where they would go. Camps were all well and good for short-term housing, but no one would want to live here indefinitely. Certainly not once winter came. Though as he got closer, he saw it was only the outskirts that were tents: some stone structures cropped up closer to the city walls, permanent residences that might one day be swallowed by the city itself. The walls hardly seemed necessary anymore, as no one had attacked the city since a generation after the wall was built. Perhaps it was time to tear them down and grow in a more natural way than Havardr's conquests.

Once he entered the city proper, the capital looked much the same as he remembered it: the high walls surrounding the city casting long shadows, the ancient brick and stone buildings lining the streets, and the castle high on the hill overlooking it all. As a boy, he'd thought it was a mountain like the ones in the distance, and it only made him prouder to call it home. It wasn't a mountain, of course—Stigandr had seen *real* mountains, and this one was a sad mockery of the name—but it was elevated above the surrounding plains enough to give it a fair vantage point. The keep had never been taken by force, so his forefathers had chosen wisely to build Yfirgardr where they had, mountain or not.

Stigandr kept his cloak low over his face, though he was certain no one would recognize him. Aside from his nearly six-year absence from the city, he still bore the same magical disguise he'd cast when he left the mountains. It'd been unnecessary while he was out among small villages and homesteads—if he'd merely shown up with his face dirty, his cloak well-worn, and his simple clothing, no one would've expected him as a pampered and spoiled prince, and certainly not in their humble homes—but it'd been good practice. Maintaining the magic wasn't easy, and he'd had to build up his ability to hold the disguise for long periods without completely draining his energy reserves. Now it was crucial: in Yfirgardr, there was the very real possibility that he would come across someone he knew.

The day was well underway when he arrived in the large market square past the large fountain by the city gates. No one batted an eye at him as he pressed through the masses of people. It seemed more crowded than he remembered, but he couldn't tell if that was simply because he'd spent so much time in Bjardleith that he'd lost the ability to gauge what a large group actually looked like. The market was claustrophobic, and the miasma of scents overwhelmed his senses. He could stand barely a minute of it before making his way to the eastern edge so he could hopefully bypass the mass of people as he made his way up to the castle.

As soon as he stepped out of the square, a boy no more than eight darted in front of him.

"I can help you find your way, sir," he said cheerfully. "Bet a man such as yourself is off to the keep, eh?"

Stigandr looked at the boy. He had raven hair and dark eyes with a mischievous gleam. Though his clothes were made of a sturdy, gray wool and seemed to fit him, they were dirty and unornamented. Not a street rat or an orphan, then; probably a boy looking to make a few coins for his family by helping visitors through the city. He had a familiar look, and Stigandr wondered if he'd seen the boy's family among the castle servants.

"I am," Stigandr said. "And how much might a guide cost?"

The boy grinned widely, exposing a missing tooth. "As much as you can spare, sir."

Stigandr reached into his pocket and pulled out a silver coin with an eagle's wings spread on it—the mark of his great-grandmother—and tossed it to him. "More when we arrive at the keep."

The boy caught the coin and pocketed it so quickly it looked like sleight of hand, then he scampered off without a word. It was up to Stigandr to keep up, and a good thing he already knew the way or he would've lost the boy as he zigzagged through the streets and alleys. Once they'd left the main merchant areas and the inns and taverns surrounding them, the roads grew steeper and everything was built at an angle. It was only then that the boy slowed down, and he smiled up impishly.

"What brings you to the city, sir? Business with the Lady?"

Although Stigandr was curious about the woman his brother had left in charge, he couldn't approach her until he better understood her. If she was one of Havardr's puppets, there was no point in speaking to her at all, at least not until he'd learned how best to manipulate her.

"I hope to join the city guard," he said. "Are they taking new recruits?"

"Oh, they'll take anyone who can hold a sword and do what they're told." The boy looked over his shoulder at him and winked. "I bet I'd be a terrible city guard."

His cheeky comment startled a laugh from Stigandr. "Why? Because you're too small to hold a sword, or because you never do what you're told?"

"I don't need a sword." The boy patted a dagger at his belt. Stigandr hadn't noticed it before. It was in a silver sheath that was too nice for a peasant boy, and there was a design on the hilt that looked far too intricate for anyone but a noble to commission: a dog biting its own tail.

Had he stolen it? was his first thought, followed by, *What did it matter if he had?*

The dagger was gone in a flash, back under the boy's cloak, the wool laying over it so seamlessly that even knowing it was there, Stigandr couldn't spot its outline.

"So it's mischief that'll keep you out of the barracks, then?" Stigandr asked.

"Aye, sir. Even my ma can't keep me in line, and I like her a lot more than the officers."

Is that why she gave you the dagger? Easier to give you a way back out of trouble because there's no way to keep you from going into it?

They continued through the streets, winding their way up to the keep. It was only in the last two hundred feet of the journey that they rounded a corner and plopped out on the main road, much less crowded here than it'd been by the market.

The boy grinned up at him and held out a hand expectantly. "I expect you'll find I did a good job."

"More than adequate," Stigandr said as he fished another couple of coins out of his pocket. He rubbed them between his fingers, eyeing the boy. There was something about him he couldn't quite put his finger on, and he thought perhaps if he drew out the moment a little longer, he would be able to work out what he was missing. "What's your name?"

"Egil," he said and wiggled his fingers.

A familiar name, though he couldn't place it. "Your parents from around here?"

Egil snorted. "Sort of. They're in the city, if that's what you mean."

With no more excuses, Stigandr laid the coins in the boy's hand. "Be good, you hear? If I join the guard, I'll be on the lookout for little troublemakers like yourself."

Egil barked a laugh and saluted before running down an alley, his dark hair bobbing behind him until he disappeared into the shadows.

Stigandr had never entered the castle gates without everyone knowing exactly who he was, and it was strange to mingle so easily among the men and women there. A few guards stopped him after he passed through the grand archway leading into the courtyard, and his breath caught for a moment until he realized they only wanted to know his business. He handed them his citizenship papers—forged, of course—and waited patiently as they read them.

"If you're here to petition, the line's over there. Lady Tessa'll see as many people as she can until noon, then there's a break and bread'll be handed out if you're still in line. If there's urgent business, she might not see anyone else after."

"I'm here to join the guard," he said, though he considered waiting in line with the others to get a look at this Tessa.

The guard looked him up and down. He must've liked what he saw, because he handed back the papers and nodded approvingly. "Head to the barracks"—he pointed to the right, and Stigandr looked over to mask that he knew damn well where the barracks were—"and give your papers to one of the officers. Ove with the red hair'll be on duty. He'll get you situated."

Stigandr did as he was told, muttering his thanks and trudging off to the barracks. The building took up the whole eastern side of the castle, yet he'd only ever been inside when he'd played hide and seek with other children. Even when he'd practiced and sparred in the courtyard, the closest he ever got to the barracks was the armory at the northeast end of the courtyard. These buildings were ones that had been added to the original keep that had been built centuries ago: it used to be a stone wall with a longhouse that contained the Great Hall and the rooms attached to it on the western edge of the castle. Everything else had been added by later kings and queens, expanding to match the city's growth over the years.

The officers weren't always easy to spot. They had the same gruff look as the other fighters, and a wealthier family or a successful raider could afford better armor than many officers. It was more their bearing, the freedom to stand around leisurely or bark orders at others, that gave them away. Soon he found a man with short red hair and a beard that fit that description.

"Are you Ove?" he asked and handed over his papers. "I was told—"

"New recruit?" the man asked. He appraised him more intently than the guards at the gate had, and he seemed less inclined to approve of him.

He didn't take the papers, so Stigandr put them away. "Yes, sir."

"Name?"

"Ashk. I'm from—"

"Do you have any experience with a blade?"

Stigandr paused, reeling himself in from responding rudely to the man's brusque manners. "Some. Mostly hunting knives and bows. Barely handled a sword."

Ove scowled. "You here for raiding or for guarding? I got more use for one than the other these days. And if you're here for glory with the prince's army, tough luck. He's been gone for nearly a year now and sounds like he'll be gone another at least."

So long? Havardr must feel mighty confident that he had Hjorrfold under his thumb. Whatever was going on with their father and Randel, he didn't expect any trouble from them. Nor did he seem to expect Ragnhild or Stigandr to return. He'd left a regent in charge, and no doubt she'd been instructed how to handle the royal family if they reemerged. Still, that was a lot of trust to place in a stranger.

"Guarding," Stigandr said. "I don't think I have sea legs, and I don't know that I trust my life on a sword just yet."

Finally, Ove gave a slight nod of approval. "Good. Find an empty bed in the barracks. There might be some in the back. There'll be rations given out at noon, and we take dinner in the Great Hall after sunset. You can join the other new recruits in the courtyard. Practice your sword work. In a few days, all of you will be gathered to see if you're up to snuff. If Lady Tessa approves of you, then you'll start guard duty as early as next week."

"And if she doesn't?"

Ove shrugged. "Then I hope you know a trade," he said and then walked away without a backward glance.

26
Havardr

521

HAVARDR GRUNTED IN annoyance as liquid cold pulsed through his ribs. In the battle today, he'd taken an arrow to the chest that would've killed him if not for the tonics his mother had given him as a boy. As it was, he'd only spat out a quart of blood and felt like he was drowning for the last hour. He'd stubbornly finished the battle, charging for the archer who'd hit him and choking him with his own bowstring, and now regretted the extra strain.

The soldiers had applauded him for his theatrics, so perhaps it was worth it. He'd managed to stay standing until he was safely hidden within his tent behind the battle lines. He was in so much pain that he didn't yet know if today's battle had gained them any ground or not. All he remembered was grabbing a servant by the collar and demanding they fetch him herbs. Half-mad from blood loss, he'd cursed Tessa and her insistence they needed healers with the troops. Because, damn it all, she'd been right.

It'd been easy to ignore her when he was never the one getting injured; now he was hacking up blood and stuffing herbs into his chest while chanting half-remembered spells to seal the wound.

"Fucking archers," he hissed. His breathing was more normal now, though the air in his lungs felt warmer and thinner than it should. Each breath spread the heat throughout his chest. He picked up the broken arrow that had been lodged between his ribs. He didn't remember pulling it out, but he must have. He'd have punched anyone who'd tried, and there were no dead or unconscious bodies in his tent.

Havardr looked at the pointed tip, covered in dried blood, then threw it on the ground.

This western campaign wasn't his first time dealing with arrows. He'd raided plenty of villages that had archers, though there were rarely any arrows shot their way. Raiding was a matter of surprise. Strike quickly, catch your target unawares, and make off with everything you want before they can muster a counterattack. Terrified villagers didn't have the best aim, and over the years, he'd seen few arrow wounds and taken none.

He'd seen hundreds since coming to Fjarriheimr. It was the bastards' weapon of choice, riding about on horseback too fast for the soldiers of Hjorrfold to catch them and striking from afar. How many men and women had died in the first battle because they'd been so unprepared for this type of warfare?

"If they didn't have archers and their horses, we'd have won this war by now, mark my words," he said. No one was there to hear it, but he'd say it again and again. It helped rally the troops, he thought, to know it wasn't their fault. The Fjarriheimr army was cheating. In a fair fight, they'd lose every time.

This war was dragging on. He'd known how large Fjarriheimr was, but hadn't rightly accounted for its size when he planned this campaign. The three islands they'd taken were large, too. He'd assumed it would take a similar number of soldiers and time. Twice as big, so double the numbers, right? But this was a unified kingdom, with an army to protect it and walls to keep them at bay. It took twice as much effort, if not more, to gain any ground, and then there was always more ground to take after.

They'd bested the Fjarriheimr in battle several times, but it was never enough. You couldn't just beat them; you had to do it so thoroughly that they surrendered. Otherwise, they would retreat on horseback to the nearest town—fortified, of course—and hide behind the walls to do it all over again, but with fresh horses and fighters.

And when they did conquer a town and have them bend the knee, he had to crush their spirits. He'd made the mistake of moving on too quickly from the first two, and they'd rebelled as soon as the bulk of his army was out of sight. Then he'd had to double back and retake those same towns, which were more defiant for having deceived him.

It was a nightmare. An embarrassing, never-ending nightmare.

He'd lost his temper that second time and razed the town to the ground and salted the earth. Hjorrfold had no room for slaves, but he was tempted to sell off the surviving rebels so they'd know how good they'd had it. Instead, he'd had them tied together, the first to the back of a supply wagon and the rest following behind in a long line, forced to march behind the army. They'd been much more compliant after a weeklong march with only half-rations.

"My prince?"

Havardr's attention snapped to the entrance of his tent. A servant stood there, possibly the same one he'd sent for herbs earlier. Though Havardr was in a more generous mood than before, he wasn't pleased to have been seen at such a weak moment by someone so far beneath him he didn't even know their name.

"What?" he barked, then forced himself to cast aside his anger. This peasant wasn't worth his ire; he needed to bottle it up and save it for battle.

Too late, though: the boy cowered and looked like he'd like nothing more than to flee the tent. But he gulped and took a step inside. "Your generals would like to see you."

"They're just officers," he snapped. This fool was hitting every nerve. "Send them in."

'General' was a term the soldiers had picked up from the Fjarriheimr. People who commanded armies and bore authority over the shape of a battle. The Fjarriheimr weren't conquerors and never intended to be, but after centuries of sharing a border with Hjorrfold, they'd long ago learned the importance of an organized army to keep themselves safe from raids. 'General' was only one of many words his people had stolen from their enemy, including a variety of colorful swear words. As far as he was concerned, 'general' was among them. It grated on Havardr that Fjarriheimr had anything he didn't, whether it was words and concepts or the land and cities he craved.

While having 'generals' would do well if they were attacking on multiple fronts, spread out across hundreds of miles, it was absurd of his officers to think they had that kind of power. Havardr was *here*. He was the one giving orders and managing everything. They fought as he bid them, nothing more. Why, take any soldier from this campaign and they would do the job just as well. To think they thought they deserved any sort of credit for doing as they were told was outrageous.

The men entered. Three of them, all older than him, though they owed all their experience and honor to Havardr. If he hadn't taken an interest in them years ago in Yfirgardr, they'd be no better than any other common raider. They were all grim-faced and still covered in blood, sweat, and filth from battle. They looked at Havardr's bare chest, the dried-blood the only clear sign of where he'd been shot, and then at each other, daring someone to speak.

Good. They needed a healthy fear of him. It was the only respect a warrior could show another warrior, and seeing how easily he'd survived his injury only added to his renown.

"Get on with it," Havardr growled.

Kerr, who had known Havardr the longest, stepped forward. He wore dark armor that matched his dark skin and black hair. "This isn't working. We're losing too many men, and it's taking too long. We'll never take Fjarriheimr at this rate. Everyone will be dead or dying by the time winter sets in, and we'll be well and truly fucked if it's a long winter."

"There's no reason to think it'll be long," Havardr said. "We spent a winter at Midreyna, and it was barely two months in all."

"A right frigid two months," one of the other men, Hakon, grumbled. He had a long, gray beard that he kept braided. It was one of the few interesting things about his otherwise bland appearance. Stand him in a line with twenty other men from Hjorrfold and Havardr wasn't sure he'd be able to pick him out, he was so average. "Short, but colder than any I can remember."

"Because we were on an island," Havardr said, enunciating each word to make it clear he thought his complaint was horseshit. "We've taken dozens of towns and have supply lines back to Hjorrfold. What does it matter how long the winter is?"

The men looked at their feet, refusing to meet his eye.

"You came here to do more than complain." Havardr stood, and though it strained his ribs to do so, he straightened to his full height. His head touched the top of the tent, and even from a few feet away, he towered over his would-be generals. "Say something worthwhile or leave."

Kerr made a face like a man bracing for a blow. He'd clearly drawn the short straw, and the burden of pleading their case had fallen to him. "We keep hacking away at these villages, wasting our time and losing soldiers."

Havardr crossed his arms over his chest and bit back a grimace at how his newly closed skin pulled uncomfortably. "And instead you propose...?"

"We should make for the capital."

"The capital? It's nearly two hundred miles from here. Who knows how many towns lie between us and there, and untold forces. Why the fuck would we do that?"

To his credit, Kerr didn't wilt under Havardr's anger. "We should ignore the towns as much as we can and make a straight line for the capital. If we push hard, we can be there in a fortnight."

"The city has walls three feet thick, they say."

"We lay siege to the city," Sten, the third in this trio of fools, said. He had a handsome face once, but it was scarred and his nose crooked from being broken too many times. He could've had any lad or lady in the keep, once upon a time; now he had to pay to have people come to his bed. "Starve 'em out if need be."

"And how is that any better than what we're doing now?" Havardr snapped. "We sit back like cowards and wait for them to be so desperate they come to us? Where's the honor in that?"

Havardr's reputation was built on his ability to fight. How could he face his people if he won a war with a pitiful siege instead of a battle?

"The honor is in victory," Kerr said. "When you make their king submit to you, who would doubt your greatness?"

Fair enough. That would impress all the nobles and peasants at home who cared for titles. It wouldn't impress the people fighting by his side, though.

Sensing his hesitancy, Kerr took another step forward, arms outstretched. "What is a snake without its head?" he coaxed. "If we take the capital, then there would be no reason to continue these skirmishes. They're picking away at us piece by piece, and we're doing the same to them. They stand no chance of taking Yfirgardr, just like they stand no chance of killing you. We *can*, though. One more march, one final battle, and it's done. Then we can loot the capital, so our soldiers forget how many of our friends got killed and injured along the way."

Havardr stared Sten down. They had been meaning to say this for a while, he realized. They had waited for Havardr to get hurt so they might appeal to his self-interest. While he resented their manipulation, he was admittedly tiring of Fjarriheimr. The sooner he could get out of this wretched land and start collecting tribute from them, the better.

"We will head for the capital," he said at last. The relief on their faces was palpable, and he let it settle in before he added, "But we will continue to fight and pillage as we go."

"But sire—" Sten started.

"You speak of what will appease our soldiers. Marching day after day with no battle won't do that. These are warriors of Hjorrfold. They want to fight. They want to strip Fjarriheimr of its treasures and dole out retribution for the friends they've lost." He thought of the satisfaction he felt choking that archer, and knew in his heart his men and women felt the same. "I will do as you've recommended, but my way."

"Of course, Your Highness," Sten said. All three of them bowed low. Would they congratulate themselves on their successful appeal, or complain that this war wouldn't end in the fortnight they'd plotted out?

"Go tell the troops to rest. We set out at dawn." He turned his back on them, a clear dismissal, and walked to the far edge of the tent. He heard them leave, and once he was alone again, he fell heavily onto the mess of furs that passed for a bed.

He liked that they had a plan, and that it differed from what they'd been doing. Things weren't working, and Havardr wasn't so deluded that he couldn't admit they needed a change. Yet this didn't feel like the right path. Not a wrong one, per se, but Kerr had made it sound too simple. There would be complications, problems to account for that Havardr didn't have the mind to predict.

Stigandr would know, he thought, then growled at his mind's betrayal.

Yes, Stigandr would have seen all the consequences of this course of action, and he would already be working out solutions. He'd know exactly what to do after they got to the capital, how to lay siege, and what negotiations must follow. And it wasn't just idle admiration that made him think of Stigandr. Though Havardr hated to admit it, he missed his brother. Not so much the person himself, but the idea of what the two of them could have been. All that they could've accomplished together, side-by-side…if only their father had named Havardr heir. But Alvis had been stubborn and refused, and had forced Havardr to see Stigandr as competition instead of an ally.

The entire world could've been theirs…

It still could be. If Stigandr ever comes back and accepts my place as the next king—

Havardr rolled onto his back and stared at the roof of his linen tent, dyed a dark gray to keep the heat in as the days grew colder. He didn't know where Stigandr had gone or if he was still alive. If he knew his brother, if Stigandr hadn't shown up yet, then he wasn't going to.

Which meant Havardr would never see his brother again.

"Rest well, Brother," Havardr mumbled to his empty tent. "Wherever you are…"

27
Tessa

521

RULING WAS TEDIOUS business.

Tessa had been brought up to be the new mistress of Hundrfeld, but she knew and understood Hundrfeld; she was a stranger to Yfirgardr, and Hjorrfold was too large a place to know it all. She was constantly being briefed on far-flung keeps and homesteads she'd never heard of, forced to account for them in her edicts when she could barely find them on a map.

She might not like the burden of rule, but she was smart, thorough, and dedicated. As dull as it was compared to fighting and training, there was skill involved, and she appreciated the work it took for a noble or minister to navigate the channels necessary to see their vision through. As regent, she could bypass many of these needless roadblocks, and still it wasn't so simple as saying the words and making it law. She had to justify and convince anyone who thought they knew better, which was anyone who'd lived in the city longer or was older than her. Basically everyone, really.

No, she didn't enjoy serving as a regent...but she was damned good at it.

And she'd enjoyed the challenge. Much like she prided herself on overcoming obstacles, Havardr had set her up for failure in impossible circumstances, and she'd thrived. She was too stubborn to allow Havardr of all people to underestimate her, not when she was perfectly capable, so she'd thrown herself into the work. It might not *appear* that she'd put in much effort from the way she'd gone into her first Council meeting and taken over, but it had required a great deal of study and inquiry, all done in secret.

Even without the years of tutelage Havardr had received, she'd already made improvements. Aside from making sure there was enough grain to support the people of Hjorrfold, she'd reallocated funds to help the poor, began construction projects to rebuild derelict parts of the city and add more permanent structures in the grasslands outside the walls, and increased patrol routes through the city to keep the increased population in check. And it wasn't as easy as determining these things must be done: she had to work out where the money was coming from, the building supplies, the men, the time, and then either bully through the Council or convince them not only that it was for the betterment of Hjorrfold, but that it'd been their idea in the first place and she was simply seeing their vision through.

The nobles fawned upon such flattery, and though they resented her rise to power when she'd been a nobody at court all her life, they couldn't deny her lineage or the authority the prince had given her. That she offered them prestige helped grease the wheel. She was happy to let them pour their own money into projects so their names or the names of their homes might be brandished upon them—the Bridge of Eirbjod, the Orphanage of Obygdvollr, the Stables of Vittagardr, the Birger Barns—and thus their standing.

And the common people—the ones who saw her in the marketplace inspecting the construction or in the courtyard training with the soldiers or in the Great Hall listening to their pleas for justice—they knew that the new reforms were her gifts to them.

Tessa only hoped her efforts would be respected when Havardr returned.

He could take credit for them. She didn't care about that. Not much, anyway. But she worried he would undo them. Dismantle everything she'd put in place and revert back to his misguided neglect. What was the point of doing all this good if her would-be brother would tear it apart the first chance he got?

So the world would see him do it and know what kind of man he really is...

A small comfort, she supposed, though she doubted it would ever happen. Havardr was many things, but he was good at maintaining the facade of a just man destined for the throne. That was her hope: that she would keep everything in place because it suited his image, even if he would've never considered these projects himself. In truth, he might not notice them at all. If it didn't have a sword or shield attached, it might as well be invisible to him.

A knock at the door told her she was no longer alone. She'd been working in the small library she'd stolen for her own use. It had belonged to King Alvis' mother. Although kept in meticulous order by the cleaning staff, it had clearly been neglected in recent years. It was a space Tessa could claim for herself that didn't feel like she was stepping on the toes of someone who could, theoretically, return any day. The king's study and the mages' workshops and the court library, for example, could be reclaimed by Alvis or any of his children. This room, deep in the west wing, could belong to her alone. Indeed, it was often overlooked by the Council, as it had been so long out of use they never thought to look for her there. Tessa liked its solitude. No one could easily interrupt her without truly putting in the effort to find her.

Tessa looked up from the pile of scrolls laid out before her. Petitions and court cases and trade requests and requisitions for supplies…on and on her work went, leaving her sparse time for pursuits she actually enjoyed. She hadn't held a weapon in over a week.

"M'lady." Dagrun bowed as she entered.

She smiled at Dagrun, her steward who'd quickly risen through the ranks of servants over those recommended by Council members for the task. She was hardworking and loyal, the only two attributes Tessa cared for, so she'd selected Dagrun from among the servants and never had cause to regret her choice.

"Yes?" Tessa asked with genuine kindness and none of the faux sweetness she used with the Council.

"The lists you asked for." Dagrun lifted a pile of parchment and stepped into the room. The woman couldn't use a dagger to save her life (truly, Tessa had seen her wield a blade and knew Dagrun was more likely to harm himself than anyone else), but she wielded quill and parchment better than Tessa could. She wore a long woolen tunic that would do terribly in a fight but that showed her status within court with its silver buttons and embroidered hem, and she kept her brown hair short, the ends curling around her face and at the nape of her neck. Despite being a few years older than Tessa, Dagrun had a smaller frame that made Tessa tower over her. She often used her size to her advantage, often blending into the background so that no one noticed her.

"The lists." Tessa sighed. She had asked for the most recent lists of guards, patrols, and pay due, but that didn't make her any happier to have to review it. A necessary inconvenience: her job, above all, was to maintain peace. There had been centuries of peace before Havardr got it in his head to expand the borders, which was trickier than merely drawing new lines on a map. It was one thing to make someone call you lord and another to make them remember it later when tribute was due and you were a thousand miles away.

The reality of maintaining order among people so recently forced to bend the knee, people who remembered being masters of their own land, wasn't easy. It was a burden that should've fallen to Havardr, yet it was her mess to manage.

"Thank you," she said as she reached for them. "Anything of note?"

"The western pass is asking for more support against brigands. The prince's war effort is forcing refugees into other lands, and our people are not much interested in opening their homes to these strangers, which is in turn leading to thievery."

"Hmm." Tessa had expected as much and had already appealed to the nobles in the western keeps for support. Those with family in Yfirgardr were receptive to her requests; those without, less so. Havardr had raised vast numbers of soldiers since unofficially ascending to the throne and taken most of them west. As she understood it, he'd left her with fewer warriors in the city than there'd ever been, even when the city was founded. Oh, she'd done her best to continue his momentum and recruit, but if she took in the wrong sort, there were brawls in the barracks. Or worse, in the streets.

She'd settled both issues at once with some finagling. She'd given land, gold, and a dreki to the best warriors from the island campaigns that were left behind. Men and women who'd proven themselves capable fighters and loyal to her, but who were titleless and landless. They were provided with land on the newly conquered islands where they could build their own keeps and claim their own noble status should they succeed in helping civilize the area. They also were required to find competent men and women to send to Yfirgardr as soldiers, and Tessa redistributed them as needed, spreading them out so they couldn't try to mutiny anywhere they went.

It was working. Slowly, yes, but she was hearing of less unrest on the islands and had a comfortable number of warriors spread throughout Hjorrfold's western lands.

This she saw as her most important work, and had done it in a way that would be impossible for Havardr to interfere with. Like her ancestors had, she had these fledgling nobles take an oath to Hjorrfold and rewarded them with a royal gift: jewelry from the late queen. Granted, she had no idea if there was some magic rite that should go along with this exchange, but it was a tradition so etched into the history of Hjorrfold that once the gifts were given, Havardr would be powerless to undo it without seeming a monster.

"What's on the agenda for today?" Tessa asked as she placed the parchments aside. She would peruse them later, when she could give them the attention they deserved; for now, nothing seemed particularly out of order.

"Petitioners are already lined up outside the gates. Ove has about thirty new recruits for you to approve. And if you do approve of them, that'll mean a feast in the Great Hall to welcome them. I'll have to tell the cooks before midday, else it'll have to wait until tomorrow."

Tessa looked out the window and judged it to be only a few hours after dawn. There was time yet. She turned back to Dagrun. "I'll take petitions until noon, then view the new recruits after lunch. Tell the cooks to start the preparations. With thirty, I can't imagine there won't be *someone* who's qualified."

"Very good," Dagrun said with a bow—she'd never listened when Tessa argued against such needless formality—and reached for the empty plate of cheese and figs she'd eaten earlier. "Anything else?"

"I can clean up my own messes." Tessa pulled the plate closer to her and waved Dagrun off. "Stop that."

"You can do a great many things," she said. "Doesn't mean you have to." But Dagrun stepped back and held up her hands in surrender.

"If I ever get too busy to clean up after myself, you have my leave to smack me. Or if I get too full of my own importance. Either way, I'll be in need of a good smack."

Dagrun raised an eyebrow and looked at her hands. "A *good* smack?"

She laughed. "Even a bad one'll do."

Dagrun bowed again and took her leave. Tessa looked at the mess on her desk and wondered if there was ever an end to the work necessary to run a kingdom. Probably not.

"Maybe this is the real reason Alvis ran away," she grumbled to herself. "He knew he'd have to do it alone."

AFTER LUNCH, TESSA stepped into the courtyard with Dagrun at her side. She'd been inside all day, and the fresh air and bright light made her tired muscles unclench in relief. The recruits were already assembled on the training pitch, so she went to the keep walls to get a better view of them (and hopefully remove herself as a distraction).

The new recruits were *rough*. They were generally competent with a blade, and she estimated that was from practical experience versus any formal training. They'd had to protect their homes or had been hunters or had sold their strength as guards and mercenaries. They were slow to line up when Ove gave the order, and sloppy as they went through their drills. There was promise, though. They *obeyed* the orders, which was chief among her concerns. They were respectful both to the officers and to her; she would accept nearly anyone who was polite and willing to learn.

There were a few she had to dismiss outright. One woman was too old and walked with a severe limp. A young boy had only one eye. Another boy was awful, with poor coordination and instincts. A woman who was so skittish she almost stabbed herself in the foot with her training sword. For their own safety, Tessa couldn't accept them.

She pointed them out to Dagrun. "Find them work in the castle if you can," she said. "Or in the city, if not."

Dagrun nodded. Her lips barely moved as she asked, "Or Hundrfeld?"

Tessa's heart clenched. Home. How many people had she sent there in her name? Yet she was unable to go herself. She was fairly certain Havardr would ride back himself if he heard she'd gone to Hundrfeld. If her endgame was merely to kill him, she'd do it in an instant. What she had planned for him would be so much worse, and required his belief she was on his side. So she stayed put, knowing that if she went or so much as sent a letter to Trond, it would make things difficult.

She had sent word to Trond, though. Many times. But it had taken time to establish a secure means of doing so.

"Or Hundrfeld," she mouthed with a smile, then turned back to the recruits. "I think the rest will do. Let's take a walk, shall we? See who's ready for duty and who'll need some work."

Tessa led the way down from the wall. She patted Ove on the shoulder as she walked by, the old man's hair graying at his temples but otherwise still a vibrant orange that glistened in the midday sun. They would consult together after the feast to decide how best to distribute the new guards, but for now, they would observe separately.

She walked up and down the lines of men and women, with Dagrun behind her. For the most part, Tessa said very little, but sometimes she would ask someone a question about where they were from or whether they'd fought before. A few times, she corrected the stance or form. One young woman had been swinging wildly with her sword, but after a few suggestions, she fared much better. Not battle ready by any means, but taking instruction was a good sign.

She took pride in the people of Hjorrfold for that: no matter how many men and women had already come forward to fight, there were always more. They were talented and full of heart. They were more than the blunt instruments Havardr wished to use them as.

Three of the fighters proved exceptionally competent. Two men had come together, a married couple who'd been hired guards at an island keep but had heard the pay was better on the continent. Tessa would likely have them both serve within the city. Their experience would come in handy with the newer recruits.

The third fighter was a man with short blond hair and a mess of stubble. He looked strong, though wielded his blade with uncommon finesse. As they worked through drills and some sparring matches, she kept an eye on him.

There was something familiar about the way he moved, and it annoyed her that it had taken her so long to spot it. He moved like the nobles trained at court, the ones who knew no battles beyond the pitch, who had memorized and refined the movements shown them as children without knowing how to apply them in a proper fight.

He didn't look much like a noble, though. His hands were too calloused and his clothing not fine enough, his skin too weathered.

After a short match against one of the youths, she put a hand up and waved him over. He looked around as if unsure she meant him, then walked over with his sword resting against his right shoulder.

"Name?" she asked as she inspected him from head to foot.

"Ashk."

"Where do you hail from, Ashk?"

He hesitated before admitting, "Yfirgardr. My father served in the keep for many years."

"On the guard?" Ashk shook his head. "Raider?" Again, he shook his head. "Then…?"

"In the kitchens, though that was long ago. His family was from the north, by the mountains. We left when my mother died."

"And as a boy, you watched the soldiers training?"

Ashk smiled shyly. "I might have."

"And you've never been in a real fight?"

The smile vanished, and his cheeks colored. "I—" The words caught in his throat, but he eventually choked out, "I wouldn't say *never*—"

"Your form is good," she said, interrupting him and hopefully saving him from further embarrassment. She wasn't sure why she'd even said that. It'd never mattered before. Not once had she refused someone because of their lack of experience, and she certainly didn't shame them for it. "A little rigid, but your technique is quite exemplary. You fight in the same style as the old guard who were here before they all went to war."

"Do they not teach that style anymore?" At first she'd thought his eyes were brown, but there were flecks of green in the light.

"We do, though with modifications. It's just odd to see someone come in already knowing it." She pointed with her chin back to the training pitch. "Carry on."

He looked like he wanted to say more, but he gave a curt nod and went back to his partner to begin again. Tessa watched him, eyes narrowed.

"Something wrong?" Dagrun asked.

Tessa jerked slightly, so deep in thought she'd all but forgotten the other woman. "No," she said. She turned back to Ashk, then again to Dagrun. "Tell Ove to finish things here. I have to go back to the Great Hall. Ask him to pull aside the four I mentioned before and any additional ones he thinks would be a bad fit. I'll speak with them after the petitioners."

Dagrun nodded. "I'll start making inquiries about work."

"Thank you." Tessa squeezed Dagrun's arm and left for the Great Hall. She didn't look back as she left, though she felt a pair of hazel eyes watch her go.

28
Stigandr

521

There were about two dozen new recruits whom Stigandr had come to know while staying in the barracks. He practiced with them on the training pitch and sat with them at meals. Despite their enthusiasm, some of them would need to be weeded out. A few were generally unfit to fight, while others sounded overwhelmed by city-life. They'd be better suited to a keep out in the plains or in a small village, somewhere not as crowded and where they had a chance of staying out of trouble.

When they were called out onto the training pitch early in the afternoon, Ove stood in the center with a few other guards at his back. It was the same officer who'd accepted Stigandr into the barracks, though Stigandr had seen little of him since that first encounter.

"Lady Tessa will be taking the time out of her busy schedule to see what you're made of. If she thinks you're up to snuff, she and I'll be discussing how best to make use of your talents. Some of you might be dismissed from service. Some will be assigned within Yfirgardr. Others might be sent elsewhere in Hjorrfold. Know that whatever we decide, it's what we think is in not only your best interest, but in Hjorrfold's."

Ove let his words sink in, hands on his hips, as he inspected them with a scowl. Stigandr couldn't get a read on the man. He never looked happy and had frown lines etched into his face to prove it, but there were also wrinkles from laughter. Though Stigandr had never seen it, he'd heard Ove's laughter in the barracks and echoing in the Great Hall at dinner. It was clear the guards in Yfirgardr respected him, and the way he spoke of her suggested he was on close terms with Tessa, yet Stigandr couldn't remember him. Had he risen from the ranks so quickly, or was this someone she'd brought with her from Hundrfeld?

Doesn't look like he's from Hundrfeld. Not with that hair.

"You may prepare as you'd like," Ove continued and gestured to the rack of practice weapons.

Most took up swords, so Stigandr did the same. When Havardr had been leading raids, he favored a large battle axe that could cleave a man's head in two (or so he said). He also favored others who used those bigger, heavier weapons. More impressive in battle, he claimed.

"If someone's running at you with a sword, you feel you have a chance. If they have an axe, you know you're only surviving one blow..."

Havardr had locked eyes with him as he said it, and Stigandr had felt the threat in those words. He shuddered at the memory, his brother's voice still crystal clear in his mind.

The problem with those heavier weapons was, well, they were heavy. Stigandr had used them once or twice with battle masters who were determined to make him competent at everything. He didn't have his brother's size, and the axes and hammers and maces they gave him were unwieldy. Dangerous even, like when he grazed his own chest with a mace. They'd made him use a sword, because swords were more regal than knives and daggers, but those smaller weapons were where he excelled.

Not that he was likely to impress anyone in this crowd with his knife throwing. Nor could he disappear into thin air like he actually would in a fight. A sword it would have to be.

He tried to position himself in an innocuous spot, somewhere he wouldn't stand out. He hoped to be just good enough to make the cut, but not so good that Tessa or Ove would remember him in particular. There were some actual skilled fighters a row down from him, and he surrounded himself with ones who didn't look absolutely dismal, then tried to mimic their level.

After a quarter hour of practice, the doors to the Great Hall swung open. Two women appeared, one looking like a clerk or a steward, and the other… well, the other was decidedly *not*.

Stigandr didn't know what he'd expected. Another Havardr, perhaps? A warrior with a sword at her belt, but a fine cloak and jewels to show off her plunder. A glower to match, with cruelty in her gaze even when she smiled. That was the type of person Havardr respected, because that was who he was.

Tessa was none of these things.

Oh, she was indeed a warrior, and she looked the part from head to toe. Her hair, so dark it glistened in the sun, was held in place by braids that kept it from her eyes but let it drape down her back. Her complexion was fair, unblemished and smooth as befit a noble lady. Her black belt bore a large silver buckle he suspected bore the crest of Hundrfeld, though she only wore a single dagger. She wore leather boots, black breeches, and a white tunic, a color reserved for the wealthy because of how damned hard it was to keep clean without magic. It was the only outward sign of her position. No jewels, no head ornament to give the illusion of a crown, and barely any embroidery on her tunic.

She had the bearing of a warrior, too. Her stride was confident, like she knew she was the strongest person here and feared nothing. As she walked by a row of guards, she placed two fingers to her forehead, inclined her head slightly, then arched her fingers out towards them. A warrior's salute, one given in greeting between raiders and distinctly different from the one made to officers. At her rank, there was no one save Havardr that she needed to salute, yet she treated these men and women as equals.

No wonder she was popular. She ruled the city and the kingdom fairly, had proven her capabilities as a fighter, and wasn't too self-important. She'd fared better than the Council would've in her place, that was for sure.

He didn't know whether that made her more dangerous or not.

Tessa and her steward took their positions on the castle wall, a good vantage point for the courtyard that would allow her to oversee all the recruits at once. She stood there, hands behind her back, and nodded down to Ove.

"Recruits," he bellowed, raising his hand. They all looked at him, tensing as they readied themselves. Once the courtyard was as still as the dead of night, he slashed his arm downward. "Begin!"

Stigandr went through the motions he'd learned as a boy, the footwork and blows rusty but passable. He felt the weight of Lady Tessa's eyes boring into him as Ove put them through their paces, though every time he stole a glance, she wasn't looking his way. It was disappointing, though it shouldn't have been. He didn't want to be noticed.

When she moved from the wall to walk through the lines, he was painfully aware of her. He'd never been so attuned to another person, not even when he'd been in the hunting parties of Bjardleith. It was like he held his breath, waiting, but he wasn't sure if he craved her attention or to remain in obscurity.

When she called him over, his heart fluttered. The former then.

He barely paid attention to what she said, too busy staring at her.

She doesn't look much like she's from Hundrfeld, either. If I didn't know she's Sindri's daughter, I don't know that I'd ever guess it. As is, the resemblance is difficult to spot…

Sindri had been conventionally handsome, with chiseled features that many at court had swooned over. Tawny, sun-bleached hair and gray eyes, he'd charmed people with earnest gazes and kind smiles. Stigandr himself had liked Sindri because he'd always been kind to Stigandr instead of merely tolerating his presence like Havardr did.

Tessa was different. There was something of Sindri in the shape of her mouth or the line of her nose, but he couldn't be sure, not with his memory of Sindri so fuzzy. Under a generous assessment, her features might be considered pretty, but her pale skin framed by dark locks rendered her breathtaking. And her eyes, most striking of all. Black as a moonless night, endless in a way that made her seem all-seeing. Perhaps that was why he didn't care what was spoken: what she saw was more damning.

And then it was over. She'd dismissed him, and with her firmly behind him and her attention elsewhere, he could breathe again.

What had just happened? And why did he feel like he'd been struck by lightning?

AFTER TESSA LEFT them in the courtyard to continue meeting with petitioners,

Ove gathered them by the barracks.

"A few of you I'll need a word with, but the Lady liked what she saw from most of you. There'll be a feast tonight to celebrate your being welcomed into Hjorrfold's service. No, no, there'll be no oaths of loyalty to Tessa. You swear to the kingdom, since we've got no king or princes in attendance. And yes, all are welcome at the feast. If I call your name, come see me and we'll get you sorted. Everyone else, congratulations. Enjoy your last afternoon of freedom. You'll get your assignments on the morrow."

He rattled off names, and though Stigandr didn't think Ashk would be among them, he was relieved when his faux name wasn't called. There were no surprises among those who would be dismissed, but he could see their frustration and, in a few cases, their concern.

"Where'll I go?" an older woman fretted as she wrung her hands. "I've got nowhere and no one…"

Stigandr was about to offer her some coin, but Ove stepped over to her and put a gentle arm around her shoulder. "It's all right. We'll find you a place. No one leaves the keep without knowing where they're going. You have my word on that."

That was new. Normally, dismissal from the guard meant you were out on your own. Even offering them a place at the table for the welcoming feast was more generous than anything from his father's time. It was far too charitable to be Havardr's addition, either. He had no interest in people who weren't useful.

This must be Tessa's work. Oh, it might be because Havardr left her as regent while he was gone, but she wasn't putting his stamp on any of this. The people saw she was the one making these offers, giving rewards, running the entire kingdom with the attention and care even Alvis hadn't shown since Stigandr was a boy. Ingegerd had become so obsessed with prophecies and avoiding some unnamed disaster, and Alvis had clearly spent most of his effort managing her fears that even from Bjardleith, Stigandr could see the ill effects.

Whatever Havardr had thought he was doing, putting her in charge, it seemed a gross miscalculation. The real question was whether Stigandr could use his brother's mistake to his advantage.

Stigandr returned his practice sword and snuck into the Great Hall. Cloaked in shadow, he sat behind a pillar in the back corner and listened as folks appealed to Tessa to settle disputes or grant them supplies.

"My neighbor cut down my apple tree 'n I want him to pay for a new one to be planted. And for the loss of apples until the new one's able to bear fruit."

"We lost our cows in a flood from the river and would kindly ask for a loan to buy new ones from the king's herd..."

"Our daughter died, and we haven't the money to pay for the funeral rites..."

"I heard your call for healers. I'm a mage with training in potions and herbs and would like a chance to prove myself at court..."

Tessa listened patiently to everyone, occasionally asking questions but more often letting people speak. She heard both sides of any argument, and he thought he would rule much the way she did. She tended to be more generous than he was, and harsher in punishments when there was a clear wrongdoer. In one case, there was a man seeking recompense for his dead son, but the boy had been killed by accident. Stigandr expected a severe sentence since the woman admitted everything.

"You will pay all that the parents have asked," Tessa said firmly, "but I see no malicious will here. Go to the temple or sanctuary of your choosing and do the rites there to cleanse yourself, but you will be held to no further judgement for this unfortunate death after your reparations are complete."

Fair, he supposed, but more lenient than when she'd punished a man for poisoning another man's geese.

"I'm sorry I'm unable to hear you all today," she said, her voice resonating through the hall and giving him goosebumps. It sounded as if she was right beside him. "If you have traveled, please stop by The Rose and Kettle Inn and ask for rooms. The crown will cover your expenses for your room and a hot meal. Dagrun will take your names to make sure you are the first seen tomorrow."

Already, servants were coming in to lay out the long tables for dinner while guards ushered people out. The steward—Dagrun, apparently—waited by the entrance with parchment and quill in hand.

He expected grumbles about wasted time and unjust rulings. That was all one could hear when his parents ended audiences for the day, though admittedly they were more abrupt with their dismissal and kept less regular hours.

There wasn't a single ill word spoken as people filed out neatly, not even to him when a servant spotted him lurking.

"Sorry, sir," she said. "But we're clearin' everything out for dinner with the guards. You'd best head home."

Home. If only. Though he could likely sneak into the castle and to his room, he couldn't risk Ashk's absence being noted. He'd already disappeared long enough, and he couldn't very well miss the feast. He might not have any friends here yet, but his neighbors in the barracks had been cheering him on, and he had a sort of camaraderie with the other recruits.

So he apologized and left with everyone else. He would head back to the barracks and soak in the congratulations of his peers. Later, during the feast, he'd eat and drink and sing with the rest of them. And when he had to swear his oath of loyalty, he'd bend his knee and recite the words, though he was no longer sure who he'd be swearing to. The only thing that was clear was that he was a guard of Yfirgardr, and he answered to Tessa of Hundrfeld.

29
Ove

521

Ove heaved another barrel onto the back of the wagon, grunting with the effort. Three barrels of fish, ready for Hundrfeld. They'd return with salted game like boar and elk. He didn't have a mind for business and didn't know if it was a fair trade, but he knew he was tired of fish and beef; boar sounded mighty fine.

"Keep to the regular route," Ove said to the driver as he wiped sweat from his brow. "If you get stopped, you tell 'em you're headed for Obygdvollr, you hear?"

The driver rolled her eyes. "It's not my first run, Ove. Give me some credit."

Valdis was a short woman with hair the color of a wet grain field that she always wore in a bun pinned loosely on top of her head. Her skin a light almond, as were her eyes, and though she was as sturdily built as any farmhand he'd ever known, she was a merchant and the daughter of a fellow raider. Her father had saved Ove once or twice on raids, and they'd been drinking buddies before Ove gave it up. His dying when they took the first island in Havardr's name had put a damper on the friendship. Ove had known the girl and her mother lived in Yfirgardr, but there had been little he could do for them aside from making sure they weren't starving. The mother had taken up work in a tavern, and it wasn't until Tessa became regent that Ove could do something for the daughter.

Tessa needed more than fighters to maintain peace. She needed loyalty, both from the nobles and common-folk. The Council being on her side made her role as regent easier (though how, Ove couldn't say; he'd thought ruling meant having your way regardless of what people thought, but there seemed to be a lot more to it), and she'd thanked nobles again and again for their support in getting the new islands under control. It was the common-folk that were more practical, taking care of the castle and city in ways the nobles normally overlooked but that Tessa noticed and valued.

Among those practicalities was travel. Tessa couldn't step foot outside the keep without notice, and even Ove wasn't so daft as to think she could waltz over to Hundrfeld without everyone talking about it. He didn't understand *why* it should matter, but he'd been by Tessa's side from the beginning: Havardr didn't want her there, which made it dangerous for everyone involved. So she'd maintained her isolation at court until word came in that Havardr was a comfortable week's worth of travel away from Yfirgardr. Then she'd set to work.

It'd taken time to find people she could trust, but with his and Dagrun's help, she'd slowly collected merchants, hunters, and tradesmen who could travel freely without suspicion. They had no particular connection to Hundrfeld, but nothing baring their passage there. They were invaluable to Tessa when she needed to send messages, supplies, or people home, or if Trond wished to do the same. Valdis was one of the newer runners, but she had proven the most eager to make the trip.

Ove had teased her because she must have a young lad there she was courting; turned out it was a young lady.

"Don't get smart with me," he said sternly, though without any bite. "If you're such an expert, then shouldn't you—?"

She held out one hand expectantly, the other on her hip. He smiled in approval, and he dug out a gold coin from his pocket. It was one of the coins from Hundrfeld that Trond had entrusted to him years ago. Now it bore a black mark—Tessa's thumbprint marked in ink mixed, pressed right over the dog's snarling face. It was the only way for Trond to know the messages he received indeed came from Tessa. When he sent word back, it would be with a different coin stamped with his thumbprint, though of brown ink mixed with soot to look like rust. Just some dirty coins, only as valuable as the metal they were made of.

Valdis took the gold and stuffed it in her coin purse. It jingled as the new coin got lost among the others. "Just the barrels?" she asked.

"Four people, too." There'd been a total of seven recruits they'd agreed were unsuited for the job: one had experience in a kitchen, so would stay at the keep; two would serve as stable hands for the newly expanded castle stables outside the city; the rest were going to Hundrfeld, where Trond would find a place for them.

"Your fine lady of the keep got any messages…?"

This was trickier. Both Tessa and Trond refused to commit anything in writing, so the messages they sent were usually devoid of any personal sentiment since they had to be conveyed through a proxy. Occasionally, Ove would make the journey under the pretense of inspecting troops at various keeps out east, and even then, they confided very little in him. To any outsider, it would appear uncle and niece cared little for one another.

Those outsiders weren't subjected to the inquisition Ove was whenever he saw Trond in person. He asked all manner of questions about his niece—Was she eating well? How was her training going? Was the Council respecting her? Was she lonely? Did she need new clothes?—and Ove had learned to provide as much detail as possible when answering. When he returned, Tessa would give him the same treatment, demanding to know about her uncle's health, about Hundrfeld, and every tidbit about the people there he could recall.

There was a great deal of love held in their hearts for one another, and it was clear there was no place dearer to Tessa than her lost home.

But Valdis was privy to little of this except what she'd gleaned on her own.

Ove ran a hand through his beard. "She wants to know about the weather, strange as it sounds. She's got concerns about the fall being short and the winter long. And she warns her uncle to fill his larders as best he can."

As a former farmer himself, he thought Tessa a little over worried. It was still summer, and a mild one at that. To him, it seemed the weather would hold enough for two harvests, but he supposed having a whole kingdom rest on your shoulders might influence how much you worried about the harvest.

Valdis, who was at least used to the businesslike nature of Tessa and Trond's messages to each other, raised an eyebrow. "And that's all?"

"That's all," he said.

Her expression soured with disappointment. "Very well, then. I'll set out as soon as our honored guests arrive."

"See that you do. And don't linger in Hundrfeld. Never know who might be watching."

DAGRUN MET HIM at the city gates with the four departing almost-members of the guard, chattering away with them about what to expect on their journey.

Ove had no illusions about his place in Tessa's court. He'd met her early on her journey to Yfirgardr, delivered her first and only letter to Trond, and brought her things to her safely; it was like he'd imprinted on her as a surrogate uncle. It was a dash of his sufficient ability in combat mixed with a healthy amount of good timing that had made Tessa favor him over the other men and women of the keep, and he was thankful every day for his good fortune.

Dagrun, on the other hand, had become Tessa's right hand out of sheer competence. The young woman was good at what she did, overseeing everyday tasks at the castle, working with people in the city to hear their grievances and suggestions, and doing anything Tessa required that she couldn't do herself. And should Tessa ever be indisposed, Dagrun would do a fine job running things in her name.

Ove helped the four travelers into the wagon and saw Valdis off. Dagrun waited with him, and only after the wagon had wobbled out of the city proper and far enough down the road to be lost in the crowd did they turn back towards the castle.

"Why's our lass asking her uncle about the weather?" Ove asked. "Didn't think that nobles took it into consideration like farmers."

"I reckon Alvis and his brood never much did," Dagrun said darkly. She'd lived in Yfirgardr all her life. For four generations, her family had been here, and they'd seen as many generations of kings and queens and their young princes and princesses. Dagrun's family had been proud subjects of Hjorrfold, happy to be in the capital and serve. Until recently, anyway. It seemed Dagrun's opinion of the royal family was falling lower and lower every time they spoke, as though every day she found a new knot to untangle from their ill decisions. "The summer is starting well, and everyone expects it'll mean a long harvest. People over-planted, and it'll be a disaster if fall comes too soon. Too many people have moved from the land into Yfirgardr or else are out west fighting. There aren't enough people working the land to work a short harvest season."

"There's time yet," he said. They were on the steep part of the climb to the keep, and he had to shorten his stride so Dagrun could keep up.

"Let's hope so," she huffed. "Have any of the new recruits caught your eye?"

"No?" he said, more as a question than an answer. He'd get to know the ones who stayed in the city. Eventually. As of yet, none had stood out, and he thought it strange that Dagrun would ask. "Why?"

She pressed her lips into a thin line.

"You didn't bring it up to not talk about it." They were rounding the last bend in the road that led to the keep: there was nothing between them and the castle. If she wanted any sort of privacy, now was the time. "If there's someone I should keep an eye on—"

"I'm sure it's nothing." Dagrun had exceptional instincts for trouble, and they both knew it. If there was someone among the visitors in the Great Hall looking for mischief instead of justice, she would suss them out and have them removed before they could do any harm.

"And if it ain't? May as well tell me. Nothing to be gained by keeping silent, and nothing to lose by speaking your mind."

Dagrun stopped short, hands on her hips as she caught her breath. She looked up at the castle and not at him as she spoke. "There was one who seemed…strange. You remember the man she talked to? Ashk?"

"Him?" Ove scoffed. The most interesting thing about him was that Tessa had spoken to him and that he fought a little too prettily for someone who wasn't a noble, but he'd explained that well enough. His mimicking the warriors as a boy sounded a lot like something Halle would've done. "What's the matter with him?"

"Nothing." Dagrun's shoulders sagged; she seemed deflated by Ove's disbelief. "I don't see why Tessa would speak to him, though. Tease him. She doesn't do that with the recruits. She knows they're too nervous."

"So you think it's odd she'd tease him? That sounds more like something off about Tessa than—"

"It's that he didn't mind," she said. Her cheeks were red in frustrated embarrassment. Despite her youth, she carried herself with a dignity that belied her age; she looked truly young now. "He was perhaps a little put out by it, but not the way any other recruit would be. They'd stammer or be stunned silent or…or *something*. He went back in line with the others like it didn't bother him at all. I watched him. He was no worse off after they spoke than before."

Ove crossed his arms across his chest. She had a point, he supposed. That was unusual—those who'd heard of her came to Yfirgardr a little star-struck—but there was nothing inherently *wrong*. "You're right more than you're wrong," he said carefully, "but I don't know what you think's going on here. Just who do you think this lad is?"

Dagrun deflated further. "I don't know, Ove. I suppose I worry he's a spy for Havardr. I'm not saying he is," she added quickly. "And I don't even know if that would explain the way he acted. I pray I am reading too much into this."

What was there even to spy on? Ove wondered. Tessa was doing exactly what Havardr wanted. Aside from her clandestine trade with Hundrfeld, there was nothing that could upset the prince.

Yet Tessa took the precautions, anyway. Ove didn't understand why she mistrusted Havardr so, and he doubted Dagrun did either…but it made them both uneasy all the same. Even with nothing to hide, they'd help Tessa keep her secrets.

"Well," Ove said. "I was going to recommend him for duty in Yfirgardr. Want me to send him elsewhere?"

At this, Dagrun went pale.

"That a no?"

"It's just…if he *is* a spy, I don't know that I'd want to send him off with a bunch of other new recruits. What if he turned them to Havardr's side? Again, I'm not—I don't mean to *assume* anything."

Are there sides? What does it mean to be on Tessa's or Havardr's?

"So you'd rather he stayed here? Where we can watch him?" Ove offered.

Dagrun heaved a sigh. "I suppose that's all we can do."

"Unless you want him arrested, though I'm not sure what we'd do with a prisoner. And I don't think people would like a regent who arrests citizens of Hjorrfold and interrogates them without cause, especially when they're trying to do an honorable job like joining the guard."

"You're right, of course," she said and continued walking.

"I'll keep an eye on him," Ove said. Easy enough to do, especially if it would put her at ease.

"Thank you," she said, yet Dagrun looked more upset than before. She'd hidden it away by the time they reached the castle gate, the furrow in her brow gone and her shoulders relaxed. Her confident, unbothered air returned, and she only nodded to him before heading to the Great Hall while he went off to the barracks. Ove hoped this was the one time Dagrun's gut was wrong.

30
Stigandr

521

STIGANDR HAD WORRIED that he might be assigned to some keep far from Yfirgardr. If that had been the case, he would've left with that group, then disappeared during the night and circled back. He would've needed a new disguise and would have to scrap his original plans, but he was determined to stay in the capital.

Though he might've made an exception for Hundrfeld. His curiosity about Trond, Sindri's death, and Tessa would allow the trip, but he doubted he would stay long.

But to his relief, he was assigned to guard duty at the castle. Ove called all the recruits into the courtyard and divided them into groups based on their placement, with only Stigandr and three others slotted to stay. About a dozen would continue to train in Yfirgardr until they were deemed fit to go elsewhere. The rest would leave within the week, going to keeps and villages that needed protection.

Protection from what, exactly, was unclear. Based on the keeps mentioned—all on the outskirts of Hjorrfold's territory—he suspected raiders were taking advantage of the royal family's absence. There were also a significant number of villages in the west, and that likely had everything to do with Havardr's war. Driven out by the fighting and destruction, people would turn to raiding as the only thing left. Clearly an unintended consequence, something Havardr hadn't foreseen despite it being an obvious side effect.

As the group broke apart to either begin their training or pack, Stigandr's small group was led by Ove to the castle walls.

"We rotate duties," he said as they climbed the steps. The keep's walls were thirty feet tall. Because of the hill it sat upon, it gave guards a clear view of the city and surrounding land, and made the stronghold impossible to break.

Without magic, anyway. But there were no battle mages in Hjorrfold and hadn't been for centuries. There might be mages skilled enough in other kingdoms, as he'd gotten a glimpse of in Bjardleith, but that kind of magic wasn't subtle. They'd be spotted long before they got to the capital. No, the best way inside Yfirgardr was subterfuge and illusion magic.

The very things Stigandr had spent his life mastering.

"There's wall duty," Ove continued, patting warriors on the back as he passed. The four of them followed with Stigandr at the rear, attempting to look interested in the view, as if he hadn't grown up with a better one only a few hundred feet away. "You'll have either the day or the night shift, three days in a row, then the opposite shift for three days, followed by a day of rest before you start the next rotation." He stopped and gestured to the city, then to a large bell. "You watch the road. You look for trouble in the city. If there's fire or fighting, you sound the alarm. I've not once heard that bell toll, save when the queen died, and I expect not to hear it again for many years."

Ove led them across the whole wall. The southern length had a walkway for guards, but it stopped abruptly at each end, since the Great Hall took up the western side of the keep and the barracks the eastern. The wall was thinner on those sides, too narrow for anyone to walk comfortably. Not that it mattered; the only way to access the keep was through the gate in the southern wall, or up the hill's steep incline. Stigandr had climbed those ridges as a boy, playing hide and seek with Ragnhild and some of the other children living in the castle, but he'd been small enough to use the tiny footholds. An adult would have a tough go of it; armed, it'd be impossible.

Next, they went to the gate and the gatehouse. They would similarly have gate duty, three days then three nights. The night shift was easy, since you shut the doors and kept everyone out. During the day, people were free to come and go about their business, and the crowds had to be watched for troublemakers.

"It takes ten people to open and close the gate," Ove said with a hint of pride. "Morning guards open it, night guards close it. You'll be glad to have the day of leave after that rotation, I promise you."

The Great Hall was next, where guards were needed to keep order among the petitioners. There were groups huddled about the hall waiting their turns, though Tessa wasn't there. From the grumbles he overheard, it seemed a Council meeting was taking up her morning. Dagrun, the steward, was moving about them and taking notes on their complaints; Stigandr wondered if this was to order their audiences or to pre-render judgement on Tessa's behalf.

He had no time to speculate, because Ove took them out of the Great Hall and into the long corridor along the western bank of the castle. It led through the more public areas like the meeting room where Tessa currently was with the Council, as well as Alvis' study and other parlors and libraries. The healers and kitchens were also here, though a level down; a level up would be the more private libraries and workshops for the family and mages in attendance. At the far end of the hall, he spotted the tower that granted access to the northern wing, the private area of the castle.

And on top of that tower was his room, long abandoned.

"We have guards patrol these corridors. This side of the castle, it goes two floors up and one down. That end"—he pointed north—"goes both higher and deeper. Even so, it's the easiest part of your rotation," Ove said. "Your only job is to keep out people who shouldn't be here, and there's never anyone here who shouldn't be." Stigandr might have imagined it, but Ove's gaze seemed to linger on him as he said this last part.

They walked to the tower and went through the door, only enough so they could see the other wing of the castle. They took turns peeking down the long hallway—for the others, their first glimpse into the private areas of the castle—and Stigandr went last so he could look exactly as long as the others had. No more, no less.

"Last'll be patrolling the city to keep the peace. Easy enough, except near the taverns or during festivals. Each day you start a new round, you'll be assigned an officer. They'll explain the finer points of what's needed. You report to that officer at dawn or dusk each day, you hear? You're late, and you're punished with cut rations. You arrive in armor with your sword at your belt, polished and sharpened. We've got an armory, and you'll all be properly outfitted. If you don't know how to polish or sharpen a blade, you'll be shown. Questions?"

They were silent, so Stigandr raised his hand and waited for Ove to nod at him.

"You said we get a day of rest between rotations? What are we permitted to do in that time?"

"You may do as you will during your leave. You can rest. You can visit the brothels or the taverns. There's a group in the barracks who gamble at dice and cards. I recommend you spend some time on the training pitch, otherwise what little skills you have might get rusty between any attempts to use them."

Stigandr was only just able to refrain from rolling his eyes. Somehow, his performance in the courtyard had gained the attention of first Tessa and now Ove, but while Tessa had seemed impressed by his display, Ove clearly wasn't.

"Fine advice," Stigandr said blandly, because it was. But he'd lived off his skill in the mountains, where he'd have been gored by wild goats or mauled by mountain lions if he couldn't handle himself. "When do we start?"

He was perhaps too blasé in his response, because Ove colored.

"You two"—he pointed to the man and woman closest to him—"will start on wall duty tomorrow morning. You"—he pointed at the man next to Stigandr—"start at the gate, the day after tomorrow. The night shift. And you…" He gave Stigandr a once-over and a smirk. "You'll start in the Great Hall today."

"Today?" Stigandr asked, sure he'd misunderstood. "Right now?"

"Aye." Ove's expression lit in amusement, the closest to a smile he'd been all morning. "I'll take you there. Coincidentally, it's my day to serve in the hall."

They followed Ove back to the Great Hall, where the others were dismissed and Stigandr was brought to the side of the hall, an area occupied by a pair of guards sitting at a round table with three chairs.

"I didn't realize I'd be starting quite this soon," Stigandr said. He got the impression that he'd somehow misstepped and Ove thought he needed watching. Perhaps he should've shown off a little more? Or was the problem that he'd looked too good? "I apologize, but I don't have any armor or—"

Ove went to a cabinet behind the table and opened it wide. Inside were weapons, mostly swords but also some throwing axes and a crossbow as well. "Take your pick. If it doesn't suit, you can trade it out at the armory later."

There'd never been weapons kept in the Great Hall before, and Stigandr wondered who'd made the change, Tessa or Havardr. He stepped forward and took a sword, uncaring about its condition and more concerned about its size: he wanted the shortest one possible, since it most suited his fighting style. Hopefully, he would never need to use it.

"You shouldn't need any armor today," Ove said as Stigandr tied the sheath to his belt. "Never had a fight in the hall that wasn't our own men getting rowdy after too much mead at dinner. You won't be one of them, will you?"

Stigandr shook his head. "No, sir."

Ove looked disappointed. "Anyways, the crowds here won't cause trouble. If they do, your job is to make sure none of the common-folk get hurt, though they'd be more likely to hurt themselves than anyone else."

"We're here to protect the petitioners?" He'd done a fair job of keeping his tone respectfully neutral all morning, but here he couldn't help his surprise. "They aren't for the Lady?"

The guards at the table looked at him like he'd grown a second head, while Ove barked a laugh. He looked much better like that, scowl gone and mirth in his eyes, that Stigandr found he didn't mind being laughed at. "Tessa, need *our* protection? If things ever get as bad as that, it'll be the end of the world, my friend. No, it's the petitioners we're here to serve." He paused in consideration. "Maybe the Council."

What a strange notion, that the guards served the people. His father had been a warrior and raider in his youth, though that was many years behind him by the time Stigandr was born. Alvis was a capable fighter, experienced and strong, yet no one would've doubted for a second that the guards were there for him. While it might have been a matter of intimidation, if there'd been an incident in the Great Hall, those men and women would've closed ranks around the king and queen and taken out anyone—citizen or not—who posed a threat.

"This is Ashk," Ove said to the other guards, placing a heavy hand on

Stigandr's shoulder and squeezing too hard to be friendly. "He'll be joining us the next few days. He's a fresh recruit, so make sure you watch him and help. I've got to check on Tessa and make sure she's not about to make any poor noble cry."

The two guards snickered as Ove left. One kicked out a chair for Stigandr, and they both nodded cordially. They at least didn't seem wary of him.

When Tessa arrived in the Great Hall a quarter hour later, with both Ove and Dagrun at her heels, the other guards stood and directed Stigandr to his assigned position near the door. He'd be able to hear very little of what was said with the noise of the courtyard at his back, but he didn't mind: he had a good view.

Tessa carried herself with a dignity that reminded him of his mother, though she had the bearing of a warrior. It was in her stance, her assessing gaze, and he'd have thought her cold if he didn't see her encouraging people to speak or smiling at the little girl who'd come with her father. Havardr had chosen well, leaving her in charge, but Stigandr couldn't make sense of it. His brother favored men like Ove, though louder, meaner, and crasser. It wasn't her gender alone that made her a strange choice for his brother, but also her competence. Havardr would look inadequate by comparison, unless he'd done a great deal of work to tie their images together.

He assumed Havardr had tried, but he highly doubted it was as successful as his brother thought. Being here in the Great Hall, Stigandr saw firsthand how she treated the people and how they treated her. Not once did he hear his father or brother's names. If he were a visiting foreigner, he'd assume she was the ruler not by proxy, but in truth.

The real question was whether she was as loyal to Havardr as he assumed. Should her dedication equal her capabilities, Stigandr needed to be ready to kill her.

ALTHOUGH HE HAD assumed guard duty would be tedious, Stigandr was pleased to see how many opportunities it offered him. Aside from getting to know the current dynamics of rule, it turned out guards were quite popular in Yfirgardr. If he wore his armor (brown leather that was too loose and not nearly as nice as the metal breastplate in his own room, but alas, Ashk could never wear it), he could venture out of the keep and find the citizens more than obliging. Their words flowed freely, all their praise for the good lady of Hundrfeld and the care that she'd taken to make sure all the people of Hjorrfold were well-protected and fed.

"Not easy, given the prince's war."

"Takes better care of us than the king's own children."

"A fine fighter and rider. My son, he tends the horses in the stables, and she's gentle with 'em. Always can tell a person's kindhearted, if they treat the animals right."

And that was what they offered unprompted. When he asked his own questions, they were equally truthful.

"And what of Alvis' children?" Stigandr asked over his mug of mead. He hated mead, but oh well. A necessity at a tavern. "Not Havardr. The other ones."

"What of them indeed," the lad behind the bar said. "The merchants sometimes come in with rumors of the fair lady Ragnhild, but it's all nonsense, if you ask me. Cavorting about the southern continent? Total hogwash. She's either back in Vaettfangkirk training girls like Miss Tessa, or she's fucked off to marry that lady friend of hers."

Or both, Stigandr thought, though he doubted it. Well, he didn't doubt the marrying part. That was probably spot on. But Ragnhild was quiet in her devotion to Hjorrfold: wherever their parents had sent her, she was no doubt still there, doing what they'd asked of her. He wished he understood why his parents had sent them away, but he assumed it was of prophetic import.

"But the other brothers?" he needled. "What of them?"

The lad leaned over and faux-whispered, "I think the lil' one's dead. Sickly sort. Left to mourn his dear ma and couldn't recover. With the others gone, they don't want us to worry, so they keep it quiet."

Stigandr tried not to wince. He didn't agree with the assessment that his younger brother was sickly, but Randel was in many ways more fragile than the rest of them.

“The other one, though.” The lad shrugged and began wiping down the bar. “No one right knows, do they? If he didn’t come back for his ma’s funeral”—here Stigandr did flinch—“then there ain’t anything that could bring him back, is there?”

“I suppose not,” he agreed and tipped him well.

The other benefit of being a guard in the barracks was his access to the castle. It wasn’t quite like years ago, when he’d been able to come and go as he pleased with people scampering out of his way, but he was rarely questioned. If he walked with the stiff posture of a guard on duty, no one gave him a second glance. It only required him to know Ove’s schedule to avoid the older man and his suspicions, but aside from that, it was quite easy.

And while he craved to be locked away in his room, to sleep in his own bed after so long and look out at the sea from his favorite place by the window, he deemed it too risky. The upper floors of the northern wing were seldom patrolled, but if he was caught poking about, he could offer no justification.

The middle floor, where he assumed Tessa was housed with other visiting nobles and Council members, was patrolled too often as part of regular guard duty. He admittedly had little interest there. Though Tessa’s room no doubt held more insight into who she was—and if she could be persuaded to turn on Havardr—it would be impossible to sneak about without the use of magic. He had no idea what state the protective charms in the castle were in, but some might still be active. Besides, his personal magic was running low from the strain of his disguise; he couldn’t take such a risk for no better reason than his curiosity.

The ground floor held servant quarters, which were useless to him. The lower ones were mostly used for storage, with the more valuable treasures closer to the surface and the forgotten ones buried deeper within the keep. They kept that treasure close at hand so they could show it off or spend it as needed, moving things lower down if it was deemed too precious or too unique to part with. No one patrolled more than two levels down, since no one knew what was down there. No one save Stigandr, who had one particular spot in mind.

He meandered through the servants’ hall as though with no aim. This was how he and the other guards roamed the corridors when they had castle duty, as if bored but needing to make their presence known. At this time of day, the hall was all but empty. Everyone was in the kitchens preparing lunch, or cleaning the rooms upstairs, or attending Tessa and the Council. No one saw him as he went to the tower that housed the main staircase and walked down, down, down to the bottom floor of the keep.

Or at least, what everyone thought was the bottom.

There were windows set high in the walls, carved right through the cliff face. He'd occasionally found one as he'd climbed outside as a boy, looking in with giddiness that he had found them, this secret in plain sight. But the door he sought was well away from these windows, at the farthest end of the corridor. They were directly under the armory, he thought, and his father's rooms above that. A nondescript door that his father had shown him many years ago…

The increasingly irregular seasons concerned him. There'd been no trouble in Bjardleith, but he'd heard the peasants complaining of the absurdly harsh (but thankfully short) winters of late. The weather was never quite predictable in Hjorrfold, but there was a pattern. The farmers were very familiar with how long the seasons should be based on the stars, the moon, and the previous year. If they were skittish, it was with reason. Along with the strange weather, there were increasing raids and pillaging on the western borders of Hjorrfold.

The attacks he could explain away as his brother's doing; the weather he couldn't. It could be a coincidence, but Stigandr wanted to check the wards to be sure.

With his father's absence, he worried they hadn't been properly maintained in some time. It could account for the fluctuating weather, and it might explain how easily brigands were making their way into Hjorrfold. In theory, anyway. In practice, he wasn't sure the wards did anything at all. But if it were possible to fix Hjorrfold's problems with such a simple thing, he might as well try.

Stigandr spared a look up and down the hallway. Confirming it was empty, he kneeled in front of the door and flipped over the mat—

The key was gone.

He flung the mat aside, then scanned the ground. He must be mistaken. It *had* to be here. He felt around the edges of the door frame, checked the mats under nearby doors. Still, there was nothing but dust. Heart in his threat, he flung himself against the door—it didn't budge against his weight—and sank to the ground. Head in his hands, his mind whirled.

If this were any regular lock, he could open it. He was more than skilled with the necessary magic, and had even taken the time to practice the more traditional means of lock picking. Alas, this was no regular lock. It was too old, the magic enchanting it far too strong to be tricked into unlocking. Without the key, there was no way in.

His father would never have removed it. Alvis believed too firmly in the wards and wouldn't risk them failing. He would've left it right here, where it had always been, just in case.

But his father had gone to Pegjajord. He would've gone knowing he was unlikely to return for some time, which meant he would've had to pass on the duty to someone else. With Stigandr and Ragnhild gone, and with Randel retreating to the sanctuary with their father, that left…

"Havardr," he hissed. "You selfish bastard."

Stigandr looked up at the ceiling, resting his head against the door. He was more convinced than ever that he needed to get through this door. He just needed to figure out where his brother would've hidden the key.

31
Tessa

521

THERE WAS SO much work to be done in Yfirgardr and for Hjorrfold that Tessa often felt she was losing herself in an effort to keep things going. From dawn until dusk, she wasn't just Tessa. She was Tessa the Regent, who had to do everything to manage a kingdom while its rightful rulers shirked their responsibilities. All of herself was given to these people, not on behalf of their king or prince (who could go fuck themselves as far as she was concerned) but because she didn't have it in her to make them fend for themselves. It wasn't the work that she minded—she'd never been one to avoid the hard way, and Vaettfangkirk had done a great deal to toughen her up. It was that she didn't get time to be her true self, and she felt it whittling away at her.

She missed Hundrfeld. She missed Trond. She missed her dogs, Flekkr and Jotunn. Sometimes she almost missed training at Vaettfangkirk, as much as she hated to admit it, because that was the only place she'd ever been able to hone her skills with a proper challenge.

She refused to spar with the other warriors here. Not after Sixten. When her schedule allowed, she would go through the training drills with Ove and the others, in part for herself, but also because she could tell the men and women in the barracks loved to train with her. It kept her from getting too out of practice, but it wasn't enough. She would need hours and hours under the sun before her muscles felt the strain, and she missed that familiar ache.

The best she could do was train at night on her own. It was the only time her schedule allowed, and she could practice alone. Without having to worry about others keeping up with her, she could let go and do what she needed to.

When they'd expanded the stables outside of the city, she'd spent weeks practicing every night. She could ride tolerably, but she couldn't fight from horseback. There were no horses at Vaettfangkirk, and at Hundrfeld she'd used them for travel, not hunting. So she'd ridden and ridden, then put up scarecrows and targets to practice with her bow, then spear, then sword. It had taken her a great deal of time to perfect these things even at a trot, and longer still to be confident enough to do it at a canter and then a gallop. It also helped her prescribe to Ove the drills she wanted the guards to do; she feared that a basic competence battling from horseback would be necessary to protect the villages in the plains from brigands.

Sooner or later, the fragile peace of Hjorrfold would break under Havardr's axe. The people needed to be ready to endure what followed.

She still went to the stables now and then, but not as often as she'd like. It was too hard to arrange, so far from the keep, and she so often lost track of time while training that she wouldn't stop until the first rays of sunlight crested over the horizon. The best decision she'd made since assuming control was to invite the healers back: she'd depended on their energy draughts on those days just to make it through her busy mornings until she could steal an hour or two of sleep at midday.

There was a great deal she wished to practice on the training pitch, which was more conveniently situated. She wouldn't have to run through the whole city if she lost track of the hour: her bed was waiting only a few hundred feet away. The problem was that everything she needed to practice required a partner. Yes, she could go through the motions, but some things couldn't be done alone. There needed to be pressure on her blade, or the possibility of a counter, something to force her to stay on her guard.

No matter. Some practice was better than none, and even at her most frustrated, she couldn't truly miss the creatures of shadow and ash that had been her partners in Vaettfangkirk.

The courtyard was quiet under the night sky, the only sound the guttering of the torches. The guards had been in the Great Hall well after dusk enjoying the new ale the crown had been gifted by Lengraey, the largest and final island she'd helped conquer. Perhaps she'd been presumptuous to have given out so much of Havardr's tribute, but it wasn't as though he were here to complain. Besides, it wouldn't do to let such a quality drink go sour. It'd be an insult to the poor citizens of Lengraey to waste it.

The guards and servants had gladly drunk their fill, and those not on duty had staggered back to the barracks. It was quieter than usual, given the hour, as they slept away their dinners.

Perfect, as far as Tessa was concerned.

She bypassed the swords on the rack entirely. Swords were traditional, and the expected choice for women to wield, so she'd used one in every battle Havardr had dragged her to. Not a bad weapon, simply not her preferred one. She passed the throwing knives and small axes as well, though her aim was likely rusty from neglect, and grabbed a large war hammer. It'd always been her favorite weapon. There was something satisfying about the *thud* it made as it connected, the comfortable weight of it in her hands. They felt unbreakable, which in turn made her feel stronger.

Her uncle had sent her the one he'd commissioned for her eighteenth name day, and she kept it in her room with her armor. This one was a practice hammer, heavier than her own and less balanced: the head was a good thirty pounds of wood encasing an iron center to add the weight, then wrapped in leather and wool to soften the blows. You still wanted to avoid a hit to the head or chest, but it might spare you a broken bone and wouldn't shatter your shield.

The real trick was being able to switch from one-handed to two-handed swings. The shaft of most war hammers was two feet long, but she'd wrapped a knob of leather around the end so that it wouldn't fly out of her hand when she swung. Her real one had a spike on one end, though this one was flat on every side. Because of the weight, few would attempt to wield a hammer one-handed. She'd never seen it firsthand, and they hadn't taught her the technique at Vaettfangkirk, which meant no one would expect it when she did it in battle. She meant to be ready.

She went through a few swings while standing at the center of the pitch, only shifting her weight as she focused on how the weapon felt as she went from two hands to just her right, two hands then left, over and over. When she was warmed up, she took a few strides as she repeated the motions, going faster and faster. The sweet burn in her muscles and the sweat gathering at her brow were welcome reminders of who she was. Not some regent or pawn in Havardr's quest for conquest and fame, but a warrior.

She was Tessa of Hundrfeld.

"Are we to be fighting with war hammers now?"

Tessa nearly stumbled. She'd been mid-swing, and though she aborted the move, the follow-through left her unbalanced. When she turned to face the intruder, she found Ashk, one of the new members of the guard. How had he sneaked up on her?

"What do you mean?" she asked and ran a hand through the unbraided side of her hair to get it out of her face. She didn't mind her messy appearance—plenty of guards in Yfirgardr had seen her looking worse—but she was thrown by his sudden arrival. Had she really been so distracted?

"You go down to the stables to practice, then the next week, Ove's ordering all of us onto horseback for drills. Are war hammers next for us?" There was the hint of a smirk tugging at his lips, and she wondered if he was teasing her. There were very few who took such liberties with her, and she wasn't sure what to make of him for the attempt.

"With the number of raids we've been getting, all of you will need to be able to ride into battle." She put the hammer down, the head resting on the ground with the shaft upright and ready for use, and rubbed her sweaty hands on her tunic. She should've chalked them. "If you can use a bow and sword, there's no need to worry about hammers."

"You mean we're not good enough to handle them."

Definitely teasing. If it had been any other recruit, she might've bristled at the implied challenge. It didn't bother her with Ashk, though, and she didn't know why.

Tessa shrugged. "You're welcome to try it, but no, few are. And you're perfectly reasonable with a sword. Why change something that's working?"

"Oh, I agree." He held up his hands in surrender. "I would be terrible with a war hammer. I prefer throwing knives, honestly, but that's more of a parlor trick at a tavern than a useful skill in a battle."

"Not useless, though." She looked around the empty courtyard. There would be guards on the walls and at the gate, but no one was in sight but the two of them. "Are you on duty?"

He shook his head. "Returning from the city. I have gate duty tomorrow night." He hesitated, then said, "Do you need a partner?"

She blinked at him. "What?"

"A partner. To spar with. I'm sure it's difficult to master blocks and parries with a war hammer, and it's impossible to do so on your own. If you just need a body to swing a sword at you, I can help."

He was right on both counts: it was difficult to master, and she had no feasible way of practicing alone. She was tempted, more than she'd like to admit.

He smiled, both mischievous and charming as he sensed her indecision. He wasn't a particularly handsome man, but his smile was endearing. "I'm 'perfectly reasonable with a sword,' or so I'm told."

"That you are," she agreed. "I'm glad a wise person told you such, and you listened." She turned to look behind her at the training pitch, to the spot where Sixten had died three years ago. Although she'd almost forgiven herself for her foolishness, she was loath to repeat the same mistake.

"I know about the boy," Ashk said quietly.

She whirled back around to face him, hands clenched into fists at her side. She had the crazy worry that he'd read her mind, then realized it was likely clear as day on her face where her thoughts were: everyone in Hjorrfold would've heard about Sixten and been able to piece it together.

"It was years ago," he said. "If you trust yourself, then I trust you."

Trust. A funny thing, that. Dagrun didn't trust Ashk, as she'd made clear a few weeks ago when they'd exited the Council chamber and found him lurking there. Or at least that's what Dagrun said he was doing, when it very much seemed like he'd been on patrol. He hadn't broken his stride when he passed them, hadn't even looked their way. But Tessa couldn't ignore one of her most loyal companions disliking him, and it made her wary now.

But what could he possibly do? The dangers Tessa feared weren't in battle. The only way he could hurt her here was by getting hurt himself. Even if he tried his hardest, he wouldn't be able to overpower or outmaneuver her. There'd be no assassination here, and with her reputation, only a fool would attempt it. Whatever anyone thought of Ashk, Tessa knew he was no fool.

He waited patiently as she considered. She met his gaze and tried to see into his mind, to figure out why he'd offered, why he would so readily trust her with his life. But instead of answers, she saw the man before her. His eyes were a drab brown, dull and a little ugly if not for the cleverness that shone through. The only thing interesting about his appearance was the green flecks hiding in the brown. Perhaps it was her imagination, or her growing familiarity with him, but she swore the green was growing, like the first leaves in spring coming to life.

A good omen, if there were such things.

Eventually, she nodded. "All right. Grab a sword."

As Ashk walked to the weapons rack and picked a training sword, Tessa took a few deep breaths to center herself. This wasn't like Sixten. She knew better, understood her own strength and the comparative fragility of others. If Sixten hadn't taught her the lesson, she'd have learned it again and again while fighting on Thrireyna. How easy it'd been to slaughter her way through the villages' best fighters...

"Ready?"

Tessa startled, unaware that she'd been so lost in memory. She grasped her hammer, positioning her hands—one at the base of the head, the other lower—so that a foot of the shaft was free for blocking. "Whenever you are."

His approach was deliberate, each movement telegraphed before he struck. She absorbed the blows with so little trouble she wondered if this practice was worth the effort. No opponent would go so easy on her. Ashk stopped after a dozen blows and took a step back.

"Warmed up?" he asked.

"Warmed up?" she repeated in confusion. "I've been out here over an hour already. I—"

There was no warning when he leaped forward and struck. If her hands hadn't been in position, she might not have reacted in time to block his attack. Another three blows landed in quick succession, each forcing her to retreat a step before she recovered and could put more finesse behind her movements. She concentrated on each of his swings and her own, looking for the minute flaws in his attack she could exploit and the ways her own form needed to be perfected.

Again, he backed away after a dozen or so blows; this time, she had to stop herself from pursuing.

"You're stronger than you look," she said. She looked him over from head to toe, wondering what else she'd missed about him. Had she not seen him when he first joined the guard? Shouldn't she have known he was this good? "Faster too."

"I'm not sure if that's a compliment or an insult. Did I seem weak and slow before?" To her satisfaction, he sounded out of breath.

"Compliment. And it's not a bad thing to be underestimated. Might save your life in a fight." Until a few moments ago, she wouldn't have given him good odds against her. While they hadn't improved to surviving an actual fight, she'd at least have to try, which is more than she could say for most. She nodded in approval. This would do nicely. "Another round like that."

They went again and again, with Ashk charging and her fending him off. When she was satisfied with her form, she'd make a slight change—blocking with one hand on her hammer, him attacking from behind, her moving quickly from a swing to a parry, and so on—until they must have done it a hundred times. By the end, she was sweat-soaked, and her heart pounded as if she'd been in battle.

She hadn't felt so alive in months. Not since they'd finished their work at Lengraey. She almost went to wipe the soot from her face with her elbow, then remembered she hadn't put any on.

Ashk had taken off his cloak early on, and he was panting from the exertion. His hair was damp, and his shoulders hunched as though he could no longer stand up straight. To his credit, he hadn't complained. He'd kept going because she had, albeit gradually slower and slower.

"You did well," she told him as he staggered over to the weapons rack and put away his sword with a slight tremble in his hands. She was glad he wouldn't be on duty until tomorrow night; he'd probably need to sleep well into the afternoon to recover. "I'll admit I didn't think you could keep up."

"Ha!" He turned to her, hands on his hips. His pulse beat wildly in his neck, and perhaps it was a trick of the moonlight, but his eyes were different. Gone was the sepia she cared little for, and in its place was a muddy green. Then the light changed, and they were brown once more. "I'll be lucky if I can move tomorrow."

Tessa patted him on the back as she passed, returning her hammer. "Good thing you'll have three days to recover before our next practice."

"Three—you'd practice with me again?" He seemed adorably pleased by the idea, as if he'd earned some coveted prize instead of the chance to be put through his paces again. Though he had earned something: he'd proven himself a good sparring partner, something she thought impossible.

"If you're up for it. I know I push harder than Ove and the other officers do."

"You have high standards for yourself," Ashk said with a hint of admiration.

Her cheeks burned. "I'm here to serve Hjorrfold. If this is how I can do that, I'm happy to oblige." He stretched, and she could hear an unpleasant pop.

"You might be, but your back isn't." She jerked her head towards the barracks. "Get some rest. I'll have a servant send you lunch and a restorative potion."

"Not breakfast?"

"You think you'll be up before noon?" The night sky wasn't as dark above them as it had been when they'd started. Tessa was satisfied she'd get a few hours of rest, but her body was used to such punishment.

"Fair point," Ashk said, suddenly sounding weary, as though he was finally giving in to the exhaustion he'd felt the whole time. "Lunch and that potion would be spectacular. Good night, my lady." He saluted her and ambled off.

Tessa didn't know why she watched him go.

32
Stigandr

521

STIGANDR WOKE TO the sun in his eyes, brighter than it had any right to be. He rolled over, intent on sleeping some more, but the movement made his whole body ache. Every muscle seemed made of putty, and he groaned at how weak and helpless he felt. Now that his body and mind had reconnected, he knew he'd never go back to sleep; he begrudgingly pushed himself up.

As he rubbed the sleep from his eyes, he caught sight of the bowl of stew and the steaming mug on the floor next to his bed. He froze mid-stretch as he remembered how he'd spent the night and Tessa's promise of a meal waiting for him. Grateful, he reached down and took it.

Stigandr was ravenous every day. The Great Hall was full of hungry men and women, most taking second or third helpings on days they'd trained in the courtyard, and Stigandr regularly changed his seat at dinner so it was hard to notice he took extra portions every night, regardless of whether he'd set foot on the pitch. It wasn't physical exertion that made his belly ache each day; it was the deep hunger that came with maintaining his disguise that drained him.

Never had he exerted himself this long with constant magic. Day and night, he wore this strange face. As he'd traveled across the plains, he'd had solitary moments where he was safely alone, with a door to guard him or miles upon miles of empty grassland, and he could let the magic slip. Now he slept in a bed tucked between two others in a room that housed twelve identical beds with their shabby wool blankets. Even the privy lacked privacy. There was not a single moment of the day when he could let his true face show.

Before he slept, he would check his reflection in the window above his bed and look carefully for any sign that his spellwork was cracking from the effort, but he knew this face so little that he feared he would only notice a large shift in features. Hopefully, any changes would be too gradual to notice.

With the prior night's physical toil added to the magical one, his body was rebelling. Scraping the bowl clean and licking the spoon clean, he hadn't put a dent in his hunger. He still had some coin left and hours before duty. Perhaps he'd head into the city to buy a couple of meals at his favorite taverns. He really should plan on visiting his bedroom soon to get more gold if nothing else, and he still needed to sneak into Havardr's room to find the ward key.

What to do, what to do, he wondered as he placed the bowl at the foot of the bed and picked up his drink. The wooden mug was warm to the touch, and he caught the scent of magic-drenched herbs. A restorative potion, just as Tessa had promised. It wouldn't solve his hunger, but he appreciated what it would do for his poor muscles. He drank deeply, sighing in contentment when the warm, bitter liquid hit his tongue. Magicked to the perfect temperature.

As far as he could tell, the only mages in the keep were healers. If there were any other mages or witches in the Yfirgardr, they kept their own shops in the city and didn't much advertise their talents. Gone were the illusionists, the conjurers, the magic smiths, and the binders. Every type of mage was once found here, and not long ago. As a boy, Stigandr had had his choice of tutors in any magical field he wished. The only type of magic no one practiced was divination, and that was because his mother had driven them all out. Too many people reading omens in one place 'muddied the waters,' so to get the full scope of the future, it was best there was only one. Books of prophecy had been locked away so that no one could claim any of the realm Ingegerd ruled. Not even Stigandr or Randel were permitted to learn her secrets.

Though that was partly because Stigandr had proven terrible at it.

Wandering seers were allowed, but only to consult with Ingegerd behind closed doors. They never stayed the night within the castle walls, and he suspected they were ushered out of the city proper as quickly as was polite.

So this small healing draught, simple as it was, was like being wrapped in a warm blanket: a reminder of his youth and simpler days, when magic was common in the keep and there were people looking out for him.

He could feel the potion doing its work before he'd finished it. His legs didn't rebel when he stood, and he wasn't as stiff as he should've been. Wherever Tessa had found the castle healers, they were worth whatever she was paying them. Feeling none the worse for wear, Stigandr gathered his empty bowl and mug, as well as his near-empty coin purse. Today he would waste the last of his money on a trip to the bathhouse and at least four men's worth of food. And tomorrow and the day after, he would take things easy so that he might be ready for his next bout in the courtyard with Tessa.

THE NEXT DAY, he looked for a chance to make his way into the castle, but the courtyard was too crowded for him to risk it. No opportunities presented themselves to sneak to his room, so he ended up reporting for duty at the gates with dark circles under his eyes and a longing in his heart for the comforts of his childhood. Within sight, yet completely out of reach.

He was down to his last three bronze coins. The guards were paid out monthly, so he only had a few days left until he received his three silver coins, but he couldn't wait that long. After a life as a prince and then years in Bjardleith, finances had never been a concern. Neither had hunger: there'd been no years of famine since his birth, and in the mountains, you went hunting. His current options were limited unless he was willing to risk revealing himself.

He wasn't. As much as he respected what Tessa had done for Hjorrfold, he couldn't bring himself to trust her with his identity. Not yet, anyway.

But something would have to give, and sooner rather than later. He couldn't go on like this indefinitely.

Continuing to train with Tessa seemed instrumental in understanding her. She might've become an attentive regent, but she hadn't started that way: she was a warrior first and foremost, and the only way to know a warrior was on the battlefield. It was far more honest than court, since in battle you were too busy fighting for your life to worry about what you did or didn't reveal. He was thankful his disguise allowed him the opportunity to get to know her in this language of muscle and steel.

Granted, they weren't fighting for their lives on the training pitch, but he already felt he knew her better for their single night together. He looked forward to the next, and it became a welcome distraction from how weak he felt. Aside from the gnawing hunger, he was tired and slept more than usual. If only he could sleep in his true face, he might actually wake up rested.

Maybe that was what he needed to do with the money he earned: spend a night at an inn, locked in a private room where he could be Stigandr once more and let Ashk go for a few hours.

As he slumped against the wall of the gatehouse, mind wandering yet again, he amended the plan: it would likely take a whole day.

"You're late," Tessa said. She had the wooden war hammer again and was going through the same routine of swings and jabs he'd caught her doing last time. Though she acknowledged his arrival, she continued her practice.

Like everything else about her, he'd been impressed by what he saw. Though not a warrior himself, he'd spent his fair share of afternoons on the training pitch. Most practiced only when required, and only as hard as they were driven. Havardr had done more, always practicing a technique until he could do it correctly.

Tessa practiced until she couldn't do it wrong.

She was methodical, her gaze discerning and as meticulous with fighting as she was with ruling. She was a rare gem, and somehow Havardr had found her. More than that, he'd found her and convinced her to fight for him, to rule for him, to be his instrument of conquest. Stigandr still couldn't figure out why she allowed it.

"Apologies," he said. "I lost track of the hour." True enough; he'd been fast asleep and barely woken in time. If he hoped to survive Tessa's level of training, he would need every ounce of energy he could muster. Especially since… "I thought perhaps we could spar?"

Tessa froze. Impressive, given she was currently holding her war hammer one-handed above her head, halfway through its arc. It lasted only two breaths, then she released hold of the shaft and let it slide through her hand, catching the hammer just below the head and lowering it to the ground.

"I've told you," she said, voice hard as flint, "I don't spar."

"Well," he said, "you did a little the last time."

She narrowed her eyes at him; he held her gaze and resisted the urge to turn away. "That was just you attacking."

"And this would be the next logical progression," he insisted. "You can't practice isolated movements and expect it to mean anything in a real fight. You won't just be attacking, and you won't just be defending. There's a natural ebb and flow between the two. We could go through routines, if that would make you more comfortable."

In his youth, his training had consisted mostly of these memorized routines with instructors overseeing him. Almost like a dance, there was a stock pattern of movements that simulated an actual fight with its footwork, blows, and proper form. Not once had they helped him when he'd moved on to sparring with his brother and sister, except to instill in him a false sense of confidence.

Tessa was appraising him, and the slight crook in her nose made it clear she found him wanting. "What if you're not strong enough?"

"I can survive a single blow, surely." He was certain he could survive a great deal more, but he couldn't say that. "I'm not a young boy trying to prove myself. I wouldn't offer if I didn't think I could handle it. I'll tell you if that changes, and I'm tired of being knocked around."

She didn't look convinced.

"Tessa, my lady," he said gently, approaching with his hands up like he would a spooked horse or a mountain lion cub. "If you hurt me, we'll stop. There are healers just inside the keep. I'll be fine. I trust you."

He hadn't meant to say that last part, because he'd been confident he didn't; he was surprised to find it the truth. In this, at least, he trusted her completely. She wouldn't hurt him except by accident, and he doubted that was likely. He wasn't unprotected.

"We'll see," was the only concession she made. "We'll start the same as last time. I need to work on my blocks, anyway."

Stigandr inclined his head.

After an hour or so of the same blocking practice—the night was cloudy, and it was impossible for him to measure the time with only torchlight to guide him—he felt that *he* had mastered the downward sword swings he'd done hundreds of times. He didn't bother to ask whether Tessa was satisfied. Every time they finished a round and she walked back to her starting position without a word, he knew she wasn't. He saw nothing wrong in her form, no mistakes that needed to be worked out. It seemed perfect. Perhaps perfection was unattainable, a moving target that Tessa didn't feel she could ever reach.

"I need a break," he said and tossed his sword onto the sand. It was no act to stumble over to the benches and sit down heavily. He'd brought a water flagon this time, and he guzzled it down. Tessa came over and stood before him, her dark eyes reflecting the torches.

"You're tired," she commented.

"I'm human. Unsure if you are." He said it lightly, so she'd know it was a jest.

"How can you suggest we fight when you look about to fall over? I haven't even attacked you."

"Nobody actually attacks in a duel," Stigandr pointed out. "I'll be no more tired from that than this, and you can't deny it'll help you."Whether she needed the help was another matter, but he wouldn't mention that.

"We can try it." Before he could relish his small victory, she added, "Once. If I think you're not up for it, we stop immediately."

"As you like." He pushed himself off the bench and went to retrieve his sword. "How shall we start?"

She grabbed it first and used the blunted tip to push him back onto the bench. He sat obediently and watched as she demonstrated the routine she had in mind. She pantomimed his part, calling out what she would be doing. It wasn't complicated, a succession of five hits and then a retreat as the other had their turn to attack.

"You go first." She tossed him the wooden sword, and he caught it easily. "If this goes well, we can keep going."

They lined up facing each other, about five paces apart. Stigandr readied his sword and lowered into a fighter's stance. He waited for her to do the same, her hammer raised with her right hand higher than the left, and then attacked.

It was much like the last time, where he did exactly as instructed. She was wary of him, and not just because of the accident years ago. Everyone had whispered in awe of how she'd skewered some poor boy with a training sword, and she hadn't sparred with anyone since. No, he suspected she distrusted anyone so willing to fight her after that, so he'd stayed within the narrow space she'd allotted for him.

When they switched and it was her turn to go on the offensive, he thought he'd have to hold back. He'd been imbued with superhuman strength and speed since he was a baby, courtesy of his mother's potions. Though he had drunk none in over a decade, it had built up enough that he was still stronger and faster than the average man or woman. Even in Bjardleith, when he'd sparred with Drusilla's hunters for sport, he always won in contests of brute strength.

It took one strike from her hammer for him to realize an unfortunate truth: he was not stronger than Tessa of Hundrfeld.

Secretly, he'd thought once or twice about killing Tessa. He didn't want to, obviously, but if he *needed* to, he'd planned to do it during one of these sparring sessions. It would be so easy to take advantage of her trust and make it seem an accident. Within seconds, that ill-formed plan was dashed to shreds. The strength and skill he'd held in reserve against her, the great tools he'd hoped to wield against her, were worthless.

She'd beat him in a fight every time.

As they parried, he used more effort than he had against anyone but his siblings in a match. She struck with brutal force and efficiency, making him stagger back as he scrambled to keep up. Even knowing what she was going to do, he barely held her off. She was trying to prove a point, to show him why no one sparred with her, and still he could see she was holding back.

It was exhilarating, in all honesty, to realize he truly was at someone else's mercy, that victory wasn't guaranteed and he'd have to work for it. He'd only ever felt that uncertainty when up against big game like mountain lions or the giant billy goats whose hooves could crush a man's skull, and only with the latter had he ever been in fear of his life.

He wasn't afraid now, either. Perhaps that was why he was able to enjoy it.

After she'd finished her turn to attack, she stepped back and frowned.

"Upset I'm not hurt?" he asked, surprised that he wasn't panting.

Her expression immediately softened. "What? No, I—"

"You're just surprised I'm not." Her denial wasn't so quick this time. "It's all right. I told you. I'm tougher than I look."

"So it would seem." After a moment's hesitation, when he worried she might end their session altogether, or worse, accuse him of being a mage or a spy or (most dangerously exciting of all) Prince Stigandr in disguise, she said, "Let's go again. Five and five, same as before."

I've impressed her, he thought. He didn't dissect why it pleased him so much to have done so.

More hours passed, though with a more equal balance. They kept to Tessa's rigid routines until the end, when Stigandr broke from the complex set. He caught her off guard and nearly forced her to retreat, he'd swear he did, but she merely cocked her head and adjusted. Soon he was the one on the defensive as she veered as wildly from the plan as he had. Freed from the confines of structured practice, he tapped into his own repertoire of attacks. If she was surprised when he rolled away from her attack and almost struck her back, she showed no sign. If anything, she looked delighted, a smile spreading wider and wider as she lunged again and again, more and more amused at the clever ways he dodged her and attempted his own attacks.

They might've gone on like that until dawn if he weren't so tired. As fun as it was, it was draining him faster than his illusions. When she raised her hammer above her head, whole body poised to deal a crushing two-handed blow, he readied himself. His plan was to block the attack with his sword, bracing the flat edge of the blade against his left palm and catching the hammer's shaft so the hammer wouldn't land. Dangerous, but it would get him close to her exposed ribs to deal a hit of his own.

When her hammer fell, it was with such speed and strength, some part of him panicked. This was no common raider. This was one of the strongest people he'd ever faced. Forgotten were her promises not to hurt him, and all he felt was impending danger. Without thinking about the consequences, he tapped into his magic to create a shield and push her back.

The smallest pulse of magic shot through him, just enough to do the job: a thin, invisible shield pulsed between them, absorbing most of the blow before it hit his sword. He heaved a sigh of relief, sure now that the wooden blade would have broken if he hadn't cheated, but the reprieve was short-lived. One moment he was on his feet and the next he was kneeling and coughing, so spent, he worried he might pass out.

"Spirits above," Tessa cursed. He heard the thud of something heavy hitting the ground, and then he was being manhandled to his feet. "Come on, then."

"I—wait." He was helpless as she dragged him bodily towards the keep. "Where—?"

"The kitchens," she said brusquely. Instead of going up the steps to the Great Hall, they went to one of the unassuming doors farther down the stone wall. Despite the hour, light trickled out, and he could smell the irresistible aroma of bread and smoked meat.

Tessa kicked the door open. A small boy jolted out of a chair by the fire, looking terrified at the intrusion.

"Sorry if I woke you," Tessa soothed and led Stigandr to a bench next to the long table where the servants ate their meals. "My friend here is tired. Could you see if any of the healers are awake and fetch an energy draught?"

There was a bowl of figs and pears set out, and Stigandr swiped a few figs while Tessa was distracted. He popped them into his mouth one after the other either, too quickly to properly savor them.

The boy scampered off, and then Tessa set to work grabbing food. She knew her way around the kitchen about as well as he did—he'd often sneaked in here as a boy to steal sweets before disappearing to climb the walls and craigs outside the keep, or so he'd have a snack as he hid during games of hide-and-seek—and soon there was a mountain of food piled onto a plate in front of him.

"Eat," she ordered.

"I'm not hungry," he protested, even as his mouth watered and he reached for a loaf of dark, nutty bread covered with sunflower seeds. His favorite, though he hadn't had it in ages.

"Course not,"Tessa said. She sat across from him and took a pear for herself, biting into it and watching him. "You should've told me you were getting hungry. We didn't have to keep going."

"I didn't know," he said honestly. He took a huge bite of the bread, stuffing his mouth and holding back a moan at the familiar, beloved flavor. Nothing tasted so good as home. He ate and ate, almost forgetting Tessa across the table, watching.

The boy returned with two steaming mugs of that same herbal potion, then fled as soon as Tessa thanked him. She pushed them both toward Stigandr.

"You don't need one?" he asked. He'd gladly take them both, but he shouldn't. He'd practically gorged himself and should've been embarrassed, but this was the first time he'd felt full in days and couldn't bring himself to regret it. That didn't mean he needed to take what wasn't his.

"I'll be fine," she said. Then, "You've lost weight since you've come here."

"Have I?" He looked down at himself, unsure if he even could alter his disguise that subtly without consciously deciding to.

She nodded. "You eat nearly as much as I do. In the Great Hall, I mean, so I know the food agrees with you. I know when I first went to sea, I felt like I was starving. Never had so much fish in my life. And everything tasted like salt. I swear, if I never eat a fish again, it'll be too soon."

Stigandr chuckled at that, brought back to a time many years ago. He remembered being a boy and eavesdropping on Havardr and Sindri. Sindri loved being out at sea, but he hated the dried rations and fish, and had voiced a similar complaint. They shared little resemblance, but there was something of her father in her if you knew where to look. "Not much fish in Hundrfeld, I take it."

"River fish, but we prefer game. The elk out east are larger than the bears. One elk'll feed a family for over a month." She looked at her hands. "My first kill was an elk. A smaller one, though. We had a feast to celebrate. It's always been my favorite food."

He wondered how old she'd been, but before he could ask, her unnaturally dark eyes were back on him.

"It's not the food," she repeated. "You're much more tired now than even a few days ago. It's training with me. You're capable, but it tires you out too much. Whatever you were doing before you came here, you're not used to this type of exertion."

In Bjardleith, he'd been no stranger to physical labor, but he could hardly say that. Besides, she was right: it was the magical exertion that he wasn't used to, and it was taking its toll.

"I suppose not," he said. And then, because he needed to get her attention off of him, he said, "You've had potions." He wasn't sure how—his mother had been the only one to know those secrets, brought with her from her homeland, and she'd taught him very little—nor to what end. Why would Havardr want her stronger than them? When he saw her frown in confusion, he gestured to her arms. "To make you stronger."

She looked down at her arms, then back at him. "Potions can make you stronger?"

"If you know how to brew the right ones," he said. He wondered if she was a good liar or if she was naturally this strong. He wasn't sure which was more dangerous. "All of Alvis' children had them when they were young. It's why Havardr is unconquered in battle and why the others have been sent alone on their secret missions. They're a lot harder to kill than the rest of us."

He said it like a joke that they could share, two outsiders gossiping about the king's family. He hadn't expected her face to darken.

"Havardr's been given magical potions to make him invincible?"

"Well, not invincible. Just...mostly invincible."

Her lips pursed in displeasure as she took in this information, then her expression was washed clean. It startled him how quickly she could school her features. "How fortunate for Hjorrfold that their royal family is so well protected."

"Indeed," he agreed. She was lying, he realized. She wasn't happy at all to have learned this, nor did she like its implications. "I'm surprised you didn't notice his strength when you practiced together. When I was here as a boy, he was always showing off in the courtyard with the warriors. We'd sit and watch and cheer for our favorites."

"And was Havardr yours?" There was a dangerous undercurrent in the way she said it, and he was tempted to push and say he was.

"I preferred the younger one," he said instead. "Stigandr. More nimble. Could dance circles around Havardr, though more often than not, he ended up flat on his back like everyone else. Even when he used magic."

He felt like a fool for having said his name aloud. His heart hammered in his throat, and he longed to hear her say it, too.

She didn't.

"Havardr doesn't practice anymore. The only time I've seen him fight is in battle, and that was always against people who never stood a chance." She stood from the table and looked down her nose at him. "Eat as much as you'd like and drink both of those potions. I'll see you on the pitch tomorrow night if you're up for it. If not, I understand."Then she left without another word or backward glance.

33
Tessa

521

TESSA DUCKED UNDER the water, no longer steaming but still deliciously warm, until she was completely submerged. Looking up through the bathwater, she blew a few bubbles and watched them race to the surface. At Vaettfangkirk, she'd become quite adept at holding her breath. Sometimes, that was the best way to put off a beating.

She would've stayed under longer, but she heard a knock and then voices. Dagrun and someone else. She came back up silently and listened. Even without the water, the words were indistinct behind the wooden screen that stood around the metal tub for her privacy. As far as she was concerned, it was unnecessary. She bathed in her room with only a few servants to help, and anyone who'd been in battle with her had seen her strip from armor to clean wounds or to get out of the blood and muck. But a noble's state of undress was of grave import, apparently, and Dagrun wouldn't hear of her ignoring the protocol.

Leaning over the side of the copper tub, Tessa held her breath and finally caught the words.

"I don't care who they are," Dagrun said indignantly. She must be at the door to Tessa's room, arguing with someone. "They can go to the Great Hall like everyone else and wait their turn."

"They're not a petitioner." Ashk's voice. Her breath caught and her heart thudded uncomfortably in her chest, so loud it was a shock it didn't make the water ripple around her. Her nakedness seemed more important than it had a moment ago.

If it were anyone else, she would let Dagrun handle them. Ashk was one of the few people she would allow to intrude on her private time, so she slipped from the water. She was clean enough, anyway.

"If they seek an audience, they're petitioning for the lady's time. This is highly irregular—"

"They're a seer. Seers have always been granted access to the court, a precedent that Queen Ingegerd set."

"I'm not barring their access. There are proper channels—"

"This *is* the proper channel," Ashk insisted. She admired that he could be both firm and gentle; there was none of the condescension that had plagued her early interactions among the Council, only patient determination. "Audiences in the Great Hall are public. Seers…" He paused as though delicately sorting through words. "They say what they think is coming, uncaring how those words might be taken by the listener."

Dagrun heaved a sigh. "Seers aren't diplomatic," she said, frustrated.

"They are not," Ashk confirmed. "If they foresee doom and gloom, they won't be quiet about it. And if there are believers among those assembled in the Great Hall today…"

"It'll cause trouble," Tessa said as she walked around the screen, her purple silken robe already dripping with water. She was surprised they hadn't heard her, a surprise mirrored on their faces when they saw her before them in nothing but the damp cloth to cover her. Water puddled at her feet, and she had to hold the top of the robe closed to keep her so-called virtue intact.

Dagrun's cheeks flushed before she respectfully cast her gaze away; Ashk colored faintly, but he met her eye. To his credit, his eyes didn't drift lower.

"You may send them to my room," Tessa said. "I would hate to break with the queen's custom by sending them away, but I agree that having them prophesying before the court could be disastrous, whether favorable or not."

Ashk's eyes never left hers as he nodded. "Yes, my lady." He turned on his heel and left, closing the door behind him without looking back.

It was well after his footsteps had disappeared that Dagrun rounded on her. "Tessa," she hissed. "You encourage him too much."

Tessa dropped her robe and went to the outfit laid out on her bed. Her belt, breeches, and a tunic, tan with a purple hem embroidered with a trail of golden dogs chasing a rabbit. "I encourage him to do what, exactly? His job?"

"You appear half-naked before him—"

"I had a robe!" She pulled on her tunic and gestured at the low neckline, lack of sleeves, and the hem that fell to her mid-thigh. "If *that* upsets you, you'll shudder to think of how many warriors on Thrireyna saw me in a much worse state of undress."

Dagrun looked less than convinced. "You like him too much. I don't understand why. He's not handsome."

Indeed, he wasn't. His appearance was quite unremarkable, except for the radiance of his eyes and the little crook in his smile that always hinted at mischief. There were several far more handsome men and women in the barracks and among the nobility. If she were looking for a lover—which she very much was *not*—he shouldn't be her first choice.

Except he put his life in her hands every night to help her practice.

"I didn't think you so shallow," Tessa teased as she pulled on her breeches of loose black linen and then began the leg wrappings that would go from her feet up to her knee. "You and I both know there's far more to someone than their appearance."

"Aye, but I'm not sure there's much to him at all. If he were at least handsome, I could understand."

"He's loyal." Tessa pulled on one boot. "He's a good soldier." She pulled on the other. "And he's been nothing but kind." She stood and flicked her hair over her shoulder, wishing there was time to have it brushed and braided before this mysterious seer appeared. "I'm not seeking a husband or even a bed partner."

"Then what do you seek?" Dagrun asked dubiously. She picked up Tessa's belt and helped her with the bindings.

A good question. Men and women who'd follow me, even should their king or prince return. It was the truth, but she could hardly say it. She didn't want to push away Dagrun or put her at risk, so she'd kept her plans to herself. Dagrun was no fool and could sense Tessa's... complicated feelings regarding Havardr, but she had no idea Tessa longed to bury a blade in his gut.

With no answer to offer, she gave none.

"I know you have your doubts about Ashk, but has he done anything to warrant that doubt?"

"No," she admitted. "There's *something* about him I don't like, but there's nothing he's done to earn my mistrust."

Tessa stepped forward and took Dagrun's hands in hers. "Please know I value your instincts. I couldn't ask for a better steward or friend. I have heard your misgivings, and I have watched him as closely as you have. I appreciate your doubts, but I cannot rightly send a man from the city without cause. Should he ever step out of line, you need only say the word and I will act."

"I understand," Dagrun said, then huffed. "That's why the people like you. You give people the benefit of the doubt."

And she would give anyone that chance…but if Ashk was working for Havardr, she'd kill him herself.

It was Dagrun and not Ashk who brought the seer to her chamber shortly after. She bowed before disappearing back into the corridor and closing the door behind her.

The seer was two heads shorter than Tessa. Their face bore wrinkles upon wrinkles, and their eyes were glassy with cataracts. It was a wonder they could see at all, though that perhaps lent credence to their skills as a reader. Instead of a tunic, they wore a thick fur that was a mix of a cloak and a dress; it puffed out so much that there could have been at least five layers concealed beneath. Beads of every color were sewn into the fur, like a thousand constellations glistening like a rainbow. They wore their faded auburn hair in a loose bun, strands falling every which way. They looked both haggard and wizened.

Not knowing the customs for a mage's visit, Tessa gestured at the small sitting table set between windows. "Are you hungry? May I get you a drink?" It was the offer Trond always made to the healers and witches who sometimes visited Hundrfeld, a meal before work.

The seer flicked their hand as if a fly irritated them. "Where's the queen?"

"She's dead." Because the seer didn't sit, Tessa didn't either. "Queen Ingegerd passed away several years ago."

"Dead? Ingegerd?" The seer quirked their head, glassy eyes focusing on Tessa for the first time. "Too early," they muttered. "Too early by a long shot. Doesn't bode well at all."

It didn't bode well for this meeting, Tessa thought, *if they hadn't foreseen Ingegerd's death four years ago. What will they do, predict my arrival at Vaettfangkirk?*

But it was unkind, and she scolded herself. The seer had clearly lived a hard life. Tessa had already invited them into her room. She could do the courtesy of listening politely and compensating them for their trouble, just as she could discard whatever they said as nonsense once they were gone.

The seer waddled over to the sheepskin by Tessa's bed and more fell than sat upon it. Their fur cloak-dress billowed around them like a sail. "Where's Reka?" they asked, patting the ground and making a clicking sound with their teeth. "Reka! Reka! Come, darling."

"Reka?" Tessa asked. She sat cross-legged on the other side of the sheepskin and clasped a hand over each knee. The seer left her feeling unbalanced, and she needed to grab a hold of something to steady herself.

"The dog." They held their hands in circles around their eyes. "Big blue eyes with black spots around them."

Tessa shook her head. "There are no dogs here." She swallowed hard and gripped her knees tighter. "There are no dogs at all in Yfirgardr."

The seer scoffed. "I am too far behind, then too far ahead." Instead of explaining what they meant, they reached into the mass of furs and pulled out a leather pouch. They shook it and something jangled inside. "Why do I bother with guessing at all, eh? Better to just read the truth."

"I don't—"

With a twist of their wrist, they opened the bag and scooped out a handful from inside. Their eyes glowed faintly, and the room grew darker. It was only a few hours past dawn, yet suddenly there was no sunlight, no candlelight, no light at all except from the seer's eyes. Tessa's skin tickled, all the hairs on her arm and the back of her neck rising in anticipation, and she regretted her earlier doubts. Whatever else she might say of this seer, there was indeed magic in them.

"I bring you the past, the present, and the future, Tessa of Hundrfeld," the seer said, voice echoing in Tessa's mind, though their lips didn't move at all. "What is it you wish to know? I will answer one question for each."

There was so much in all three that was unknown to her, and she didn't know where to start. Would the war be the most prudent thing to ask about? Or perhaps the raids on Hjorrfold. No, the upcoming winter and their stores of food—

Did Havardr really kill my father?

The question came from deep within her. A young girl staring at lights dancing across the sky with her uncle, trying to piece together what it all meant.

The seer rattled the items in her hand and then tossed them into the air. Several fell to the ground, rolling across the sheepskin until they got caught in the wool. Others clung to the air, hovering and spinning in a yellow mist-like fog that seeped from the seer. Some whirled like a top, others swirled in a slow arc, and one stood still in the center above them all.

"Prince Havardr killed your father," the seer said, this time aloud, and the words thundered into Tessa's skull. "On a hunt. He killed him to keep you to himself. He wanted all your loyalty, and only gave you up to Trond because he didn't want to raise a child. To him, you are a tool, not a person."

Tessa closed her eyes and let out a breath through her nose. She knew all of that, or had guessed it, but hearing it was so much harder than bearing it in silence. For three heartbeats, she let herself feel it. Then she locked the anger and pain away, back where it'd been hidden for years, and opened her eyes.

"Is Ashk a threat to me?"

The beads and bone and marbles shifted in midair. Some dropped while others rose from the sheepskin in a beautiful, horrible dance.

"The man you know as Ashk means you no harm, lest you mean it to him. You have no enemies in Hjorrfold except those you choose to make."

That was a relief. She didn't know there'd been a vise around her heart until this moment when it was gone. And while the best news had nothing to do with Ashk, that was the part that made her blood sing.

"One more question." The seer held up a gnarled finger, the nail long and black, the color seeming to spread into her skin. "There are many paths before you, all hidden in shadows. Which do you wish to cast light upon?"

There was only one future for her, and she'd barely started out along that path. She would destroy Havardr, inside and out, or die trying. There was no need to ask if she would succeed; she didn't want to know. Such foreknowledge wouldn't deter her, should she fail, and she didn't want a promised victory to make her sloppy. Practical, short-term matters were her concern.

"When does winter come?"

The items floated through their orbits, all of them jumping in the air as they danced to some silent melody.

"Winter falls as a royal union is consummated, and it will be a long, cruel winter. It can only end with a prince's death. Be careful, lest it be your princeling you lose. Hide him well."

The seer held out their hand and, one by one, the trinkets bobbled over to her and fell into her palm. All but the last, a metal crescent, which shot itself right at Tessa's face. She caught it before it could hit her and felt the unnatural cold of it.

"Princeling?" She opened her hand. The metal rested there, holes poked through the crescent, not unlike a compass. The outside edge was smooth, but the inside of the crescent was jagged, like the metal had been part of a bigger piece but ripped apart. "*My* princeling?"

"Hide him," the seer said again, voice cracking. "As long as you can."

Deciding there was no point in asking for more or arguing, she accepted the warning and pocketed the crescent. "I thank you. What can I offer—?"

"You will leave my home be," the seer said with a desperate note that made her voice shake. "You will know it when you find it. You. Will. Leave. It. Be. I have given you everything you need, *everything*, and I ask for but one place to be spared."

Tessa blushed so hard it felt as though she'd been slapped. "I don't understand. I'm no conqueror or destroyer." *I'm no Havardr*. "I wouldn't—"

"We never know what we will or won't do until the time comes." They pushed themselves up to their knees, then their feet. "I have chosen to help and trust you. I hope you will repay my goodwill with your own."

"Of course,"Tessa said, though she didn't know how she could when the seer spoke so obscurely. "You have my word. No harm will come to your home. I won't meddle with it."

The seer nodded, their lips quivering. "Thank you. They said you were a good lady. A fair one. Stars willing, you'll prove them right."

WITH THE SEER and their oppressive presence gone, it was hard to cling to what they'd said. Tessa wrote it down, realized how damning the words looked printed on a page—*Havardr killed him*—and burned the parchment. She wasn't even sure she believed it anymore, this long winter. The only reason she'd believed it at all was because the seer had told her what she wanted to hear about Havardr and Ashk. But she could hardly pick and choose, could she? Either she took it all as truth or ignored it all and made her own decisions.

"Prophecies aren't real," Dagrun said, interrupting Tessa's thoughts.

Tessa was supposed to be reading over the latest reports from the keeps, but as she refocused her eyes, she realized she'd been staring into space. "Sorry," she said. "What?"

"Prophecies. They're not real. Queen Ingegerd spent most of her life holed up in this keep trying to suss out the future, and she still died in her bed without warning. All it ever did was make her act contrary to who she'd been before."

"What do you mean? Who was she before?"

Dagrun hesitated, then said, "My family's been in Yfirgardr for more than a hundred years. My ma worked in the castle, a little chamber girl when the queen first arrived newly married. She loved the sea, and she loved riding. Two things she'd never had in Andiby. She spent every day she could at the shore or riding across the plains...until she started casting bones and reading the stars. By the time I was born, she never left the keep. I don't think she even went into the courtyard anymore, just stayed indoors day and night, locked away so she could read the future instead of living in the present."

Tessa had never heard of any Ingegerd but the one who'd been obsessed with the future. She wondered if anyone had mourned that young woman who'd loved the sea, or if she'd been lost too long ago for her family to remember.

"And is this why you didn't want the seer brought in?" Tessa asked. "You're worried I'll become like that?"

Dagrun huffed. "I don't care about the seer or what they said, and I know you've got a good head on you. I thought it was presumptuous of Ashk to interrupt, and now I see you fretting over what they said like it matters when it doesn't. What could they have possibly said that's more important than this?" She leaned over and tapped a finger on the parchment.

They said the man I'm supposed to serve is the man who killed my father... there is nothing more important than that. If Havardr hadn't killed him, I wouldn't be here.

But she saw Dagrun's point, and as much as she adored and trusted Dagrun, that was a secret Tessa wasn't ready to reveal. She might never, though not to protect Havardr; it was Trond she worried for, a man who'd already had to burn his whole family but her. She wouldn't go digging up ghosts to haunt him.

"You're right," Tessa said and turned her attention back to the reports. Almost instantly, she looked back up at Dagrun. "There have been earthquakes?"

"See how I knew you weren't reading them?" she teased. Then, more seriously, she said, "Yes. I've sent off messengers to verify, but that report seems genuine. As do the rest."

"The rest?" Tessa groaned as she read the other disturbing news: once unpassable rivers now nearly dry; hunting grounds empty as the animals fled; disease at the fringes of the kingdom, only in the west but slowly making its way east as people fled. And brigands, more and more, as hungry people took desperate measures. The seer's words echoed in her ears once more: *it will be a long, cruel winter*.

"We'll need to consult with the healers about what ingredients they'll need to fend off disease." Tessa let the papers fall onto the table as she wracked her brain for all they needed to do. "Food stores in the city are adequate. We'll need to limit hoarding and price gouging. For the rivers and tremors, I don't know what to do. Put out a call for elemental mages. If we can find a few earth or water ones, they might have a solution. But all of this, all at once, it's unnatural. Why has bad luck befallen Hjorrfold so suddenly? There must be some cause, and we must root it out."

"If the land has turned against us," Dagrun said, "it would have to be something very wrong. Murder or treachery. A stain like that isn't easy to wipe away."

Tessa thought of the queen's sudden death and the king's disappearance. There was her father too, and she doubted that was the only murder Havardr had committed to get his way. But perhaps it was a deeper, older stain than that. She remembered Bergunn's warning that no skjaldmaer who fought for Hjorrfold could return, as if Hjorrfold were the blight and not any one person.

"If the land has turned against us"—Tessa rose and started towards the door with Dagrun falling into step beside her—"then it would take a powerful mage to undo it. Without one, there's only so much we can do."

34
Stigandr

521

"FUCK," STIGANDR HISSED as Tessa's hammer hit his ribs. It was a glancing blow and not a direct hit, but he didn't enjoy it. She immediately backed off.

"You were sloppy," she said. It was gratifying that she was almost out of breath. Not panting like him, but not as composed as she was in the Great Hall. A small victory. "You keep your elbow too high when you attack."

He glared at her as he felt his tender ribs. They'd be black and blue by the morning. "And how long ago did you notice that tendency?"

"Four nights ago." There was a note of amusement in her tone.

"Lovely. So glad you warned me of it so I could correct it."

She swung her hammer so that it rested over her shoulders behind her neck, hands loose on the shaft. "You know now, and you're more likely to remember it this way."

"Well, I'll be remembering it for the next week at least," he grumbled. "Is that how you learned?"

"No. If I made that kind of mistake, they exploited it to knock me down and didn't stop when I fell."

Stigandr froze as her words sank in. Ragnhild had never talked much about Vaettfangkirk, but he saw the haunted look in her eyes and heard her scream at night. Only ever one scream, a sharp, piercing cry that must've woken half the household, before it was muffled as quickly as it'd come. The first few times it had woken him, he thought he'd dreamed it; it never stopped, not even months after her return. He'd tried asking her about it, and she'd nearly stabbed him with a knife at the dining table for it. He couldn't tell if letting it go made him a good brother or a bad one.

"You trained as a skjaldmaer," he said dumbly, as though they both didn't already know that, but he was equally uncertain what to say to her as he had been with Ragnhild.

"I did," she said with a note of finality, closing the door on the conversation. "Are you too hurt to continue?"

"Wounded pride never killed anyone." Stigandr squared his feet and lifted his sword. "Shall we?"

Their practice together had become routine, and the highlight of his days. Of all the reasons to enjoy it, his favorite was what came after: sitting with Tessa in the kitchens, eating and talking. The kitchen boy had mercifully caught on after the second time Tessa had woken him by the fire, and tonight there were cheeses, bread, and cold meats waiting for them, along with a kettle of tea that smelled medicinal but tasted of honey.

"You spoil me," Stigandr said as he took his customary seat. The mug of tea was warm against his calloused hands, a simple pleasure. "If word gets out, you'll have dozens of soldiers training with you."

Tessa was by the washstand, pumping water into a tankard for herself. "The fact that you've held up this long is to your credit. I don't think anyone else in Yfirgardr is up for it, even if I bribed them with a meal after."

"You underestimate your charm. They'd be lining up around the courtyard for their chance. Granted, they might not come back a second time." When she sat, he nudged over the plate of cheese. "Why don't you train with Ove? He's a better fighter than I am."

"You're right. He doesn't need the practice."

He put a hand to his chest. "I'm wounded." His heart skipped a beat when she smiled.

"I've tasked Ove with enough already," she said more seriously. "I won't ask anyone for more than they can give. That goes for you, too. If you want to stop or need a break—"

"I'm well aware I can tell you that," he said. Unlike when his father had said it to his underlings, he knew Tessa meant it. She was indeed a better ruler than his family had been in recent times, and he saw the injustice of her doing it when she'd rather be in Hundrfeld.

"You're quiet tonight," she said. She grabbed a few slices of cheese and pushed the plate so far onto his side of the table, he knew she wouldn't take more. "Tired?"

He shrugged. "No more than usual." A pause. "Do you miss Hundrfeld?"

Though he would swear she didn't move, he could sense her stiffen. The air was electric, like before a lightning strike. "I haven't been there in years."

"But do you miss it?" he pressed. "I grew up in Yfirgardr, and I was gone for years. I won't deny I found a kind of peace in the mountains. It wasn't home, but it was close enough. Then I returned. I didn't realize how much I missed this place until I was back."

"My duty is here," Tessa said. She sounded hollow, so unlike herself, that Stigandr regretted bringing it up.

"Well, I'm sorry that you feel you can't or shouldn't go home. It can't be easy, and it's not fair that you have to give it up to help the people when their prince won't do it himself."

Silence reigned, and he worried he'd ruined the evening, until she said, "I sometimes forget you grew up in the kitchens. You've seen more of the royal family than I have."

More than you can imagine, he thought wryly. "It's not as though we were on speaking terms. Their attention hardly ever turned my way. But yes, I saw them. All of them."

"What were they like?"

He had to admit, she had a demeanor for diplomacy. He could tell she was interested in his answer, but he couldn't divine what she actually wished to know.

"The royal family?" *Ah, where to begin?* "You'll know Havardr better than I. He was either in the courtyard with the warriors or off raiding. The king and queen were just, and the queen especially always had a kind word for the servants and their children." He smiled fondly, remembering the woman she'd once been...before she and his father had sent first Ragnhild, then him away.

Scared of their own children.

But no, that wasn't fair. His mother had turned cold well before that. Their dismissals had merely been the end of any pretense of motherly affection.

"And the other princes and princess?" she pressed. "It seems there's no one left who met them."

There were indeed no familiar faces in the keep, except men and women he perhaps had seen but never spoken to. Ove, for example, would've been here before Stigandr left. If they'd crossed paths, Ove had made no impression on him. He wondered what that said about himself. He doubted there were many names in the keep that Tessa didn't know, and fewer faces.

"Ragnhild was quiet," he said. He'd liked that about her. A woman of few words, it had made people listen when she spoke. Except their father. "Like Havardr, she was often in the courtyard, though she didn't mingle with the other warriors. She was a very skilled fighter, but you could tell she didn't enjoy it the way Havardr does. Don't think she ever went on any raids, except maybe one when she returned from Vaettfangkirk."

He missed her. The two of them were closest in age, and she'd never held his magic against him.

"The other princes," he said, continuing before his throat could constrict too much, "were the mages. Very scholarly. Always with tutors or in the libraries or workrooms. Traveled little. The queen spent more time with them on account of their shared magic. Probably had a magic bond—"

"Magic bond?"

"Oh." Stigandr's cheeks burned. He'd forgotten he was a lowly guard with no magic to speak of; what would he know of bonding? "They say those with potent magic can form bonds with one another. I don't know what the bonds do," he added quickly, "but talk was that Havardr envied his brothers for the way their mother favored them. Especially when it didn't seem to be balanced by any particular favor from the king."

Tessa nodded. "And where do you think they are? Ragnhild and Stigandr, I mean."

His name on her lips was like music. He was so caught up in that swell of glee that it took him longer than it should have to understand what she was really getting at.

"No one knows," Stigandr said carefully, and it was true. Even he couldn't guess where his parents had sent Ragnhild or why, and there were so many rumors that it was impossible to sort out the truth. "Are you worried what'll happen if they return?"

"Shouldn't I? They didn't return for their mother's funeral—"

"They probably hadn't heard of it. If they've been gone this long, they're probably quite far away."

"—and now their father has more or less yielded the throne to their brother, who in turn has left it in my care. Me, some woman from Hundrfeld that they've never met before."

"Don't sell yourself short. You're hardly just a woman from Hundrfeld. And aren't you Havardr's best friend's daughter?"

The look she gave him hurt more than the blow to his ribs had. "Am I?" she asked darkly; it gave him chills. "But you can see the position I'd be put in if they returned. I am happy to yield authority to the rightful rulers of Hjorrfold, but who is the rightful ruler aside from Alvis?"

Indeed. Stigandr was more than willing to contest his brother on the matter, but after so long an absence, he was unknown by his own people. Why would they side with him over Havardr? Though thanks to his blood, they might very well prefer him over Tessa. Together...

He put the thought aside. He knew they would work well together, but he didn't see how to get there. The better he knew her, the more he wanted to trust her. He didn't understand her, though. She did Havardr's bidding, but it wasn't clear she even liked him. So why was she doing it? Why was she here as regent and not at home in Hundrfeld, where her heart so clearly ached to be?

What was he missing?

"The one benefit of being a guard," he said evenly, "is that I don't have to know such things. I get to trust in better minds to work it out, and fight who they tell me to fight."

"And who do you fight *for*, Ashk?"

Without hesitation, he said, "You, my lady. I fight for you."

Stigandr had put off everything in favor of getting to know Tessa, and he might've done so indefinitely if not for the whispers around the barracks and the city. Drought, famine, sickness, tremors…Hjorrfold was in growing danger, and he couldn't shake his fear that it was because of the wards. He *needed* to get into the chamber below the castle to investigate, to spill his blood if need be, and that meant he needed to go into his brother's room to find the key.

The next time he had guard duty in the castle, he made his way through the private corridors until he reached the third floor. Alone, he started at the far end of the hall: his father's room.

Despite being Alvis' son, Stigandr could count on one hand how many times he'd been in his father's private chambers. Grand and stately, they were everything one might expect from a king. They were also, in his opinion, devoid of personality. Much like his father, so perhaps it fit. He'd always felt uneasy here, in part because of his father's cold presence, but he thought his discomfort was something else. This room represented possibilities. It currently belonged to Alvis, but who would be its next master?

Not that it seemed to have a master now. It stunk of must and the air felt heavy, like years of emptiness accumulating and trying to push him away. His father had loved his mother, but it had never struck Stigandr as a particularly romantic kind of love. There was affection, with a partnership built upon respect and companionship. It was no great love story, and the idea that his father had disappeared to mourn was strange. That he would be gone for so long was impossible.

Looking at his father's room, he didn't know what to think. Nothing had been taken with him, it seemed. It was as if he were the one who'd died, his space left as it was to preserve his memory.

Unsettled, Stigandr cast a tracking spell. Anything magical would glow and have a magnetic pull towards it. His father, being not magically inclined, had very little to sort through. It took Stigandr only a few minutes to account for everything, and none of it was of much use: invisible ink, crystals for augmenting torchlight, an embalmed eye (that one he didn't understand at all and was glad for it), and silver ribbon with runes embroidered in red. No key, not that he'd expected his search to end so easily.

There was no point in searching Ragnhild or Randel's rooms, but he did anyway. He didn't think Havardr that clever, nor did he think him secure enough to hide anything outside of his own domain. The spell produced numerous questionable magic items in his brother's room, and nothing in his sister's.

He lingered outside his mother's room, heart pounding in his chest. He almost hoped someone would come to stop his search, but as the minutes dragged on and no one appeared, he resolved to do what he needed to: he pushed inside.

Throughout his boyhood, he'd spent hours here learning magic craft at his mother's knee. Their interests and strengths were different, but the core principles of magic he'd learned from her in this very room. That was what scared him about entering. This was where their magical bond, that intangible connection that had made her favor Stigandr above all her children, was forged... and this was where she'd died.

Magical bonds connected mages in many ways, but the most common way was through feelings. Pain, touch, emotions, all of them had the potential to be shared. The more intense the feeling, the more of it that echoed through the bond. And the bonds didn't break when one party died. There were echoes that lingered in important places, on shared objects, and within the other person. Going into her room was inviting all those ebbing pieces to potentially reignite. While that might be a comfort to some, Stigandr couldn't imagine anything worse than experiencing his mother's last moments. Didn't he have enough guilt to bear?

Except it didn't happen. He pushed open the door and felt... nothing.

His mother's magic was everywhere, the room suffocating with the afterimages of the woman who'd once lived there, and he walked through it as one would fog. Yet where was the pull of her death? He sensed nothing amiss. It was as if, as if...

As if his mother hadn't died here.

He sat on the edge of her bed—the bed everyone said she'd died in—and reached for the slight indentation where she'd last slept. Nothing, not even a flicker of magic. He was certain: Ingegerd, daughter of Andiby and Queen of Hjorrfold, had not died in this room. Where then? And why the lies?

He didn't bother casting the tracking spell here. Havardr never would've hidden the key here. He hated this room, and all it represented. The room crackled in warning whenever Havardr got too close, as though it could sense his disdain. Their mother had joked about it, the unmagical prince scared of a room. Even her death wouldn't have persuaded the leftover magic to be any kinder to her least favorite child. There might be no place safer from Havardr than Ingegerd's room.

When Stigandr was a boy, his mother's ambivalence towards Havardr had confused him. He'd adored his older brother back then and didn't understand why his mother had merely tolerated him. Ingegerd and Havardr were both alike in their stubbornness, in their drive, but because their ambition took them on divergent paths, they couldn't see eye to eye.

Though he was tempted to take a memento, Stigandr ignored the impulse. This room felt like a tomb; he didn't want to be a grave robber.

Havardr's room was the only one that was locked—no surprise there—but it took little more than the flick of his wrist to unlock the mechanism. It was almost disappointing how easy it was, a slight nudge with his magic, and the door clicked open. The hinges squeaked, but the room had a lived-in feeling to it that the others hadn't.

It was also a damned mess.

"Of course," Stigandr muttered and snapped his fingers to enact the tracking spell. Predictably, dozens of items glowed, and he resigned himself to sorting through them all one by one. Not necessarily because he thought the key was here—he assumed it wasn't and was only being thorough—but because he wanted to see what his brother was up to. He started in one corner of the room and worked his way outward, inspecting each magical item (a dozen charms that looked pretty but did very little, but also a surprising amount of medicinal creams and tonics) before determining it all rubbish. Then he went through the stacks of parchment. He'd hoped for a journal that conveniently outlined his brother's plans and chronicled all the ill deeds he'd committed so far, but alas, no such luck.

The closest he found were some maps with scribbled notes and a tightly rolled parchment hidden under his mattress. It glowed as if it were magic, though Stigandr could read no spellwork in the paper or ink, and the words themselves—they were notes about people, some in runic but mostly in Havardr's handwriting—were innocuous enough.

Njal's marriage in a full moon will end in poverty...

Tove bears five children, all to die in battle....

Alvis will succumb to the will of his family...

"Hang on..." He'd been about to put the parchment back, but did a double take as some words caught his eye. As Stigandr read them more carefully, he noted they had the distinct air of prophecy to them, which might be why the paper bore a hint of magic. True prophecies did that, carrying the weight of magic even when the diviners themselves were no longer the one repeating them.

Where had Havardr gotten these? Did this account for some of his actions? His wars and conquests? To fulfill some prophecy he'd gotten from spirits knew where? His brother, who could barely satisfy their tutors with his ability to read and write...

"Oh brother," Stigandr sighed and pocketed the parchment. What a fool Havardr was. Their mother, who'd dedicated her adult life to such magic, had worked night and day to interpret the visions and signs she read, only to die without warning. Yet Havardr in his arrogance thought he could piece together a map of his future and manipulate the circumstances of the world to his bidding based on a few words he'd pilfered from somewhere. "You never could accept your place in the world, high as it was. You always thought you could go higher."

He left and waved his hand to lock the door once more.

Stigandr had already pushed his luck being here for so long, but he couldn't resist: his room called to him like a beacon, and he was so very tired. He wanted his bed, he wanted his books, he wanted the safety of his own space.

He wanted to be Stigandr again.

Though he shouldn't exert more magic than he already had, he cast a spell to make sure there was no one nearby. It knocked the air out of him, his magic reserves almost running dry, but the world around him lit up with glowing red dots. Each represented a person, and the larger and brighter they glowed, the closer they were. His own hands, when he looked down at them, were a burning scarlet.

A quick glance around him showed dozens gathered in the barracks and courtyard. The Great Hall was filled with petitioners, and the kitchens with servants preparing the midday meal. In the private parts of the castle, he saw far fewer people: no one was in the stairwell that led to the third floor, and all the bedrooms below him were empty save one, where it appeared someone was sleeping. But no one approached, and no guards were nearby who might note his absence, so he flicked his wrist to end the spell and marched to his room.

The door swung open on his approach, and the faint creak on its hinges was like music to his ears. He sighed in relief as he reached the threshold, then stopped short when he passed the magical barrier he'd put in place to keep people out. It tickled at his skin, and goosebumps rose along his arm. Frowning, he kneeled to check the wards drawn onto the tiles with wax. When he poked at one, he saw it hadn't been damaged but it had shifted slightly, the way it would to accommodate his mother visiting.

Someone had been in his room, and a mage at that.

But there were no mages in Yfirgardr, and his mother's presence was stronger than whoever had entered—there would be the oppressive feel of her magic lingering in the doorway. Even Randel would've left more of a mark; this was subtle, almost like a non-magic user had entered. Which was, of course, impossible: only someone with active magic in them could have opened the door with the enchantment he'd put on it.

While everyone had the potential for magic, the amount needed to pass these wards unscathed was no paltry amount. It was far more than the average person would naturally possess. His mother had put a similar charm on a box and presented it to him on his fifth name day, saying that when he could open it on his own, she could start teaching him. It had taken three years of daily practice with the court mages before he could, revealing a set of divination cards he, to this day, couldn't read properly.

"Who are you, my mystery guest?" he asked and stepped further into his room. The door swung shut behind him, the deadbolt locking with a satisfying *click*. Stigandr went to his bed and collapsed on it, his curiosity briefly giving way to exhaustion. Oh, how he longed to sleep for the rest of the day, if not a whole week. His fingers ran over the soft quilted blanket that had once belonged to his grandmother in Andiby, a family he'd never met and that his mother had rarely spoken of, but whose keepsake had comforted him throughout his childhood.

"I want to go back to how things were," he grumbled into the mattress, breathing in the scent of home before pushing himself up. Time travel was a coveted magic that no one had ever possessed; he didn't think so highly of himself to assume he'd be the first.

"All right," he said as he walked over to the window, where thin tendrils clung to the frame like a spiderweb. He waved his fingers before them like a minstrel would their instrument, plucking out any words that had been spoken within these walls since he was last here.

"Being a mage must be hard work," the voice whispered. He repeated it several times, straining his ears to recognize its owner. A female mage...perhaps someone he'd known before he'd left? Someone who'd been here before his mother's death but had since departed? But no, the words were quiet but not so faint as that: this person was here more recently.

And then it clicked.

"Being a mage must be hard work," Tessa whispered to him from the past. Stigandr stood at his window, frozen in shock. Then he caught himself and thought how foolish it was to be at the window of an abandoned room and stepped away as he scrambled to collect his thoughts.

Tessa wasn't a mage, that much was certain, but she must possess innate magic to a staggering degree if she'd entered his room with no ill effects. That kind of raw talent...she was an exceptional fighter, strong, fast, and dedicated to the craft. If she were to learn magic as well...already she might be able to best Havardr in a fight, but with magic on her side—

The wheels in his head were turning, and he had to grind them to a halt.

There was a reason no one learned both magic and warcraft. The toll it took on one's body was enough to dissuade people from trying; the sheer damage they could do made it taboo. Those types of fighters, the ones like his ancestors who'd forged Yfirgardr in a land overrun by warlords brandishing staffs in one hand and swords in the other, they were a cancer on the world. That was why Hjorrfold had been founded: to bring peace and order in a time when such promises had been a dream. How could he even think it? That kind of strain might kill Tessa…and would be the ruin of Yfirgardr if she took it too far.

"Havardr's already taking it that far," he whispered, swatting away the words before they could crystallize in his webs. "She could stop before it overcame her."

It was an idea, at least. A possibility that might help them defeat Havardr and set Hjorrfold on a path to peace once more. No more wars or conquering, just minding after the people who called Hjorrfold home.

He pocketed a few items before he left. Coins, obviously, but also crystals and powders that he could use to overcome some of his exhaustion. Buy him more time while he muddled over how to proceed. Ashk's time in Yfirgardr was limited, though he didn't know how Stigandr would be received in his place.

Distracted as he was, he'd only just closed his door before he heard footsteps in the stairwell. The stairwell that was *right next to his room*. Someone was coming, and he had nowhere to hide except his own room, but surely whoever was coming would hear. Best to face them head-on. Ashk was allowed to be here, after all. He was on duty. He lifted his chin, fully prepared to seem like a guard on patrol, but the wind was taken out of his sails when a familiar face rounded the final bend in the stairwell and caught sight of him.

"What are you doing here?" Tessa asked.

35
Tessa

521

"PATROLLING THE CASTLE," Ashk said with a look of mild boredom. Not that she could blame him. While on Thrireyna, she'd taken her turn at watch often enough to know it was mind-numbingly dull. And that was on islands where half the inhabitants were trying to kill them; here in the castle, with no enemies within a week's ride, it must've been far worse.

"Poking about the royal bedchambers?" She wasn't sure if she was teasing or not, but she kept her voice light so he could choose to interpret it however he wished. If he felt guilty, it would show.

But his expression was impeccably unreadable. "I assumed they were locked," he said with a faint note of surprise.

"You didn't check?" she asked, her own guilt for snooping coloring her cheeks.

"No? Should I have looked in?" He seemed genuinely confused. "I thought walking through the hallway was more than adequate. Do people often sneak up here?"

"Not often." *Just the two of us, it would seem.* She weighed Dagrun's suspicions and the seer's words against his appearance here. Letting out a breath, she let herself relax minutely. He was her friend, and she was determined to treat him as such. "They're not locked," she said, and tried to muster more kindness. "Except Havardr's, they're all open."

Ashk frowned. "Are you sure? I'd worry the mages booby trapped their rooms with spells or charms or something. Stigandr especially seemed the type, and he didn't leave in a hurry like the little one. His, I assumed, would turn me into a newt if I so much as reached for the handle." Though he said it like a joke, his expression was deadly serious. He really was concerned about traps.

"Randel's not that little. He's fourteen. You've been gone a long time. And I promise, only Havardr's is locked. Here, look." Stigandr's room was the closest, so she went over and pushed down on the handle until the door creaked open. She didn't open it much—barely an inch—before she pulled it shut again. She wasn't sure why she felt the need to protect the prince's privacy, but it seemed appropriate. "See? They're all like that. I've been in all the rooms here, and last I checked, I'm no newt."

"All of them?" he asked skeptically. He was staring at the door to Stigandr's room like he couldn't believe what he'd just witnessed.

"I never thought you'd be so superstitious."

"It's not superstitious to worry about mages, even absent or dead ones."

"Perhaps," she conceded. "I admire your caution. Having never met a true mage myself, I can't share it."

Ashk frowned. "There are mages that visit court, aren't there?"

"Aye, but they all practice 'small magic', as they say. The Ingegerds and Stigandrs and Randels of the world have eluded me thus far. Speaking of…" She started back down the corridor to Ingegerd's room. "I'm here on a very specific task. If you fear I risk dismemberment or enchantment entering these rooms, you are welcome to follow and stand watch."

He hesitated before falling into step behind her. "I'm happy to assist, my lady." She could tell he wanted to ask more, that his curiosity was greater than the average guard's might be, but he said no more. She appreciated his restraint. However, her business today was no secret, so she saw no reason to withhold it.

"I have taken it upon the crown's behalf to give out land on the new islands, as well as financial grants to build on that land," she said as they neared Ingegerd's room. "The short-term purpose is to help pacify the peoples of Thrireyna. The long-term goal is to fold them into Hjorrfold with less resistance."

"And the long-term effect is you're creating new noble houses and keeps,"

Ashk said. They stopped at the door, and she turned to face him. His eyes had a green sheen to them today. She rarely saw him during the day, and she wondered if the sunlight cast in through the windows was the culprit. "Does Havardr know?"

Tessa raised an eyebrow. "He has access to the information," she said. "Reports are sent out west every few months, but my messengers return without ever seeing Havardr for themselves. We receive no response, so I suppose I can't say for sure what he does or doesn't know about Hjorrfold. I'm sure amid battles in a foreign land, it's the least of his concerns."

"Whose room is this?" Ashk asked, tilting his head to indicate the door but not looking away from her.

"Queen Ingegerd's." Tessa opened the door and stepped inside, intent on her task once more and uncaring if Ashk did or didn't follow. She went to the wooden table with the gilded edges by the window adorned with a mirror and several small chests. Picking one at random, she opened it and pushed the jewelry around with her index finger until she found an adequate one: a blood-red brooch the size of her thumb, with a gold border made to look like a snake eating its tail. When she turned back around, Ashk was still in the doorway, looking around the room uneasily.

"I would like to point out that I am completely unharmed," Tessa said and spread her arms to prove the point. "You may enter if you wish."

"I'm not sure I do. Wish to, that is." But after another moment of indecision, he stepped inside. "Why are we in the queen's bedchamber?"

"I'm sending another new noble to Lengraey with their household and several warriors to establish a new keep. The other two islands, as well as Havardr's earlier, smaller acquisitions, are settling down. Lengraey is by far the largest island, and as the last to fall, many refugees from the neighboring islands fled there. There are more people and more pockets of resistance, so as a precaution, I'm sending more people." Tessa held up the brooch. "It's tradition to establish a new noble household with a gift from the royal family. Since I act on their behalf, I cannot give my own jewelry without it seeming like I'm usurping their authority."

Never mind that I have *no jewelry.*

"So you've been using the queen's." Ashk's face lit up in understanding. "I suppose she won't be missing it."

"Given the absence of her children, I wonder if anyone would ever notice it's gone." She saw Ashk biting his lip and looking warily at the chest. "What?"

"The queen was a mage, yes? Could any of those items be…I don't want to say cursed, but, well."

Tessa frowned. She hadn't considered that. She looked down at the brooch in her hand, then back at the chests of jewelry. *Could* they be cursed? Or enchanted in some way that might be harmful?

"I guess it's possible…" she said slowly as she thought it through. "But why would the queen curse her own jewels? Isn't it more likely that they would be charmed to help the wearer?"

"I suppose. I believe the gifts to nobles were often enchanted to give boons or, in rare cases, to put restrictions on the family receiving the gift."

"Were they?" Tessa thought of the necklace she'd given to Sixten's family. Was there some sort of magic in place that had helped or hurt her family all this time? They seemed no better or worse off than before, so she doubted it. If there had been any magical endowment, it must've worn off over the centuries.

But if she hadn't been aware of the possibility and she'd owned such a keepsake, how did Ashk?

"How do you know about all this?" she asked.

"When I was a boy, a family's oath-swearing keepsake was returned to the king and queen because the line had died out," he explained. "It was all anyone could talk about, including the magic imbued in the ring that was returned. Something about virility, all the good it did them."

"Well, this will hardly be the first item I've given out from the queen's collection, and I've heard no reports of curses. The queen was a prophetess, not a…" The word failed her.

"Alchemist?" Ashk offered.

"Thank you. She wasn't known for her alchemy"—the word tasted strange on her tongue—"so I don't know that it matters."

"Probably not," he agreed; he was quick to retreat back to the corridor.

She thought of how he'd been so adamant that the seer be brought to see her. Ashk's fear (or was it reverence?) was unlike anyone else she'd met thus far in Yfirgardr. Mostly, they didn't acknowledge that anything other than 'small magic' existed. Anything bigger was more legend than reality and certainly not present here.

"You're welcome to check this hall when you have castle duty," she said as she led the way back to the stairs. "Though it's likely unnecessary. I don't think even the cleaners come up this way except to sweep every now and then."

"With how little trouble I've seen since coming home," Ashk said, "most of my duties feel rather unnecessary."

"We are fortunate to live during peaceful times." Here, at least. The capital remained untouched by the ill effects of Havardr's war and the portents plaguing the rest of Hjorrfold. For now. "Let's not allow ourselves to become complacent because things seem easy. I'm sure Fjarriheimr has lasted this long because they never deceived themselves that Hjorrfold was a friendly neighbor."

Finding Ashk on the third floor lingered in her mind. Most of the people she'd met in Yfirgardr had little interest in magic, but many from farther afield had a healthy respect for mages and the wonders they could work. Tessa's own limited experience with witches and healers told her little about the type of magic Ashk feared. There had been a mass exodus of magic wielders after the queen's death, and before that, they'd kept to themselves and hidden within the keep. Ove had been in the city for years, well before all this mess had started, and the mages were so reclusive, he'd seen little of them.

So that left Ashk, returning after years away, as her eyes into that former world. And unfortunately, it appeared it wasn't a safe one.

Even dead, he feared the queen's lingering magic. Stigandr and Randel were still alive, and they might very well be unhappy with how their eldest brother had managed the kingdom during their absence. If they took out their wrath on her or the people, could she stop them?

Not a single mage could best her in a fair fight, of that she was confident, but did mages even have the same concepts of what made a fight fair? She couldn't help but picture her bout with Sixten from years ago: he'd expected a duel between equals and had been destroyed by that hubris. She couldn't afford the same mistake.

"You're distracted," Ashk said during their practice that night. She'd been too busy fighting phantoms and their magic rather than the man before her, and it was making her careless. She could handle anyone else easily, even with her mind elsewhere; Ashk was too familiar with her style, and had used her distraction to land more blows than usual.

"I am," she confessed. He waited, giving her the chance to say more, and it was his lack of pressure that made her speak. "I'm worried about Stigandr and Randel."

"Why?" he asked, bewildered. "Isn't Havardr the dangerous one?"

It was her turn to be surprised. At worst, Havardr was deemed reckless and greedy. Dangerous? To her? No one would ever think it, let alone say it. No one except her and Trond, anyway.

"Havardr's no threat," she said. "I don't know these mage princes. I've never fought a mage, save once or twice on the islands. I can't prepare for that on the training pitch."

He raised an eyebrow. "You fought battle mages?"

"They were mages, and it was in a battle, but no. They hurled stones at us. It was one of the few times I used a shield, but they were mostly ineffectual."

She'd remembered those rocks lifting from the ground and flying towards her, but they'd wobbled so much on their path and gotten slower and slower as they traveled that she'd easily dodged the biggest. The smaller ones flew as fast as arrows, and once she'd been nicked along her cheek dangerously close to her eye. She'd started wearing a helmet after that.

"They could hurl stones at you, and it was ineffectual?"

"They weren't fighters," she said. "They used their magic to defend themselves and their villages, but there was no strategy. When we got within striking distance, they panicked and fled like everyone else. Or worse, they reached for their weapons and found themselves on the wrong end of my sword."

"Your sword?" Ashk gestured to her hammer on the ground, her foot resting on the head and her calf pressed against the shaft. "You didn't use…?"

Tessa snorted. She would've loved to, but she was too skilled with a hammer and didn't want Havardr to know that. He assumed women fought with swords or bows, and she was all too happy to play into that assumption. Let him doubt her when she raised her hammer against him; it would make savoring the first blow and his fear all the sweeter.

Not that she could admit any of this to Ashk. She trusted none here more than Dagrun and Ove, and they were unaware of her plans regarding Havardr. It was better that way; should she fail, they could claim genuine ignorance. Even to Trond, who would sooner die than betray her, she had never spoken the words aloud. It was a silent understanding between them that needed no voice to give it life.

Ashk, as fond of him as she was, couldn't know. No matter what that seer thought.

"My real hammer didn't arrive from Hundrfeld until after we'd returned. I would rather have an untested sword than a hammer. They're hard to balance right. This one"—she tapped the practice hammer with her foot—"is after five attempts by the blacksmiths here. I'm sure they were quite happy to be done with me."

"On the contrary. I'm sure they were glad to have guidance from an expert. There aren't many, I'd imagine." His brow furrowed. "Are you sure you're worried about the princes, or is it mages in general that trouble you?"

Tessa considered. She appreciated that he asked these sorts of questions. Like Dagrun, he didn't dismiss her concerns, and he made her think them through.

"Both," she said. "I don't want to be put in the middle of a feud between brothers, but I want to do right by the people of Hjorrfold. It feels inevitable that I will face a mage in battle, whether it's the princes or someone else. No one here knows anything of magic, and it was the one thing I wasn't trained for in Vaettfangkirk."

"They didn't have mages there?"

She shook her head. "Just the one who healed me and made the shadows I fought against. They teach no magic or how to fend against it. It's one of their strictest tenets." *That and not fighting for Hjorrfold, yet here I am...*

"Is there anything that says you can't learn magic now that you've left?"

Her breath caught. Her, learn magic? "No, there isn't. And that's not what I—"

"I'm not telling you to become a mage," he reassured her. "But isn't it common for nobles to teach their children a little of each? Magic and blade? If you studied enough to understand how others might use it, wouldn't you feel better?"

"No son or daughter of Hundrfeld has learned magic," she said, as if that was that. "There's little magic in us."

"Oh, I'm sure there's plenty in your blood," he said with a certainty she envied, but he raised his hands in surrender. "It was a suggestion. I wouldn't even know where to start learning about magic. The princes had tutors and their mother to guide them, none of whom are currently available."

"No, they aren't." She rolled her shoulders, popped her back, and picked her hammer back up. "Let's get back to it. I might not know anything about magic, but I'd very much like to know everything about this."

Ashk inclined his head slightly. "Of course, my lady. At your service."

36
Stigandr

521

STIGANDR HAD A plan.

Actually, he had several plans, and they all revolved around Tessa of Hundrfeld. His brother might think she was the key to his conquest, but the more Stigandr got to know her, the more he suspected the opposite. Tessa would be his undoing, with or without Stigandr's help. If he could nudge her along...

He'd placed the idea of magic in her head and would leave the decision to her if she pursued it. If he ever revealed himself, he could offer to help her with magic like he had on the training pitch, though his magical talents weren't useful on a battlefield. But that was a conversation that only Stigandr could have with Tessa; Ashk had no magic to spare, not even small magic.

In the meantime, he could try to win Tessa to his side. The practices helped, as did their time together afterward. She liked him, he knew. Though perhaps not as much as Dagrun and Ove, she still preferred his company over most in Yfirgardr. They were friends of a sort, and if he had any hope of becoming allies, he wanted to solidify that friendship.

So that brought him to his current plan.

With his pay in his pocket (and some coins he'd taken from his own room after a second visit), he left the keep on his next day off and began the long path down the hill to the city. The ground was smooth, dirt packed down tightly: foot traffic, carts, horses, the constant travel to and from the castle, all this had honed the path over the centuries. Only a line of stones marked out the road and kept people from wandering too close to the sheer drops that appeared at random on the pathway down.

Because of how uneven the land on the hill was, Stigandr was often eye level with the second or third floor of some of the homes built between the peaks (or sometimes directly into them). He waved at some children watching him over the edge of a windowsill. They waved back shyly.

It didn't take long before the true aim of his trip appeared in the narrow gap between a tea shop and an inn. Two dark eyes seemed to glow from the shadows, a little boy with hair so dark that he was all but invisible.

"Egil," Stigandr said amicably. He stopped and put his hands on his hips, staring right at the boy hiding in the alley. "Just the lad I was hoping to come across."

Egil stepped out into the sunlight, looking as mischievous as ever. He wore the same clothing and cloak as the last time, though he appeared a few inches taller. Quite the growth spurt, and Stigandr hoped that meant the boy was eating well.

"Me?" He looked both pleased and suspicious that Stigandr had remembered him at all, much less wanted to see him. In truth, Stigandr had noticed the boy lurking about the city on several of his trips to the tavern, no doubt looking for repeat business. It was only now that he had a task and the gold to fund it. "What can I do for you, sir?"

"You know that Lady Tessa is from Hundrfeld, don't you?" he asked as he crouched down before the boy so they were eye level. His eyes were so dark that even this close and under the bright sun, Stigandr couldn't make out his pupils.

Egil frowned. "The whole world knows that." He spoke slowly, as if he thought Stigandr was particularly stupid.

"Many do," he agreed, "but not everyone's as smart as you. It's why I wanted to find you. I need a clever lad who knows the city to help me with a task for our Lady."

Egil, who had preened at the word 'clever', now wrinkled his nose. "What kind of task?"

"Lady Tessa sends messages to Hundrfeld"—he didn't bother phrasing it as a question, because he was quite certain she did and there was no point in asking this boy anyway—"and I need to know what merchant or trader she uses to do so."

"Why do you need to know that?" he asked dubiously, hands crossed over his chest. It gave him an imperious look that didn't match his dirty clothes. It actually reminded Stigandr quite a bit of himself when he was that age, frustrated when the other children questioned his princely authority. "Couldn't you just ask her or someone in the keep?"

Stigandr had expected some pushback and was more than prepared. With anyone else, he would've tried threatening or bribing them; with a little boy so starstruck by Tessa, he hoped the truth would be a better tool.

"I'm getting her a gift," he said. "Something that can only be found in Hundrfeld. And I want it to be a surprise, so I can't ask anyone in the keep."

"Oh?" Egil looked intrigued. Perhaps not yet convinced to help, but definitely interested in hearing Stigandr out. It was a start.

After looking up and down the street dramatically, he motioned for Egil to come closer. When the boy did, Stigandr whispered the idea into his ear. First, Egil's eyes grew wide, then his grin wider. He nodded eagerly, vibrating with excitement, before saluting Stigandr and rushing back into the alley, disappearing into the shadows as surely as if they'd devoured him.

It had taken two days for Egil to find out what Stigandr needed, and then another week for the opportunity to present itself: an evening of freedom to visit a tavern.

The girl—Valdis, according to Egil—preferred this tavern because her mother worked there. As Stigandr watched her from the far side of the bar, the girl gambled and drank with her friends until her mother stopped serving her, then she pouted and got one last mug of ale. A watered-down mug, if her furrowed brow was any indication.

After her drink, she made several rounds of farewells before leaving the tavern, and Stigandr slipped out behind her. He didn't know where she lived or where she was going—probably another tavern where they might still serve her—but he'd wait until they were suitably alone before he approached her.

Most who traveled the streets at night carried a weapon of some sort, especially women and anyone as small as Valdis. Daggers were the most common, and none were shy about wearing them. Valdis had but a small knife, hidden under her cloak. It was a little thing (only four inches, barely enough to pierce someone's heart), a testament to how much she trusted the peace in Yfirgardr. Even so, she drew it quick as a cat when she heard footsteps behind her.

"I'm here on behalf of a mutual friend," he said, hands raised. "I have a business proposal."

"I'm not interested," she growled. Then, "What friend?"

He motioned with his eyes up to the keep, then winked. That got her attention. She lowered the knife a hair.

"What business proposal? Why come to me and not O—" She cut herself off and looked behind him. Stigandr could hear a couple of drunkards stumbling out of the tavern. Stigandr thought he and Valdis were far enough away that they'd be ignored, but Valdis went rigid with tension. Her eyes darted back and forth between him and the loud, babbling oafs before she grabbed Stigandr by his tunic and pulled him in. To anyone passing by, it would appear a lover's embrace; to Stigandr, all he could feel was the edge of the knife pressing against his ribcage. "Speak quickly," she hissed.

He liked this one. No wonder Ove trusted her.

"You go to Hundrfeld soon." He took advantage of their proximity to breathe out the words. "I'd like you to acquire something for the lady of the keep while you're there. I'll pay you."

Valdis stepped away from him, confusion plain in her features. "What do you mean?"

He didn't bother to explain how he knew about her trips and focused on the only part he cared about. "I want to get her a dog," he said. "There aren't any in Yfirgardr anymore, and I imagine the best are in Hundrfeld."

"There aren't any because they're not allowed," Valdis said.

Oh, he knew that well. Stigandr remembered his mother's edict that there should be no dogs within the city walls, and he equally remembered everyone's bewilderment. There were appeals first to her, then, when she remained cold and firm, to the king. Alvis supported his wife, as he always did when she made demands. The only leniency he gave was to allow the dogs currently in Yfirgardr to stay until they died. There were likely a few ancient dogs left in the city, but it'd been years since the nights echoed with barks.

Stigandr had always found the proclamation strange. He didn't question it, because his mother never confided anything prophetic to anyone besides Alvis, and he hadn't cared either way. Unlike sending him off to the mountains, this prophetic concern had no impact on him. Sure, they'd had dogs at the keep, but they belonged to the servants in the kitchen or the guards at the gate. For Stigandr, it had changed very little.

Though he'd never been to Hundrfeld, he'd known Sindri. Briefly, and only as the annoying kid brother of his friend, but Sindri had been so kind to him. There were a few absolute certainties about whenever Sindri would visit: he would spend all his time with Havardr; they would go hunt or raid; and Sindri would bring at least one dog with him. Stigandr remembered the time he'd brought five, and they'd followed behind Sindri the way he followed behind Havardr, loyal and loving to a fault.

The decree from his mother had come two years after Sindri had stopped appearing at court, so perhaps that was why Stigandr had never thought to connect the two. He still didn't know if they were connected, but it was a striking coincidence if they weren't.

His mother hadn't particularly liked Sindri, though Stigandr couldn't understand why. He was far more respectful to her than Havardr, that was for sure.

Not that it mattered. Stigandr's request had nothing to do with Sindri or his mother or even Havardr: Tessa was his friend, and she surely missed having dogs. She would never break the queen's edict on her own behalf—she understood too well how precarious her situation was—but who better than him to do it for her? If he could only lend his own name to the plan, all the better; for now, the gesture would have to come from a much humbler origin.

"Says who?" he challenged.

"The law," Valdis said. "You asking me to break the law?"

"It isn't actually a law," he said. "The queen ordered it, but it was never written into law. Much like when Princess Randi, in the reign of King Halfdan, demanded that the color purple be banned from the city because it reminded her of her dead fiancé. The King, her would-be father-in-law, allowed the ban, but it was lifted a few years after Randi returned to her home on Hvalreyna. Even during the two-year period when the ban was in effect, it was punished very mildly."

He was met with silence for a solid minute before Valdis asked, "Are you a barrister or something?" She gave him a once-over. "Look like a guard to me."

"I'm a guard," he assured her. "But a guard who can read. I checked the archives in the castle. There's precedence—"

She held up a hand to shut him up. "I don't want a legal treatise," she snapped. She pinched her lips together as she considered him. "So you want me to bring back a dog? A gift for…our mutual friend…that you'll pay for. Am I understanding you correctly?"

"You are. Though there's actually a bit more to it than that. Just in case others are less interested in the legal history of royal embargoes." And as he explained what he wanted, counting out more than adequate coin to make it happen, he was pleased to watch as Valdis moved from baffled astonishment to reluctant acceptance to giddy enthusiasm.

37
Trond

521

TRONDS STARED AT the pile of parchment, weighted down by a small but heavy brown figurine of a dog. The dog in question, Bita, had been Sindri's first, and the four year old had named her 'bite' because of how she liked to gnaw on the bones after dinner. Trond had carved the figure himself, though with a much less skilled hand than he'd later perfect. It was worn smooth decades ago from his little brother's playing, and now it sat here at his table, guarding a pile of letters and staring mournfully at him.

He stared at the pile of parchment, grinding his teeth.

Within a moon of Tessa's arrival at Yfirgardr, the letters had started. Expressions of sympathy and surprise at Sindri's death from noble families throughout Hjorrfold had arrived nearly every day for weeks. Men and women who seemed to think his death recent, and that their condolences were timely. Trond had been baffled by the first, then slowly understood the narrative being spun at court.

Hundrfeld kept to themselves, but they had friends. Friends who'd many years ago visited to pay their respects in person when they'd found out about Sindri. It was all the northeastern keeps, the ones lining the mountains and who didn't often send their sons and daughters to Yfirgardr. They could govern themselves quite well, thank you, without representation on the Council. Perhaps Trond had naively thought that his brother's death was widely known, because everyone he encountered knew of it; he forgot how large Hjorrfold truly was.

And getting larger still…

He kept the letters as a reminder not of the friends he had elsewhere, but of the keeps he couldn't quite trust. It unfortunately set him in a foul mood more often than not. It was a rather large pile, after all.

"Here, m'lord." A wooden tray of fruits and meats was placed on the table before him, along with a stone kettle. He blinked out of his angry reverie and thanked the serving boys who'd brought him his meal, though he was more thankful they'd pulled him from his spiraling thoughts.

Trond never felt as old as he did in the mornings, eating breakfast alone. On the second floor of the keep, there was an alcove fitted with a table and benches, lit from above by a stained-glass window—the only one in all of Hundrfeld. The alcove was outside his room and the long-empty room of his wife Reidun, and across from the other family rooms: Sindri's and that of Trond's infant son were also empty and would so, but Tessa might yet come home to reclaim hers. Still, this was a place where Trond was alone, each and every morning, surrounded by the ghosts of loved ones who were no longer there with him.

But he wouldn't abandon this place. Not when it was filled with the memories of that same beloved family. Hundreds of meals shared with his parents, his brother, his wife, his niece… those times were a balm to his soul even as his joints ached from the cold and his stomach rebelled against the too-tart jams he spread across his bread. He was old, and he felt it, but he reminded himself that in his life, he'd had more years with family than without, and that was no small blessing.

A dog, black with a white tail, whimpered and put her head in his lap, looking up at him with big brown eyes.

"No, I didn't forget you," he said, petting her and then slipping her a piece of bacon. There were three dogs with him this morning—the rest were probably out playing in the courtyard, the menaces—as there were every morning, afternoon, and evening. The dogs of Hundrfeld loved their master, and he was grateful that he was never completely alone. "Let's see what they want from us today."

"There are few petitioners," his steward said when Trond arrived in the great hall. Only one of the outer doors was open, signifying that Lord Trond was not yet at his grand seat to take callers, but that they were welcome inside. Several had taken the offer, escaping the morning chill and enjoying a bread roll and mug of hot tea. "No disputes, just requests for alms."

Trond grunted. There had been more of that lately, which didn't bode well. The lords of Hundrfeld had always been generous, willing to buy any goods their people made but couldn't sell elsewhere. It was charity disguised as business so as not to offend those in need. He'd bought skinny cattle not worth the effort of butchering them, bushels of crops he'd rather not eat, and skins and wool enough to clothe everyone in the keep thrice over, but he'd done it so that the people selling it could walk away with enough coin in their hand to try again. It was important, keeping people's hopes alive.

Of late, there were those seeking charity outright, ashamed to have nothing left to offer him but the clothes on their backs and their sworn oaths to do any service he asked of them. They were people displaced by tragedy, like the tremors in the woods that had nearly wiped out a clan of hunters, or the blight that had ruined a whole orchard within a week. They came on their knees begging for help or they would have nothing, already had nothing, with no prospects for the future.

He gave them what he could and found work for them whenever possible, but if this continued, he would soon run out of options. He couldn't very well house them all at the keep, not when every job was taken, and every bed filled in the small village outside the walls. They might have to build more…that would at least provide some work for the displaced and then give them a roof over their heads come winter.

Winter. He shuddered at the thought. How could he possibly feed everyone? Keep them warm? And beyond winter…well, he'd figure that out later.

"Anything else?" The dogs had followed him from breakfast and were walking anxious circles around his feet. They wanted their own food, no doubt, and a chance to run about the courtyard. Only the older dogs stayed inside during petitions, content to lie at his feet while the younger ones came and went. He whistled and nudged the nearest with his boot; the trio took the hint and ran out the door, barking excitedly and nipping at each other.

"There's a merchant from Yfirgardr who'd like a word with you, my lord," the steward said.

Trond kept his expression neutral. He couldn't deny that he looked forward to any visitor with news from the capital. The only thing he wished for more was news of Tessa's return or Havardr's death, though he suspected he'd hear the former on the heels of the latter.

"And who brings this news?" he asked.

"The girl. Valdis."

He let out the breath he hadn't realized he was holding. Valdis was both loyal and shrewd, her discretion impeccable within the capital, and the insights she shared were invaluable. Oh, she shared the messages she'd been told to, exactly as instructed, but she was all too happy to tell him what rumors were circulating in Yfirgardr. With Havardr off west, there were many rumors indeed.

"Lead the way."

There were four nooks set into the longest side of the hall, each with a curtain that could be drawn to give some semblance of privacy. Trond met the petitioners with more sensitive demands here, and occasionally the spaces were converted to makeshift guest rooms during festivals like the Ondljosbod when the keep overflowed with visitors. Today, his steward brought him to the first nook, the thick curtain already drawn tight; he held the cloth aside, just enough room for Trond to pass, and then pulled it closed behind him.

"No people this time," Valdis said. She was leaning back in her chair, feet crossed on the table before her, and rubbing behind the ears of a dog. That was how Trond had known to trust the young woman: his dogs were good at sniffing out the bad ones. Theirs was a special breed, magically endowed to be good war dogs and protectors long before there was ever a keep in Hundrfeld. They might not go to war anymore, but the dogs were as skilled as they ever were. He didn't envy Tessa the task of weeding out the loyal from the mercenary all on her own, but he was glad she had proven up to the task.

Trond crossed his arms and waited.

"Really?" she huffed after a drawn-out moment of silence. She dug into her pocket and then flipped a coin to him. He caught it from the air and checked for Tessa's thumbprint. He ran his finger along the black mark. It always brought with it the recollection of his brother finger painting. It was a memory so old he was no longer sure it was real or he'd imagined it. He pocketed the coin.

"You were saying?" he asked as he took the seat across from her.

"You know damn well what I said," she grumbled, but Valdis sat up straighter and pulled her feet from the table. "I travel alone this time."

"Good. We'll take anyone who needs a home, but we are not without our own troubles." A servant entered discreetly and left a plate of tarts and two mugs of mulled wine. Trond drummed his fingers against the table, thanked the servant, but didn't speak again until they were alone. "What news from my niece?"

"None." Valdis picked up a fruit tart—no doubt her favorite; the kitchen staff always remembered frequent guests' favorite treats—and took a bite. "Since you both refuse sentimentality and there is no new business to discuss," she said as she chewed, "I was given no well wishes or inquiries after your health or tokens of affection to pass on."

Trond rolled his eyes. As much as Valdis encouraged him to pen a real missive to Tessa, he would put no one at risk by doing so. He was in no doubt of Tessa's love, and he hoped she had no doubts of his. The point was that Havardr should doubt it. That was his only concern.

"I can send twelve cattle, skins, and bushels of acorns, damsons, and turnips."

If she found the collection odd, she didn't comment. "And I bring the usual fish, gold, and imports. Though I've been sent with a special request." She produced a leather pouch and opened it so that gold and silver spread across the table.

One rolled to a stop by Trond's hand, and he placed his palm over it to stop its rattling. He picked it up and inspected the royal seal on one side and a dreki on the other. "What request?" He rubbed his thumb over the imprint showing the year 412. Though over a century old, the coin shone in the dim light.

"I've been asked to bring your niece a pup, and to bring as many dogs as you can spare to sell in the capital."

It wasn't easy to take Trond by surprise, and harder still to make him show it; he dropped the coin.

"The Queen banned dogs in Yfirgardr," he said. He remembered when he'd gotten the news, and how he'd gritted his teeth in anger. First her son took his brother, then Ingegerd forbade his people's primary source of income. How many other keeps and homesteads outside of Hundrfeld had stopped going to their breeders after that? If the queen couldn't bear a single dog in her city, why should they? Dozens of dog farms had been forced to find other means of keeping food on the table. It had been a bad year in Hundrfeld, and so soon after Sindri's death that Trond had taken it harder than he might have otherwise.

Not that there weren't still hundreds of dogs across Hundrfeld and thousands still across Hjorrfold. They were used for hunting, herding, protection, and companionship. But the breeders needed to be careful, making sure they knew they'd find a place for the pups before a dog went into heat.

"I'm aware, but seeing as the Queen's dead"—she made a gesture to ward off ill omens—"her ban doesn't apply anymore. Or at least, there's no one there currently who'd be likely to enforce it."

"So you've been sent to bring dogs back to Yfirgardr and give one to my niece." He scanned the table. There was more than enough coin here to accomplish the task. Not just the dogs, but the food to last them the trip and the leashes to manage them. This was no small feat, and this was no paltry amount of gold, either. "And who makes this request?"

Valdis shrugged. "A member of the city guard. His name's Ashk. I asked Ove about him, but he didn't know much. Used to live in the city as a boy. His parents worked in the castle. Lady Tessa is fond of him because they train together in the courtyard. It's unclear if she knows Ove knows that last bit, though. Ashk approached me about the task, and it's equally unclear how he knew I make this run for her."

"And none of this concerned you?"

She shrugged again. "He paid me. He's paying you. And though some might argue it's against the law, it's a pretty stupid law. I suspect your little lady likes these mutts"—she patted the dog's side, and it whimpered for more—"as much as you do. I see no harm in it."

"You don't think this might expose your part?"

"Ah, but here's the brilliant part... I'm a humble merchant trying to make a living. Hundrfeld isn't profitable currently, but if your dogs are as popular in the city as they're likely to be, that would give me reason to come this way more often. In fact, it would allow me to travel *just* to Hundrfeld. I don't mind making my way to a half dozen other keeps to throw 'em off my trail, but it'd be nice if I could come and go direct. And more often."

Trond considered. Tessa would indeed love a dog. From Ove, he knew she tried to get her pair, Flekkr and Jotunn, on the way to Yfirgardr, but hadn't been allowed to because of that asinine law. It would help Hundrfeld to breed and trade dogs once more, and, as biased as he was, he thought the people of Yfirgardr would benefit from having them back in the city. There were risks, of course, but it seemed the good outweighed the bad.

Besides, if Tessa was regent, who was there to challenge her? When Havardr returned, he might not be happy to be undermined, but the history between himself and Hundrfeld was complicated enough that he likely wouldn't push. Not publicly, anyway. That was a thread he wouldn't want pulled.

But this was a puzzling development. Strange that he knew nothing about the man responsible for it.

"This Ashk...are you sure he's a mere city guard?"

"That's what Ove said. He would know."

The coins, though...and someone strong enough to match Tessa on the training pitch (and either brave or foolish enough to attempt it)...a man who would know how much Tessa would want a dog and how to work around the law...a man willing to undermine the royal house and question its decrees...

"What color are his eyes?" Trond asked and held his breath.

Valdis at last looked surprised, a rarity for the young woman. "His eyes? I don't know. Brown. Maybe hazel. Why?"

"Not green?"

"Don't think so."

Trond nodded. He stroked his beard as he tried to work out the dangers. Both Valdis and Tessa seemed to trust this Ashk, and neither was easily won over. If Valdis was on board, and she the one in most obvious danger...

"I'll make all the arrangements." Trond pushed up from the table. "Go visit your lady friend. Ask if she wants to go with you. You'll need someone to mind the dogs for you."

"Oh, I'm sure she'll be amenable. You just make sure you find a good dog for Lady Tessa. I'd hate to break the law and not even have a pup for her."

"Oh, I've got just the one…"

38
Havardr

521

FJARRIHEIMR'S MARBLE PALACE glistened in the rising sun. The city walls rose fifty feet tall from the flat landscape of Fjarriheimr, yet the palace's spires were visible a great distance from the city, so high did they stretch into the sky. Havardr had noticed them miles out, well before the scouts had returned with news that the people had fled inside and sealed the gates shut.

Everyone was in awe of how beautiful those spires were. What a marvel of architecture! Havardr found them gaudy and a waste. All those resources squandered on a pretty building, when instead they could've sold the lot of it and bought something more useful. Like dreki or blacksmiths who could craft sturdier weapons than bows and arrows. But all the better for him that they hadn't.

Havardr's army had driven to the capital like a ship's bow cutting through water. He begrudgingly had to admit that it had been the more effective stratagem: they needn't waste time subjugating each tiny village or town or homestead between them and the city—and there were many such towns, more than in Hjorrfold, and their tribute would indeed be a boon once secured—and it had allowed them to make good progress toward the palace. The city was under siege, and soon the king would surrender. Or the inhabitants might do the job for him, handing over their king and begging for mercy once the food and water ran out.

The last problem that plagued Havardr's army as they lay siege was that all those countless settlements that they had ignored on their march had banded together. Night after night, the attacks would come on the outskirts of their camp. Never the same place two nights in a row, and never did it end without casualties on both sides.

"There'd be no one to attack us if we'd conquered them properly on our way through," Havardr growled as he inspected the latest damage. He poked at a body with his boot, one of a dozen of his men with their throats slit. The rebels were getting better. The last few nights, no one had heard their ambushes, and it was only when dawn broke that they found the bodies and smoldering tents.

His would-be generals had followed him. If they'd figured out a way to stop these nightly attacks, they might've earned the title.

"We'd be a hundred miles from here if we'd continued on like that," Kerr said coldly. He was right, but Havardr still wanted to bash his head in for saying so. "Autumn has come, and winter is fast on its heels. Our scouts say the sea storms have already made the water off the coast impassable for the dreki."

"Not that they'd do us much good," Sten grumbled. Fjarriheimr was on the sea, same as Hjorrfold, but centuries ago they'd had their mages raise rocks along the shore so that it was impossible to safely approach by water in anything larger than a rowboat. They'd known the dangers of Hjorrfold's dreki and had protected themselves accordingly. Those elemental mages had also died out since then, thank the dead, or Havardr's troops would've been in a worse position than they already were.

"My point," Kerr said, talking over Sten, "is that we need to take the city before winter. We're starving them out of their food stores. We take the city at the wrong time, and we've trapped ourselves. What's shelter with no food?"

"We can conserve our own supplies," Havardr said dismissively. What was the alternative? He didn't come this far to give up. Besides, the villages they'd left unmolested on their march would surely have enough to feed them. They could take what they needed on their return to Yfirgardr.

"We already are," Hakon said. Havardr had almost forgotten he was there. "We're on half rations for everyone. I send groups to pillage the surrounding countryside, and they come back empty-handed. All the villagers fled with everything they could carry and burned the rest."

Havardr let out his breath through his nose to contain his temper. He understood that as prince, the management of the army was his burden, but such trivial concerns frustrated him. He was a warrior, not some steward who oversaw food stores and dealt with these logistical matters. These were distractions from the real issues that required his attention. It was the only time he missed the Council. More and more, he understood his father's reliance on them, if only to pass off this sort of thing to hands that might not be more capable but were certainly more interested.

"The answer is simple," Havardr said after a moment's consideration. "We have injured. Anyone who can't fight, we send them back to Yfirgardr. Hjorrfold can feed and house them come winter, and they can send us more troops and supplies to replace them. We solve all our problems, aside from the city gates, in one fell swoop."

The men shared a look.

"And if Yfirgardr has no soldiers or supplies to send us?" Hakon asked.

"Why would they not? The Council has watched over Hjorrfold before in times of need—"

"You already gathered most of the able-bodied men and women who wanted to fight," Kerr interrupted with the condescending air elders often held when explaining something to a stubborn child. Havardr gritted his teeth and kept his hand away from the hilt of his sword. "Any who have joined the guard since then will be necessary for the defense of the city and—"

"Defense of the city?" Havardr balked at such an idea. "And what, pray tell, might the people of Hjorrfold need defending from? Have I not expanded our control of the sea? And pushed our western border farther than it's ever gone?"

The men were quiet. They wouldn't meet his gaze, nor would they speak, yet their disagreement was palpable. Havardr stared at them each in turn to see if they dared argue further. When he was satisfied they wouldn't, he continued.

"Have the bodies burned. Send everyone who's injured back to Yfirgardr."

"Will they make it back alive?" Sten challenged. He'd always been too stupid to know when to shut the fuck up. "Some are too injured to walk unaided. With the locals rebelling against us, surely they will see an opportunity to kill them off."

Havardr wanted to slap him. After all Havardr had done to lift him up above his peers, taking him on raids, giving him authority, and this was how he repaid that generosity. Questioning him openly as if they were equals. Had anyone ever challenged his father this way? Even when his parents disagreed, they were careful not to do it too publicly.

Havardr stepped forward, so close to Sten that he uneasily took a step back, though he didn't dare go farther.

"Your concern is noted." Havardr kept his voice low and even, not quite a whisper, but quiet enough that the others would have to hold their breath to hear. "Get a count of the injured and for every dozen, find an able-bodied soldier to escort them to Yfirgardr so they might have protection as they travel through the wasteland of Fjarriheimr. You, Sten of Eirbjod, will go with them and deliver the news to the Council. Spend no more than a fortnight in the city to get what's needed. You leave at noon."

Sten kept his eyes downcast. Their chests nearly touched, no more than a hand's breadth between them, so there was nowhere to look but Havardr's breastplate. Havardr saw clearly as Sten swallowed thickly, a vein popping out at his temple. "Yes, sire."

"Good." He turned his back on them so he could go back to his tent and draft letters to the Council. He'd made it three feet when his patience was tested once more.

"And what of Tessa?" Kerr asked.

Havardr froze mid-step. It would be a lie to say he'd forgotten her, his insurance against his siblings and a necessary piece in dominating the entire continent (and hopefully the southern one too), but he'd wanted the soldiers to. *He* was to be their champion, the one they looked to in battle. Tessa could have her admirers, so long as they all knew her place was second. By the time they'd taken Lengraey, her following was alarmingly large; he'd thought this grander western campaign without her would settle any doubts about who the better warrior was.

Except this damned kingdom wouldn't fall.

Were they questioning why he hadn't brought her? Did they want her here to finish the job? They'd almost broken the capital, cracked it like a stubborn nut. If he sent for her now, with victory within reach, they'd give her all the praise for doing none of the work.

"What about her?" he asked darkly and looked over his shoulder.

Kerr seemed to sense he was wading through dangerous waters. He licked his lips and said, "She is in Yfirgardr, is she not? Any message for her?"

"To do as I ask and make sure the city is ready for my return." He stalked away before his waning self-control eroded further.

39
Tessa

521

TESSA HAD NO aspirations to be a mage. Having mastered one craft, she couldn't imagine starting anew. It had taken years of blood, sweat, and tears to become the warrior she was. She wasn't sure she had it in her to do it again with magic.

Nor could she let the idea rest once it'd been laid before her.

She started with inquiries among the kitchen servants. They were the most skilled at the house magic that was widespread across Hjorrfold. When they had time, Tessa would ask some of the older cooks to teach her.

"Something simple," Tessa said.

"Lady can't light a fire?" one elderly matron asked skeptically as she wiped her hands clean on her apron. "We teach the children that."

"Not without flint and steel, no. Could you show me how?"

Despite Ashk's assertion that there was magic in her blood, it didn't much feel like it. Her lessons went slowly, with a week passing before she could conjure even the barest spark of heat. There was an art to it, no matter how simple the cooks claimed it was. The flick of a wrist, the conjuring of magic from deep within, the combination of words and intent necessary to work the thought into reality.

"Well, Lady has other talents," they would soothe when she'd fail. "No one needs to light a fire when they can wield a sword. Prince can't do it either."

"Won't," someone muttered, and they agreed Havardr perhaps could but refused to, and it didn't matter. If he didn't need magic, why should Tessa?

Far from easing her concerns, it only strengthened her resolve. It was a matter of practice, she was certain, and so she practiced in her room each night until she could conjure a flame (almost) every time.

It was exhausting and reminded her exactly why she had no wish to master a new art.

Yet the idea, once planted, refused to stop growing.

The more she considered Ashk's suggestion, the more intrigued she was. Who said she had to master it? There were many who practiced small magic to make their day-to-day lives easier. Did witches not use magic to make healing tonics? And didn't the best blacksmiths use magic to enchant their wares? What shipbuilder didn't know charms to strengthen the hull of their ship? She could do the same, but focusing on the magic that would complement her skills in battle. She needn't learn how to light a torch or plug a hole in a bucket, but she could learn shield magic to counter blows.

In fact, to truly be the best fighter in all of Hjorrfold, she *had* to learn this type of magic.

Once she'd set her mind to it, the problem became clear: there was no one in Yfirgardr who knew the battle and defensive magic she sought.

Though there *had* been someone who might've been able to help her. And while Stigandr was long gone, his things weren't.

She dug out the scroll she'd taken from his room over a year ago. *Defensive Shields and Warding* read the title, and that was exactly what she wanted. Ways to attack and counter, unexpected and powerful ways to surprise her opponent. She was confident she could beat Havardr in a fight, but she wanted a guarantee. *This* was her guarantee.

Except the words were complete gibberish. They relied on principles she didn't know. Stigandr's notes in the margins were extremely helpful, but she could no more cast these shields than she could step off the edge of the keep's walls and fly. There were steps in-between she was missing, and she must bridge that gap.

"I hate magic," she grumbled as she pushed into Stigandr's room once more. It didn't feel as oppressive as the first time, though she suspected that was her comfort with the castle as opposed to any actual difference in the room itself. She knew little of Stigandr besides what she'd heard secondhand, but she could see from his things he was an organized, methodical sort of man. There were dusty tomes on the far left wall, and the highest bookshelf seemed more elementary in their approach to magic; she started there.

The notes here were written in a larger, more childish version of the same hand, and contained more questions than notes. She smiled, imagining a young prince dedicated to his craft. It reminded her of how she'd had to approach statecraft when she'd been thrust into the role of regent. More and more, she wished it was Stigandr who'd been the one in Yfirgardr instead of his brother. Though they'd never met, everything she'd learned of him had convinced her they would be well suited to each other, unlike her and Havardr.

Or at the very least, she was less likely to want him dead.

She worked on the basics of hand movements, recitations, and the meditation that seemed to be required to draw from one's internal stores of energy. This was where she failed. She could practice the words and acts, but she had no gauge for whether she was 'looking inward' properly. When her flames sputtered and the trinkets she levitated wobbled before clattering to the ground, she knew it was this internal piece that had failed her.

At Vaettfangkirk, the only meditation she'd learned was where she disconnected from herself. Disappearing from the present as completely as she could to avoid the pain of her training, that was how she'd survived. That type of dissociation seemed the antithesis of what was needed for magic.

"Always unlearning and relearning," she grumbled to herself as she cracked her neck and tried again.

THERE WAS AN altar outside the city walls, around the back of the hill upon which the keep sat. It was carved into the stone, not so deep as a cave but enough that it lay in shadow most of the day. If you looked straight up, you'd see little bits of the northern wall of the castle. This side of the city was left completely undefended, and though Tessa didn't like it, she understood why: it would be difficult to climb the sheer, rocky crags, and harder still if you were carrying any weapons.

There were no altars in Hundrfeld. Some left offerings for spirits on their windowsills or outside their gates, but there was never any place they gathered to pray aside from the Ondljosbod. When Tessa first heard of this place, she'd been surprised. Then she'd learned how ancient it was—older than the city itself—and she understood Hjorrfold better.

This was an altar to the dead lost in battle.

The path from the city gate to the altar was so worn that it was nearly a foot lower than the surrounding ground. Once they passed the first bend, wildflowers lined the path. The noise from the city was all but deadened by the walls, and only the sound of other pilgrims and the breeze accompanied her and Ove as they walked.

Ove didn't go often to the altar. The first time she'd seen him go, she'd found him alone in the Great Hall long after everyone else had gone for the night. He'd been clutching a mug of mead like his life depended on it. On Thrireyna, when everyone had celebrated victories or drank away the cold from their bones, not once had he reached for any drink but water. Alarmed, Tessa had gently coaxed away the mug—so full still that it sloshed over the brim, so old that it had long gone warm—and asked him what was wrong.

"My poor brother," he'd said, shame etched into every word. "What if he thinks I've forgotten him? My poor Halle..."

Then he'd thrown his head into his hands and cried. Between the sobs, he'd babbled on and on about his younger brother who'd died on a raid some years ago. She sat beside him, at a loss. He'd helped her so much since her arrival in Yfirgardr, and she wanted to return the favor.

"What can we do?" she'd asked after his tears had died down to sniffles. And he'd told her about the altar, and they'd set out at once. Even in the dead of night, they hadn't been alone walking that strange path around the eastern edge of the city. When they'd arrived, Ove had poured coins onto the tray before the carvings of a shield and sword. Candles were crammed into every nook in the stone, lighting the offerings others had left behind.

When she'd kneeled beside the altar and pulled out her own offering of coins, Ove had put a hand on her shoulder.

"Only for those lost in battle," Ove had mumbled apologetically. She'd nodded and turned back to the altar. Not for her father, then, or her mother. But there was someone she could mourn.

"For Sixten," she'd whispered, and dropped the coins one by one amongst the rest.

Today they made the journey again, as they did whenever Ove felt particularly melancholy. He'd recently received a letter from home, and Tessa had been expecting this trek to the altar for several days. He carried not only his usual purse of coins, but a bottle of mead and a horseshoe that his mother had sent for this very purpose.

The offerings could be anything, but they were best if it was something the dead would miss. The tray was often covered with coins, food, and bottles of drink, and sometimes jewelry or clothing hung from the rocks. Once there'd even been a sword still in its sheath. After that first impromptu visit, Tessa had asked around the barracks about Sixten. Since then, she'd kept her preferred gifts on hand: sand from the shores of Hjaeyna and sea buckthorn.

This was not her manner of worship, so she laid the items down and stepped aside for Ove. He knelt down so low his forehead touched the ground, and she didn't have to look to know his lips were moving as he spoke to his dead brother; she turned away to offer him privacy and to allow the other mourners their time.

It was difficult, since she felt no spiritual connection to this place. Even the people whose deaths she carried in her—her parents, her grandparents, Trond's wife and son—were barely more than names and portraits to her. Sixten was the closest she had to the type of loss the rest ofYfirgardr came here to honor, and she knew it wasn't the same.

She jumped when someone touched her elbow, hand reaching for the dagger at her belt before she could stop herself. It was Ove, of course, and he graciously pretended he hadn't noticed her reaction.

"I'm done," he said, not unkindly. "Shall we head back?"

That was what she liked about Ove: he had seen her at her best and her worst, and he had never judged her for either extreme. He saw her more as herself, the woman capable of good and bad in equal measure but who tried to do the right thing.

She hoped she wouldn't disappoint him too much when he learned the real reason she'd come to Yfirgardr was far less noble.

"Ready if you are," she said, and they picked their way through the crowd to find the path once more.

Her favorite part of these visits to the altar was how irrelevant she was. No one paid them any mind as they returned to the city gates, and she knew no one would do more than glance their way until they were back within the walls. Once they were, all bets were off; an honor guard waited to escort them back to the castle, though they would trail behind to give the illusion of privacy. If citizens approached Tessa then, she would allow it. Not to settle their disputes or help decide matters like she did in the Great Hall, but she felt it was important people see she was real, that she lived outside of her role as regent, and that she was a person no different from them.

"You've been in better spirits lately," Ove said with a lightness that she could tell was feigned.

"Have I?" she asked warily. In the past few months, she'd had a lot on her mind between Yfirgardr and the incidents appearing throughout Hjorrfold, but she couldn't deny she felt…not happy or even content, but more balanced, perhaps? Like she'd finally found her footing, able to endure the attack until she could counter.

"You made a friend in that Ashk," Ove said. "He's been good for you."

"Good for me?" Where was this coming from? She didn't disagree by any means—it was always good to have a friend, someone who wasn't there because he had to be, but because he chose to—but she wouldn't have expected Ove to say it. "I thought you and Dagrun didn't like him."

Ove spit. "I never said I didn't like him. Dagrun doesn't trust him, and so I said I'd keep an eye on him for her. It's my job, isn't it?"

It was *not* his job to be rude to members of the guard or citizens of Hjorrfold, though keeping the peace was within his jurisdiction. As far as meddling went, this was rather benign.

"I suppose," she said. "So you've warmed to him?"

"Like I said, I never disliked him. I did my part, like Dagrun asked, but Ashk has never stepped out of line. The worst that can be said is he eats more than anyone his size has any right to, but I know he practices with you at night, so I suppose I understand it."

Tessa glared at him as heat rose in her cheeks. "You know about that?"

"You put me in command of the guard. It's my job to know what's going on in the keep. I know you can handle yourself, but I worry. About you on the pitch with someone."

She was hardly in a position to argue. Not on the way back from the altar where she'd left offerings in Sixten's name. In fact, Ove had probably chosen this very moment for this discussion because she was least able to protest.

"I feel like a sword on the anvil, waiting for the hammer to fall," she said. "I'm at your mercy. So tell me, why do you mention Ashk?"

"I have no purpose." He paused long enough that she almost believed him. "Only wanted to say I…approve of the lad. Not that it's my place to approve or disapprove," he added hastily. "It isn't, and I know it isn't. As a friend, I'm happy to see you've found someone with whom you can be Tessa the woman and not Tessa the regent and Havardr's right hand."

Havardr's right hand.

She cringed. She knew that was how some viewed her, that it was a necessity that they did, but she hated to hear it. "So you're happy with him, even if Dagrun still doesn't trust him," she said bitterly and hoped he would think it was her words and not his that had caused her sour mood.

"Don't you mind Dagrun. She forgets people might have interests that aren't…*political*."

Tessa's foot caught on a rock, and her step faltered. "Are you implying that my relationship with Ashk is romantic?"

"Or sexual. Or neither. It's not my business, and I'm happier knowing no more than I already do. Whether he's a lover or a sparring partner, he's made you smile more than I've ever seen. That's worth something."

They'd reached the city gate, and she changed the subject lest anyone overhear them. There was no semblance of privacy inside the city, and she'd rather not have anyone besides Dagrun and Ove judging the company she kept.

"Autumn has come already," she said. "More than a month early. If winter does as well and it's as bad as the last one..."

"Aye," Ove sighed. "I remember."

Everyone who'd been on Thrireyna fighting would be hard pressed to forget it. Tessa was no stranger to snow or cold—it often fell so high in Hundrfeld that it climbed as high as the keep's walls—but that last winter had felt worse than all her previous ones combined. As she understood it, things had been milder on the continent, but not by much.

"What do we do?" he asked.

"We pray and hope for the best," she said, for there was no better answer. "Maybe good fortune will find us."

"What is it you say? Luck is made. How do we make our own luck?"

Tessa clenched her fists. What could they do? She was a warrior, and a damned fine one, but this wasn't a battle that could be fought with weapons. She could hardly grab her hammer and beat the winds into submission. This was beyond what she was capable of.

And yet...well, she hadn't thought herself capable of managing a city, much less a kingdom. She'd had no training or interest, yet when the position had been thrust upon her, she'd taken up the challenge. By no means was she perfect at it—one need only ask the Council for a list of her faults and they'd readily provide one—but they were surviving. Thriving, even.

There was great magic, she knew, that could temper the weather. She wasn't so naive to think she was anywhere near that skill level, not when most of the servants were better mages than her, but it was a tempting fantasy.

"I don't know," she said. "I don't know."

40
Stigandr

521

When Stigandr had made the arrangements with Valdis, he'd hoped to be there to see it all come to fruition, but he'd known it wasn't likely. No longer master of his own time, he was at the mercy of his duty and couldn't putter about the Great Hall waiting for Valdis' return. Indeed, he was seldom in the Great Hall, except for meals or if it was his turn to stand guard. Because his turn to watch over the petitioners fell shortly after the merchant's departure, it was highly unlikely he would be so fortunate upon her return.

Luckily for him, Valdis' arrival happened during the midday meal, while he and other guards were sitting in the courtyard with their bowls of stew. Luckier still, it was on one of those rare occasions when Tessa was eating lunch among them.

Sometimes the guards would duel to practice and entertain, and when possible, Tessa would come watch. That was one of the reasons she was such a good fighter: she genuinely enjoyed it, enough that she loved watching others showcase their skill. She would cheer with the rest of them when there was a particularly good bout. You'd have been hard pressed to find Havardr or Alvis watching anyone except the most noble or lauded of fighters. Ragnhild as a girl might have, though after Vaettfangkirk, it'd been hard to coax her out of her room.

Today it was Ove going at it with another older member of the guard, a man named Viggo, who'd recently arrived from one of the newly conquered islands.

He'd been helping pacify the locals, decided he didn't care for the climate, and returned home to stay. Stigandr had observed him carefully to see how he fit in among Tessa's court. There was no other way to describe it—aside from the Council, everyone with any power in Yfirgardr had been given said power by Tessa. Even the Council, he found, responded well to her style of leadership. Oh, they grumbled as much as they had under Alvis when they didn't get their way, but overall they enjoyed having a regent who listened to them. Unlike their absent prince, who didn't, remained unsaid.

If Viggo, a relative outsider to the new order of things, bristled at the changes, it would be a good indication that others would as well. Sooner or later, Havardr and his army would return, and the old and the new would have to blend somehow.

...or they wouldn't. At all. Stigandr was more and more certain of Tessa's dislike for Havardr. She was deferential when she spoke of him, or neutral when asked to give opinions on his policies or the western war. If she spoke well of anything related to him, it was to talk about the soldiers themselves, the men and women of the army that she had the utmost faith in. It was always well done, impressing Stigandr despite his years of seeing equally politic answers in court.

Viggo, like all soldiers in Hjorrfold, seemed enchanted with Tessa's attention.

"You're faster than Ove!" Tessa called through cupped hands. "Use it to your advantage!"

"I'd prefer you didn't fight from the sidelines," Ove called back. "Let an old man have his fun!"

It was only a few more jabs after that before Ove was disarmed and held up his hands in surrender.

"Well done," Tessa congratulated Viggo and offered him a warrior's salute. "Your footwork's gotten better since I last saw you."

"The only advantage of being on Fyrrey," he said, out of breath, "is learning to fight like them."

"You'll have to teach us," she said. Viggo preened at the praise and was about to respond, but they were interrupted by a commotion at the gate. Stigandr thought nothing of it—it wasn't uncommon for late petitioners to arrive after midday, hoping to seek an audience after the morning crowd had thinned—until a loud bark echoed off the walls. Stigandr had just enough time to turn towards Tessa and caught her head whirl around towards the gate.

"My lady," Valdis called as she appeared with a large dog at the end of a leash, pulling slightly against her and sniffing absolutely everything. "I have a gift for you." And then, no longer able to contain the excited dog, she let go of the leash.

Men and women staggered out of the way, their shock moving like a wave down the line as the dog sprinted right to Tessa. A few had panicked looks and reached for their weapons as though they feared the attack of a savage animal. It was decidedly not a savage animal, and its assault was welcome: as it neared Tessa, it leapt and she caught the furry beast in a fit of laughter as it licked her face again and again.

"What a beautiful girl," Tessa cooed at the dog, who seemed delighted at the praise. The dog was large, dark gray except for black spots around the eyes and light blue eyes. The dog wagged its tail and continued trying to devour Tessa, one lick at a time. It was only when she put the dog down (the poor thing looked heartbroken until it realized it could now sniff about her feet, and it did so while happily wagging its tail) that Tessa regained the composure of a regent.

"To what honor do I owe this gift?"

A woman with brown braids and gray eyes stepped forward. She had slanted eyebrows and wore a dress of thick linen with a long apron. It was a farmer's garb, and unusual for this area. It was too plain, all neutral colors with no sign of the blues and greens currently in style, and no decorative embroidery or ribbons or lace to be found. No fur trim, and no leather except for her belt, and from it hung strange metal clips. Whoever she was, she didn't live within fifty miles of Yfirgardr. She bowed to Tessa, and even in that she stuck out because her arm swept low as if to graze the ground.

"My name is Bodil," the woman said. She sounded younger than she looked. Despite her posture and formal tone, there were cracks that hinted at how scared she was to address Tessa. Or, more likely, how terrified she was of Yfirgardr. "My family is from the lowlands of Hundrfeld, and we are dog breeders."

"You have fine stock if this lady here is one of yours,"Tessa said. Her hand had never left the dog since putting her down, nor had the smile quite left her face. Or perhaps it was seeing a fellow countryman that lit her with happiness. "What's her name?"

"Reka. A gift so that you might show me favor and allow me to sell more of my family's dogs in the city. It has been a long time since we have been able to do business within the capital."

"Reka,"Tessa repeated, the joy suddenly gone from her as she grew pale and looked down at the dog.

"Yes, m'lady." Bodil frowned at Tessa's reaction. "Is there a prob—?"

Tessa snapped her gaze back to Bodil. "No. It's a lovely name. Do you know who sired her?"

"Flekkr and Jotunn," Bodil said, eyes twinkling like she'd shared some great secret.

"Good names,"Tessa said mildly, though she looked at the dog with more affection than she had before (a feat Stigandr wouldn't have thought possible). "Are you sure she's mine? If she's as well-trained as she is friendly, she'd fetch you a rather handsome price."

"If you would allow the sale of the other dogs I have brought with me, and allow others to reestablish trade in Yfirgardr, it would be well worth it." Again she bowed with that sweeping hand. Though Stigandr knew more than most here about this little show of generosity, he realized he'd never be able to understand it all. Bodil and Tessa shared a common heritage and were clearly using it to say more than what their audience heard. Who knew what they'd already communicated through gestures and in the way they talked around the truth?

"My inclination is to say yes,"Tessa said, "for I know all too well the value of a loyal dog. Alas, I feel I would be overstepping to do so without consulting the Council. I don't know the reason the late queen forbade dogs from the city, but if the Council doesn't object, then I will gladly lift the ban."

"I thank you for your consideration, my lady."

"Please leave word with the guards at the gate of where you'll be staying. I'll meet with the Council tomorrow morning, and I'll let you know their decision as soon as I can. You should take Reka and—"

"She is yours, whatever you decide," Bodil said with her hands behind her back. "I cannot take back what's been given."

Tessa looked pleased by this answer, no doubt because her hands were tied on the matter of Reka. For now, at least, the dog was hers, and it would be a lot harder to force them to part once the dog had stayed. "I humbly accept," she said, her hand twitching as though she wanted to return the sweeping bow but didn't want to appear too aligned with Hundrfeld by doing so. "I hope to see more of you soon, Bodil of Hundrfeld."

STIGANDR WOULDN'T BE privy to the Council meeting, but he watched that happy dog follow an equally happy Tessa around the rest of the day. She sat patiently at Tessa's side in the Great Hall throughout the afternoon audiences, ate happily from Tessa's hand at dinner, and then accompanied Tessa to the courtyard for their nightly practice. They were both already on the training pitch when he arrived, fresh from the kitchens and belly heavy from an energy draught (and the irony wasn't lost on him that he needed magic to restore the energy drained by magic). They were playing fetch with a wooden ball, Tessa throwing it with inhuman strength and Reka bounding after it with uncanny speed. They were a good pair, and he was glad for the minor part he'd played in bringing them together.

"I'm not sure who's more pleased by her arrival," Stigandr said, "you or Reka."

Tessa pried the ball from Reka's mouth, ignoring the dog's dramatic whines when she lost her grip.

"She's the pup of my last two dogs. The ones I wasn't allowed to bring to Yfirgardr."

"Your family gets dogs from Bodil?"

Tessa snorted. "There are many good breeders in Hundrfeld, but we breed our own."

Ah. So that was why she was so pleased to hear the dog's lineage; Bodil had told her to show her uncle was aware of and supported this endeavor.

"So she really was meant for you. No wonder she's taken to you so keenly."

"I've never met a dog who didn't like me," she said. "And that includes on Thrireyna, where some locals had war dogs. They wouldn't turn on their masters on my account, but they didn't attack me. Just everyone else." She kneeled and wrapped her arms around Reka's neck to pull her close. "You would've done so well on the islands, wouldn't you? You fierce war bitch," she cooed. The dog licked Tessa's chin.

"She might need some training before you take her into battle," Stigandr said. "Unless she's going to kill them with kindness."

"Oh, if I know my uncle, she's trained. At the keep, we only breed dogs for fighting. The same line that we've had since my ancestors built the place. Granted, she'll need some refinement because she's so young. Just a baby, aren't you?"

If the dog stood on its hind legs, she could comfortably put her paws on Stigandr's shoulders and see over his head. He might not know how old she was, but nothing that big could reasonably be called a baby.

"I didn't think the people of Hundrfeld raided much. You still train war dogs?"

"It's what we do. They're decent at hunting, though they don't really have the nose for it. They're meant for battle, though we rarely get to use them for more than guard duty."

"Ah, so Reka's here to replace me," he said with a wink at the dog. She quirked her head at him. Tessa might've never met a dog who didn't like her, but Stigandr hadn't interacted with many dogs. He'd never ventured too close to Sindri and his pack when they'd visited, since Havardr had guarded Sindri's time possessively. Even before his mother's peculiar, paranoid decree, there had never been many animals of any sort in the keep, at least outside of the servants' hall. Even the horses never lingered, staying instead in the stables outside the city. "She'll do a fine job of it, and I imagine her wages are far cheaper."

"You needn't be jealous. She could never replace you." A pause. "She can't very well hold a practice sword, now can she?"

Stigandr laughed, pleased that Tessa was pleased. He wanted to ask what she would do if the Council denied her request to repeal the ban, but he didn't want to ruin her good mood.

"Is she spectator then?"

"Until I can put her through her paces and see how far along her training is, yes."

"You plan to fight *with* her?" He'd thought Reka would be a companion, a reminder of home to comfort Tessa since she couldn't return. Though he shouldn't be surprised. Leave it to Tessa to turn even a dog to training. "I'm already out-manned."

"She's a war dog," Tessa said simply. She placed a kiss on Reka's head before standing, and Stigandr was surprised to learn he envied a dog. "She'll be the first of her line in decades to be used for her true purpose. None of our pups have left Hundrfeld since my father took some raiding." She gestured to Reka, now panting where she lay across Tessa's feet. "That'll be her great-grandparents."

"You didn't take any dogs with you to Vaettfangkirk?" he asked. It seemed ideal to send Tessa with her pets to keep her company and protect her while away from home. In fact, he couldn't imagine Trond sending her without an escort of some kind, and there would be no one more loyal than the dogs bred with an ancient magic that bound them to the lords of Hundrfeld.

"I did take them," Tessa said, the words dropping from her lips like a stone into a well. "They weren't welcome. The skjaldmaer told me to kill them. Instead, I set them free and hoped they'd be smart enough not to come back to the marsh. When I next went home, I was relieved to find them there, waiting for me. It's a wonder Trond didn't come for me when they turned up alone."

"Why didn't he?"

"Because they were unharmed and, other than being hungry, they weren't in any distress. That bought me the time necessary to send him a letter. Letters may leave Vaettfangkirk but rarely are admitted. I told him in vague terms that they weren't welcome and had sent them home. Trond never much liked Vaettfangkirk, but because I'd agreed to go, he did his best to…ignore the things that might cause him unease. As I did my best to shield him from them."

Stigandr was silent for a long moment. He tried to imagine Tessa as a teenager, going out of her way to be strong and protect the only adult in her life who seemed to care for her. The skjaldmaer were fantastic warriors—the very best, as he'd seen firsthand with Ragnhild—but at what cost? What had they done to her? What had they done to his sister that had made her an angry, quiet shell of who she'd once been?

But there was nowhere to funnel his anger, his guilt, his indignation at their treatment. It had already happened, and both women had come up with their own ways to cope with the trauma of their past. The best he could do was make sure their futures weren't so bleak, in whatever ways he could.

He missed his sister. He hoped he got to see her again.

"So," he said, his voice so thick that he had to work to steady it. "How can I help you train her?"

Tessa's answering smile was radiant, her excitement contagious. "Today we should practice together, so I can see how she reacts. If she can't sit patiently and watch, she's not ready for more. Like a warhorse or any warrior, she'll need to endure the sounds and frenzy of battle before I can trust her to fight."

"Very well," he said with a slight bow. "I'm ready when you are."

"I'm always ready." She guided Reka to a bench and tied her leash to it; he was glad she didn't see his blush at her words. Once she had her hammer and he his sword, he could again pretend to be Ashk, a guard helping a comrade practice. It was much safer than admitting he was Stigandr, a prince smitten with his brother's regent.

41
Havardr

521

Havardr strode across the polished marble floors of the palace. He'd walked through the market and the adjoining neighborhoods, littered with squalor and the starved dead. There was blood, too, from the few resistors who'd tried to repel them after the palace guards had opened the gates and let them in. His soldiers had made an example of those desperate fools, and soon the rest were resigned enough to their fate not to throw their lives away.

Now all that remained was to put the royal family in order, though it appeared the siege that had ruined the city hadn't touched the palace. There was still defiance in the gazes of the nobility, and their faces weren't as pale and gaunt as the peasants dying in the streets. These men and women had enjoyed the royal stores; they'd known no deprivation except escape.

Havardr was glad a trail of mud followed him. This place needed a little dirtying.

The great hall of Fjarriheimr was larger than the whole keep of Yfirgardr, the ceilings so impossibly high it didn't feel like they were indoors at all. The vaulted windows high above didn't have any glass in them, and birds flew in and out as they pleased. It was, admittedly, impressive in scale, like a house made for giants. Grand…and utterly bland. White floors, cream pillars, pearl furniture. It was ridiculous, all show with no substance beneath. It felt like a place devoid of history and personality, devoted to its own opulence.

He wouldn't mind owning it, but he could never live here. Whoever he positioned as his puppet in Fjarriheimr would be given specific orders to tear down as much as they could and make it more human in scale. The people here needed to be reminded that they weren't giants in any sense, and that any pride they'd held was misplaced.

A throne stood in the very center of the hall on a platform that rose fifty feet above the ground. Here was the only color to be found: the steps were each lined with a ribbon of gold. The king of Fjarriheimr sat on his throne, leaning heavily on an ivory cane. Havardr shouldn't have been surprised that the man was dressed in loose white robes and an alabaster crown, yet he was. Even his hair was silver, though Havardr suspected that had more to do with his age than commitment to aesthetics.

Or so he thought: he reconsidered when the princess approached him from the foot of the dais, her hair as silvery-white as her father's, so long it hung well past her waist. The woman was of a dark complexion, but still pale, as though she'd never set foot in the sun; another brief burst of color in this sterile space, though the paleness gave the appearance that her body saw the color as treasonous. Her eyes glistened a brown that was almost red, radiating old magic. Untapped magic, he suspected, since there had been no mages to protect the city.

And of course, she wore white earrings that hung to her shoulders and a long white dress without a speck of dust.

"King Havardr," she said as she curtsied. Not in the way of Hjorrfold, where the women bobbed down quickly to pay respect; this was more about spreading wide her skirts to put them on display. Indeed, they were impressive, as far as cloth went—intricate patterns of lace and pearls—and the movement highlighted the graceful bend of the princess' waiflike beauty. Instead of showing deference, it focused the attention on the lady.

"I'm no king," he said dismissively. Not yet, and he could hardly claim the title too early without alienating his people. His would-be generals were behind him, watching and listening and judging. Kerr and Hakon would be all too glad to spread rumors of Havardr's missteps, so he refused to make any. "I am a prince of Hjorrfold. The eldest son of King Alvis."

Her expression pinched slightly. "You are to become king of Fjarriheimr when my father cedes power."

Havardr snorted. He liked the sound of it, but he balked at the presumption that any of their customs and traditions still mattered. "That's not how it works in Hjorrfold. You're part of our kingdom now, beholden to our laws and our king."

She gritted her teeth and looked about to object, but one look at Havardr's icy stare and she wisely reconsidered. Instead, she cast her eyes down and mumbled, "Of course, my lord."

He stepped closer and put a hand on her shoulder, enjoying the way she flinched at the contact. "Good girl," he said, leaning in so she'd feel his breath on her ear, then cast his eyes up to the throne. The old man was slumped over so much he might be asleep. From a distance it was hard to tell, but he looked older than anyone Havardr had ever seen before.

"I'm older than you," she whispered, so faint he wouldn't have heard her at all if he hadn't been so close.

"And how old is that?" he asked.

"Nearly sixty."

Ah, so that was where their magic lay: in maintaining their youth and extending their lives. "And your father, then? How old is he?"

"One hundred eighty-five."

"Impressive," he said, the only genuine praise he expected to offer. Unfortunate that he wouldn't be able to wield it for himself. "Why does he still sit on his gilded throne if you're ready to call me king?"

The princess reached into the pocket of her long gown and produced a bleached piece of parchment with a golden band. She offered it to him on both palms, eyes downcast. "This is my father's descension. It lists you as the rightful holder of power, and that our people and wealth now belong to Hjorrfold. Written in his blood and sanctified by our holy men."

Havardr took it and stepped back, gesturing with the parchment at the empty space before him. "I will accept your surrender when your father kneels before me and says as much himself."

The princess staggered back as if struck. "Sir," she said, her expression horrified. "The indignity—"

"There is no dignity in being conquered. Just ask your people left starving in the city, the dead left behind in the villages we destroyed on our way here. Why should your father get to preserve his when it's already been stripped from his people? Wouldn't some argue he *must* give it up with his crown?" He pointed with his chin at the dais. "He certainly has no right to sit in that seat. This tells me you think that this is all a farce. That you are only pretending to give up your power but plan instead to hold it and continue on as things were before."

"I—I—" She floundered for a moment before she fell to her knees and clasped his left hand in both of hers. "You are right. Of course you are right. It was impudent of us. A thousand apologies. But please, my father is too old and weak. He cannot bow down—"

"He can get off his high throne," Havardr growled and pulled his hand from her grasp. "I wonder if he wasn't too weak to rule, since such a task is beyond him. He can walk or fall or be dragged down, but he will find his way before me to surrender his kingdom and beg for my mercy."

The princess—he'd never bothered learning her name, nor the name of her father, or anyone from this forsaken land—turned away from him, to hide her anger or her disgust at his demand, or her frustration at her own impudence. If she'd been a woman of Hjorrfold, she'd have tried to claw his eyes out or spat at him. Her lack of spirit was a fault of her upbringing. A true sign of weakness, not to keep fighting until the very end. Pathetic.

At least it would mean less work for him to break her. He could respect resistance, but he would only accept obedience.

She signaled for two servants to assist her father. They marched up the steps and lifted the old man to his feet, then escorted him down at a snail's pace until Havardr snarled at them to hurry. They carried him down the rest of the way, nearly stumbling under his weight on the high steps. Finally, he was before Havardr, a pathetic old man that wasn't worth the effort his people had put into defending him. Even on firm ground, the servants supported his weight as he stood before Havardr, his eyes a milky white though he appeared still able to see.

"Kneel," Havardr said. He placed a hand on the hilt of his sword and waited.

The king didn't kneel. He squinted as he took in Havardr. "I have been king longer than you've been alive. Longer than your father's been alive." His tone wasn't angry or condescending—that would've earned him a sharp slap across the face—more contemplative. As if he was in wonder that such things had come to pass.

"A man who cannot stand on his own shouldn't be king. Perhaps it's why the rest of us have more *natural* lifespans. To keep us from becoming decrepit." He waited to see the king's reaction, but the old man merely licked his dry lips and stared at Havardr serenely. "Kneel," he said again. "Give up your crown and swear your loyalty to Hjorrfold so that your people no longer have to endure hunger and death."

This earned him a frown. "Kneel? I have already signed over all my holdings and titles with a blood oath. I can't—"

"Let him go," Havardr said. When the servants hesitated, he drew an inch of his sword in warning. They did as they were ordered, letting go of the old man and stepping back. Immediately, he fell to the ground. He gasped and tried to catch himself, but only managed to slow his fall. He lay there, wheezing and prostrated before Havardr in a far worse position than if he'd kneeled as ordered. His daughter, in a show of solidarity with her father's frailty, kneeled beside him. She placed a hand on his back and then dipped forward so low that her forehead touched the cold marble.

Finally, Havardr thought, and grinned in satisfaction.

"We are your humblest of subjects," the princess murmured. She nudged her father, and it sounded as though she whispered something in a soothing tone.

"Our kingdom is yours," he said. He sounded even older and weaker than he looked, and Havardr wondered how much longer this man could live. Havardr understood better the ridiculously high throne and the daughter who spoke for him, all to obscure his weakness. "Fjarriheimr bows to Hjorrfold. Our people will do the same, and we beg for your mercy."

Mollified, Havardr decided he would indeed be merciful. He wouldn't kill this old man or his daughter. Not yet anyway. Not while they were still useful.

"I accept your surrender," he said gleefully. They rose just enough to look up at him. "You will publicly tell your people everything you have told me. That you have given up your right to the throne and that all the people of Fjarriheimr need to bow to Hjorrfold's might. We aren't unreasonable masters"—both flinched at his choice of words—"and will be fair to all who yield to the new way of things. Any who don't…well, disobedience will be dealt with swiftly and harshly."

"Of course," the princess said. "They will listen to my father when he tells them to obey."

Havardr continued on as if she hadn't spoken. "We will arrange a wedding ceremony between myself and the princess to take place in three day's time in conjunction with your speech to the people. This display of unity should help smooth things over."

Of all their reactions thus far, this was his favorite. He savored as the princess' face blanched. There had been some discussion of this among the nobles who'd negotiated the opening of the gate, so it couldn't be a surprise. It had been one of the requirements on both sides, for it gave the illusion of cooperation between the kingdoms instead of Fjarriheimr being absorbed into Hjorrfold. They no doubt hoped that the princess' influence would temper any plans Havardr held for them. It wouldn't, but he'd encouraged the idea.

But in their talks, the marriage had been made to sound like a distant event. A long engagement as matters were settled (and he was sure in her heart, the princess hoped Havardr would never follow through with the actual ceremony). An engagement would be enough to show unity and assure both of their needs were met. Havardr, who in no way wanted a wife, might've agreed to such an arrangement. It was only his imminent return to Yfirgardr that had made him reconsider. Though he was king in all but name, his position was not without its perils. If his siblings returned, he would have to convince them to cede their claim to the throne or otherwise dispose of them. If he were gravely injured or went on another long campaign, it would give them the opportunity they needed to supplant him.

What Havardr needed was a legacy. He needed his own heir to ensure that his was the stronger claim. He was the prince who was present, and if he had a son or daughter, it would show that the next transition between kings would be seamless. Why back Stigandr or Ragnhild, childless and long absent, when there was a line of succession in place?

A visibly pregnant wife would do just as well as a child, so soon the wedding must be.

"We can do the ceremony as your people wish," he said, throwing her a bone to soothe her vanity. "So long as it can be managed quickly, you may handle all the details."

When he looked at her expectantly, she muttered a soulless, "Thank you." She looked to her father, this time with none of the filial affection she'd shown before. At last, she saw his weakness because it affected her.

Havardr turned his back on them and walked back to where his own men and women waited, stone-faced. "Find the treasury and take everything worthwhile," he said as he continued walking, everyone trailing behind him. "Divide it among the soldiers. Try to get the citizens fed, but anything you give them, make sure they know it's from us. Invite the people to the palace so they might hear the king's abdication and witness my wedding. We'll need to discuss how the city and kingdom will be run once I return to Yfirgardr, but we'll put that off for a few days. Best to get a lay of the land first, though I refuse to stay longer than necessary. I'm not spending another fucking winter outside the keep."

There were muttered agreements as they broke off to do as he'd ordered. For all he cared, they could squabble amongst themselves over who did what, so long as everything got done. For his part, he was going to find himself a hot bath and sleep on a proper bed. He'd earned it.

At the doorway that led out of the great hall and presumably to the living quarters—the only thing about the room that was of reasonable proportions—he stopped and looked back. The vast space was empty, save for the king still lying on the ground, and his daughter bent over him as silent sobs wracked her body.

She was pretty, at least. A small consolation when he didn't want a wife. And there was magic in her blood, which should produce strong children. Though he supposed he'd have to learn her name…

42
Alvis

521

ALVIS DREAMED.

He didn't know it was a dream at first. It felt so real, though nothing made sense; that was the only way he knew it was a dream.

He dreamed his wife died, and they burned poor Ingegerd in the courtyard. She would've hated that. Her people buried their dead, especially the seers, because they thought the spirits of the dead clung to the living world and could be contacted at their graves. She'd planned on a grave outside the city when she'd first come to Yfirgardr, but when she learned neither Stigandr nor Randel were gifted in death magic, she'd planned to be returned to Andiby.

Alvis dreamed he gave the power of the crown to Havardr, heard his own voice say the words, though of course he would never do that. Not after the attack in the tomb below the city (though had that too been a dream?), and likely not before it, either. Ever since the boy turned twelve, danger and his ambition had gone hand in hand. Alvis had tried to direct it towards raiding, hoping that glory and riches would satisfy his eldest, all the while knowing it never could.

He watched his youngest son disappear into the mountains, wearing the wrong face and working magic that never should be worked.

And he watched his daughter travel the southern continent with her lover, content to be doing her part from afar, while dreading when she'd be called back home.

Alvis dreamed of Stigandr living just as happily in the mountains, a life he would've never chosen but that fit him so well that Alvis mourned when the boy left it behind...and was thankful he did, because what would come of Hjorrfold without him? Ingegerd had worried he'd destroy it, but Alvis had always thought the opposite; if some great mage was coming to break apart the keep, it wouldn't be Stigandr. Stigandr would be the glue that might hold it all together.

He saw Stigandr returning to Yfirgardr, hiding in plain sight. But who did he hide from? Havardr wasn't there. Alvis could see nothing but the Council, and surely they would welcome the boy.

But then he noticed a shadow in the castle, a blind spot he couldn't see no matter how hard he looked or how the dream shifted. Even Stigandr, always clear as day to him now that he was home, became hidden in dark fog when he passed too close to the shadow. It even looked like he pulled wisps of it away with him each time, little slivers of shadow diluting his light... and the shadow took little tendrils of his light with him. He could never make out the shape of the creature, but it became easier to find for all the pieces of Stigandr it dragged in its wake.

But the dream, strange as the visions in it were, had never been a nightmare. Not until the night he dreamed he was the land. Yfirgardr was the heart, and each breath he took was the city breathing. He grew weary with the weight of such a body, so large and spread out, but strong. Except something kept pulling at his edges, as though it was stretching his skin to cover more and more limbs that someone tried to attach to him. He felt a mangled, bloody mess, a monster of someone's terrible creation.

When Havardr finally took Fjarriheimr, it was like his body was ripped apart and another man stuffed inside it. The strain was unbearable. He could feel his skin splitting apart, his body succumbing to its wounds. There was no magic that could properly heal him from what had been done, not unless they undid it all: took out all the pieces that didn't belong, so the original might have a chance to recover. Weaker than before, but with the hope of survival.

In a brief moment of clarity, he almost jerked himself awake. He remembered the wards and could feel how weak they were. There was something outside of Hjorrfold trying to get in, and Havardr was opening the door for it. Every mile he pushed his foolish need for conquest was another crack in the armor that protected them all.

But then Alvis remembered he was only dreaming and he needn't worry. There was nothing coming for Hjorrfold. All was well.

43
Tessa

521

"THE COUNCIL AGREES that the queen's ban can be lifted," Tessa said, the Great Hall silent. She used the same carefully neutral tone she always did when delivering news from the Council, but she couldn't quite rein in her smile. "Since the queen had never given any explanation as to why she wanted the ban, they saw no reason to continue it. Dogs are once again welcome in Yfirgardr. Bodil, you may sell your dogs whenever and wherever you choose."

Bodil bowed in the Hundrfeld style, this time her fingertips brushing the ground and hem of her dress to show how deeply she appreciated Tessa's words. "Thank you, my lady. I will convey your words to my fellows."

It was an unfortunate necessity that Tessa stayed on the dais to continue the daily audiences with the others who'd come to the keep. She watched Bodil depart, stopped along the way by a few nobles who undoubtedly wanted to arrange their own purchase of a dog or two, and wondered if she would have the chance to actually speak with Bodil. Tessa so rarely encountered people from Hundrfeld. She knew this was good news—it wasn't her people that were being displaced by the disasters befalling the kingdom—but she coveted these rare opportunities. Few merchants from any quarter came to speak with her directly, and she found she missed the drawling sounds of her people. Much better than the sharper accent of the capital, and more distinct than some of the other areas where whole syllables seemed to disappear when they spoke.

And because there was simply no way Bodil had acquired Reka without meeting with Trond, Tessa dearly wanted to hear news of her uncle from the lips of someone who could reasonably affect his words.

But she forced such hopes from her mind and listened to the petitioners seeking her aid. Unlike Havardr, Tessa never sat on the thrones. Indeed, she rarely sat at all, standing only on the first or second step of the dais so she could be seen but not so high that people had to look up overmuch to speak to her. Today, though, she sat at the edge of the dais with Reka's head resting across her lap. Whenever a child would timidly come and ask to pet the happy pup, Tessa would nod and grin widely when their little faces lit up as they felt the soft fur and enjoyed licks and nuzzles from Reka.

It reminded her of home, enough that she could ignore the empty thrones behind her and see only her future: back at Hundrfeld, performing this duty for her own people.

When the Great Hall was cleared out at midday, Ove appeared at the door and nodded towards the kitchens. Tessa took the hint and left the hall, Reka at her heels.

It wasn't Bodil she found there, but the young woman who'd escorted her to the keep.

"Valdis," the woman said, bending forward just enough to be considered a bow. Her sandy hair spilled over her shoulders as she straightened up. "I'm the one Ove usually sends."

Tessa looked around, but the servants were too busy in the hustle and bustle of preparing the midday meal to pay them any mind. They paid attention only to Reka, sniffing around and begging for treats. A welcome distraction.

"Thank you," Tessa said warmly. "It can't be an easy task, and your discretion and service are much appreciated."

"As is your gold," Valdis said. "I wanted to speak with you about this change in our arrangement and make sure you weren't upset for it to be more . . . public that there is at least one person in Yfirgardr making the rounds to Hundrfeld."

It was certainly a risk, but it seemed it was one both Ove and Trond considered acceptable. Whenever Havardr reappeared, they might need to reassess. Hopefully by then things would be well established.

"You take as much risk as I do. More, even." More quietly, Tessa said, "Next time you see him, thank my uncle for Reka. She is a very welcome gift."

Valdis looked at her with an arched brow. "I can pass on any message you wish," she said, "but I feel I would be doing a disservice if I let you think it was his idea."

"What do you mean?"

"Lord Trond picked the pup," Valdis said, her voice equally quiet and forcing Tessa to lean in to hear her over the hubbub, "but it wasn't his idea. Someone from Yfirgardr commissioned me for this task. I suspect he wished for his part to remain unknown to you, but if you're looking to pass along your thanks, they shouldn't go to your lord uncle."

Suddenly, the kitchen, crowded and busy as it was, seemed muted and distant. If not her uncle, then who? Neither Ove nor Dagrun, for all their loyalty and friendship, would've known what this meant to her. They couldn't have understood the hole in her heart this helped mend, nor was it like them to take such a risk on her behalf without her knowing.

"Who?" she asked, but in her heart she knew before Valdis said it.

"Ashk," Valdis said. "He arranged the whole thing with me. Paid for the dog. Explained the legality of the endeavor. Clever one, he is. And kind-hearted, if you're as happy with Reka as you seem."

At the sound of her name, Reka hopped back over and sat happily between them.

"I am," Tessa said, though she wasn't sure what to do with this news. This was such a kind gesture, and so very welcome. Why the secrecy? "But why wouldn't he want me to know?"

"Perhaps he thought you wouldn't like it and didn't want to face the consequences," Valdis said.

Anyone who *knew* her, really knew her, couldn't believe that. And Ashk was no fool: he must have known Valdis would've sold him out if Tessa were upset.

"Or," Valdis said, when she saw Tessa's doubt, "if someone does something nice in secret, it's because they want you to have the nice thing without feeling any obligation to them for procuring it. Course, he probably wasn't accounting for me telling you, but your young man did me a good turn, letting me travel with my lady and openly visit Hundrfeld. I wanted him to reap his due rewards."

There was something suggestive in her tone, which Tessa chose to ignore, though she thanked Valdis. And paid her, though the merchant insisted she'd been well compensated already.

"I'm sure you have."Tessa stopped at the door to the Great Hall. "But not by me. Thank you for all you've done, but please understand we can't meet again."

ALL DAY, TESSA considered what she'd learned. She wanted to thank Ashk—and would, regardless of his intentions—but she wasn't ready to face him yet. Not until things had settled more.

Though she finished her day as usual, she skipped dinner in the Great Hall and had a small tray of bread, cheese, and meats sent to her room. The meat mostly went to Reka, who had mastered begging with her wide blue eyes, staring mournfully into Tessa's soul.

"What a spoiled girl you are," Tessa cooed, both hands cupping Reka's muzzle. She kissed the dog's head between her ears. "We'll have work to do soon. I can't have a war dog who wouldn't survive in a real fight. What would they say in Hundrfeld?"

Reka woofed.

A sudden jolt of happiness made something settle inside her. As though she'd been trying to tie a knot with a piece of string that wasn't quite long enough, and now the length had doubled.

She looked at her hand, flicked her fingers, and a flame appeared.

"Ah!" she huffed in delight. She flexed her fingers, and the flame disappeared. She held a breath and tried again. Then again, and again, worried this would be the time it didn't work; every time, the flame came when called.

Looking at her hands and then Reka in wonder, she said, "I think we have a lot of practice to do, indeed."

Tessa was no stranger to hard work. She took the same approach that'd been forced upon her at Vaettfangkirk, channeling magic through her newfound happiness whenever she could. She kept her practice to solitary moments alone, with only Reka as witness. Within a few days, she'd mastered all the house magic she'd been shown in the kitchens. Emboldened, she returned to Stigandr's scrolls and notes to try defensive magic.

She didn't go to her nightly sessions with Ashk. She didn't know what to do with him. She remembered all too well the seer who'd said she could trust him, and how they'd been looking for Reka. Too early, they'd said. They'd been right: they'd arrived too early to find Reka, but arrive she did. And if the seer had been right about Reka, then it followed that she'd been right about Ashk as well.

Tessa wanted to trust Ashk…but she was scared to. He was the one who'd suggested she try magic. He didn't know about her attempts and failures, but he'd solved the problem for her with Reka. Again, she couldn't be certain of his intent. He might genuinely believe magic would be useful for her and, quite separately, that she longed for a companion. Yet the coincidences made her worry. It all fit together too nicely.

So if she entertained the idea he'd *wanted* her to learn magic *and* helped her do so…the question became why. What did he stand to gain if she became a mage?

It was childish, but she avoided him. She attended the large dinners in the Great Hall—she could hardly justify her absence and the slight against the entire guard on account of one man—but she stopped coming to the training pitch at night. It didn't take long to miss it, but she remained firm in her resolve.

Even if it left an ache in her chest and made her dream of a hammer in her hands, as well as the pleasant burn in her muscles from a good fight, and kind, hazel eyes.

"You given up on practice?" Ove asked her after a few weeks. She had never told him she'd started sparring with Ashk; it shouldn't be a surprise he'd noticed it'd ended as well. "Or is it your partner that you've given up?"

"I don't know," she answered, because it was easier than explaining. She *was* training, but her focus was on defensive wards and controlling fire bursts. Her skill was limited, and she refused to practice where she might be seen, not until she was confident she wouldn't embarrass herself with her rudimentary abilities. She hadn't considered herself to have much ego, but never had there been witnesses to her learning, aside from her tutors in Hundrfeld and the skjaldmaer, both groups having known her long before she'd perfected their lessons. In Yfirgardr, they'd only ever known the warrior that'd been forged by years of work, and perhaps it reflected poorly upon her vanity, but she wasn't keen to dispel that image. She was the best and enjoyed the respect and awe that garnered her.

But she would soon exhaust what she could accomplish alone in her room. She was liable to break something or set the entire castle ablaze. And what good was a shield if she couldn't conjure it while wielding a weapon and in the heat of battle?

Reka whined and pawed at the door. She too was tired of being cooped up at night, and she would need proper training. Watching Tessa awkwardly fumble through shields did the dog no good.

"All right," Tessa said when the autumn chill seemed more inviting than her over-warm room. "We'll go."

It had been so long, she had no expectations of seeing Ashk there. She both longed for and dreaded the reunion, but she doubted any man would wait around after such an obvious snub. After a few nights, he must've thought she'd grown bored with him and in turn given up waiting. It was with the assumption of an empty training pitch that she went outside a few hours after dusk, Reka at her heel, and stopped short when she saw Ashk there.

He was going through the motions of his preferred routine. She'd never understood why he favored it so much, when it was a set of moves that worked best with a dagger and not a sword, but he moved through it fluently. She supposed that, as the son of a cook, he'd had more opportunity to work with knives than swords. Swords were the weapon of the city guard and the warriors Havardr had taken west, not kitchen boys and servants.

Not wanting to interrupt him, Tessa approached slowly. She got as far as the benches, took a seat with Reka at her side, and watched for a good ten minutes before Ashk noticed her. He startled as he swung the sword in an arc, unbalancing himself. He scrambled to stay upright and preserve some dignity as he tried to salvage the swing. In obvious embarrassment, he put the sword—a real sword, she noted, and not the wooden practice ones they'd always used together—in the ground and rested against the hilt. It was endearing how bashful he seemed.

"How long have you been watching, exactly?" he asked. His face was red from exertion, and his voice a little shaky.

Tessa ran her hand down Reka's back. "Long enough to know you don't mess up *every* time you swing your sword."

Ashk chuckled, though it still sounded racked with nerves. "It doesn't bode well that I startle easily, does it?"

"I'm very intimidating," she said. "It could be overlooked."

Silence fell upon them. A pride she'd never before known herself to have made her lips stay shut. Ashk must have sensed there was no alternative, because he spoke first: "I hope all is well. You must be quite busy to have stayed away from the training pitch for so long."

A flicker of guilt squeezed her heart. "I have been busy," she admitted. "With a different kind of training. I'll confess, I didn't expect to find you here."

"I'm pleased you think my skill with a sword is so good that I didn't need the practice," he said breezily.

She pushed off the bench and walked towards him, Reka huffing at being disturbed. "That's not what I meant."

Ashk shrugged but cast his gaze to the ground. "I wasn't sure if I'd displeased you," he admitted, "but I do need the practice. And I thought perhaps, if I was diligent enough in my visits, you would return and I would have a chance to…apologize if I had wronged you." He gulped and chanced a look at her. "Have I?"

Tessa sighed. It was her turn to look away. "No, you have not," she said. "I owe you thanks for Reka, as I understand it, so quite the opposite." Out of the corner of her eye, she watched him carefully. He showed no reaction, to the point that she wondered if Valdis had been mistaken, except that any true ignorance would be met with confusion.

"I..." He licked his lips and cleared his throat. "You are very welcome, but please know I didn't do it for praise or thanks or any sort of obligation. It didn't sit well with me that you were allowed so few reminders of home. And you needn't argue that nothing prevents you," he said hastily. "I understand that technically there might be nothing opposing it. It just seemed...that you have considerations beyond what one can see that might be making it...difficult."

He'd hit the nail on the head, though she could hardly admit it.

"I see," she said coolly. "Well, you have my sincere thanks."

Ashk leaned forward in a slight bow. "My lady."

She let the moment linger, then walked towards the weapon rack. There might be further opportunity to show her thanks later, but the hard part was done. Now they could go back to the way things were.

But she knew that wasn't quite true either. With time, they might overcome and fall back into their old habits...but what if she didn't want to? What if it were time to press forward, not back?

She lifted her practice hammer. What she was about to do...there was no coming back from.

When Ashk started over to exchange his blade for a practice sword, she waved him off. "It's fine," she said. "Use the real one."

He froze. "While I don't doubt your ability to defend against the likes of me—"

"Then line up." Her tone was more imperious than usual, like when she spoke on the battlefield. She walked over to her own starting point, whistling sharply to Reka. "Stay," she ordered. "You're not ready to play along."

Though Ashk did as he was told, raising his sword to the ready, his brow was furrowed. He stood ten paces away, but she thought she saw a slight tremor in his hands.

"No one will get hurt," she promised. *Not mortally wounded*, she amended silently; she resolved not to use any of the more dangerous forms of magic that she'd been practicing.

With her hammer gripped in both hands, she dug her feet in. "Don't hold back," she said. She didn't know why she said it—never had she suspected Ashk of going easy on her—but it seemed important. She wasn't sure she'd be able to muster the energy for a true shield if she didn't feel threatened, so threatened she must be.

Whatever Ashk thought of her request, he said nothing. He narrowed his eyes, gave a curt nod, then came at her. He was... faster than she remembered. His blade cut through the air with a metallic hiss, sometimes so close that she felt the air rushing past as it kissed her skin. With liquid grace, he dodged her attacks. Her blood thrilled at the challenge, and she relished the difficulty in avoiding him.

And then she went on the attack.

She deftly kept him at the perfect distance to swing her hammer freely, forcing him to dodge because his sword stood no chance, real or not, of absorbing a single blow. Sweat beaded on his brow as he staggered back. But he'd never yield, not until he'd been disarmed, and she pressed her advantage. He was fast, yes, but if she never let up enough for him to use that speed, it didn't matter.

Soon he made a desperate attack. He swung with full force at her unguarded ribs during the follow-through of her own swing. A real blade, sharpened metal, came searing in on her—

And landed firmly in the shaft of her hammer, barely there in time.

The blade was stuck, and though Ashk desperately shook it, hoping to free it, there was nothing he could do. She pulled her hammer as she stepped backward, wrenching the sword out of his grasp, and then kicked him in the chest to knock him down.

"You could've hurt me," she said mildly as she wiggled the blade free.

Ashk looked up at her from the sand. "And yet I'm the one on the ground," he grunted.

She tossed the sword at his feet. "You should use daggers," she said. "A sword doesn't suit you."

His eyes went from her, to Reka, to the sword, then back to her. "Why do you say that?"

And this—the words said and the ones not said—felt like the true battle. An accusation here, a suggestion there, all glancing blows as they prodded for weaknesses.

"Just a feeling," she said.

"And wouldn't I be terribly outmatched with daggers against a war hammer?"

"You're already outmatched," she pointed out with a smirk. "Does it really matter by how much?"

"How is it," he said while picking himself up and reclaiming his sword, "that even when I have a real sword, you're still the more dangerous one?"

"Years of practice. They can be real daggers, if that'd help."

Ashk walked over to the weapons rack, muttering something that sounded suspiciously like 'bossy' under his breath. He exchanged the sword for a set of four daggers, sticking two through his belt loops and holding the other two so expertly she wondered briefly if he was an assassin. He was a rather poor one, given how many opportunities he'd had to kill her so far, but still, the image stuck.

"You planning on throwing them?" she asked as he returned to his side of the pitch.

"Don't think you could dodge them?" he asked, but then said, "I won't throw them."

This time, she attacked first. She charged him with the hammer behind her back. She held it one-handed so she could swing it but still use the other hand for balance and attacking. Since Ashk only had daggers, if she got a hand on his wrist, she could eliminate half the danger.

As she rushed him, Tessa swung the hammer around to hit him hard in the chest. He deflected with a swat of his hand and used his daggers to trap the base of her hammer. Criss-crossed blades wrenched the weapon from her grasp, but she swung her other hand around to grab the hammer's shaft before he could cast it aside. She shook the tangle of weapons so much that one of Ashk's daggers was cast aside, but he'd pulled the other free and unsheathed a third before Tessa had properly regained control of her hammer.

Though she wanted to compliment him, she had no time: she planted her feet to prepare for the next strike, her mind racing as she recalibrated her strategy. The unexpected move by Ashk had thrown her off balance, a move that thrilled her more than worried her. She analyzed his stance to anticipate his next move. As Ashk lunged towards her, she swiftly sidestepped, narrowly avoiding his blades.

Blades aimed right for her chest. She didn't truly believe he meant to harm her, but the possibility of it was very real. It was far more exciting than it should've been.

Tessa spun around, her hammer now gripped tightly in both hands. With calculated precision, she aimed for Ashk's exposed side. As she swung toward Ashk, she hesitated, concern for Ashk momentarily holding her back just enough that he was able to parry the attack, the clash of metal and wood reverberating through the air.

Back and forth they went, Tessa unable to follow through when the chances came to knock Ashk down. If the same dilemma faced him, she saw no sign of it. He moved with equal fury, whether on the attack or defending. It was like a dance, steps they knew intimately, though Tessa didn't much like where they led. Each time they clashed, she grew more frustrated with her own reluctance to end things.

It made her sloppy.

It wasn't just her frustration. She had to admit, Ashk was talented. His prowess with the smaller blades was far beyond anything she'd seen from him when he wielded a sword. Every movement was more fluid, as though before he'd been thinking too hard as he fought, and now he could rely on muscle memory and instinct. With each exchange, the exhilaration of the fight coursed through her veins, igniting a fire within her that burned brighter with every passing moment. It made her push herself more and more to match him, though still she held back.

I might hurt him…

He brandishes daggers of real steel, and you worry about him? Finish this, or back down enough to bait him. You're not here to be impressed. You're here to practice.

She took a deep breath. She *wasn't* here for their usual practice; she had more planned.

As they circled each other, she made herself hold steady. It wasn't easy to give Ashk control of the fight, but she did. She forced herself to react, to follow the pace he set and to allow herself to be moved wherever he wanted. Only when her arms burned and her legs ached did she start to draw on the pool of magic she'd been cultivating for the past few weeks.

As Tessa retreated, she allowed herself to be overwhelmed by Ashk's onslaught. Her instincts begged her to counter, but she backed away, fell into a defensive posture where she could do little more than fend off his continued onslaught. As her body screamed in desperation, she knew the next blow would actually land. It was now or never.

Ashk struck. She held out a hand, willing the invisible shield to form, knowing if she didn't, she might very well lose an eye.

His blades froze midair.

She pictured the barrier between them pushing outward, and his daggers trembled.

When Tessa dipped into the well of magic inside her, the one she'd spent the last few weeks cultivating drop by drop, and drew her hand back one inch, then another, drawing his blades with them. Then, when it felt like a bow drawn taut, she pushed forward, and Ashk went flying.

Tessa wanted to jump and cry out in victory. She'd done it! The shield had worked. More than worked: it had protected her one moment, and the next cast aside her assailant. If she could do that in battle—

And that was when the world grew black. All her strength left her in a rush. Her hammer fell first, her vision blurred, then it was her tumbling to the ground. As her eyes fluttered closed, she was glad it was Ashk here with her and not Havardr; otherwise, this mistake would've cost her life.

44
Stigandr

521

Stigandr landed hard on his back. He groaned as he dropped his daggers and pushed himself back up, ears ringing. He'd just managed a sitting position—though he had yet to figure out what had just happened—when he saw Tessa stumble and fall. Stigandr jumped to his feet and managed to keep her from crashing to the ground.

Reka was at their side, fretting as she poked Tessa with her nose and then making a strange whine at Stigandr as though to say *take care of her fix her help her*.

"Are you all right?" he asked Tessa, cupping her face in his hand. It was impossible to see her pupils in the black depths of her eyes, but her gaze seemed cloudy, as though she couldn't see him. She'd done magic, no doubt about that, and a powerful burst of it at that: she was reeling from the aftershocks. Stigandr had seen this dozens of times before as a boy (had even experienced it himself once or twice), that unleashing of raw power that left a mage spent and defenseless.

A mage. Something Tessa was not.

It didn't matter. She'd obviously been doing magic work on her own, and the remedy was the same for inexperienced and expert mages alike. Stigandr slung her arm around his shoulders. She couldn't get up on her own, so he bore her weight and carried her to her feet. "Let's get you to the healers—"

"No!" she hissed, suddenly more alert. "My room."

He hesitated, but only briefly. Against his better judgement, he hobbled them towards the door at the far end of the courtyard, leading to the private quarters instead of to the much nearer door to the kitchens with a straight path to the healers. Reka followed, walking anxious circles around them and whimpering as she sniffed at Tessa.

"You're stubborn," he mumbled. She was at least trying to walk, though she could barely manage one full step for every five he took. "No one knows you've been practicing magic, do they?"

"No."

It took some work to heave open the heavy door with his left shoulder, but he managed it. The stairs were their own challenge. Giving up the pretense of her walking, he swung her into his arms—one hand holding her legs, the other tucked around her back—and carried her. She was wobbly on her feet when he had to put her down to open the door to her room. Thankfully, it wasn't locked, and her trusting nature made his heart throb as much as his tired arms. She managed two whole steps before she stumbled; Stigandr caught her once more and guided her to the nearest chair.

"Stay here," he ordered, pointing a finger at her. "I'll get you some potions. Try not to pass out. I'd rather not force-feed you."

She groaned but nodded, head in her hand as she leaned over the armrest. She was quite pale. More so than usual. He'd bring her some food as well. Potions did a fine job, but sometimes more practical, traditional methods were better.

"Watch her. I'll be back soon," he said to Reka, who seemed no less distressed than in the courtyard. She licked at Tessa and nuzzled her, though Tessa trembled with exhaustion and couldn't reciprocate the poor dog's affection. "She'll be all right," he soothed, hoping the dog was as smart as the legends of Hundrfeld would have him believe.

Reka huffed, walked in a tight circle at Tessa's feet, then lay there with her head resting on her paws. She looked very sad.

"Good girl," he praised, then slipped out of the room. At the stairwell, he hesitated. He should go straight down to the healers and the kitchen, then come back as quickly as possible; instead, he went up to his room and snagged some of the more potent remedies he'd been saving for himself. His supplies were limited, so he'd been using them sparingly, but he was used to magical drainage. Even with his faux face, he was in a better position to handle the exertion than a new mage.

It took him nearly an hour to acquire everything he needed. When he knocked on Tessa's door, he got no response, so he carefully pushed his way inside. Tessa was right where he'd left her, dozing with a faint snore. Reka perked up and wagged her tail.

"You're a smart girl, aren't you?" Stigandr pushed the door open wider with his foot. "Could you stand guard for us?" If Tessa wanted any hope of secrecy, he probably shouldn't be caught in her room administering draughts while she looked like death.

Reka padded over, sniffed him and the tray he carried, then went to sit in the hallway right outside the door. She cast him a look over her shoulder, and he got the impression it was a warning to do her mistress no harm.

"I'll take good care of her," he promised. "I know what I'm doing." He shut the door as quietly as he could, hoping they hadn't woken any of Tessa's neighbors among the nobles and Council. What a disaster *that* would be.

He had to kneel before Tessa to put the tray down on the small table nearby, and he gently shook her. She didn't stir.

"Tessa," he said softly but firmly. "Wake up. I know you're tired, but this will help." He held a steaming mug up to her lips, the smell strong and overly sweet. She wrinkled her nose and blinked her eyes open.

"That smells terrible," she grumbled.

"It doesn't. Drink it."

She took the mug, but her hands shook so badly he had to cup his around hers to keep it steady. After a few sips, she could manage on her own; he flexed his hands to dispel the feel of her skin against his.

"What happened?" Her voice was thick. "We were in the courtyard..."

"You used a magic shield to block my attack. A very good one, actually. It held me in place for three seconds before pushing me back." He nodded to the tray, and she took a pastry to nibble on. "Magic isn't much different from using your body. It's exertion, and if you're not careful, you'll exhaust yourself. Like you did."

She frowned and took a proper bite and then sipped from the mug.

"You must have been practicing a lot to get it that strong. Have you noticed you've been more tired lately? Hungrier? Sleeping deeper?"

"Yes." She finished the last of her drink. When she placed it back on the tray, Stigandr refilled it from the pitcher he'd brought. The healers were used to making late-night draughts after their practices, and they hadn't batted an eye when he'd asked for a fresh brew, extra strong. "How do powerful mages account for it? If a single barrier could incapacitate me, it's hardly practical."

"I'm sure if I handed someone a war hammer for the first time, a few swings and they'd be on their knees panting. It takes time to build up your endurance, and there are crystals and spells that help you supplement your energy or siphon it from other sources. Moderation is also important: the larger the magic, the more sporadically you're able to use it."

He took a jar of ointment out of his pocket and held out his hand for hers. Rubbing her eyes with the back of one hand, she offered the other palm up.

"Since we use our hands for magic, that's where we lose a lot of energy." He opened the jar with his free hand and dipped his fingers in. He worked the ointment into her skin, trying not to map out each callus. "This ointment will stem the loss of energy now that you're done, and will slowly restore it."

Unfortunately, this jar was the last he had; the ingredients weren't easy to harvest, and it was time-consuming to make. The healers might have what he needed, but he'd have to steal it and wait until a new moon to make more. He wasn't a good alchemist, either; he'd need extra to account for errors in his brews.

"We?" she asked, interrupting his train of thought. When she noticed his confusion, she said, "You said since *we* use our hands for magic."

Stigandr hoped he didn't hesitate when he answered, "I can do small magic, same as most."

"No one who uses small magic ever mentions it making them tired," she said.

"Most don't use it enough. Using a knife to cut your steak is hardly as taxing as wielding one in a fight."

She watched him keenly as he finished with her right hand and moved on to the left. "You know so much about this, though."

"There were many mages here when I was a boy. Not just the princes and queen, mind you. At any time, there were a great many who were there either to tutor the princes, or to use the books kept in the library, or even to perform in the Great Hall. Not unlike when warriors duel for sport. I saw many mages casting illusions, and we all clapped and cheered for the best ones. You learn a thing or two watching such talented people perform their craft."

Tessa inspected her right hand, then sniffed it. "Smells like lavender."

Stigandr hummed.

"Smells like you," she added.

"I'm sure I smell more like sweat and the barracks," he said. He placed the lid back on the jar and put it on the tray. "You should put that on *before* you cast magic. It works better as a preventative measure."

She assessed him with her cold, dark eyes. They didn't seem to reflect even the dim candlelight, and there was no hint of what she was thinking. "Why do your eyes change color?" she asked. He wished there was a trace of exhaustion still in her voice; there was none, unfortunately, which meant he needed to give a real answer.

"Do they?" he hedged.

"They're usually brown with green flecks," she said. She gestured at his face. "Sometimes they're more green than brown. It's not the light. It happens day and night in equal measure, though they seem greener these days."

Fuck.

"You pay a lot of attention to my eyes."

"I pay a lot of attention to *you*, and your eyes are attached."

Stigandr remained still. He went so far as to hold his breath. But he realized the longer he hesitated, the more damning it was. Any chance of using this moment to maintain her trust was slipping away.

Decision made, he lifted his slightly glowing fingers and wiggled them to get her attention. He'd gotten enough of the ointment on his own hands that this wouldn't completely waste his energy, because this display of magic would cost him. Her gaze followed his hand as he drew it through the air, trails of light following. Without a word, he lifted his hand to the tip of his head and then lowered it over his face, concentrating as he pictured in his mind's eye Ove's face instead of Ashk's.

Tessa's breath hitched when the illusion settled in, but said nothing.

Taking it as an invitation to continue, he repeated the motion, this time imagining Dagrun as he moved his hand down and felt the tickle of magic shifting over his features. When he saw fascination and not fear or anger, he went through a few more faces: an innkeeper, another guard, a servant from the kitchens. Finally, she reached out and caught his wrist. Whatever exhaustion had overcome her in the courtyard was long gone.

"That's very good," she said, then bit her lip. He could see the wheels in her head turning as she put together everything he'd said and shown her, and he felt her hold tighten. "Now show me Stigandr," Tessa whispered.

The air came out of him in a rush. She didn't let him go, but he had no need of his hand to perform the trick, and certainly not to undo it. Like a muscle unclenching, he let go of the illusion he'd worn for months now, the constant leech on his energy and concentration. It scattered like dust around them, revealing his own features: the aquiline nose he'd inherited from his mother, the umber of his hair, and the vivid green eyes all children of the royal household bore, an everlasting sign of the magic that had founded first Yfirgardr and then Hjorrfold.

He'd never felt more naked than he did then, waiting for her to condemn him for his deceit and his blood.

She did neither. Instead, Tessa's gaze was like a caress as she traced every line of his face. Abruptly she let go of his wrist, and then her hands followed as she mapped out each plane, every curve. He stayed very still, frozen where he kneeled before her as she memorized him, scarcely breathing as he waited and hoped to still be found worthy.

"Ah," she said, brushing a stray hand of hair behind his ear. "There you are."

Then she pulled him in and brushed her lips against his, that first kiss that sealed his fate.

When their lips met, it was like a vise constricted around his heart. He gasped at the shock of it, the strength of a magical bond locking them together.

It took him by surprise not so much that it would happen, but the speed and strength of it meant he'd already given himself to her and was waiting for her magic—her hitherto untapped magic—to provide a foothold to latch onto.

For better or worse, he was bonded to Tessa of Hundrfeld.

Well, he thought as he deepened the kiss to savor the taste of her, *no reason to hold back*…

So he didn't. He let himself melt into her kiss, heart open as he accepted anything she was willing to give him. When she pulled him closer so they rested chest to chest, she broke away.

"Take me to bed," she whispered, lips still so close that each word tickled along his skin.

He made a needy sound, pitiful and desperate. "Are you sure?" he asked as he kissed along her neck. He nuzzled against the collar of her tunic, greedily breathing in her scent. He had never allowed himself to imagine such intimacy with her, perhaps out of some sense of self-preservation, because now that he'd been this close, he wasn't sure he could do without her.

By way of answer, she undid the buckle of her belt. She pulled the heavy leather aside and dropped it onto the floor beside them.

"Take me to bed," she repeated. As regent, she'd ordered him about many times; he'd never been more eager to serve. "Stigandr."

Hearing his name once more on her lips, he was done for. He would've given her anything and everything, and he would've needed nothing in return except to know he'd pleased her. "Yes, my lady." He lifted her into his arms. "Whatever you wish…"

Part Three

45
Ingegerd

521

In Andiby, death wasn't seen as an ending. Those with the right mindset—stubborn, self-important, driven people with magic deep in their bones—could cling to the world of the living long after their bodies had died. Granted, most weren't so determined and went somewhere no magic could find them.

It'd been that way with Ingegerd's father. Ingegerd, with the confidence of any ten-year-old, had been so *certain* he would linger. Had she not heard the whispers of her grandparents and great-grandparents in the graveyard? Why should her father be any different? But no matter how many times she'd gone to his grave, he wouldn't answer her. New moon, full moon, midnight, the winter solstice, with charms and offerings to conjure him, nothing could bring him back. She tried for years before she gave up, and she decided then and there it wouldn't be the same for her.

Though prophecy became her expertise, as a young girl, her passion had been in death magic. She'd read every book of the dead and performed every rite that bound the soul more tightly to the body. It would take more than death to rip her from this world.

But she'd have no way of knowing how effective the rites were without experimentation. Ingegerd had no interest in dying, even to prove a point, but there were elders among her people whose knowledge would die with them if they completely left the tribe. With the rites, the charms, the meditation to create that proper mindset, she worked it all to preserve their souls, and in exchange they taught her prophecy so she could avoid her death as long as possible.

When they'd passed away one by one, Ingegerd and the others had worked to contact them. If a connection could be established even once, it was easier to keep them grounded in the present. Ingegerd had determined early on that link was essential. After an elder had died in the dead of winter, they hadn't been able to bury her for months because the ground was frozen solid. Everything else had been done properly, yet they couldn't coax her spirit back come spring no matter how hard they tried.

Over the years, Ingegerd had refined her methods and taught them to her sisters so that when she left Andiby—and she had no doubt she would leave Andiby, the omens were quite certain—everything she'd set in motion would continue.

Somewhere along the way, she'd misread her future.

She'd expected to live to an old, grizzled age with her children and grandchildren by her side, but when she nearly died in childbirth after her second, she worried about what other miscalculations she'd made. She put aside her death magic and focused on prophecy. Knowing and controlling the future would give her the time necessary to teach her sons how to perform the death rites later. Stigandr, having almost killed her, would be more attuned to that kind of witchcraft than even she was, with her years of practice. He would be a natural, she was certain, and so it made it easy to let him pursue his other interests while she pursued hers.

Her husband's end, that she'd seen from the first moment she'd cast his fates: the skjaldmaer who would slaughter him and the blood she'd wear. Never when or where or even the face of the skjaldmaer, but the same vision every time, never changing. When Ragnhild returned from Vaettfangkirk, her eyes darkened with hate, Ingegerd thought for sure the vision would solidify more in her mind's eye; it didn't, but she didn't need it to. Ragnhild would kill her father, and so Ragnhild would need to go to save them both from that shame.

The only other glimpse she saw with any clarity was a giant, three-headed dog, massive and powerful, that swallowed the entire world in its greed. The dog was made of shadows with eyes darker than the deepest pit. It would gaze at her coldly, as if it truly could see her, when she tried to look for it looming in the future. Ingegerd shivered every time she slipped into that vision. She couldn't stand to look at any dog because of the uncomfortable reminder, always worried *that* dog was the one staring back at her.

It would be a great mage who unleashed this beast upon them all, so Stigandr needed to be sent away. It'd broken her heart to see glimpses of his future self in her visions, powerful and so very capable of the destruction she'd foreseen. And she'd seen happiness in his future tangled up with all the misfortunes. That happiness began on a path through the mountains, so she'd put him onto that path, satisfied her favorite child would be safe from doing harm or being in harm's way. It meant she'd have to teach the death rites to Randel instead, but so be it. There was time yet, and he was capable and pliable, though not particularly enthusiastic.

There'd always been more time...

It wasn't that she didn't care about her own fate. She did, but more effort was put into Hjorrfold and, therefore, her husband. She foresaw a bright future for Hjorrfold, where it glimmered and shone like the brightest star in the night sky. It was all but guaranteed. She only needed to safeguard her family and occasionally nudge things back onto the right path. There were so many strings to pull, so many mingling pieces. It'd required so much of her attention. She'd cast her gaze too far ahead; she'd forgotten to look where she was placing her feet.

After all her work with death, she hadn't recognized what it felt like until it was too late.

The strange tunnel leading under the city killed her. Step by step, it'd drained the life from her without her noticing. Like a fool, she'd thought nothing in Yfirgardr could harm her. She was the queen, a mistress of death, a true seer of Andiby. She could sniff out treachery a mile away, which was perhaps what had done her in. Havardr, so secretive in his doings but so simple in his motivations, wouldn't have been able to conceal any ill will towards her. When she'd followed him, she'd sensed something amiss, but never in a thousand years did she think he meant her any harm. Strained as their relationship was, his plots were aimed at lifting himself over his siblings; they were the ones who should fear him.

She died in her son's arms, weaker than she'd ever felt in her life. She had much to regret—that she hadn't seen her own death, that her preparations were incomplete, that she'd sent away her best shields against Havardr—but that wasn't what made her blood boil.

It was rage. Rage that this had been her end, might be her permanent end, and she held it tight. It might be the only thing strong enough to give her a foothold back to this world.

TIME PASSED. SHE knew not how long: whether for seconds or an eternity, she was in no state to understand the difference.

Havardr's occasional visits disturbed the space enough to rouse her. Or maybe it was because he was her son, and something in her soul reached out for something in his. It didn't matter: his appearances were the catalyst that allowed her to will herself back together. Slowly, she collected the little pieces of herself and became not quite Ingegerd, but something close.

As some semblance of consciousness reasserted itself, she took in the space that served as her tomb.

She surveyed the wards, her nose inches away from them as she tried to work out their meaning. She didn't understand she was dead until she realized she was at the ceiling, floating dozens of feet in the air to investigate the spellwork.

Then she realized she had no nose, or any shape at all.

Her husband lay dead on the ground. She noticed him with a cold, detached sort of understanding. He'd gotten them into this mess, of that she was certain, though she barely remembered that he was her husband. Nor could she remember how she'd ended up as a detached spirit in some strange vault under the castle, so her sympathy was limited to herself. Hers, she felt, was the worse predicament.

Each subsequent revelation came gradually. It was difficult to care, her initial rage ebbing away along with her pride and aspirations. But crumbs of understanding scattered her way from time to time, and she took them when she could.

Alvis wasn't dead; he was in a magical sleep. He was dying, yes, but slowly; he could be saved if someone found him and wished to help. She didn't think anyone would help him, though was unsure if that was because he was hidden or because they didn't care.

This chamber under Yfirgardr was a magical siphon, strongest here at its core. It drew magic from mages to fuel the protective wards that encased Hjorrfold. When she'd entered the stairwell, it had started draining her magic in earnest. By the time she'd reached the chamber, she was as good as dead.

Her body was gone. She was trapped at the place of her death because the shock had rendered her from her body. But that physical tie should've still been strong enough to draw her in, unless it'd been burned to ash. There was no hope of her leaving this place, not with the hold it had on her.

Except…perhaps she could escape. Cracks were forming in the wards. They were so small, like spiderwebs glistening over the glow of magic, that she couldn't trust that they were there at all. But as time—that immeasurable force that continued to propel the world outside the darkness forward—passed, the fissures grew. They eroded the magic, and soon, wisps of the outside became apparent. She no longer held a physical form, so it was unclear how big they would need to be for her to slip out. If she waited, they would grow, and then—

And then what, exactly?

Her own, albeit limited, recollection of the world told her this place was a blessing and a curse. Unbound spirits had something akin to freedom, but they had no tether. They roamed, aimless unless the living could somehow contain them long enough to give them purpose. With no grave beyond this place, she would be a leaf on the wind, at the mercy of forces beyond her control. She'd gotten a taste of helplessness already in this tomb, but at least she was slowly regaining herself. Outside…would it undo all her progress?

There were greater concerns than her own sanity. The wards kept her in, but they also kept something *out* of Hjorrfold. Her skill at ancient runes was by no means small, and she'd pieced together the desperate necessity that had driven the former kings and queens to create this space of power. There was something terrible outside that was trying to claw its way in, something that craved the ruin of Yfirgardr. Was her own desperation to exist worth losing the kingdom she'd worked so hard to protect?

"Wake up," she hissed at her husband. If he were awake, he could *do* something. Whatever was destroying the wards, he could stop it. Whatever doom awaited their kingdom, he could take charge and act. Magicless as he was, he wasn't incompetent. He must know why his ancestors had built this place. He'd maintained it, hadn't he? Alvis could do what was necessary, and then she could worry about herself.

"Husband, there is work to be done."

But he couldn't hear her. More dead than alive, he should've been receptive to the shades of the dead, but he slept on. Even Havardr, far less magically inclined than Alvis, seemed to sense her presence; he was always looking over his shoulder when he came to administer a tonic to his father and drain his blood. If she whispered in his ear, the hairs at the back of his neck prickled, and she could taste his unease.

"You killed me . . ."

He ran away each time.

Eventually, a hole grew so large she could stick her fingers through it. Not that she had fingers, not truly, but it was hard to free herself of the physical limitations that had bound her. She didn't need a shape to drift about, yet she often clung to the ghostly visage of her former self. If she could shed her mind's need for a body, perhaps she could wiggle through—

"Alvis," she hissed as she kneeled beside him. He didn't stir, but she was out of patience. He needed to know, so she reached her ghoulish hands into his head. She couldn't feel the hard, cold stone of this chamber. She couldn't smell the dried blood or musty bones. But she could feel the squishy insides of her husband, wet and pliable as she wiggled her fingers.

She closed her eyes and thought of the failing wards, the cracks and their dimming light, of Havardr's visits and her husband's prone form. She pushed each memory through her being into Alvis. When she finished, she watched him carefully.

He frowned, his peace finally disturbed.

Satisfied that she'd done what was necessary (more than anyone should expect of her, given the circumstances), she flew to the crack. She'd given years of her dedication and talents to Hjorrfold. Given her life for this land, really, and she was done with it. In Andiby, they appreciated her. In Andiby, they had the skill and insight to notice her presence.

Ingegerd would never again draw breath, but in Andiby she might find a new life for herself, born from the dregs of her death.

It took all her concentration to let go of her insistence on form. Bit by bit, she whittled away the appearance of hands and feet, the limbs and torso and head she'd never been without. She no longer needed any of it; so long as she could keep hold of her essence, her true self, she would continue on. Once she'd shed those last little bits of her human form, she pushed through the crack and fled east.

Not once did she look back.

46
Stigandr

521

Tessa was lovely, so peaceful with sleep and the morning light softening her features. There was no scowl or calculating look that she often wore in the Great Hall, just her ebony hair framing her face, her lips curled into an almost smile.

This is your last chance to kill her, Stigandr thought. *This is the last chance. She knows who you are. She knows everything. If she turns against you . . .*

The voice, the words, they didn't sound like his. Was that his mother's voice? He didn't know, and he couldn't stop his hand from coming up to rest at her throat. Her breathing was even, deep, unbothered. It would be so easy to take her by surprise, to choke the life out of her. Use the confusion to take what was rightfully his—

He jolted upright in alarm, yanking himself so far away from Tessa that he nearly fell out of the bed. His heart beat erratically in his chest, his breathing painful as he drew in lungfuls of air.

There was no morning light creeping through the windows: outside, the night sky was tinted with the first whispers of drawn. And Tessa lay in the bed, her back to him, blissfully unaware of his panicked state.

A nightmare.

A fucking awful one at that. He buried his face in his hands and stifled a groan. He didn't know where the sudden, unwelcome dream had come from. It'd been born of fear, and the irreversible nature of what had happened. Death was the only way to break their newly forged bond. Death was the only guarantee of her secrecy. Death was the best impetus to force everyone's hand.

It was what Drusilla would do. It was, in a way, what she had done to her husband's kin to become clan leader. He'd seen it firsthand, even helped. Her counsel to him would be to forget his heart and instead secure his birthright. His mother, a woman who'd spent his life sniffing out prophecies and eliminating anyone who threatened their family's power, would've wanted the same.

He couldn't, though. Death might be necessary to set things right in Hjorrfold, but Stigandr would do whatever possible to ensure it wouldn't be her death. Never hers.

When he felt more himself again, he lowered his hands and watched her sleep until he was sure he'd chased away the echoes of that dream.

"No one will harm you," he whispered. "I promise. Not even me."

Deciding to seal the oath with a kiss, he leaned in and placed his lips against her temple.

No sooner had he kissed her than Reka began barking in the hallway.

"Tessa," he said, but she was already rousing. "Someone's coming."

Tessa cursed under her breath as she pulled out of his grasp and climbed out of the bed. He suspected she was still half-asleep as she pulled a robe over her naked form and walked towards the door. Stigandr, well-rested from sleeping in his true form for the first time in months, slipped from her bed as well and concealed himself with an invisibility spell. It wouldn't fool anyone who got close, but he suspected no one would. By the time the knock came, Tessa was presentable, and Stigandr was nowhere to be seen.

"Yes?" Tessa asked gruffly when she opened the door, and Reka rushed inside. It was Ove in full armor, grim-faced as ever, but with a touch of nerves Stigandr had never seen in him before. Tessa must not have liked what she saw either, because her shoulders tensed at the sight of him. "What is it?"

"Raiders have been spotted northwest of the keep," he said in a strained voice. Too formal, his words clipped as if he wished to get them out so quickly he didn't quite finish them. "They've gone through two homesteads already, killing and burning and taking all they can. A rider came—"

"Wake the barracks," she snapped. "Send someone to the stables. We'll need at least twenty horses saddled and ready to ride within a half hour. Find as many guards as you can who are ready to help. I'll meet you in the courtyard."

It looked like Tessa was about to slam the door in his face, but she noticed his hesitation and stopped short.

"What?"

"Ashk is missing," he said. "We've already rounded up everyone in the barracks and those that went to town. I don't know if something happened to him—"

While he spoke, Tessa peeked over her shoulder. Stigandr could see her slight frown at the empty bed and the way her eyes scanned the room to find him, but it seemed Ove noticed nothing amiss.

"I'm sure he's fine," she interrupted. "Give me ten minutes."

Ove was off before she'd shut the door, but Stigandr waited until the latch clicked to dissolve his invisibility illusion. Reka, who had jumped on the bed and was lying there as if she owned it, perked up and barked at him excitedly. Tessa froze, only for an instant, and then continued over to the wardrobe.

"Get dressed," she said and discarded her robe. "I assume you heard."

"I did." He remembered he too was naked, and looked for his scattered clothing and armor. "I hope I didn't...offend you by hiding. I thought it best not to be discovered like this."

"I agree." Her back was to him as she pulled on her tunic and breeches with remarkable speed. Her braids were messier than usual, but there'd be no time to fix them; they'd be out of her way once a helmet was in place, anyway. He got distracted watching her pull on her belt with its great silver dog emblem. She cast him a disapproving look when she caught him not only staring at her, but completely disregarding his own state of undress.

"You ride with us," she said as she reached for her armor—thick leather pressed with patterns that he longed to rub his fingers over, wondering what tales they would tell of her past battles.

She was far more impressive in her armor than he was in his. She was the very embodiment of a skjaldmaer, especially when she picked up her war hammer. Her helmet was a thing of beauty, charcoal metal with ram's horns framing her face, a gold frame where it traced along her cheekbones, around her eyes, and down to the tip of her nose. It brought out her pale skin and the dark depths of her eyes. He looked like one of a dozen, an average guard with whatever armor they could scrape together, repaired where needed and mismatched decorative touches.

"Can you use a bow?" she asked as she kneeled by the hearth, the fire low and dim.

"I was a hunter when I was in Bjardleith."

She paused, a full three heartbeats as she took in this information and its implications, then placed it aside. "Good. Take a bow and quiver from the armory. Get one for me as well." She reached into the soot and dirtied her fingers, then ran them down her cheeks and below her chin so there were three lines of ash. He raised an eyebrow at her, but she shrugged. "Tradition. Since my first fight in Fyrrey. Do you have a helmet?"

"I don't need a helmet for guard duty."

She walked over to him and clapped him on the shoulder. "You need a helmet for raiders," she said. Her hand lingered.

He took it in his and brought it to his lips, kissing the back of it. "It will be an honor to fight by your side, Tessa of Hundrfeld."

"It will be an honor to have you," she said, "Stigandr of Yfirgardr. Though you're likely to give everyone a heart attack if you go out there like that."

It felt good to wear his own face, but he agreed; it wasn't the time to reveal himself to the castle at large. Closing his eyes as he concentrated, he tried to piece together Ashk's features to cover his own; his skin tingled at the effort. When he opened his eyes, she was looking at him in puzzlement.

"I can...I can still see you underneath it. Like a mask made of fog."

Oh. She was feeling the effect of their bond. He'd have a lot harder time deceiving her with magic, and he couldn't really regret that. It was comforting to know she could see him through his glamor.

"You can do magic now," he said, hinting at their bond but too afraid to say it outright. "And you've already seen my face. You know me."

Despite a fierce warrior standing before him, about to ride out to defend and likely kill, her expression softened. "Do I?" She leaned in and cupped his cheeks in her hands, rubbing one thumb across his skin, almost as if to wipe away the magic clouding it. "I liked Ashk's face," she whispered before dipping in for a kiss. "But I might like Stigandr's more."

Reka was annoyed to be left behind, pacing in a circle when they closed the door on her. Tessa and Stigandr parted when they reached the courtyard, Tessa rushing over to the gathered guards while Stigandr went to the armory for bows, arrows, and the first helmet he could find that almost fit. It was a tad too tight and would give him a headache, but it didn't fall over his eyes, so it would have to do. He arrived as Tessa finished yelling out orders.

She locked eyes with him, and he tossed her a bow and quiver. Ove did a double take when he spotted Stigandr approaching.

"Ashk! Where have you been?" he barked.

"Why weren't you at your post?" Tessa said, voice like steel.

"I—"

"He wasn't on duty," Ove said in his defense. "I rounded everyone up, and he was the only one unaccounted for. Had me worried to death you were lying dead in an alley!"

Something about the way he said it, the sharp gleam of haunted memories peeking out, made it seem he dreaded it from experience. Before Stigandr could apologize, Tessa snapped, "Scold him on the way. Innocent people may very well be dying while you complain about how a man on leave spends his time."

They jogged down the great hill of Yfirgardr, a half mile of winding roads through the sleeping city. Despite the early hour, the sound of so many boots moving in unison drew some onlookers to their windows and doors, earning them both worried and curious gazes. At the city gate, horses were waiting for them, and Tessa was the first to mount. She stood in the stirrups and cupped a hand around her mouth.

"If you ride well, ride with me! Know that we go to fight. You may need to take a life today, but know you do so to protect those who need us. This is why we joined the guard! To wield our weapons to serve the land that bore us and our families.

"If you stay behind, don't feel ashamed: we need people to defend Yfirgardr and its people. With raiders this close, your strength is needed here to safeguard our home. All of Hjorrfold does its part, and we are no different." She raised her hammer above her head as easily as if it weighed nothing. "For Hjorrfold!" she bellowed, voice like thunder.

"For Hjorrfold!" they all cried, lifting their own weapons. Stigandr joined in as well, adding his voice to the chants. "For Hjorrfold! Hjorrfold!"

There were plenty of horses across Hjorrfold, but it was the merchants and the farmers and the hunters who rode them with any regularity; the king's raiders didn't need to know how to ride as their raiding was all by sea, and the city guard had no need of horses within the walls. If a band had set out when Stigandr was last at the keep, he wouldn't expect more than a handful to be able to ride at all.

But because of circumstances, Tessa had been forced to recruit guards from beyond those who usually enlisted. There were a great number of merchants and farmers and hunters among them. As the dozen or so who could ride rushed to find horses, Stigandr was prepared to push his way through them if need be—he wouldn't let Tessa leave without him—but was able to get one without much difficulty. He found a light-brown mare with a thick white mane. She looked gentle but fleet-footed, and she was calm despite the ruckus. A good mount.

Tessa whistled and raced off with Ove close behind. They all hurried to catch up, driving the poor horses hard so they could get to the fight as quickly as possible. Every moment lost could mean someone's life, their home, their livelihood, and he could practically taste Tessa's anxious worry through their bond. It wasn't glory she rode for; she had meant what she'd said about helping people.

That alone made her more worthy than Havardr.

They rode north, Tessa in the lead. She checked each small homestead they passed. Most were quiet, with only a few men and women awake to begin the day's work. Tessa would slow down enough to speak with the wary peasants.

"Raiders were spotted north of here," Tessa would tell them. "Stay armed and close to home. Someone from the guard will check on you before the day is out to let you know all is well."

Stigandr watched again and again as their faces grew pale with fear and they scurried back into their homes. Often he could hear the door bolted shut, though sometimes they reappeared with pitchforks and axes to stand guard over the small patch of land that was their life.

After an hour of cantering northward, the sun brightening more and more of the way, they came across a homestead where no one was out and about for chores. This time, Tessa held up a hand to warn them to keep their distance and nudged her own mount closer.

"My name is Tessa," she called, voice even and smooth, weaponless hands plain as day. "I come with warriors from the city guard at Yfirgardr. We've been told there are raiders nearby. Are you well?"

A slit opened in the door to reveal a pair of eyes. "We are well here," a man's muffled voice called back. "But we have men and women who escaped from Leidby. The raiders got their village, then went—" The eyes disappeared and there was the sound of hushed conversation before the man reappeared. "They were going east, toward Marrtoft."

Ove, who was a few paces in front of Stigandr, tensed so much his horse threw its mane and snorted.

"Is anyone injured?" Tessa asked. "Do you need a healer?"

The man shook his head, dark eyes going back and forth in the slit. "As I said, we're well." A pause, then a hesitating voice, "Would any of your guards be able to stay? We've many children and no means to fight or run off with them if we're attacked."

"Of course," Tessa said with a curt nod, and Stigandr balked as she pointed to five in quick succession to step forward. She introduced them, each bowing awkwardly in turn from their saddles, though they preened at being personally selected for such a task. "They will patrol the area and protect you should the need arise."

"That's a quarter of your men," Stigandr muttered as they started back to the flattened dirt that passed for a road. "You don't even know how many raiders—"

"They were never coming with me to fight," she said, a faint hint of annoyance until she saw either who she was talking to or something in his expression. Her tone was kinder when she said, "You're all here for this very thing: to help the people out here. I can't be everywhere at once." Then she whistled and nudged her horse, off so fast that Stigandr's poor mare couldn't hope to catch up.

The land in Hjorrfold was not a single flat plain, but miles and miles of grassland interrupted by stony hills and rivers, sometimes so abruptly that you could fall right off the edge of a crag or into a river if you were unfamiliar with the land. They were well away from Yfirgardr by now, stretching their party's knowledge of the area. Their progress was slowed as more and more rocky hills jutted out into the path, no longer safe for the horses to run at more than a trot.

Smoke started to peek out on the horizon between hills, and Stigandr could feel Tessa's frustration. But when they rounded a bend and found a clear stretch of flat-appearing land with a cluster of smoldering buildings a mile out, Tessa took off at a gallop. They all urged on their own horses, but there was no catching her. She yelled a wordless war cry as they drew near, the wind amplifying it so much he was certain she must be using magic to do it.

Specks rushed from the buildings, men and women who shouted back in a pale imitation of Tessa's cry. They raised their weapons and shook them as if to scare her off, little good it did them. It was only when Tessa took off her own bow and nocked an arrow that Stigandr remembered *he* had a bow, too. Tessa had let two arrows fly before he'd readied his own bow off his back, and both had hit their targets before he'd gotten an arrow out. Then there was the uncomfortable balancing act of riding at a gallop without holding on while also trying to hold the bow, never mind aim and fire.

A few of the other guards shot, though some went well short, and those that were closest stuck into the ground and walls near the raiders. Three more arrows flew from Tessa's bow in quick succession. When they hit arms and legs and shoulders, never the chest or head of their armor-clad enemies, Stigandr knew that was not because Tessa's aim had faltered: she was targeting the less protected areas... and the less lethal ones. She wasn't trying to kill them.

Stigandr gave up on the arrow. He wasn't a good enough shot to compensate for his riding. He was better off making it there in one piece so he could actually help, so he focused on small magical pushes to redirect the few arrows and spears sent their way so that they fell aside harmlessly.

Tessa soon tossed away her own bow, quiver empty. She'd almost reached the wooden wall that enclosed half the settlement, and Stigandr concentrated all his energy on knocking aside any weapon thrown her way. With impossible grace, she crouched low on her saddle, one hand still on the reins as she guided her horse to the wall, then sprang onto it. She pulled her war hammer off her back as she ran along the thin stone wall.

The rest of them had arrived at the opening, those skilled with bows staying mounted to shoot at the cornered raiders while others dismounted and drew their swords.

"Protect the livestock!" Ove bellowed, leading those on foot to the pen at the far end of the village. "Look for survivors!"

Stigandr, the least used to following orders, dismounted and followed Tessa. He held his shield up to protect his right side while he kept his left to the wall, a dagger in hand. Tessa, it appeared, didn't much care for shields: she hadn't even brought one.

The curve of the wall brought her to where a wagon was overladen with cargo. Instead of precious treasures like coins and jewelry and furniture, it seemed stuffed with food and furs. A circle of six large, burly men who would dwarf even Havardr stood protectively around their prize with swords drawn. Stigandr raced to help as Tessa landed on the ground only three paces away from them.

"Go now, and I'll let you," she said. Stigandr was panting as he ran, but she stood there, no more breathless than if she'd been idly watching the events unfold.

One man scoffed at her. "Take your own advice, love," he said, though not unkindly. "Leave us be. We don't want trouble."

"You want at least a little," she said. "Thieves know trouble finds them."

Stigandr halted when he was finally close enough; able to join the fight at any time, he remained distant to maintain a safe position for spell casting. With their reach and his dagger, he was of more use with his magic than his blade.

"Don't bother," another man grumbled. "They're from the capital. They can't understand."

"Don't presume," Tessa said. "Last warning. You're lucky I offer any at all."

"We can't walk away without this wagon," the first man said. "If you'll let us leave with it—"

"I won't allow people under my protection to starve because you can't be bothered to find honest work." Her hands tightened on the shaft of her hammer, and she dug her feet into the dirt. Such small shifts that Stigandr recognized all too well from the training pitch, but the men before her didn't notice at all; they faced great danger, yet they couldn't see Tessa for what she was.

She was more than fair, letting them make the first move. One man dove at her, and she even let him get a step before she sprang into action. She ducked his attack and swung the blunted edge of the hammer hard into his belly. He cried out and collapsed in pain, his own weapon forgotten as he choked up blood. The other five were on her, circling her as if she might change her mind and wish to flee.

Without a hint of fear, she ducked and swung to take out the legs of another man. Still, they thought they had the upper hand, even as she kicked her second victim in the gut before pulling back her hammer for another blow. With a swift, fluid motion, she spun around and sent two more of the men staggering back from the fury of her attack. While they struggled to regain their ground, the remaining two hesitated; uncertainty flickered in their eyes as they shared a panicked look.

Their indecision evaporated when she knocked one of their comrades so hard he flew ten feet through the air before hitting their own wagon. It shook violently on its wheels, and a barrel rolled out and shattered on the ground, potatoes spilling everywhere. They grabbed their still-mobile friend and ran toward the gate, abandoning their weapons and injured friends in their haste to escape.

They ran past Stigandr, no more concerned about his presence than if he were a rabbit at the side of the road. He cast a look at Tessa, who merely shrugged as if their escape didn't bother her. As soon as they'd disappeared through the gate and out into the open, she turned her attention back to the three she'd felled.

"If I leave you here, will you do anything foolish until I come back?" she asked, though only groans answered her. When she was satisfied they would indeed stay put, she relaxed and walked over to Stigandr. She swatted his arm. "What's the point of all that practice if you aren't going to help fight?"

His chest clenched tightly around his heart. For months, he'd known he'd admired and respected Tessa; it'd been weeks since he'd been forced to acknowledge the more tender feelings he felt for her. In that instant, he understood it was more than that. Despite the urgency of the day, she'd remained unrattled. He'd seen her skill firsthand every night they'd sparred together, yet nothing could have prepared him for her sheer grace in battle. She was beautiful, strong, and so damned dedicated to any task laid before her. She'd had every right to kill them, but she'd let those men go.

Stigandr was in love with her, and the weight of the realization hit him as hard as her hammer. Harder even, because at least that was a blow he might recover from. This revelation changed him forever; there would be no coming back from loving Tessa of Hundrfeld.

"You seem to have handled it just fine on your own." How could he speak when his world had crashed around him? He sheathed his dagger as he tried to regain his composure. He felt a little embarrassed that he hadn't contributed at all, not from the moment they'd set out from Yfirgardr, but in all honesty, he couldn't have done anything better than she had. He couldn't muster the guard or order them about as efficiently as her, and if it had been left to him to fight off those six men, the fight would still be going on, and not much in his favor. "You done this before?"

"Fight?" She looked affronted, and he couldn't help but laugh.

"No, I meant..." He gestured at the poor ruined village. The guards had rounded up a few of the other raiders and, along with the villagers, had put out the fires. He wasn't even sure what to call it. Leading? Providing aid? Defending people? These were all things she'd been doing in Yfirgardr, though it was one thing to do it in the safety of the Great Hall. His father had excelled at it, never getting his hands dirty but getting the credit all the same. Stigandr had never quite seen the hypocrisy of such rule before.

"Oh." Tessa gave a one-shoulder shrug. "There's never been raiders this close." She appraised him, and for a wild moment, he feared she could see the change in his heart, but she said, "I thought once or twice an arrow was going to hit me."

"There were many arrows that flew," he acknowledged and glanced over his shoulder. "Strange you noticed they were coming for you, but didn't think to dodge them."

"Aye, I noticed them, but when the first few took an abrupt turn from my skull, I thought perhaps I needn't worry about them." She put her hammer on her back, wielding it like it weighed nothing at all. She took off her helmet—hair wild and sweat-dampened—to wipe her brow.

"How fortunate, then, that their aim was so poor." He put his hands on his hips to mask the sudden worry he felt now that his heart lived in someone else, someone who rode headlong into danger with so little regard for her own safety. "Why wouldn't a seasoned warrior bring a shield with her, I wonder?"

"Because hammers require two hands, and shields are too bulky when you want to ride and run at speed." She opened her mouth to speak again, but something behind him caught her eye and she stopped.

"The village is secure, m'lady," Ove said. He had a splatter of blood on his cheek and his chest was covered in mud; despite the victory, he still sounded tense.

Tessa nodded and put her helmet back on. "I'll question the prisoners. See if there are more of them or if this is it. Take ten guards to check the other homesteads nearby. Start east of here."

Ove huffed. "I needn't—"

"Go east first," she said firmly. Stigandr looked between them in confusion, but held his tongue. "That was the direction they were moving. We'll settle things here, and when you return, we'll move west to help the settlements already attacked. Hopefully, the worst has passed, but we won't know until I question the prisoners."

Ove clenched his fists, then abruptly relaxed. He bowed his head. "Yes, m'lady. Thank you."

She pointedly didn't respond. "I'm sending Ashk back to Yfirgardr."

Stigandr reeled as if slapped. She was sending him away? Ove looked equally surprised, though no doubt for different reasons.

"Ashk is a skilled warrior," Ove said. "Are you sure you want him to go?"

"I don't need extra protection," she said mildly. "Yes, he's skilled, which is why I can send him alone and know he'll arrive safely. He's an excellent rider, and Dagrun will know he speaks for me when he brings my orders." Then more firmly, she said, "Ove, go. With speed."

Ove hesitated only a few more breaths before he nodded and was off, barking orders to the men and women he wished to take with him.

"His family lives a few miles east of here," Tessa whispered. "He doesn't want any special treatment, so he resists whenever I offer them support. Granted, they need very little help, but he's earned any and every courtesy I bestow upon them."

Ah. That put his unusual disquiet today into better perspective.

"He's a decent man," Stigandr said. "Too honest for his own good."

"Warriors can afford to be honest," she said and gave him a once-over. "Princes seem to be the most duplicitous, in my experience."

Stigandr's cheeks went hot. "I—"

She cut him off. "Later. You need to head to Yfirgardr as soon as we can find you a suitable horse. We'll need supplies. Food first and foremost. Whatever can be spared. Load as many wagons as you can and have them ready to depart by morning. I don't want anyone traveling in the dark if we can help it. We'll need volunteers from among the citizens to help with the repairs as well. Offer a week's wages to anyone willing to come. If there are more in the guard able to ride, have them escort you. Your little arrow trick won't help if you're the only one there to fend off an attack."

"My arrow trick?" he asked, amused.

Tessa's lips twitched, but otherwise she ignored his interruption. "Arrange with Dagrun for grain distribution to increase both in the capital and in the larger towns. That should help those displaced by the attacks and deter future ones."

"How will it deter more attacks?"

"Did you see their loot?" Tessa pointed at the wagon. A chicken was fluttering down from it, clucking indignantly. "They're just hungry. It's a short harvest this year, and Havardr's war has pushed many from their own lands. If they're fed, they'll have no reason to raid these people." Her expression hardened. "And if they do, they'll find I won't be so accommodating the next time."

A chill ran through him. Tessa had much of the mercy and justness that Trond and the nobles of Hundrfeld were known for, but there was a dark streak that lurked beneath. He'd noticed it before when she talked about Havardr. It reminded him of Drusilla, though in Drusilla, it had always been about practicality; Tessa's motivations seemed less charitable.

"Tessa," he said, though he didn't know what he would say. Luckily, he was interrupted by surprised cries, and when they looked around, they found the rather benign source of the commotion. Not another attack, not an escaped prisoner or a new building catching ablaze: it had begun to snow.

The first snowfall of the year.

"Winter's come," Tessa whispered. She lifted a hand to catch a snowflake and frowned down at it. "A royal union and a cruel winter. A prince's..."

His neck prickled. Her words had the air of prophecy to them, and she bore the same faraway look his mother had worn when her foreseen future unfolded before her.

"The seer in the keep," he guessed. "What did they tell you?"

Tessa blinked rapidly before she met his gaze. She coughed and rubbed her hand against her thigh. "We'll discuss it later. I need to talk to those raiders, and you need to get to Yfirgardr. Time isn't our friend, I fear."

"No," he said. "I suppose it isn't." He resisted the urge to take her into his arms. He craved to caress her cheek and kiss her goodbye, to reassure her that together they could work everything out. Fully aware of how public their farewell was, instead he put a hand on her shoulder and squeezed through her armor. "Stay safe," he said. "I'll be back on the morrow. Try to dodge any errant arrows until then, please."

With a put-upon sigh, she placed her hand over his briefly. "I'll do my best. Go. We both have much to do." She stepped into his space, close enough that he could smell her sweat and see that even in sunlight, her eyes were black pits of darkness. "It goes both ways. You need to stay safe, too."

"I will," he promised, and then he turned on his heel and walked away before he did anything stupid.

47
Tessa

521

HANDLING THE RAIDER situation, blessedly, took all of Tessa's attention for several days. She camped in Marrtoft—the village where she'd scared off the raiders—as she oversaw all the necessary work. It took many sweeps of the land before she was satisfied the danger was over, but still she coordinated with the local villages to arm them and, when necessary, station guards there for protection. The repair efforts were no simple matter either, now that winter had fallen: it was getting too cold to mend the worst of the damage, and so people had to be relocated. Families like Ove's took in those with nowhere to go, though many elected to try their luck in Yfirgardr.

Trond had always shown her that generosity and understanding went further than punishing desperate people. If the choice was starvation or theft, it was hardly a choice at all. The grain distribution would hopefully deter future raids. Why take by force what was freely given?

Only when she'd managed everything and yet still lingered in the northern homesteads was she forced to acknowledge the truth: she was avoiding the return to Yfirgardr.

She, of course, wanted to be thorough in her efforts to support the common people, but she'd exhausted every reasonable excuse for delay. The longer she was away, the more she risked the Council eroding her place within Yfirgardr. Worse, she risked missing any news of Havardr. She couldn't afford to have him catch her unawares, nor did she want anyone else getting any news before her.

But she felt weak for admitting the true reason for her reluctance.

Stigandr.

He'd returned from Yfirgardr with everything she'd asked for. She could have ordered him away again, back to the city, but she didn't. She could've claimed she kept him close out of fear he might usurp her as regent; in truth, she liked having him nearby. It was comforting, reminding her of the charge into Marrtoft when he'd protected her.

Out in the countryside, it was easy to maintain distance. When they returned to the city, there'd be no more excuses.

To his credit, he didn't act any differently than he had before. He was, as ever, Ashk. He was loyal and quietly competent, and he was there if needed, but didn't impose himself on her. She could sense he wished to speak with her, felt it in a way that made her wonder whether magic was involved, but while her heart longed for that as well, her head dreaded it.

Could she trust Stigandr the way she had Ashk? Was all she'd come to feel a deception?

Dagrun was right to suspect him.

But he's earned Ove's respect through his work in the guard. A prince working such a menial job and performing it as though it's not beneath him...

The seer said I could trust him.

Little one, Trond's voice whispered to her. *Why do you seek everyone else's opinions? Talk to him yourself and trust your own instincts. That is what we do in Hundrfeld: we sniff out those who are worthy and ignore the rest.*

And are you worthy, Stigandr of Yfirgardr? she asked herself again and again, never sure of the right answer but knowing what she wished it to be.

On the eve of their return, she walked among the people of Marrtoft. Since this was the most intact of the plundered homesteads, it was easiest to repair. It consisted of some twenty or so stone buildings with mossy roofs, and she found the place quite charming and its people wonderfully kind. The hustle and bustle, the people amicably sharing the too-cramped spaces, it reminded her of the rough winters in Hundrfeld when the farmers would come to stay at the keep, sometimes cramming inside the courtyard walls during the worst storms. That feeling of community had always stuck with her, a reminder of how the lord of a keep was meant to serve and protect his people, not the other way around.

The people greeted her as she passed, though she was pleased to note they no longer had urgent need of her. For days, she'd had barely two spare moments together before someone was seeking her aid or counsel. The relative calm that had settled was a good sign, and further proof that she should return to Yfirgardr.

"Everyone should learn to wield a knife."

Tessa stopped short when she heard Stigandr's voice. She followed it behind a row of small huts and found Stigandr surrounded by a dozen children. The youngest of them looked to be about five, the oldest a teenage boy that didn't quite reach Stigandr's shoulder. They all had knives in their hands and stood in a line like warriors doing drills.

"I cut vegetables with my ma," one small boy said. Indeed, his knife looked more suited for a kitchen than a fight.

"Excellent," Stigandr said. "Who else has used a knife before? In the kitchen or for hunting or whittling?"

Several of the children raised their hands, and Stigandr nodded approvingly.

"Very good. Using a knife is very useful, yes? It can also save your life if your home is attacked and your parents aren't around to defend you. Now, let's do some practice."

Tessa stood there, leaning against the hut and watching as Stigandr taught peasant children how to use a knife. His patience with them, the care he took to teach them, and the way they looked so thoroughly enchanted with him, were so endearing she could almost forgive him for his lies and deceptions. There was a kind heart in him.

"Now remember," he said when the lesson was over, "the first thing you should do is run or hide. Knowing how to defend yourself doesn't mean it's the best option. It's a last resort. Understood?"

"Yes, sir," they said, not quite in unison. A few looked relieved that he'd given them permission not to fight, and she appreciated that he'd made such an offer. Trond had left the choice to her if she wanted to fight, and she'd taken it because it seemed the only way to get close to Havardr; if left solely to Havardr, she'd have spent years in Vaettfangkirk with no escape until they'd deemed her finished. It was good to see that not all of Alvis' children were so callous in how they treated their subjects.

As the children scattered, Stigandr finally turned enough to notice her in the shadows. He looked around and saw what she already knew: they were alone.

"I didn't realize we had an audience," he said wryly.

"You were doing so well. I didn't want to interrupt." Now that she knew who he was, it was difficult to look at him head-on. She could see Ashk's familiar face over Stigandr's true one, a strange effect where his skin seemed to shimmer and his features changed depending on the way the light hit him. He was both men and neither at the same time. The only consistent thing was his green eyes shining like emeralds through his magic, no longer contained by Ashk's muddy brown.

"Your presence is never unwanted," he said, then hesitated. "I should apologize—"

"Walk with me." They were alone, yes, but who knew what ears and eyes hid behind these walls, so Tessa turned on her heel and started toward the main entrance into the village. Without looking, she sensed Stigandr rushing to catch up to her before he fell into step just behind her. They weaved through the more congested square where the guard was camped and the supplies of wagons were being unloaded to return to Yfirgardr for more grain. Carefully, she picked her way through the crowd past the wall, then walked along it until the noise had all but died out behind them. Soon the only sound was their boots crunching on the recently fallen snow.

"Do you know any magic that can keep this conversation private?" she asked and slowed so they were side by side. She kept walking, though, because it gave her a way to expend some of her nervous energy.

He didn't react at first, then raised a glowing hand and muttered words she didn't understand. His hand glowed faintly, and she felt a slight tickle as something passed over her like a wave, invisible yet there, no matter how gently it pushed over her.

"People can still hear us," he said. "Though they won't be able to make out the words." He paused, then began: "Tessa, I'm sorry for deceiving you for so long. You have every right to be angry with—"

She cut him off, because she *did* have every right and she *was* angry, but she had secrets of her own and could perhaps be persuaded he was justified in lying. She kept her voice level and devoid of any feeling as she asked, "And why did you conceal yourself? I cannot consider your apology without an explanation, no matter how heartfelt your words might seem."

"Why did I conceal myself?" He was so shocked that he came to a stop, and she had to stop with him. "Wouldn't you? My brother all but stole the throne for himself and brought war upon Hjorrfold and our neighbors. I know what they say about my mother's death and my brother and my father's disappearance, but I know Havardr, and I can only guess at what part he played in things. A man so willing to send his people to war and do spirits know what to his own kin…

"And then there was his regent, some woman I'd never heard of and the daughter of his dearest friend. Aye, you kept the peace for him, but what else might you have been obligated to do? My brother would like nothing more than to see me in chains or in exile, if not outright dead. I couldn't risk my life on chance until I'd gotten to know you for myself."

Fair points, all of them, though she hadn't quite expected him to be aware of his brother's character. Havardr had never hidden his ambitious and devious nature in his visits to Hundrfeld, but he'd been a different sort of man in Yfirgardr. Charming in the way he spoke to the Council, respectful to the warriors. He was the type of man who appealed to the masses, a champion for the common citizens who could take pride in his exploits. He didn't need to hide before Tessa and Trond, but he would've had reason to deceive his family.

He *had* deceived them, about her father's death at the very least.

But here was Stigandr, openly acknowledging his brother was dangerous. It showed he didn't lack sense.

"And how long did it take to learn my character?" she asked. It was the only line of questioning she had any right to pursue, given she agreed Havardr would not be pleased to have his brother in Yfirgardr. He would certainly hate knowing they were talking, sharing their dislike of him.

Conspiring.

"Not long," he admitted. "I hadn't known you for a week, and I knew you were not at all like my brother."

Her first reaction was relief that he'd realized so early on that she wasn't at all like Havardr; then she counted the months and days that had intervened since his realization, and his continued silence. "Then why—?"

"It wasn't your character that was in question, but your loyalty," he said urgently. He tentatively reached for her hands, and she allowed him to take them in his. "You might not be as bloodthirsty or greedy as Havardr, but if you'd sworn him your oath, you'd be compelled to follow his command, just or unjust. It isn't my life but my kingdom that I risk."

He looked desperate to make her understand, and with that single word, she knew all too well what he'd feared.

Loyalty.

Hundrfeld had been loyal to Yfirgardr since the capital was built, and her ancestors had helped carve out the first borders of Hjorrfold centuries ago. Loyalty was built into the foundations of Hundrfeld, and if she appeared to have given that loyalty to Havardr as her father had, Stigandr would be right to doubt her.

"You needn't fear," she said as she soaked in the warmth of his hands. "I've sworn that man no oath, nor will I. My family swore to serve Hjorrfold five hundred years ago, and that's what I've done. What I'll continue to do, in the manner I think best suits the people and not some haughty prince."

While she'd tried to remain calm, by the end she was practically spitting the words with the vehemence of her disgust for Havardr.

Stigandr frowned, his grip on her hands loosening. "You don't like my brother, yet you serve in his name."

Tessa snorted before she could help herself. "I despise that man," she said, helpless to contain her sneer as she said it.

Stigandr opened his mouth to speak, hesitated, then said, "I don't mean to sound insensitive, given my own feelings for Havardr, but... what has he done to earn your ill regard?"

"You think it's unwarranted?"

"No," Stigandr said, and it immediately soothed her flash of anger that he might doubt her. "I'm sure he's earned it, but I can't help but wonder how. He and Sindri..." Again, he seemed to struggle for words. "Your father and Havardr were so devoted to each other that I assumed you would feel something of that as well. An obligation to your father's memory, perhaps, or to the way he's lifted you before the court. All we've seen is the good he's done for your family, and no doubt that's by his own machinations, but it leaves no ground for your dislike to stand on."

Her body went rigid. In all her plans to ruin Havardr, she'd only thought about the people of Hjorrfold in the sense that they were something she would take from him: their trust, their admiration, their loyalty. He was so obviously a despicable man in her eyes that it hadn't occurred to her that *she* might seem traitorous for acting against him. The world hadn't seen what he'd done to her family behind closed doors. Would she seem the villain of this story?

"Whatever it was," Stigandr soothed, pulling her closer to him by their joined hands, "I believe it. You're too just a woman to hate a man for some meager slight."

She blinked away the frustrated tears that had formed and looked up into Stigandr's earnest green eyes. "He killed my father," she whispered. "Havardr used him, then killed him when he was done, and now he means to use me. For what, I don't know. I thought he wanted me to be his weapon of conquest, but he's gone to Fjarriheimr without me..."

"Probably so he doesn't have to share the glory," Stigandr said, and then frowned. "Hang on. Did you say Havardr killed Sindri? Are you certain?"

"They went hunting together." Her voice was as cold as ice. She could picture it all too well, the image as clear as any of her own childhood memories. The two youths walking through the forest together. Her father laughing and enjoying the time with his friend. And then the spear in his back, the confusion in his eyes until they grew dark. She doubted he believed it even when Havardr stood over him. "It wasn't my father who came back, but his body. Havardr said a boar gored him, but Trond says the wound looked like it was from a spear. The seer who visited, they let me ask questions about the past, present, and future. When I asked about my father..."

"They confirmed it," he whispered. He took her hands to his lips and placed the lightest of kisses there, his gaze never leaving hers. "I'm sorry," he said with a grief that echoed her own. "I knew Sindri when I was a boy. Kinder by far than my brother. I...I didn't even know he was dead. He'd stopped coming to the castle, but Havardr still visited him in Hundrfeld, or so he claimed—"

It was too much, looking at him, so she pulled away and continued their walk around the wall. She kept her pace slow and her back to him so she could collect herself.

"He visited to make sure I was progressing as the little warrior he wanted." This time, there was scorn lurking beneath the surface. "I truly don't know what he plans to do with me, but he's spent too much time at the grindstone sharpening me into a blade."

Stigandr grabbed her arm and held her tight. When she tried to keep walking, he pulled and swung her towards him. "If you knew this, why did you come to Yfirgardr? Why this act of submission to him? Tessa, *why* would you do this to yourself? Whatever duty you feel to Hjorrfold, no one would fault you for refusing him."

Her heart ached. She imagined that world where she'd walked away. Where she wasn't forced into this sham of doing Havardr's bidding. It was a peaceful kind of life...and one where she wouldn't have met Stigandr. Where there was no one in Yfirgardr to help the people while Havardr fucked off to the ends of the world. Even if it'd been possible, knowing what she knew now, she wouldn't have been able to make a different choice.

"You know I don't walk away from a challenge," she said ruefully. "Compliance bought my uncle his life and my people more gold than any other keep in Hjorrfold can claim. Now that I'm in Yfirgardr, Havardr no more looks at Hundrfeld than any other distant keep. They're safe in obscurity." A faint smile crossed her lips as she imagined Havardr's ignorance lasting until it was too late. "He'll never see it coming when I slash his throat and leave everything he loves in ruins. He cares for his name and his glory, as you say. I will lift mine and yours and Ragnhild's and Randel's and everyone else's above his so that his name is less than the dirt beneath his feet. Once everyone sees how rotten his heart is, only then will I use my father's dagger to kill him like the treacherous rat he is."

Stigandr swallowed thickly, and Tessa realized how cold-hearted she must seem. As righteous as her quest for vengeance was, Havardr was still his brother. Tessa had no such family to speak of, but she could only imagine listening to someone threaten Trond with the same intensity.

She stepped out of his arms. "I shouldn't have burdened you with this. It isn't fair of me. For better or worse, he's your brother. I would never expect you to help me."

Stigandr took in a ragged breath. "He is my brother," he agreed, an admission that seemed to pain him. "I...I don't know that I could ever kill him myself. I've killed people before, but only in defense of myself or others. And they were strangers in the heat of battle. My brother..." He shook his head and clenched his fists. "He'd destroy Hjorrfold to get what he wants, without ever acknowledging the destruction he's wrought. He would walk through this village and the others, some razed to the ground by raiders driven here because of his damned war, and he would rather cast the blame on those villagers for not defending themselves or us for not getting there sooner. The consequences of his actions are never his to confront, and it will be all our ruin. I might not be able to strike the blow, but I won't stand in the way of what needs to be done."

He offered her his hand. Not in the tender way he had before, but in the way merchants did when they struck a deal or the nobles when they made a pact.

"We work together to stop Havardr," he offered.

Her fingers stretched out to accept his offer, but she hesitated. "And when it's done?"

"You can go back to Hundrfeld or stay in Yfirgardr. I'll need to find out the truth about what happened to my family. I'll want to visit my father and Randel, find my sister...but I can do none of this until I know Hjorrfold is safe."

It was both reassuring and disappointing. What more could she want from him? A partnership benefited them both, especially when their aim was the same.

She took his hand and clasped it tightly; he didn't flinch.

"I accept," she said. "Together, we stop your brother and save Hjorrfold."

48
Havardr

521

HAVARDR'S BRIDE LAY on the low bed, her silver hair cascading over her bare back. He watched the gentle rise and fall of her ribs as she breathed deeply. It had been a long day, filled with wedding rituals Havardr neither cared for nor understood. He'd been washed and anointed in oils, then dressed in a long tunic that resembled his mother's gowns more than anything a warrior might wear. The sash around his waist had been too long and too tight, and it had annoyed him the whole time he'd been stuck in their too-white temple enduring hours of prayer in a language he didn't think a single one of them understood, the priest included.

And that was simply to 'bless' the marriage: the wedding itself came later at dusk, when they'd stood before the king's high throne. His bride had undone his sash and then tied one end around his hand, wrapping it all the way to his forearm. He'd done the same to her, binding them together for the rest of the night as they sat on the ground before the low tables barely a foot off the ground and ate the wedding feast, feeding each other the first bites from each dish.

He supposed there was poetry in the ceremony. He could appreciate the meaning behind it. It didn't make him enjoy the process, though, and in very Hjorrfold-fashion, he'd lifted his bride at the end of it, swung her over his shoulder, and marched her to the wedding chambers while his men and women whistled and the Fjarriheimr nobility tried not to appear too offended by the bawdy jeers.

His bride—Idonea, he'd learned during the ceremony, and he supposed he should remember it—had gone to bed willingly enough. Not enthusiastically, but he'd had no need of that. So long as she feigned devotion in public, even in the muted way of Fjarriheimr, he would be satisfied. He needed heirs, not a happy wife, and if she valued her place in this new order of things, she would want those heirs as well.

The bed was little more than a feather mattress on the ground. Comfortable in its way, but disorienting to wake up on. It was like being in the tents at camp until he opened his eyes and found not damp canvas and barren walls, but silk curtains and splendid furniture. When he'd reached to rub the sleep from his eyes, he remembered his arm was still bound to Idonea's.

He unwound the sash and left her to sleep. The damned thing had gotten in the way, and he'd had to rip Idonea's clothes off before he took her. His own clothes were stiflingly hot; he removed them with his newly freed hand and strode across the floor to the large balcony that overlooked the city. Fjarriheimr's capital wasn't as pristine as its palace, though it had been laid out with more intention than Yfirgardr. Yfirgardr had sprung up piecemeal over centuries, people building what they needed when they needed it, wherever they could find the space to do so; this city was laid out like a star with the palace at its center, long streets stretching out to the city walls with such precision he was sure he could walk them blindfolded and not get lost.

It was a strange place, this. And it belonged to him.

Havardr smiled, gratified by his success. There had been moments when he'd doubted, moments when he'd regretted leaving Tessa in Yfirgardr because he could have unleashed her on this hostile land. But as impressive as this conquest was, he knew greater things were to come: he needed to show that he was the true architect of Hjorrfold's glory. In the wars to come, her part was as his weapon, and what a weapon she was foretold to be.

His mind wandered to images of that magnificent future, and he reveled in the possibilities that awaited him. He was so lost in thought, it was a chill wind that snapped him back to reality. He shivered, recognizing how deeply the cold had already settled, and when he looked out to the night sky, he saw fluffy wisps of snow dancing to the ground. He blinked in the vain hope he was mistaken.

He wasn't.

"Bjarngrim's ass," he cursed and stormed back inside.

His steps were so loud, Idonea jerked awake. She reached blindly for the blankets, but froze when she saw him. It took visible effort for her to relax and not cling to the wrinkled silk.

"Husband?" she murmured, eyes downcast. Her displays of submission, especially after her arrogance when they first met, were the most attractive thing about her. "What's the matter?"

He was searching the room for anything more reasonable to wear than that ridiculous wedding gown, but it seemed few of his things had been brought in. He'd rather go naked than wear anything from Fjarriheimr ever again. Finally, he found a light tunic that would have to do. "We must return to Yfirgardr. Immediately. The first snow has come. It's only a matter of time before we're trapped out here."

In this bizarre land where we'll all grow soft and meek like you…

There was a flash of something akin to relief in her eyes. "What supplies will you need? If there's anything you need of me while you're gone—"

Havardr pulled the tunic in place and glared at her, his stare so hard the words died in her throat.

"You're coming with me," he said firmly, so that she couldn't mistake his departure as her escape from her wifely duties. When she stiffened, he huffed in amusement before turning his back on her; he still needed to find a belt and boots. "As my wife, you'll need to be with me until you've produced several heirs. Then, assuming things are settled in Fjarriheimr, you might be able to return under guard."

"Of course," she said, voice hollow.

"I'll leave Kerr in charge here. Your father may… *advise* him." Havardr wasn't convinced the old man knew he'd lost his kingdom. Any wisdom he offered would need to be taken with several grains of salt. "Have your servants pack whatever you wish to bring. You may take a few of your maids with you, but no more than a wagon can be spared for you and your attendants."

He fastened his belt, a thick leather one he'd had made last year—the buckle showed the fall of Thrireyna—and turned to her. He'd expected a flash of hatred or desolation in her gaze before she'd mastered herself; instead, it was more of the resignation she'd worn throughout their wedding. He could almost pity her…if only her father's weakness hadn't been what had put her here.

Havardr, with more courtesy than he felt she deserved, nodded curtly before leaving the room to find Kerr and Hakon.

Sten should've already arrived in Yfirgardr. The roads were fair, but the injured would've slowed them down. Havardr's journey might take longer still: the soldiers were tired from war, lazy from celebrating, and at any moment a storm could bury the roads and force them to camp lest they risk freezing to death. Though if the storms were as bad as they'd gotten on Thrireyna, it was a matter of choosing between freezing while sitting in their tents versus while marching on. Havardr would always pick the latter.

He wouldn't let it happen. They'd leave quickly and gain as much ground as possible before the weather turned on them.

The former king of Fjarriheimr must be kept under heavy guard. Havardr would rather kill him outright, but the old fool was more useful as a hostage. He didn't deserve to become a martyr, and Havardr refused to consider the humiliation of having to reconquer what he'd already won. He'd rather burn it all to the ground than give it up, even temporarily.

The army would have to be divided. A large force would need to stay to maintain the peace here, though food would be scarce. Under the new law, they could demand tribute from the locals who lived farther west than the capital, in the lands unravaged by war. Yes, that would work. It would force them to come to the capital for food, and then Kerr could keep better watch over them. It would also be a good show of force, the first edict in the name of their new prince.

So much to be done…he'd planned on remaining another month to oversee such details before departing. Perhaps this was for the better. He was done with Fjarriheimr, after all. Best return to Yfirgardr to regroup and plan his next campaign. It was too soon to go for the southern continent, which left the eastern or southern islands, or perhaps Bjardleith or Andiby.

Andiby. He shuddered to think of an entire land filled with people like his mother. A more impressive target than more islands, but they wouldn't be an easy people to subdue.

He thought of Tessa, and the way she'd destroyed whole villages single-handedly. Maybe he'd been thinking of her wrong. She needn't always be a weapon. He should use her as a shield, protecting himself from the dangerous, mage-infested lands while sending her to do the dirty work. Andiby was small. Its conquest wouldn't be nearly as impressive as Fjarriheimr or even Thrireyna. An acceptable trophy to allow Tessa.

That was it. He would return, enjoy a small reprieve from fighting while his wife bore him a child, and meanwhile he could send Tessa off to Andiby once spring came.

Cheered by having a plan in place, he felt no remorse barging into the banquet hall to demand his generals meet with him. It would be a long night.

49
Stigandr

521

ASIDE FROM THE new frenetic energy that had taken hold of the city, Yfirgardr was much the same as they'd left it. There was an underlying sense of anxiety now that winter had arrived, not only for the turning weather but how it might strain Hjorrfold's resources to combat storms and inland raiders. Thankfully, people were too busy going about their day, living as best they could despite the strain of new faces trying to find their way in the city they'd only ever heard of but never seen.

Though Stigandr wanted nothing more than to stay with Tessa in the Great Hall as she listened to the petitioners and caught up on the never-ending tasks of running a kingdom, there was more need than ever for the city guard. There were too many people, all troubled and some looking for an excuse to take out their worries on others. He and the guards patrolled the streets, especially near the taverns and markets. Stigandr was pleased to see several dogs happily sitting in doorways, watching with interest anyone who approached their new homes. Stigandr was glad he could help in the small ways, but it irked him not to do more.

Was this not his kingdom to safeguard? Would Tessa and his people not blame him for sitting idly by while she dealt with the Council and shouldered the burden of rule? He was *right here*, yet he did nothing. At least Tessa didn't seem to begrudge him his secrecy. And given her independent streak, he wasn't sure any interference would be welcome should he offer.

Ask her, you fool, he told himself. *She knows the truth now. Show her you're committed to making up for the deception.*

Despite his specific skills in magic, he preferred hiding and not outright lying. This was an opportunity to be the man he truly was, and he should take it.

Easier said than done, of course. When he returned to the keep for dinner and rest, there was no chance to approach Tessa. She was surrounded at all times, so much so that she barely had a spare moment to eat. Reka, back at her mistress' side, seemed just as annoyed as he that Tessa was constantly bombarded by requests. It was only when Dagrun appeared and shooed people away that Tessa could eat the stew and bread growing cold before her, and Stigandr didn't have the heart to invade her moment of reprieve.

Later, when they all left the Great Hall for their evening duties or the barracks, he finally found his chance: instead of leaving with the rest of the guards to the courtyard, he slipped into the hall that led to the meeting rooms.

"Tessa," he called, relieved that she stopped and waited for him. "How are you?"

"Busy, though little more than usual." She squinted at him, as though trying to see through the magic masking his face. When she settled on his eyes, he couldn't tell if she'd been successful or not. "How's the city?"

"Adjusting, but people are nervous." Reka poked at his hand and licked it, so he patted her head and rubbed behind her ears. "Better, I think, now that you've returned. They hear raiders and they're afraid, but you give them confidence."

Tessa was at a loss for words.

"Do you…" He hesitated. "Would it help if…if Stigandr were here to help you?"

Her expression softened. "I appreciate your offering, but there is so much upheaval already that I fear the return of a lost prince would only make things worse."

"I understand," he said, and hoped she heard his sincerity. "The offer stands, whenever you think the benefits outweigh the drawbacks."

She raised her eyebrows. "And how quickly upon your return before Havardr arrives with the full force of his army behind him?"

"Depends," he said.

"On?"

"How far away he is."

The hustle and bustle of the Great Hall followed them into the corridor, several nobles crashing through the door and giving them curious looks as they went to the Council chambers. Tessa straightened up to her full height and crossed her arms over her chest, her warning scowl and Reka's low growl keeping them silent as they passed. Alone once more, it seemed their time together was at an end.

"They seem eager to monopolize your evening," he said cheerfully.

Tessa rolled her eyes. "They usually are. They have concerns about the aid I've given out, as though the grain wasn't collected from the very people I gave it to. And naturally, the prospect of their own homes being attacked has them all on edge. As if being lord of a keep doesn't make that same keep your responsibility."

"Hjorrfold has known centuries of peace except at the farthest edges," he said. None of the few Council meetings he'd attended had ever broached the topic of safety. "And even then, it hasn't been so very dangerous. It's easy to become complacent under such circumstances."

"I suppose," she said, though it sounded like she disagreed. She no doubt thought of how her family had not, in that same span of time, neglected the defenses of Hundrfeld. After a last glare at the closed Council doors, she turned back to him. "Will I see you on the pitch tonight?" she asked lightly so it would fool anyone who might overhear.

"I think we have much to practice," he agreed amiably. He angled his chest so that only she could see his hands as he worked the spell he had in Marrtoft that would muffle their words. "But perhaps we should go elsewhere. I think we've exhausted how much you can improve your fighting skills without magic."

Her eyes stayed fixed on his hands and the faint glow around them. "Do you wish to make me your apprentice?"

Stigandr had taught no novice anything magical in his life—how would one begin to do so?—but he supposed he should have made such considerations before he'd encouraged Tessa to learn magic. Who but he in Yfirgardr could help her work on the magic she sought for battle, even if he knew very little of it himself? The fundamentals he could impart readily enough.

"Not an apprentice," he said. They weren't pupil and teacher, just like when they'd practiced and sparred together. They were equals, only offset in experience. "But I can help. The courtyard is a rather...public space to refine your skills."

She looked back at him. "And where might we go instead? I've nearly set fire to my room a dozen times."

A couple of servants walked past them, pressing against the walls so as not to disrupt them. Stigandr waited until they were at the far end of the long corridor before he next spoke.

"My room has been enchanted so that no one can enter unless they have magic, and there are charms to protect against magical damage." The only other place that might be safer would be his mother's chambers, but he didn't want to go in there again, regardless.

She considered. "And you'd be able to remove your disguise. I'm sure that will be some relief to you."

"It would." Did she want to see his face? His heart leapt at the possibility. He had a strange sort of jealousy that she might prefer Ashk over him, as though they weren't one and the same.

"Very well. The usual time, but in your room." She started to walk off, then called over her shoulder, "Bring a weapon."

With no shame, Stigandr watched her disappear into the Council chambers and left him back to his life as Ashk, the city guard. Still, it was with no small amount of anticipation that he went back to duty, whistling and smiling the rest of the day.

STIGANDR WAITED UNTIL the castle had settled for the night before slipping away from the barracks. There was still pink in the sky, and he took the most direct route to the third floor, yet he was late: the door was ajar when he arrived. He found Tessa sitting at his desk, a small thing that had suited him just fine as a young boy but that he'd outgrown by the time he was twelve. He'd kept it, since it at least provided him a flat surface on which to write, though it'd hurt his legs to sit there too long. It was wholly inadequate for anything else—he'd had to use the floor or some of the alchemist workshops many times—though Tessa looked at home.

It was a cozy image, and it struck him so hard he stopped dead in the doorway.

Tessa, in his room, as comfortable as if it were her own.

"Do you need an invitation?" she teased, and it jerked him back into action. Quickly, he shut the door and removed Ashk's face, shuddering with the dissipating magic. It always felt good to shed that faux skin and the burden of maintaining it; with Tessa's keen gaze on him, it was not unlike undressing.

He spread out his hands to reveal the real him. "Better?" he asked and hoped she did indeed find his true self more intriguing than the fake.

Her head tilted so she could inspect him from head to toe before saying, "That nose suits you more. And the eyes." She stood from the desk and gestured to the neat pile of scrolls stacked there. "When you suggested I practice magic, I didn't know where to turn. The kitchen servants helped me with house magic, which was useful as a starting point, but so far from what I wanted. The only mage I knew of in Yfirgardr was, well, *you*."

Stigandr walked over, a slight heat rising in his cheeks, and picked up one of the scrolls. He unrolled it, fairly certain what he would find when he did so, and was unsurprised when his own scribbled notes greeted him. "Defensive Shields and Warding," he read aloud, a faint smile pulling at his lips. "You read this?"

"And a few others. I'll admit, your notes helped clarify the confounding language these ancient elders used to conceal their true wisdom. What is the point of writing all this down to share with others if they won't be able to understand a word of it?"

"The language of the learned is meant to be difficult, to keep the unworthy, aka the less educated and the poor, from accessing it. I had the best tutors and the best magical minds in Hjorrfold to help me, and still look at all the notes I had to take just to make sense of it. These"—he placed a hand on the pile of scrolls—"are the defensive and offensive magics I never meant to master myself. Reading these works and going through the process of analyzing them was more an exercise I undertook to better my understanding of magic as a whole."

"So you can't teach them to me?" She made no effort to hide her disappointment, and he was tempted to lie and oversell his abilities just to have her esteem once more.

"I have no particular knack for that kind of magic and have practiced it very little, so I can't teach it to you the way I can the ointments to conserve your energy or the wards I placed in my room. I am, however, able to help you manage your magic and can work through them with you. Think of it as though you were teaching me to use a longsword. It's not your weapon of choice, but you have enough skill in similar weapons and in fighting as a whole that your instruction would be far better than if I attempted it on my own."

Tessa considered before nodding. "All right. Where do we start?"

"At the beginning," he said regretfully. "That shield you produced was impressive, but how much it drained your energy tells me you weren't ready for that level of exertion. We should work on more basic magic to increase your endurance and slowly work on the shields and attacks that will most help you in battle."

Though disappointed, Tessa didn't protest.

He tested her knowledge to better understand what she'd learned already. There was reluctance in her answers, and she hesitated to demonstrate anything. He'd never seen her so unsure of herself, and he credited it to her years at Vaettfangkirk, where inadequacies were handled with brutal efficiency. But his easy acceptance of whatever she said or did, whether successful or not, helped her relax, and soon she was more forthcoming.

She was unrefined in her methods. Her hand motions were jerky, and she frowned as she worked, as though concentrating very hard. If speaking was necessary for a spell, her voice lacked its usual confidence. But still, she had a great well of power to draw from. Raw talent was on her side, as well as her thorough nature. As they worked on harder spells and he corrected her, she asked question after question, and would practice several more times after he'd been satisfied with her performance.

"You said it was difficult to start?" He offered her a drink. He'd pilfered a flask from the kitchens that morning, hoping to share it with her. Not mead, but an aged wine that his parents had favored at celebrations. "The magic didn't come to you easily?"

She took a swig, handed it back, and nodded. "I did everything the servants had shown me, but I could barely light a flame. It was like something was missing inside. This necessary piece to make it all come together."

"And you found it," he said more than asked. "Everyone needs something different to access their magic. For some, it's a clear mind. For others, they draw from what's around them. Nature, perhaps, or a talisman. But for most, strong emotions channel their power. Anger, love, desperation, pride, I've seen many of these fuel the mages at court. It's best for lighting a spark but becomes difficult to control after that."

"Which is it for you?"

Stigandr shrugged. "I learned magic before I could read. Little things, of course. I don't remember what it was to start, though I suspect it was a desire to make my mother proud. I was her favorite, and I suppose I wanted to repay that affection in the only way I knew how. Now, magic is like walking or breathing: I just do it." Then, his curiosity got the better of him. "What about you? Clearly, it's been coming together for you since you started. Where does your power come from?"

If he'd had to guess, he'd have expected it would be clarity. He saw her determination on the training pitch, the way she could narrow her focus to what was in front of her. He could picture her meditating, forcing that same clarity into her magical practice. Sheer determination and a refusal to accept failure.

"Happiness," she said simply. "I got Reka, and I remembered how proud my uncle is of me, and that I have friends here who support me...and that was it. I was happy despite all the pressure and the challenges still before me. It brought a sort of peace that calmed everything enough that I could find the magic." She shook her head. "I never knew that kind of power could be inside me. In anyone, really. I hadn't thought about where it comes from when a mage casts their spells."

Happiness... Reka and friends... I helped make her happy, in some small way...

"Magical education in Hjorrfold is rather lacking," he agreed. Over his own lifetime, he'd seen it fall in eminence. The respected scholarly mages who'd been employed to tutor the royal princes had been the last vestiges of that old way, but his mother's descent into obsession had tainted the court's view of magic at the same time Havardr's raids laid honors upon those who lived by their blade. His ancestor, Bjarngrim, who'd founded Yfirgardr a half-millennium ago, had been a great warrior mage, yet it was also he who'd forced his children to pick one or the other: magic or sword. Perhaps he didn't want the competition, but it had become a tradition so deep-rooted that Stigandr himself was the closest of a blend between the two arts, and he was by his own admission a poor warrior.

"Is there any reason?" she asked. "We barely use small magic in Hundrfeld. It's all tonics and charms, left to healers and midwives. If it can do so much, why is it so little practiced?"

Stigandr huffed in amusement. "I have about a dozen books on my shelves that discuss that very question, each filled with history and opinions and sermonizing on how things ought to be instead of describing how things are."

"But I didn't ask for their thoughts on the matter," she challenged. "I wanted yours."

"Well..." He'd often been scolded by tutors for doing just that: giving his thoughts. Magic was about study and pursuing knowledge. Only the true masters might dare voice their opinions, because they were no longer considered opinions but observations of fact. Until one had reached such a lofty position, it was better to keep one's mouth shut. Though that had never stopped him from having opinions. "For all its history, for all the magic in the land and its people, Hjorrfold at its root prides itself on its raiders and warriors. We've begrudgingly taken up trade and farming, because we've grown too big to rely solely on what we can take, but every little boy and girl plays at raider. You can throw swords and shields and plunder onto a warrior's funeral pyre. What could they throw on a mage's?"

"You wouldn't want them to throw all your scrolls and books on there with you?"

Though she said it in jest, he answered seriously. "Preferably not. Though perhaps if you were to use battle magic, it might pique people's interest to have a warrior mage once more."

Their practice done, Stigandr lectured her on the most boring but necessary part: recovery. Before the raids up north, he'd started to gather the ingredients necessary to make more ointment; he'd found the rest while out among the homesteads. Together, they made a new batch as he spoke of the other methods he could show her and harped on the importance of rest.

"Sleep is the best cure, as is a hearty meal." He finished rubbing the ointment onto his hands. When he offered her the jar, she instead gave him her hands. He tried to rein in his smirk as he applied the ointment for her. In her wrists, he could see her pulse fluttering.

"You seem nervous," he said. It was strange to think he could make her nervous when she didn't hesitate to run headlong into battle or stand before petitioners in the Great Hall. She was in the least danger around him.

Tessa's smile was weak, and she flexed her hands in his, only accentuating her nerves. "I've never taken anyone to bed besides you. I'm... not familiar with the best way to do this."

"You've never taken anyone to bed before," he repeated, trying out the words and enjoying how they tasted. He'd finished with the ointment, but he kept hold of her hands.

"I've had little opportunity," she said defensively. "And when I did, I didn't like anyone enough to."

He grinned wide. It was no love confession, but it warmed him immensely to hear. "You like me, then?"

"Against my better judgement," she said wryly, though at least she seemed more at ease.

He stepped closer to her, hesitating before placing his hands on her shoulders. "You need never be nervous on my account. I've not taken many lovers either, so we can learn this together."

Tessa raised an eyebrow. "The handsome prince hasn't taken many lovers?"

"Am I handsome?" He couldn't contain his delight at the compliment.

"You know you are."

"Maybe, but I only care that you think so." He lifted her chin and leaned in. "I've been enchanted by your beauty and strength since I met you. It's gratifying to know at least some measure of my affection is returned."

It was Tessa who closed the small distance and kissed him. It was as electric as the first time, his skin alight everywhere they touched and his magic rejoicing as it reached for hers. He wondered if she could feel it too, their nascent bond rejoicing whenever they were close. His blood had been singing with joy when they'd practiced magic earlier—could Tessa recognize what was happening?

The kiss was soft at first before Tessa's lips parted, and he greedily took advantage. Greedy as he was, he let her set the pace as their kisses deepened and their hands roamed in hungry exploration. Tessa was the one who removed his armor and tunic while directing him to do the same to hers. When she was naked before him, beautiful and strong, he fell to his knees before her.

"I'm yours, my lady," he breathed against her navel and kissed her soft skin.

She threaded her fingers through his hair. "Show me," she ordered, and he was all too willing to comply…

Afterwards, they lay tangled together on Stigandr's bed. Even as his breathing calmed, he couldn't imagine his heart would ever stop its wild rhythm. Tessa of Hundrfeld was in his bed.

She held his hand against her chest—her heartbeat not so erratic as his—as her eyelids fluttered shut. She wasn't asleep, he knew, but he took the opportunity to drink in his fill of her. There wasn't much of Sindri in her, he thought. Little pieces that reminded him of his brother's friend, but so little that he would never have found them without knowing to look. Some of it was the way she carried herself, far more serious than Stigandr had ever seen Sindri, even when paying respect to Alvis and Ingegerd. Sindri had always seemed to him a carefree youth chasing adventure and enjoying ample freedom as the younger son of a noble house.

She must get the hair and eyes from her mother, he mused, *and the scowl from her uncle.*

The responsibility she'd borne from a young age, even without Havardr's imposition on her education and training...he supposed it was natural enough she wasn't prone to smiles.

His woolen cover masked most of her body, but as she shifted to wiggle closer to him, it slipped and exposed her right shoulder. The puckered line of a scar, long healed but without magic, glinted in the silver moonlight.

"How'd you get this?" he whispered, rubbing his thumb over it. It was so perfectly straight it must've been a weapon, and deep if it had left such a mark.

"In my first battle on Fyrrey. I was sloppy." More quietly, she mumbled, "Never had to fight for my life before."

He remembered the first time he'd had to fight to survive; it wasn't a feeling easily forgotten, sometimes chasing him into his dreams years after he'd thought he'd overcome it.

"The healers here are quite good," he said. "Couldn't you get the scar removed?"

Some wore their battle scars as a mark of pride, but only those that were likely to be seen. Besides, most nobles didn't. Their lack of scars, despite their battles, was what was sought. The marks on their shield and blade were evidence of their prowess, not blemishes marring their skin.

Tessa opened her eyes and stared at him, as if she were trying to wheedle his thoughts out of him. "I like the reminder," she eventually said, the sleepy note in her voice gone.

He leaned over to kiss the scar and settled back so he could meet her gaze. "Of what? The risks of battle?"

She shook her head. "That I'm not in Vaettfangkirk anymore."

Vaettfangkirk...he wished he'd asked his sister more about that wretched place and what they'd done to her. He had half a mind to raze the sanctuary to the ground on their behalf, though he suspected neither woman would much appreciate it.

"What happened to the person who did it?"

"Dead," she said flatly, her voice free of anger or pride. A matter of fact, and unrelated to the wound she bore.

"Ah. I should've guessed." He had in fact known there was no other answer to that question. If Havardr had been injured like that, he'd have been less than merciful. He would've taken out his angry embarrassment on the poor fool, making sure it hurt. Tessa's answer was so disinterested, he imagined she hadn't even broken her stride as she slit his throat and moved on to the next victim.

"I don't enjoy killing," she said, as if reading his mind. Whether it was their bond at work or she simply knew him well enough to guess, he couldn't say. "I let plenty of people go if they surrendered. But he'd drawn blood, and no one surrenders when they think they stand a chance. Though his death might've bought a few of his comrades their lives, having seen it."

"Like the raiders at Marrtoft." The men who'd only given up once they'd seen her take down three large men in quick succession. If one of them had injured her, he wondered if they'd have pressed their luck.

"What's this?" she asked. Her fingers ran across his left arm; he didn't have to look to know she meant the tattoo so few had seen.

"A warding," he said. He remembered all too well the day he got it. The stink of the magic ink and the shock of the first needle prick before the real pain set in. "My father made all four of us get it when we were children. It's to protect us when we're outside of Hjorrfold. From vengeful spirits and ill omens." This last part he said with a mockery of his father's severe tone.

Tessa traced the runic letters, ancient like the ones in the tomb beneath the city and equally indecipherable. "Does it work?" she asked.

"Well, I'm still alive after living outside Hjorrfold for years, so perhaps. Havardr comes and goes all the time with no ghosts bearing down on him, as far as I know. Now, if Ragnhild ever comes home safe and sound, that might give it more credence. I doubt Randel will ever go far enough to test it."

"It's magic, then? It looks like symbols I've seen in your scrolls." She looked at him for confirmation, and he nodded. "I thought your mother was the mage, not your father."

"She was," he said. Stigandr still wasn't used to her being gone. If he knew any death magic, perhaps he'd be able to find her spirit, but all her magic from Andiby she'd kept from him. Always 'not yet' or 'you're not ready.' Now it was too late. "But my father knows some. Old magic that's been with our family since the keep was first built." Again, he thought of the tomb and the damn lock. What was his father thinking, leaving? Who was maintaining the wards?

"He doesn't understand it, though. Follows the rituals as he knows them. Like the tattoos. It might just be superstition at this point, honestly. You follow what your parents did, as they followed theirs, on and on, but along the way, someone gets it wrong. An errant mark or a forgotten line, and then it's worthless."

She leaned in and kissed the inked skin; her warmth spread through him like a brand. "Not worthless," she said. "It shows you're loved."

Stigandr swallowed thickly, words escaping him.

"And what did your mother give you to protect you?" she asked.

"A compass."

"A compass?" Her confusion was adorable and not unfounded; he didn't understand the gift much either.

He rolled away from her to reach over the edge of the bed. He dug through his clothes until he found the small chain he wore looped on the inside of his belt and carefully extracted it. On it was the compass from his mother, the snowflake from Drusilla, and a small flat metal seal like a coin that bore a crude rendition of his portrait along with the details of his name and birth on one side, the royal seal on the other. The 'proof' of his identity his father had given him years ago before unceremoniously sending him from Hjorrfold. He handed them to her, and she inspected each before settling on the compass.

"Your mother gave this to you?" She dragged her thumb along the grooves that marked the outer edge, looking uncannily like Ingegerd when she did so that he had to shake his head to dispel the image.

"She said it'd always point the way home."

"It won't point you anywhere." She pulled away from him and got out of bed, rummaging through her own clothing. Stigandr stole a moment to trace the lines of muscle in her arms, the sweep of her collarbones, the swell of her breasts, before she returned and sat cross-legged on the bed. She tossed him his compass and held up a second.

"This is the compass I used on the way back from Thrireyna," she said and offered it to him. He sat up to inspect the two metal discs.

At first, they seemed identical. The same size, the same weight, the same polished gold with holes and indentations to mark stars. He knew sailors used them to navigate, but he'd so rarely been at sea and never himself been in charge of navigating the way. If he were ever lost and couldn't use the sun to get his bearings, the compass would be useless to him. When he put them side by side in his palm, he could see they weren't the same. The star charts were different, in a few places by a small shift, but in others, they showed completely different constellations.

Tessa took hers back. "Perhaps the view of the sky is different in Andiby," she said, though she sounded skeptical.

"Perhaps," he agreed. Strange that his mother would give him the charm like a precious talisman without explaining it. He tied it back onto his belt. Just another secret of his mother's that he'd never be able to unravel. "Though I don't plan on getting so lost that I need to find out."

"Good," she purred and pulled him close. "I like you right where you are…"

50
Tessa

521

TESSA HAD NEVER taken a lover before, and she hoarded her time with Stigandr. It was rare that they could share moments as their true selves, Tessa without the burden of regency and Stigandr without the guise of Ashk. They spent almost every night in Stigandr's childhood room, sharing a meal, working on magic, and then tumbling into bed together more often than not.

It was the happiest time of her whole life.

She felt guilty thinking so, given the deepening winter and the fear that grew among the people. Her days were filled with meetings and reports, pleas and petitioners, with barely a spare moment for herself. Yet no one could say she didn't work her hardest: no matter how much she craved her nights with Stigandr, she neglected no aspect of her responsibilities.

But her heart and her soul lived for dusk.

She craved everything about their time together. Tessa had always loved the feel of tired muscles after a day's hard work, a desire to earn her rest so deep-seated in her blood that she didn't think Vaettfangkirk had given it to her. Exploited it, yes, but it was too intrinsic a part of her. She sought it still, despite there being no threat of punishment if she chose not to push herself to the brink. This magical strain was different while being the same, and she leaned into it with Stigandr's help: she would be a warrior like none had seen for centuries, and Havardr would rue the day he'd thought to use her.

The softer, quieter parts delighted her, too. The thrill of sex and the tired embrace afterward carried with it a peace she had never known. She'd never imagined a partner for herself, and though she'd not thought of herself as above anyone else, there was something gratifying about finding an equal.

They shared and shared, and each new revelation endeared him to her more.

He told her about how he had been sent to Bjardleith by his parents, and all that he'd learned there and his suspicions about why he'd been sent. He talked about his childhood, his siblings, and his deep wish that Havardr was the boy he'd once been and not the man he'd become. And her favorite was when he told her stories of his childhood, ones completely disconnected from the throne and their current troubles. Climbing the cliffs at the back of the city. Playing hide and seek with the other children of the keep. The songs the nannies would sing while they played games in the courtyard.

And she in turn wove a tapestry of her life before Yfirgardr. What it was like to grow up in Hundrfeld with her uncle, as loved as any child could wish to be and spoiled by everyone in the keep. The dogs that would trail after her, the other children who didn't care about her distinction as future lady of the keep, and the travel around the homesteads and farms that paid tribute to Hundrfeld. She even told him of her first hunt, the adventure of taking down the elk bare-handed, and then her uncle's concern, so palpable she could practically smell it over the beast's blood.

By the end of that first week, she felt she'd never known anyone better in all the world. Not even herself. But it couldn't last, their secret affair: his presence in Hundrfeld was too important to keep to herself.

She'd made the decision in the early morning when she had to sneak out of Stigandr's room back to her own so that the servants could find her. The secrecy gnawed at her, made her feel so dirty that she asked that a bath be made so she could scrub her guilt away. It didn't work, of course, but by the end she knew what she needed to do. Stigandr's presence could no longer be her confidence to keep, though she wouldn't break his trust by announcing it to anyone without first speaking with him. Tessa resolved to discuss it with him that night, if only to give herself one last day where Stigandr was hers and hers alone.

Even when they were safely tucked away in the tower, she greedily took the full night without mentioning it. What did it matter if she asked first thing upon seeing those green eyes or before they fell asleep tangled together? She wouldn't force him into the Great Hall to reveal himself in the middle of the night, so why ruin their time together?

And still, when the moment came, she let it slip by. Instead, she slept in his arms, head on his chest as his heart soothed her worries.

Guilt woke her in the dead of night. She slipped out of the bed, careful not to disturb Stigandr. As silently as she could, she pulled on a robe and went to the window. The moon was a thin, pale crescent in a clear sky glistening with stars: the first cloudless night since their return from the villages. Unblemished snow blanketed the land in every direction, but Tessa didn't look down at the valley behind the city. Instead, she looked outward into the dark, towards where the northerly mountains lay beyond sight, hidden beneath the invisible horizon. Somewhere out there to the northeast was Hundrfeld.

She stared so long, at first she thought she imagined the slight glimmer in the sky. A flash of green that made her blink and try to chase its afterimage. Soon there was another. Like a lightning bolt, almost, but gentler. A wave of yellowish-green light, so familiar her body ached with longing.

She held her breath and put a hand to the glass, willing the lights to come back, to prove they weren't some cruel trick of her imagination.

They did come back, flickers that grew more rhythmic as she watched, their shape distorted by the glass. In a fit of desperation, she found the window latch and pushed it open. The night was frigid and snatched the air right from her lungs, but she leaned out to be those precious few inches closer, closer…

It was too early for the true Ondljosbod, but there were the first hints of it, so distant Tessa didn't know if it hurt or soothed her to see this little tease of it, but there it was. She pulled the robe tighter around her with one hand and reached out with the other as if it was possible to beckon the lights closer. A laugh (or a cry) welled up inside her throat but got stuck on the way out, some shaky noise escaping instead, and the lights seemed to answer by sparkling orange for a second before dancing back into green.

"Aren't you cold?"

Tessa jumped as she was engulfed from behind, first by strong arms, then by a wool blanket. She glanced over her shoulder at Stigandr and offered an embarrassed smile.

"Yes, but it's worth it." She pointed to the farthest edge of the sky. "I never missed the Ondljosbod, even when I went to Vaettfangkirk. Not until I had to go to Thrireyna with your brother." She sighed, more melancholy than angry for once. "Just another thing to hold against him."

She felt Stigandr nod. "In this rare circumstance, I can offer in my brother's defense that the Ondljosbod has never been part of our traditions. The lights are so hard to see here that those who celebrate travel to see them, though I don't think there are many here who do. He likely didn't know it meant anything to you."

"So it wasn't an act of malice but of ignorance," she said. "He's so good at both, is he not?"

"Unfortunately," he agreed, and they fell silent as they watched. She preferred it this way, with Stigandr pressed against her, his presence and warmth making up for the homesickness welling up inside her. Better than watching alone, even if he couldn't quite keep the chill at bay.

"Do you look for anyone?" Stigandr asked, interrupting the silence. "Or do you simply enjoy the beauty of it?"

"Both. I look for my father. And my aunt and my cousin. And my mother. People whose faces I've never known and couldn't recognize, even if I did see them." She swallowed thickly.

"I've never had a connection to anyone who's died. Now, I suppose I'd look for my mother. She was fascinated with death. Mostly avoiding it, but she'd spoken at length about the traditions in Andiby. All the dead spirits she'd communed with. Her certainty that would be her fate. A dead guide to the living, always benefiting from her never-ending wisdom." He made a noise. Without seeing him, she couldn't tell if it was a scoff or a show of fondness. "She never said as much, though. My mother liked her secrets, and few were worthy of them. Not even my father, I think, was privileged to all of them."

They stood like that for so long her face went numb. Begrudgingly, she closed the window and slowly thawed as she leaned back against Stigandr's chest.

"I have to tell Dagrun and Ove about you," she whispered, hoping it wouldn't shatter the fragile happiness they'd found. "They are my most loyal and trusted advisers. I can't in good conscience deceive them any longer."

He kissed her shoulder. "Very well. Do you want me there when you tell them?"

"Yes," she said. "I think it best. They'll have questions, and I don't want to speak for you. Besides, they'll trust you more if they get a chance to know you."

He kissed a line up her neck. She tilted her head to give him better access, and he nibbled at her earlobe. "As you wish," he whispered. When she turned to catch his lips in a kiss, all her worries melted away. It was easy to feel invincible in his arms, shielded by the magic of his room and the silence of the night.

THAT INVINCIBILITY LEFT her after they parted in the morning.

Tessa summoned Dagrun and Ove, saying it was urgent that the three of them meet, then felt as though she held her breath while she waited. She paced back and forth in Alvis' office—the king's study next to the Council chambers, a floor away from Tessa's preferred room—while she waited. The space wasn't quite up to the task, giving her a narrow path of three strides past the window before she was forced to turn around again.

How would she go about this?

She needn't mention how she spent her evenings. There was no need to justify what she did in private, not when it hurt no one. Whether or not they approved didn't matter…yet she wanted that approval. Or failing that, their understanding. Dagrun and Ove were the only people outside of Hundrfeld who felt like friends, and she valued their opinion too highly to ignore their scorn.

She very much didn't want to choose between them and Stigandr.

Logically, she knew she wouldn't have to. Regardless of their personal feelings, Dagrun especially knew the political advantages of having a prince on their side. She might not yet know that there *were* sides, but it might be time to reveal more of her plans to them. Regarding her disdain for Havardr, Ove must have his suspicions. Their year on the islands together, sharing a dreki by sea and a tent on land, had left little room for secrets. Tessa knew better than to speak ill of Havardr, but she couldn't completely conceal her distaste. He'd seen the slips in her bland expression and neutral words often enough that he must know her true feelings were less than cordial.

Given Havardr's negligence of his duty and his people, she wasn't sure how anyone could still say his name without contempt.

They don't see it, she thought woefully. *They don't see what he truly is…*

They will, though. I'll just have to make them see.

"M'lady?"

Tessa startled out of her thoughts. Reka stirred from her nap by the fire, yawning and looking pitifully at Dagrun and Ove as they entered the room. Ove succumbed to the pup's silent pleas and stooped to rub her back; Dagrun closed the door behind them.

"Thank you for coming. Both of you." She stopped her pacing and moved to stand in front of King Alvis' impossibly large desk. It could seat four, six if you had a mind to. This room was where Tessa would meet privately with Councilors to address their individual concerns, though she seldom used it otherwise. Still, she'd thought this was the right place to have this meeting. Made it feel more official, more important. She rubbed her sweaty palms on her tunic and willed her staccato heart to calm.

"Of course," Dagrun said. "You said it was urgent."

"It is," she breathed out, then very carefully mimed the hand motions Stigandr had taught her. The spell was heavy on her tongue, but her magic obeyed. Her hands glowed as she finished her work, the space sealed from eavesdroppers.

"Look at you!" Ove said with delighted surprise. "The little miss learned some magic. I must say, I'm impressed—"

"Who taught you that?" Dagrun asked. She looked around the space, as though finally registering how odd this meeting was: the timing, the location, and suddenly the magic. "What's this about?"

"A mage has come to Yfirgardr," Tessa said. She tiptoed around the full truth of it, unable to dive right in. "I've been meeting with him to work on magic. I may need some in the coming days."

Dagrun stared at her blankly. "Meeting with a mage? When? Who? I know of everyone who's come to the keep, keep track of your meetings—"

"I thought you spent your evenings with Ashk." Ove stood, abandoning Reka and concentrating more on Tessa than he had since that day at the altar, like he hadn't been looking properly before and was trying to work something out. "When you disappeared from the training pitch, I'd thought you two'd…" His cheeks went nearly as red as his hair. He started over. "You mean to tell me you've been learning magic all that time?"

Dagrun looked startled. "What? Ove, what do you mean? Training pitch? Ashk?"

Ove shrugged one shoulder. "She'd been training with him most nights. Sparring and the like. Stopped a month ago, before the raid. Couldn't tell if they'd had a falling out or…" He coughed, embarrassed, as Dagrun gawked at him. "My point being, I didn't expect there to be any *magic* involved."

"Is Ashk the mage?" Dagrun asked, putting both the right and wrong pieces together.

"Don't be daft!" Ove scoffed. When Tessa was silent a beat too long, his head whipped around. "He isn't," he said. "He couldn't possibly be."

A knock at the door momentarily saved her from answering. Dagrun and Ove froze, but after a nod from Tessa, Dagrun opened the door.

It was, by their reckoning, Ashk who stepped through. She tried to see him from their perspective, to see if he carried himself any differently than he had before. It was hard to see the veneer when she knew what was beneath so much better. But she'd known Ashk first, and even now, she saw he was the same as he ever was: mild, uninteresting features, a solid build, and an unassuming air. When the door closed once more, he locked eyes with Tessa, silently asking if it was time. After she nodded, he spread his hands and let the magic fall away.

Ashk melted away to reveal Stigandr's vivid green eyes, his tall, lean frame, and a confidence that must come hand-in-hand with royal birth. Blond hair darkened and straightened, his nose shifted, and a prince stood before them.

Dagrun stiffened, and Ove looked as if he'd been struck.

"This is Stigandr," Tessa said. "Second born of King Alvis and the late Queen Ingegerd."

"Stigandr?" they said at once, both in awe but with different feelings behind it.

Dagrun gave him a calculating look, her expression closed off. It was the same face she wore in Council meetings and in the Great Hall, when her neutrality was her greatest asset for putting people at ease and masking her true thoughts.

Ove... Tessa didn't know how he felt. He seemed more conflicted about the prospect than Dagrun, yet he spoke first. "I can't believe I was ordering around a *prince*."

Stigandr bit his lip to keep from laughing.

"Where've you been all this time, lad?" Ove frowned. "Not a lad like you were when you left."

"I was twenty. Hardly a lad then, either."

"Twenty?" Ove frowned. "Were you really?"

"He was," Dagrun cut in, voice like steel. She folded her arms over her chest. "Six years you've been gone, no word of where you were, or if you were alive or dead." While there was a distinct accusation in her words, she didn't seem angry. Again, that precise, measured voice she used to perform for nobles and peasants alike.

"Ah, and so many letters have arrived from Ragnhild. I'm sure you hear from Randel often as well. Havardr we can at least place in Fjarriheimr, though he's given up on reporting any meaningful information." He crossed his hands over his chest, mirroring her even in his blank expression. They stared at each other, unblinking and seemingly not even breathing.

"Stigandr," Tessa warned. "Dagrun. We aren't enemies here."

Both relaxed minutely, having the decency to at least look sheepish.

"I was in Bjardleith," Stigandr said. "My parents sent me to make allies there. They said they would send for me when it was time to return. Because of the secretive nature of this mission—and no doubt they used the same sort of pretense with Ragnhild—I was told not to send any messages home. When I found out about my mother's death and my father's apparent abandonment of the capital, I came back."

"Why?" Dagrun demanded. "And why did you hide yourself?"

Stigandr raised an eyebrow. "I know you're clever," he said. "Have you really no idea why?"

Dagrun's composure broke with a slight frown. "I suppose I could speculate, but I'd rather hear it from you."

Stigandr didn't look her way, but Tessa sensed his annoyance. A flash and it was gone, like he'd mastered it before it could taint his words. Yet she'd felt it as clearly as if it were her own. Interesting.

"My brother has never hidden that he wishes to be the next king of Hjorrfold. My parents never made him heir, and that was intentional on their part, though I don't know why. Then suddenly, my mother dies, and my father all but gives Havardr command of the kingdom, departing with the only other heir left. To say nothing of his wars and desperation for conquest, I had concerns about what a court under my brother's thumb might do with an errant prince who could challenge his authority."

"We are *not* under Havardr's thumb," Dagrun said with her chin raised.

"No," he agreed. "But I couldn't know that until I was here to see it myself."

"So you mean to challenge him?" Ove asked. "Is that what this is? A coup?"

Stigandr's eyes flickered to Tessa before he met Ove's gaze. "I have no intention of overthrowing anyone," he said carefully. "In my view, my father is still the king. My aim is to send word to Pegjajord requesting his presence here in Yfirgardr to restore the rightful order. Havardr can go on raids as he sees fit, but he has no right to conquer in the name of Hjorrfold when he is not doing so under the direct order of our king."

Dagrun and Ove exchanged a look, an unspoken question running between them before Dagrun turned to Tessa.

"So what exactly are we doing?" Dagrun asked. "Why are we meeting in secret?"

"You say you don't want to overthrow anyone," Ove said, eyes locked on Stigandr with a wary expression, "but you certainly wish to displace your brother."

"Even if your goal is to have your father intervene, this is ultimately a course of action that will set the eldest prince of Hjorrfold against us," Dagrun agreed. "If we fail, it will be considered treason, no matter how mildly we act or what our true purpose is."

"So you wouldn't move against Havardr?" Stigandr asked. "You say you're not under his thumb, yet—"

"We wouldn't blame you if you wished to remain uninvolved," Tessa interrupted. "You're right to point out the dangers, and you should absolutely take them into consideration before deciding. I would never compel you to act contrary to your own heart."

They were all silent for several minutes as Dagrun and Ove stood there, looking at one another in consideration. It was Ove who spoke first, turning to Tessa and asking, "Do you do this on his account or your own?"

"My own," Tessa said. "I had no specific plan to appeal to the king, but I have long thought Havardr unfit for the throne. He leaves his people at the mercy of disasters and raiders, with no thought to anything but his own glory. The whole of Yfirgardr could burn to the ground, and he would only care at his convenience. He—"

"He is a poor man for rule outside the battlefield," Ove said so gently it made her skin prickle. She could sense the blow coming before it landed, and braced for his next words like she would on the training pitch. "You disliked him well before those failings became clear. I didn't realize it until Lengraey, but looking back, I suspect you've disliked him before you even arrived in Yfirgardr." He took a step forward with beseeching eyes. "What did he do to you?"

There was a vise around her chest. She knew the reason, and had spoken it aloud with but three people. To declare it more widely felt like . . . like opening up her chest and bearing her heart for all to see, to judge if the injury to it was worth the hatred and deception and plotting. Would they think less of her if they deemed her pain not enough?

"Havardr killed her father," Stigandr said, speaking only when it became apparent that she couldn't. He waited for her thankful nod before he went on. "They were boyhood friends and went on many raids together. Then, about twenty years ago, Sindri's visits to the capital stopped. There were no more raids, no more duels in the courtyard, nothing.

"But my brother visited Hundrfeld often. Every year at the end of the raiding season, he would claim he was going hunting with his dear friend. Little did we know, Sindri had died shortly after we'd last seen him. He went on a hunt with Havardr, and his body returned home to Hundrfeld when Tessa was still a small child. Though my brother claimed it was a boar that'd gored him to death, Lord Trond thought the wound looked too much like a spear for that account to be a reasonable one."

She was glad Stigandr was the one to tell them, because that meant they weren't watching her face for any cracks in her meticulously neutral expression, waiting for the wobbles in her voice to expose her. Emotion was weakness. In battle, it could get you killed, and even in the Great Hall or with the Council, a flash of anger or spark of amusement could undermine her role as regent. It had been cut out of her at Vaettfangkirk to trust her true self to anyone, and it was a hard habit to break.

But as he finished speaking, they turned to her with a mix of shock and pity so strong she turned her back on them.

"Is this true?" Dagrun asked.

"I have always believed so," Tessa said, proud that her voice was bland. "The seer who visited confirmed it, if such can be taken as proof."

"Havardr's a right bastard," Ove hissed, then quickly added, "respectfully, Your Highness."

"You needn't apologize to me," Stigandr said. She envied him his easy show of amusement. "Few know him better than I. There's nothing you could say about him that I haven't said at one time or another."

"But what does this mean?" Dagrun asked. "My lady, why do you serve him if he's done this?"

At this, Tessa was forced to face them once more. "I serve him so I might undermine him. Distance is no friend when it comes to your enemies. I can do nothing to help Hjorrfold and limit Havardr's power from Hundrfeld. Here or at his side, I might find opportunities to do right by the people and my father's memory."

"But what does he want with you?" Ove pressed. "Why has he given you the powers he has? And taken you with such honors to Thrireyna? Was your father's death perhaps an accident, and he means to make up for his cruelty?"

You're so loyal, she thought. *He doesn't deserve you. Nor do I.*

"But why lie about it? If he feels any true shame or remorse—"

Stigandr coughed and sheepishly spread his hands in apology. "If I may…" He pulled a roll of parchment from his belt and offered it to Tessa. "This might shed some light on my brother's plans."

Tessa walked over and took it. As she unrolled it, Dagrun came to look over her shoulder. There were runes scrawled across the page in a hand as inelegant as her own, pieces circled and crossed out, arrows connecting lines together. It looked rather like Stigandr's magic notes, though less refined. At first it appeared to be nonsense, random thoughts and ideas with no obvious connection…until she saw the names: Sindri, Stigandr, Havardr, Trond, and, of course, her own.

"What is this?" Dagrun asked, though Tessa already felt the weight of the words. The same as when the seer had revealed her past, present, and future, like their truth and possibility were a physical force that insisted upon being felt.

"These are prophecies," Tessa said. "Where did you get this?"

"I found it in Havardr's room. It's in his hand, if you don't believe me—"

"And a hand cannot be faked?" Dagrun muttered.

"It can," Stigandr acknowledged.

Ove glanced at the paper, wrinkled his nose at it, and turned back to Stigandr. "These from your mother?"

"Doubtful. She used runes, but they were hardly her preferred method of casting, and she committed nothing to paper. She never would've trusted Havardr with such wisdom. They *feel* like prophecies, though. There's a certain magical weight when they're true prophecies, and this parchment has it."

"I feel it," Tessa agreed. She traced her fingers along the page. The runes would sometimes catch at her skin, though sometimes her hand ran smoothly across.

"When prophecies get written," Stigandr said, "they lose some of their potency. They're not just words, but images and ideas, things impossible to pin down properly. It's why my mother never bothered, because an incorrectly transcribed omen is dangerous. They can only properly be interpreted by the person who first saw the signs. So this"—he gestured at the paper—"can give us clues to why Havardr is acting the way he is, but *we* cannot act on what's here without a lot of speculation and risk."

"Havardr doesn't seem the type to...foresee things," Ove mumbled. "If they're not from the queen, who gave him these prophecies?"

"That I don't know," Stigandr said. "There are traveling seers, like the one who visited Tessa recently, but these are too many and too detailed. Without asking him, I couldn't even hazard a guess, and I doubt he would be forthcoming with the answer."

Dagrun took the parchment from Tessa, and Tessa let her. This realm, despite being based in magic, was more suited to Dagrun's strengths than her own. Before she could say as much, Reka jumped to her feet and barked.

There was a banging on the door.

All four of them froze, but only for the briefest of moments before they acted: Tessa dispelled the silencing enchantment, Dagrun hid the parchment behind her back, Stigandr backed away behind the door and disguised himself once more, and Ove stepped in front of Tessa while putting a hand on the hilt of his sword.

"Enter," Tessa said, and a couple of guards clambered inside and bowed clumsily.

"There's an army approaching," a woman said breathlessly. "From the west."

"They bear the banners of Hjorrfold," a man added, barely more composed than his counterpart. "We've sent a scout ahead to meet with them."

"An army?" Ove said with alarm. "How many?"

"No more than two hundred," the man said confidently, though that hardly put Tessa at ease. A party of a couple dozen raiders had wreaked havoc on the countryside. Imagine what such numbers could do.

"Could it not be the prince?" Dagrun asked.

"Too few men," Ove said. "He took several times that."

"Come," Tessa said, both to Ove and Reka. Her mind was already racing as she calculated the size of the guard, the weapons on hand, the horses, and the best way to keep the citizenry safe. "I'll need as many guards as possible at the city gates. I'll ride out to meet our guests. Send word for horses to be made ready."

"Yes, m'lady," they both said with a bow and hurried off to carry out their orders.

"Are we under attack?" Ove grumbled. "I don't know how many more surprises I can take in one day."

"Let's hope not. The city gate hasn't been closed in a few centuries," Stigandr muttered. "Should I come with you?"

Though she would prefer him with her if things went awry, it was best they weren't out together. If the worst befell them and she was injured, she wanted Stigandr safe so he could take over ruling the city.

"No. I want you and Dagrun to work through the prophecies together. By no means will I base all my decisions around them, but it appears that Havardr has. If we can better understand him and his goals, it can give us an advantage." She was nearly through the doorway when Stigandr reached out and stopped her with a hand on her arm.

"Be careful," he said.

"Oh, it's only two hundred men," she said lightly. "I think I can handle it."

51
Ove

521

THEY WERE OUT of the keep within a few minutes, flanked by every guard on duty. The rest were being roused to take over watch of the castle while everyone else fortified the entrance.

Spirits willing, it wouldn't be necessary.

Ove jogged down the road behind Tessa, trying to sneak glances out over the western wall. It was impossible to see anything through the houses, but when they'd first set out from the castle, he'd glimpsed a black smudge on the snowy fields a few miles away. He prayed they really were soldiers from Havardr's army, though he couldn't account for no word having been sent ahead and there being so few of them.

Tessa didn't seem alarmed. Yes, she'd taken every precaution and was off to meet the potential danger head-on, but she wore neither her helmet nor her war paint. Even her hammer was absent, with only a sword and dagger at her belt. It put him at ease to see she was, well, not *unconcerned*, but confident that this all would be handled without bloodshed.

It was many of the same riders who'd followed Tessa to protect the northern farmlands, buoyed by their pride at having been selected before and doing the job well. Instead of inflating their egos, they were grim-faced and severe as they chose their horses: they felt the burden of such a responsibility and the seriousness of what lay before them. These weren't men and women who'd come looking for the adventure and glory of raiding. City guards were recruited for their muscle like any warrior, but steadiness was needed for such a job. They hadn't come to Yfirgardr expecting to face their deaths on the battlefield. They'd wanted security and pay and a home, and they were willing to work for it.

Ove was proud of them, frankly. They hadn't tried to shirk their duties now that it was more dangerous than drunken brawls in the streets. They held their heads high and did what Tessa asked of them, knowing she appreciated them for it and would reward them in any way she could.

It was only eight of them who rode out to meet the coming army, their horses kicking up snow as they raced across the empty land. As they drew nearer, it became clear they were Havardr's men. Ove couldn't account for there being so few of them. Five times their number had left for Fjarriheimr, if not more, and it didn't appear Havardr was among them. He'd never known the prince not to be at the front of a procession or in a place of honor where he was visible for all to see. It sometimes seemed foolish in battle to draw such attention to himself, but Havardr thrilled in having the enemy attack him above all others. Like Tessa, he had the skill to handle such an assault.

When they drew within a quarter mile, Tessa raised her hand to slow their approach. The man at the head of the mass of soldiers did the same. They met in the middle, this man and a few others. They dismounted; Tessa did not.

"State your business in Yfirgardr," Tessa said.

"My name is Sten." He did not bow or incline his head.

Tessa didn't react.

"Of Eirbjod."

Again, she didn't so much as blink. Ove could see the man's frustration grow.

"We fought together at—"

"I know who you are," Tessa said mildly. She looked at her left hand and flexed it, as though she saw something there more interesting than the man before her. "You manned the dreki with the green dragonhead and golden coins for eyes."

The man flushed bright red, his anger rushing to escape his lips, but instead he choked on the words. Ove was embarrassed for him when he finally spat out, “Then why did you—?”

“I’m waiting for you to state your business. You march on Yfirgardr, which I’ve been charged to protect, with no small force. You tell me your name, which I already know, and neglect your purpose, which I do not. So,” she paused, to let it sink in that she thought him unworthy of this discussion, and Ove saw the older man’s hands twitch, “why have you come?”

“I come on orders from Havardr, the prince of—”

“I am also well aware of who Havardr is. I am his ward and regent, am I not?”

The poor man looked about ready to have a heart attack. Ove almost pitied him, but Seen was exactly the type Havardr favored: big, mean brutes who could crush a man’s skull in their hands if they were properly motivated, and usually it required very little motivation. This one drank too much—Ove knew him all too well from his own days in the pubs and taverns of Yfirgardr—and thought a little too highly of himself for a man with a background no more illustrious than Ove’s own. Imagine the audacity if Ove went around introducing himself as Ove of Rotby like some sort of proper nobleman instead of a raider from a farm who happened to do well with a sword.

Though it’d likely been many years since Sten had been challenged, and never by a girl half his age. He would’ve never tolerated such treatment…except that even with an army behind him, he could hardly do anything but tolerate it. So slowly, he swallowed his pride and inclined his head slightly.

“Apologies, m’lady. I have been on the road a long while and forget myself. I come with the injured from Fjarriheimr. Men and women unfit to fight in the war any longer.”

“But fit to travel a thousand miles on foot?” Tessa raised an eyebrow and turned her attention to the soldiers. They did look rather worse for wear, now that Ove considered them. “You are fortunate to have arrived before winter set in any more.”

“Fortunate,” Sten sneered.

Tessa ignored him. “The tent village is not what it was before your departure, but we will do what we can to make everyone comfortable. Have a squire go to the keep so we can discuss supplies. I’ll send down healers to tend the wounded. What news of Havardr and his war?”

Sten reached into his armor and procured a square of parchment with a blood-red seal on it. It looked sweat-dampened and muddy, though the seal was intact. When he held it out, Tessa made no move to accept it. After an awkward, drawn-out moment, Sten had to step forward and hand it to her and then backed away quickly, never meeting her eye.

Tessa inspected the seal before breaking it open, reading through the letter as if she had all the time in the world and wasn't keeping them all waiting out in the frigid cold, miles from a warm fire.

"So the war effort goes well," she said, loudly enough that their own men and women from the guard might hear. Ove thought she looked annoyed at the good news, but she hid it well enough he doubted anyone else would. "We should expect news of a victory shortly on your heels."

"Bjarngrim willing," Sten mumbled.

"I'll arrange rooms for you and the officers. Once you've had a chance to rest, meet me in the Great Hall. I would like to hear your account of Fjarriheimr, since I'm sure you can tell me much more than Havardr's letter can."

"I've been traveling for near on two months. It won't be anytime soon." Ah yes, the one tactic of those with less power to show their displeasure to those who had more: delay.

Tessa nodded and suddenly was all sympathy and good manners. "Of course. You've had a long journey after months of fighting. You may take as much time as you need. It's early yet. I think the kitchens can find a few cows to roast in your honor. Your soldiers deserve it after all they've done for Hjorrfold."

Ove suspected the men had seen nothing but wild game and dried meat for some time. A hungry gleam replaced Sten's anger; he licked his lips and puffed up his chest. "We've fought well," he agreed.

"I would expect no less from Hjorrfold's best." At this, she gave a soldier's salute not to him but to the troops gathered behind him. Several returned the gesture, though most looked dead on their feet. "Yfirgardr opens its arms to you all."

Mollified, Sten and his escort started waving on the rest of the soldiers to continue their journey.

"What are the chances of my winning over such a man from Havardr?" she whispered to Ove as they turned their horses back to Yfirgardr.

"Slim to none," Ove said. He'd liked having Sten on raids and in the taverns, but had stayed clear of him otherwise; Ove had learned Sten was not an easy man to endure while sober. "Men like him follow whoever has won the most battles and survived the most raids. Unless you fight Havardr in a duel, there's nothing you can do to sway him. You're too young."

Tessa nodded. "I do like a challenge," she said with a wink, "but I suspect you're right."

"Is that why you were so hard on him?" He'd never seen her be so imperious before. She stood her ground before the Council and in the Great Hall, but she was known for being fair and kind. While he wouldn't say she was unfair with Sten, she certainly hadn't been kind until the end.

She nudged her horse into a trot, and he did the same. "That man is a fool. No messenger sent ahead when he comes with an army? He deserved to be humbled after that. I understand it—he's a raider, and we're not a people used to armies—but those men and women were placed in his care. I was within my rights to attack them on sight, all because he never thought to use his head. Such a man has no business being in charge of anyone."

"Even so, I've never seen you humble someone before their peers or underlings before."

"You don't come with me to the Council meetings," she said. "Ask Dagrun. I've done it many times when necessary, and I'm sure there are plenty of farmers who don't like my judgement who would argue I do it often."

It wasn't the same, though Ove would be hard-pressed to explain how.

"I had to put him in his place," she said. "I saw it in his bearing that he thought his authority was superior to mine. He would've challenged me at every turn, because Havardr gave him this responsibility and he would use that to insert himself into as much as possible. Like it or not, I'm the regent, and I take orders from no one." She paused and gave him a sly look. "Except the king and prince, of course."

"Of course," he said. They rode on, her words rolling about in his head in time with their horses' hooves. "I expect some princes are more worthy than others."

Tessa cast him a sharp look. "Aye."

"And you've certain you've found a worthy one?"

"I know little of royalty," she said, her gaze fixed straight ahead once more. "But I think I can recognize if a man is worthy or not of my trust."

"I should hope so. Especially when it's more than trust you place in some, and more than you who'll have to suffer the consequences if you're mistaken."

He'd learned not to hold his tongue with Tessa. Havardr didn't appreciate people talking back to him, no matter how valid their concerns. Ove had heard of how he'd bickered with the queen when she denied him what he felt was his due, and he'd done the same with the king, though less publicly. Tessa, for all her talk of putting people in their place, wanted the truth from them...so long as they were people whose opinions she valued. The servants could speak freely without fear of rebuff on any matters concerning the castle; the merchants likewise could do so for any business concerns, the guards on security, the nobles on matters of law and rule. Dagrun and Ove had perhaps more freedom, though he never tried to overstep what was his place as one of the guards and as her friend.

Her wayward prince fell under both realms, and he would be negligent not to mention his concerns.

Ashk he'd liked and thought good for her; Stigandr he didn't know, except as this distant idea of a man. By all accounts, an even-tempered, clever man who was a skilled mage, but a man who'd disappeared for years to become spirits knew what. Lying and hiding didn't do him any favors, not in Ove's opinion.

"I've known him as himself for barely more than a month," Tessa admitted. "I hope my judgment isn't clouded in this, but my gut insists I can trust him. For whatever it's worth, the seer who visited me said I could as well."

Ove had heard some of the late queen's omens himself, a shudder always rolling through him when she worked her magic. He might not have any magical talent or training to speak of, but there were few who could be in Ingegerd's presence without sensing *something* when they got close or heard her speak. He'd felt nothing in the parchment of prophecies Stigandr had shown them, and he hadn't met the seer Dagrun had told him about. But in both, Tessa had intuited their power.

"It's unclear what you plan, my lady," Ove said. "But let's hope your prince is the ally you need."

52
Stigandr

521

STIGANDR—STUCK ONCE more as Ashk lest they be interrupted—sat at his father's desk and sighed. Of all the ways he'd imagined his introduction to rule, he'd never have predicted this.

Disguised and conspiring with a steward.

Dagrun was silent as she gathered clean parchment, ink, and quills for them to work. She was quick and efficient in the way she moved about the space, and Stigandr had seen her working enough times to know this was her manner in general. It wasn't until she sat down and started furiously transcribing the first of Havardr's notes that he finally understood how agitated she was by his presence.

"Dagrun," he said, and waited until her hand stopped moving. "If you've something to say—"

Not needing more permission than this, she slammed her quill down. Ink streaked across the page, ruining whatever she'd been writing. "Why did you not give these prophecies"—she said the word with such disdainful skepticism, Stigandr knew she'd have done poorly under his mother's court—"to Tessa sooner?"

"Honestly, I'd forgotten about them," he said. They'd been intriguing when he'd first discovered them, mostly because he found it curious Havardr would have any interest in them, but they weren't his primary concern when Havardr wasn't even in Hjorrfold. He'd been more concerned with Tessa, getting to know her while trying to understand the new dynamics of the city. Once the parchment was out of sight, it'd truly been out of mind. "I'd read over them, but couldn't make much sense of it other than what I've already said. At the time, Tessa didn't know who I was, and I could hardly show them to her without revealing my true identity."

"And how long exactly did it take you to do that?"

Stigandr stared at Dagrun. She wasn't the type of steward or servant his parents would've tolerated for long. Obedience and respect were valued among the castle servants. Even the raiders and guards would've needed to show more deference, though the occasional outburst during feasts or in the courtyard might be accepted.

Tessa's Yfirgardr was not the same as the one he'd left. Her manner of ruling differed greatly from his father's, so it was no surprise her inner circle was of a different ilk as well.

"Do you have nothing to say?" Dagrun asked, taking his silence as obstinance. He supposed it was, just as he supposed she was used to having authority over those she questioned.

"I have quite a good deal to say, but much of what you're asking has already been said to Tessa. While I appreciate your being protective and suspicious, it's Tessa's opinion that matters. If she's satisfied, then I have nothing more to say. And if you have concerns, you can bring them to her and I'll be happy to discuss them. With *her*. She's the regent, and I'm a prince. You are her steward, and I will give you all the respect that position deserves, but no more until you've earned it. I don't answer to you any more than I answer to Ove or the guards at the wall."

Without missing a beat, she said, "You wear the face of Ashk, a guard of the keep. You *do* answer to Ove—"

"Enough." Stigandr raised a hand, and the lock clicked into place. He shook his head to scatter the illusion of Ashk and stared at her with that one princely look he'd perfected decades ago when he'd learned he could use his status to his advantage. It was what had allowed him and the other children to play their games without interference, and what had afforded him the opportunities to study unmolested for hours on end.

Dagrun, for all her spirit, wilted a little.

"I'm here to help," he said, tapping his finger on the table to accentuate each word. "I promise, if I meant Tessa or Hjorrfold any ill, you would *know*. I may be adept at illusions, but I would need no deception to take what is my birthright. If I wanted the throne, I would've gone to the Council and taken it. That's *not* what I want."

"And what *do* you want?" she snapped in frustration, then seemed to think better of the outburst. "My lord," she added stiffly.

"I want Hjorrfold to be safe. I want my people to *feel* safe. My brother is not the man to do that. He will bleed this land dry to get what he wants, which is his name in the histories. He thinks it'll be for glorious conquest when I'm certain he'll be infamous for his cruelty and neglect."

Dagrun appraised him with narrowed eyes. "If you betray her..." she warned.

"I won't," he said. "I'll swear any oath you wish. To you, to her, before any altar or holy place. I promise she has nothing to fear from me."

"Truly?" she asked, a gleam in her eye as though she'd caught him.

"Whatever you need to hear in whatever way you need to hear it, yes."

She wasted no time. In a flash, she had a small dagger no longer than her finger.

"What—?"

"I want a blood oath. We both swear not to betray Tessa or her confidence." Without further preamble, she sliced her palm in one quick, efficient cut, and offered him the dagger.

Stigandr ignored her dagger and instead took out his own. Enchanted weapons were rare, but he wouldn't risk using a strange blade on himself. He slit his own palm and held out his left hand.

"*I swear on my life*," Dagrun said in the old runic language, her inflection suggesting she didn't quite understand the words. As she spoke, she reached for his hand and held it tight so their blood oozed together.

"*I swear on my life*," he repeated.

"*Not to betray Tessa of Hundrfeld.*"

"*Not to betray Tessa of Hundrfeld.*"

"*Through action or inaction.*"

"*Through action or inaction.*"

Satisfied, she gave a sharp nod and pulled her hand away. She wiped at the blood with her sleeve, though she made no move to bind the wound.

It was a peasant tradition. A misunderstanding of the uneducated watching proper mages perform binding oaths. There was more to it than words and mingled blood and intention. Without drawing on magic and using principles of binding or blood magic, it was at best a ritual, but was more akin to superstition.

"This isn't real blood magic, you know," he said. He wanted her to be happy with the oath, but he didn't want her to find out later that he'd duped her.

"My family takes this oath upon marriage. When my uncle ran off with the blacksmith's wife, he dropped dead before my aunt had even noticed he was gone," Dagrun said. "We speak of prophecies and oaths. What are those if not belief manifest? It's not for you to say what's real magic or isn't."

He raised his hands in surrender. Magic and coincidence often overlapped, and it was hard to unravel the true magic from the traditions. Dagrun had the oath she wanted, and though he knew it held no power to bind him any more than any other promise, he didn't plan to break it. They could both be satisfied without invoking ancient blood rites or awakening vengeful spirits. So instead of wasting his breath belittling her beliefs, he wrapped his hand in a piece of cloth to stop the bleeding, knowing better than to use magic to knit the skin shut.

"Which do you think are the most relevant lines?" Dagrun asked. Now that they were 'blood-sworn,' she was all professional courtesy. Not warm, but a vast improvement over her cold suspicion moments ago. Cooperation was the only thing he required, not friendliness, so he was glad to see the change.

"The ones with our names. He's transcribed a few runes as himself, me, our siblings and parents, as well as Tessa and her family. He's already acted in ways that are clearly to circumvent ones he doesn't like or guarantee the ones he does. Like this one: *a loyal dog will safeguard the child until called to court*. There's a note that indicates he thought this was Sindri, but his most current note implies it's Trond, so that's likely why Havardr had him raise Tessa instead of attempting to do so himself at court."

"*A mage of royal blood will rule over Hjorrfold and all its neighbors, united*," Dagrun read with a raised eyebrow. "I suspect he liked that last bit, but not the first part."

"Yes, and it would explain why he wasn't thrilled to have me as a rival. Though he might try to control this one by having heirs of his own and raising them to be mages."

"Would that work? Is it really so easy?"

"My mother would've thought so. There are two schools of thought on the matter: that true prophecies are set in stone and cannot be changed, and that any attempts to do so only bring about those events. Then there was my mother, who believed they were a warning that could be heeded. She saw terrible disasters in Hjorrfold's future, and she took great pains to prevent them. Of course, that assumes they were ever true to begin with and were interpreted correctly."

"So this could all be nonsense and a waste of our time?" Dagrun sighed and made crisp notes on her parchment. "Is it not strange that Ove and I aren't mentioned? Or anyone else?"

"Not *so* strange. It doesn't mean either of you aren't important or play your parts, but Havardr might not have known your significance when he received or found these prophecies. Look here at these first ones. They seem mostly irrelevant, as though he hadn't yet refined his methods. Even some of these later ones are of questionable importance. And the names aren't actually listed in the original runic. This here"—he pointed to a line of crudely copied runes—"says *'wanderer who's swift on his feet,'* but he's transcribed it as *'Stigandr.'* The same goes for all our names, really. And here, it merely says *'the king,'* but he's written *'Alvis.'* "

"So, these might not even be about you?"

"Correct. But with prophecy, that's always a risk. Misinterpretations and misunderstandings are littered throughout. That's why skilled seers are crucial in making sense of them. Needless to say, Havardr is not a skilled seer."

Dagrun trailed her finger along a line. "And they aren't guaranteed even then, are they?"

"No. My mother…she said it was a matter of connecting with the earth and the spirits around us, and listening. They give hints of what's to come, but it's not a carving set in stone, which is why she thought she could nudge it in the ways she wanted. It's more like ripples in a pond. You know it means something's disturbed the water, but not necessarily the details. The where, the how, the what. Those are just guesses, though the more adept readers are much better at their work."

"Your mother read the future from ripples?" Dagrun looked appalled by the possibility.

"I speak not literally," he said, though he wouldn't have put it past his mother to try. "I meant more to illustrate the uncertainties inherent in this sort of magic."

"Would a seer be able to do more with this?" Dagrun asked. "You make it seem like it's more than just reading the runes."

"Possibly. Without the true source, it's hard to say."

"And you are not a seer?" Dagrun pressed. "Despite your mother's talent in that type of magic, you know none of it?"

"It was the one thing my mother never taught me," Stigandr said. "She said it was because the men of her line were terrible at prophecy, and I was a good enough son to pretend I believed the lie. Though I do think I'm rubbish at it. No natural talent, though that hardly matters. Anything can be mastered with enough dedication and practice."

Dagrun put down her quill and stared at him. "You don't want to know the future?"

"Do you?"

She considered. "No. I don't see the point. Knowing all the bad things that might come to pass seems like a distraction. No offense to your mother, but I don't know that I can believe in prophecies and divination. I believe what I can see."

"A respectable point of view," Stigandr said. "I…I don't know that I can believe it either. My mother put her whole life into this, and yet she couldn't see her own death. I highly doubt this is the future she wanted."

"So you say Havardr is terrible at this. You're no better than he, and even your mother, renowned for her skill in this very thing, was not as talented as she appeared." Dagrun pushed away from the table in exasperation. "What purpose does this serve—?"

"It doesn't matter if everything here is wrong." Stigandr pointed emphatically at the paper. "It doesn't matter if everything Havardr has ever done based on these words is contrary to his true aim. It mentions, for example, a feud between brothers, which I assume is the two of us, yet there was no feud until he started one. *That* is the point. We can better understand his actions if we try to interpret what he perceives these words to mean."

"So if he thinks…" She looked down at the parchment and read, "*He must be careful to keep his eye for conquest turned outward lest war follow him back home.* Obviously, he wouldn't want this to come to pass, so we can assume he'll work to stop this. Which means we can stop him from stopping it? Is that the advantage?"

Stigandr made a noise in the back of his throat. "Not exactly. Again, the prophecies are guesswork at a tapestry few can see and fewer still can hope to weave to their liking. I don't consider any of these individual proclamations useful in and of themselves. More so that they control Havardr, and so we might use it to trap him. If he thinks the only way to keep Hjorrfold safe from war is to continue conquering, that gives us an idea of his future plans."

"To what end, though? Tessa hates him. You don't want him to be king. Where does that leave the rest of us?"

"Caught in the middle, I'm afraid. At least Tessa and I see there are other game pieces on the board. Havardr sees only what's advantageous to him. Small folk and peasants aren't. Excepting those willing to pick up a sword and march behind him, though it's their numbers that he values."

"Right now, things aren't so very bad—"

"We're at war with our nearest neighbor for the sake of one man's vanity. There are raiders daring to attack the people who live less than a day's ride from Yfirgardr, which has been unheard of in over three hundred years. You say it's not so very bad, but it's materially worse than it was before my mother's death. Havardr won't stop at a single conquest, as we have already seen."

Dagrun was quiet. "I will do as Tessa asks of me, but if you mean to overthrow—"

"My brother isn't king."

"—the established order, you will need more than this to convince people. You speak of Havardr's vanity, but what of yours? It's easy for him to claim his victories and honors as his due and part of the aggrandizement of Hjorrfold, and just as easily can he claim you're a jealous brother who seduced a young woman to take what your father willingly gave to him. Yes, there are people suffering, but they will trust your father or brother to return and set it to rights rather than support a usurper."

Stigandr opened his mouth to protest, then shut it when he realized she was right. Her questions, which had frustrated him, had been her way of working through the situation. He couldn't argue with her conclusion: the people might not see the troubling manner Havardr had come to power, nor the dangerous way he used said power. Their goodwill had been earned with his success at Thrireyna, and his dwindling support would be rekindled if he successfully conquered Fjarriheimr. The riches and glory would be enough to garner him many satisfied nobles and peasants alike.

"What do you suggest, then?" he asked.

"You must expose Havardr as an unfit ruler, which I agree these prophecies might afford you an opportunity to do. More than that, you must win over the people. Exposing him means nothing if they see you as no better. Appealing to the king can only do so much if the people are against you. Or worse, don't know you.

"Tessa's earned respect as regent. Stigandr is a lost prince who abandoned his people years ago to gallivant across the world. Havardr, however imperfect, is the prince who stayed. The *only* one of you who stayed. No matter the result or unintended consequences, he acted in ways meant to benefit Hjorrfold."

"I agree," Stigandr sighed. He suddenly felt very tired and rubbed his temple in the hopes of keeping a growing headache at bay. This was part of why he'd never wished to be king. It wasn't merely the responsibility and the burden, it was the nightmare of balancing what was right with what was necessary, all while keeping the people content enough to allow such work to be done in their favor. "Again, I ask what you suggest. Any actionable recommendations would be much appreciated."

"Well, it's simple." Dagrun shrugged. "Tell people all the terrible things he's done. If it's rumors among the taverns, you need no proof. If you wish to challenge him publicly, you'll need more. Tell them how he killed Sindri. As Ashk, question what happened to the queen and then once the doubts have set in, as Stigandr, demand to know what happened to your mother."

"That could help." Stigandr considered the possibilities. He would need to be Ashk quite a while longer as he made his way through the taverns and inns. Aptly placed graffiti. Recruiting Valdis and perhaps the boy Egil... there was much they could do to undermine Havardr among the common folk. And they would need to start well before he returned.

They worked a little more, with Dagrun making a meticulous copy of each prophecy, Havardr's notes, and their own interpretation. They classified each by its relevance, if they thought it was likely to come to pass, and if Havardr was moving towards or away from those events.

They hadn't yet finished when there was a knock at the door. Stigandr flicked his hand to unlock it and sucked in a breath before changing his face back. Each time he allowed himself to be Stigandr, it became harder to wear Ashk.

The door pushed open, revealing Tessa fuming with frustration that made his palms sweaty when he felt it.

Dagrun stood, bowing her head slightly. "My lady. I take it there was no battle?"

Stigandr realized with embarrassment that he'd forgotten to worry about Tessa. He'd taken it for granted that she would be fine and that she'd handle whatever army had alarmed the guards. Their bond was a poor excuse—it might have alerted him if she were injured or her emotions spiked—but he'd been too distracted to make any proper effort to check.

Tessa's gaze flew to him, as though she in some way sensed the turn of his thoughts, but she quickly turned her attention back to Dagrun.

"Sten of Eirbjod has arrived with all the men and women Havardr deemed too sick or injured to continue fighting. We'll need to make arrangements for them. More tents outside the city, food rations, healers..." Her lips pinched together, and she blew out a harsh breath through her nose. "Ove's already working on some of it, but the kitchens will need to prepare a welcome feast. As much meat as can be spared and cooked as quickly as possible. Rooms will need to be furnished in the keep as well, for Sten and his officers, and of course I'll have to meet with them to find out what I can of Havardr and his damned war, then meet with the Council to let them know, and that's not even to *begin*—"

"I'll handle it," Dagrun said smoothly. Where Tessa radiated nerves and exasperation strong enough Stigandr would need no bond to sense it, Dagrun was calm as she gathered parchment and a book from the desk, a quill tucked behind her ear and a bottle of ink stuffed into her pocket. "I'll prioritize accommodations to get them out of the snow," she said as she scrawled out a list. "Food, rations, healers. Before the roads get too bad, we might be able to send some people home..."

Dagrun continued muttering as she left, brow furrowed as she worked through the logistics of two hundred extra mouths to feed. While Tessa was tense with annoyance, Dagrun looked almost pleased by the challenge, and Stigandr saw once again why Tessa had chosen her as steward.

The door closed behind Dagrun, and Tessa locked it before turning back to Stigandr. "Did you make any progress?"

"Some," he said and let himself be Stigandr once more. Though nowadays with Tessa, he felt seen with or without his real face. "Though most of my effort was in convincing your steward that I'm not a scoundrel taking advantage of your kind nature."

Tessa huffed an amused laugh as she rounded the table and came to stand by him. "*My* kind nature," she said as she grabbed his left hand. "As if I haven't killed far more people than you, all the while plotting to destroy your brother. What's this?"

She'd turned his hand to see his palm and was undoing the cloth that bound his cut.

"Proof of the blood oath Dagrun made me swear not to betray you," he said with amusement. "You've done well with her and Ove. Loyal and competent advisers are difficult to—"

"I felt this." She held his hand and placed her left one next to his. Hers was unblemished but for calluses. "When you cut your hand. How?"

His fingers twitched. "Ah," he said. He'd known his own magic had latched onto hers rather strongly, but she was so new to it that he wasn't sure if she'd be able to sense it until she'd had more experience with magic. He should've known better than to underestimate her abilities. "Remember when I told you about magical bonds?"

"I remember when Ashk told me," she said with a slight pinch in her brow. "Bonds that form with other mages or something like that, right?" The pinch became an outright frown. "Are you saying that's what's happened?"

"All magic brushes against each other," he said. He lit a fire in the palm of his hand and waited until she did the same. The flames stretched toward each other, the edges licking. "The stronger the magic and the mage, the more there is to latch onto." He extinguished the flame, smothering Tessa's as well. "You're so new to magic, I knew it was likely to happen, but not for a while yet."

He held his breath as she considered and tried so very hard not to let his own worry influence her perception of this shift between them. This was a strong bond to form so quickly, and he feared the intensity was one-sided and exposed him in some way.

"So we're bonded?" she said slowly, chewing the words like she could somehow taste if they agreed with her or not. "Magically?"

He nodded. "It happens over time, sometimes without either party being aware. The first bond I ever formed was with my mother, but there were ones with my tutors and the other students learning with them. With some of the mages I met in Bjardleith as well. Because of our sparring and practice, your magic has latched onto mine and vice versa."

"When did it start?" There was an edge to her voice. He sensed nothing from her.

"Well..." He shifted uncomfortably on his feet. "I noticed it when you used that defensive shield in the courtyard. I'm sorry," he said in a rush. "I should've mentioned it. It's so normal to a mage that I forgot how... how strange it is the first time. When I was a boy—"

Tessa held up a hand to silence him. "Don't keep secrets from me," she said with a dismissive note, as though this wasn't her primary concern. "I understand why you might not have understood it was a secret, but assume in the future I know nothing about magic. You've seen I'm not skilled in it and have little foundation."

He remembered their discussion in Marrtoft, and her anger that he'd deceived her for so long. Already he'd broken her trust with another lie of omission... yet she seemed not to care. His relief was short-lived. She must be more bothered than she was letting on, yet why downplay her true feelings? He could think of but one reason why she would forgive him so easily.

She had secrets of her own, and she hoped her easy forgiveness of him would earn her the same treatment later.

No, he thought and forced away the thought. *You're thinking she's like your family. She's not like your parents or Havardr. You are allowed to take her words at face value...*

He couldn't, though. It would nag at him, he knew, but he was in no position to challenge her.

"You're actually remarkably skilled given how long you've been working at it," he said instead, "but point taken. I'll be more forthcoming with information, and you're always welcome to tell me to shut up if I'm explaining more than necessary."

"Good." She took his hand once more in both of hers and traced along the wound with her thumbs. It stung, but he made no move to stop her. "What does it do? The bond?"

"Weaker ones are..." He combed through his mind to find the right words to describe the feeling. "They're sort of... proximity-based. You know when the person is about to enter the room, for example. Or if they're close by, you can sense when they're using magic."

"And stronger bonds?"

"You sense more, and from farther away. Like when I was a boy, my mother could sense when I'd scraped my knees while climbing on the rocks outside the city. She knew if I was practicing my magic properly, because she could sense when I was using it and the general type of magic I was working. Since my mother was almost constantly using magic, I could rarely tell when she was casting, but I could usually sense her moods."

“And that was your strongest bond?” she asked. “Not to your brother?”

“Randel?” Stigandr couldn’t help but laugh. His youngest sibling, he’d always thought, suffered from the indifference of their parents, who’d spoiled him out of negligence more than fondness. It had influenced how they’d all seen him because they’d indeed so little of him at all. “He’s so much younger, and acted it too. By the time we could walk, Ragnhild and I were out on the training pitch nearly every day, even though I was destined to be a mage. My parents would let Havardr beat us bloody, uncaring that he was so much older. I think my mother thought it good for me, because I had to learn magic quicker to avoid the worst of it.

“I don’t think Randel learned to wield a blade until he was ten, and he never sparred with the rest of us. The bonds *are* stronger when there’s an emotional connection there. Any magic shared between me and my tutors was practical in nature. Same with my hunting fellows in Bjardleith. Drusilla, we were closer friends, but her magic was weaker, so there was barely anything at all. None of those people could compare. My mother…”

Stigandr couldn’t meet her eyes as he thought about his mother. The cold, empty imprint on her bed, and the certainty she hadn’t died there. “Bonds grow stronger over time spent together, but they deteriorate as well. I was gone for so long and was so far away…” He swallowed a lump in his throat. “I was shocked to hear of her death, not only because it was so unexpected, but because I hadn’t *felt* it. Our bond had withered away without me noticing it, and it was like she’d died twice.”

They stood there in silence, the crackling of the fire at the hearth the only measure of time passing around them.

“So when you’re hurt, I’ll feel it,” she whispered.

“Yes,” he whispered back. “And when you’re hurt, I’ll feel it.”

“And when one of us dies…” She let the words hang there.

Stigandr took a step forward, the last of the space between them, and tilted her chin up. She was only a few inches shorter than him, a rare feat for a woman. “If things continue the way they are,” he said quietly, reverently, “then we’ll know when the other takes their last breath.”

And it will hurt as much as if it were our own.

Dark pools of black burned into his soul, and he feared she could see or sense just how much his world had shifted when he'd felt her magic burrow into his. That was the truth of why he'd put off mentioning their bond: the raw fear that she wouldn't want it, want *him*. It would ruin him to know his love was unreturned, only valued for how he could contribute to her revenge.

He'd help her all the same, but it would wreck him. To be a pawn once more, as he'd been with his parents. Never the one kept, always the one sent away.

It was only out of self-preservation that he kept those thoughts to himself now. If she sensed anything, let her draw her own conclusions. She had his oath; hopefully not knowing she also had his heart wouldn't matter.

"Well then," she said, her breath tickling his skin. "Let's make sure that's not for a long time. I'd hate to die twice."

"Oh, are you outliving me, then?"

Her answering smile was small and shy, her face lighting up with fondness. "That's a distinction I hope neither of us will have for quite some time, least of all because we have a lot to accomplish first." She went up on her toes to kiss his nose, then stepped away. "Come, we have work to do. How well do you know your brother's raiding companions?"

"I took great pains *not* to know them at all," he confessed. "Anyone Havardr favored was likely to be an insufferable ass. The only friend he had that I ever liked was your father, and he's long since outgrown having level-headed comrades."

Tessa groaned. "I'd thought as much. I'll have to deal with this Sten fellow and get as much out of him as I can. I met him on Thrireyna, but he was so irrelevant then I could easily ignore him. How did things go here?"

"Well enough. Dagrun thinks we need to undermine Havardr as much as possible with the people. Have rumors spread—true or not—that cast him in a poor light. If you only wanted to . . . eliminate him as a threat, then we wouldn't need to worry about public opinion. But *I* want him completely removed from power, and if you mean to destroy his reputation as well as . . ."

"Rumors," she said skeptically. Then shrugged in acceptance. "Sounds like Dagrun. Seeing the problem from other angles when I just want to attack head-on. We'll need to start that as soon as possible, before these newcomers can spread any praise of his feats in Fjarriheimr."

"If they're injured and ill, perhaps they could help do the opposite."

There was commotion in the hallway, the sound of many feet and loud, gruff voices drawing nearer. They were nearly out of time. He tucked away the parchments so curious eyes wouldn't spot them. He nearly forgot to put Ashk's face back in place.

"Did the seer have any additional wisdom that might help us?" he asked.

Tessa hesitated. He couldn't tell whether she was trying to recall the right words or deciding what was relevant to share.

"Most you already know," she said. "That Havardr killed my father so he could have me as a weapon. They said I could trust you. And they said it would be a long, cruel winter that would only end with Havardr's death. Let's do our best to make sure we fulfill our end of the deal."

His heart sank. There'd be no saving Havardr, then. He was already as good as dead in Tessa's eyes.

53
Tessa

521

It had taken Sten several hours to deem Tessa's invitation worthwhile, and he'd arrived in fresh clothes and smelling faintly of mead. Since Tessa hadn't summoned him or given any instructions beyond meeting with her, she let the impudence go without comment. It had been a long and no doubt uncomfortable journey; she could be gracious and allow him some time to recover. No such courtesy had ever been given to her by Havardr, and she tried to be different in any way she could, even to those unworthy of it.

"So his war isn't going well," Tessa said. She was leaning over the enormous map on the table in Alvis' study with Sten at her side. The first half hour had been little more than Sten going on about how woefully outdated and incorrect the maps of Fjarriheimr were, and giving meticulous reports of villages and geographical features that he had a scribe draw onto the map. The paper was now damp with ink and overfull of irrelevant details. If they did acquire Fjarriheimr, perhaps the merchants and the officials charged with collecting tribute might need to know which lands had orchards and which were rich in salt, but Tessa's only concern was the war effort.

More precisely, when she could expect Havardr to return and in what state.

Sten hesitated, his muscular frame as tight as a coiled rope. "I didn't say that."

Tessa gestured to the map. "You tell me of villages conquered who then revolt. You speak of a march on the capital that should only take at best three months but has taken more than double that. You return with dozens upon dozens of soldiers unfit for duty because of injuries and illness, but with nothing to show for it but a few hundred miles of empty land. When we took Thrireyna, we had no such revolts. We fought in the dead of winter, yet after a year, had fewer dead than I now have camped outside the city walls. And for what? An unfinished war and more soldiers left dead and dying."

"He's marching on the capital as we speak," Sten said stuffily. His chest was puffed out as if he were still on the front lines and not safely within the keep, two months and a thousand miles removed from the conflict. "They'll lay siege to the city and get a surrender, mark my words. Bjarngrim's beard, it might be done already."

"And if it were done, could we expect a messenger sent ahead to tell us so, or would we have to wait until hundreds of hungry men and women arrived at our doorstep?" she asked. She kept her tone level, but there was steel behind it; she wasn't so angry that she would punish his incompetence, yet there was much to be gained from making him uncomfortable and worry that she might.

Sten's face went red, and he choked on a reply. She waited three seconds to let him stew in his discomfort, then moved on.

"And he asks for supplies and men. I can hardly provide either. He's taken all the men and women fit to fight already, and we barely have the supplies that we need on hand for winter. There's little I can spare and no way to get it to him safely without an armed escort."

This seemed unimportant to Sten. "I wouldn't bother," he said with disinterest. "It'll be done by the time anyone gets there, and they'd just have to turn back around. Best keep everything safe here."

Yes, best keep the food here where, conveniently, you are.

"What are his plans once he takes the city?" she asked. "Will he stay there to consolidate his power or return immediately?"

"He'll..." There was an uncomfortable silence.

"You don't know his plans, do you?" she grumbled. Of course the man would prove not only impudent but useless. No, that wasn't fair. He was skilled with a blade and had done well in leading the injured home. The reports indicated very few had died along the way, despite the constant threat of attack and the worsening weather. He was merely incapable of anything that required him to use his brain. "Being in his confidence, could you not hazard a guess? I'm sure there are few who know him as well as you."

The flattery worked, and he relaxed at having something to offer. "The Fjarriheimr are a restless, insolent sort. He'd do best to stay put until they've all bent the knee and he has the court well under his thumb. Depending on how long the siege lasts, it should take another moon or two before he could risk the return."

Finally, something tangible. "Will the arrival of winter concern him? Was the weather much different in Fjarriheimr than here?"

"It was a fair bit warmer." The words flowed easily now, and she could see that despite his obstinance, he wished to please. She could see why Havardr favored him, when he needed so little encouragement. He was simply out of his depth with the responsibilities given to him. Perhaps Tessa could arrange some exhibitions and duels between him and the other returning warriors, to give them a chance to regain some of their lost honor at being sent home early. "It's worse here. Seems to be moving westward, the snow. There'll be time yet before it's full winter in Fjarriheimr."

"And will he stay or go once it descends?"

"He'll stay until things are settled," Sten said confidently. "There's no rush to return if he can't beat the storms. The capital is more than big enough to accommodate the army, and they'll be wanting to take what's owed to them out of the city."

Tessa just managed not to flinch. She was all too familiar with the pillaging that happened after a battle. There were some boundaries they wouldn't cross, but much was tolerated in the euphoria of victory. It wasn't always greed that drove them. More than gold was taken, and some men and women had a taste for destruction when they were given free rein. After seeing their comrades cut down beside them, or in the longer conflicts, to see them waste away from injury or sickness, there were those who wished to punish the losing side for having had the audacity to fight back.

It was a world foreign to Tessa, despite her having lived it on Thrireyna. She wasn't a spiritual person, but the closest she ever came to inner peace was with a weapon in her hand and a challenge at her feet. The thrill of battle, the concentration it took and the strain on her body to accomplish the feats everyone so marveled at…it was just her and the moment, the world so simple and clear. In contrast, altars and rituals felt like a performative gesture that made her feel disconnected from others instead of united; when she was fighting, even on the training pitch, she was alive and one with the world.

Needing any sort of reward after seemed blasphemous.

"Thank you for your time," she said graciously. "Your insights on Fjarriheimr have been enlightening. I hope to see some of the wonders myself when Havardr returns with his spoils of war. You have made Hjorrfold proud, and we look forward to honoring you all tonight."

Sten nodded in agreement, with no sign of humility at all in his wide frame. "Aye, not easy work, dealing with those wretches. Would've killed them all if I'd had my way, but then who'd farm the land?" He scoffed as if such work was beneath the men and women of Hjorrfold. As if he wouldn't be enjoying the grains, vegetables, and meat provided by that very sort of person at the feast that evening. As if half of Havardr's so-called army weren't former farmers and hunters themselves.

As if he weren't from Eirbjod, a small town surrounded by farmland.

It disgusted her that he thought so little of the people they'd stormed through, men and women protecting their homes from invaders.

But there was no point in saying any of this. She was in no position to dismiss Sten without offending him and potentially alerting Havardr that she wouldn't blindly do as she was told. Besides, she wanted Sten cooperative so that she could use him later. Now that he had suggested not sending fresh supplies, he would at the very least be a convenient scapegoat should Havardr be displeased.

"Harder going than Thrireyna?" she asked, though she was mostly indifferent to the answer. She looked out the window to judge the time, hoping she might yet be able to call the Council together to update them. Not that she had much to tell them, but they would expect to hear it from her before it became widely known throughout the city.

"Tenfold," Sten said. "On Thrireyna, they fought respectably. Came right at you. None of this archery nonsense or this sneaking about. Cutting men and women down in the middle of the night if they wandered too far from the campfires. Like bloody wolves. Would've been a lot faster if you'd been there. Never understood why Havardr left you here, when the two of you could've driven right through Fjarriheimr in a three-month." He tsked and then spat into the fire. "Damnable waste, leaving you here to mind the city. There's a whole Council for that."

Sensing an opening, she smiled. "Missed having my sword?"

Sten slammed a fist on the table. "Not a battle went by when we didn't notice your absence. Havardr did well recruiting so many for his war, but more than half of 'em could barely fight. Not raiders like me and Hakon and Kerr and Ove. Not warriors like you."

"I'm sure they're seasoned warriors by now," she said with an amused note she didn't feel.

"Bah! If Havardr's got his sights set on more conquering"—he exchanged a meaningful look with her that suggested he very much believed Havardr did—"then I'll tell him myself. You should be there with us. Fewer, better fighters to share the glory and the riches. The way it should be."

"I do miss it," she said, the first truth she could offer him. "The battlefield. The tents. The brotherhood and sisterhood we all shared." She could picture it all so clearly. Despite being under Havardr's watchful eye, she'd been more herself there than she'd been allowed at Vaettfangkirk. It wasn't Hundrfeld, but the camps and the dreki had afforded her that same sense of belonging. And it'd been so very easy: Havardr had pointed them in a direction and let them loose on the world, and she'd been all too happy to fight.

She didn't like that about herself. That her joy came at the cost of other's lives. That she'd been happy to do Havardr's bidding in those battles.

Sten leaned forward across the table. "There'll be more chances for it," he promised, a gleam in his eyes. She suppressed a shudder at how alike the two of them really were. Difficult and frustrating as it was, being in Yfirgardr away from Havardr had been good for her: it'd given her the perspective she needed to understand who she wanted to be.

Her responsibilities kept her occupied for three nights in a row. The Council, the feast, the endless arrangements for the soldiers, all on top of her regular duties…it exhausted her. Each night, she told herself she would sneak away to Stigandr's room, and each night she fell asleep on her own bed, still fully dressed with Reka draped across her. It was Reka's wet kisses that woke her each morning instead of Stigandr's embrace. It was their bond that comforted her, that secret knowledge that they were connected in a way no one could break or take away from them. A little piece of him was hers, as a piece of her was his.

A strange, not wholly expected piece. She hoped their connection would make them both stronger, both together and apart. It was the magical nature of it, the way it'd been forced upon them both, that made her hesitant to embrace it fully. But like so many things, she had to put it to the back of her mind and focus on more immediate concerns.

If the new arrivals were surprised to see a dog following her around, they said nothing. There were some turned heads from the more seasoned raiders who'd lived in Yfirgardr, but most were from farther reaches of Hjorrfold and saw nothing strange. Many offered Reka pets and treats, so much so that Tessa worried they'd spoiled her. That, more than anything, made her combat her exhaustion to return to the courtyard that night. Magic would need to wait: Reka needed work.

It was terribly cold once the sun set, but Reka's thick fur was made for winters. Tessa wasn't, but she dressed as warmly as she could with fur-lined tunics and a heavy cloak, then tucked a warming quartz into her pocket that one of the kitchen matrons had given her when the snows started.

As they practiced some basic commands, Tessa felt a prickle at the back of her neck. She ignored it at first, testing the power of the bond. When she was certain Stigandr had reached the edge of the training pitch, she turned to greet him.

The surprise of seeing Ashk's face over Stigandr's hadn't left her yet. Both had been welcome companions, but where Ashk had been a friend and training partner, Stigandr was…more. An equal, despite their being so very different.

"Reka is already a better fighter than I am," he said as he approached. Reka whimpered where she sat a few yards away, twitching with a desire to run over and greet Stigandr but obediently waiting for permission to do so. "I don't envy the opponent who must face you both at once."

Tessa whistled a single, bright note. Before the echo had reached them, Reka was bounding over with her tongue out of her mouth and tail wagging. She stood up on her hind legs to lick affectionately at Stigandr's cheek, his ears, his nose, but gently enough that he didn't topple over.

"Yes, yes," he soothed and rubbed her back. "I've missed you too." This last part he said while eyeing Tessa, and her cheeks flushed with heat. How could he set her afire with four simple words?

She cleared her throat. "There's no need to envy anyone," she said. "You'll be our first opponent, if you're up for it. Reka needs more than shadows to work with."

"She's not really going to attack me, is she?" he asked before turning his attention back to Reka. "You wouldn't attack me, would you, sweet girl?"

Reka barked happily at the attention.

There was magic in the dogs of Hundrfeld, Trond had told her. As ancient as the stones of the keep. Was that how they bonded with their owners? And if so, could Reka sense Tessa's connection to Stigandr?

Musings for another time.

"She won't," Tessa assured him. "To begin, we always work on control. She'll work on flanking you, and any time she 'attacks', she'll poke you with her nose to mark where she would bite. The worst she might do is pull your cloak."

"Good thing it's not a nice cloak." He winked at Reka. "How do you teach her to attack?"

"With straw dummies and possibly on hunts, if the opportunity presents itself."

"And is this practice merely for Reka?" he asked, his words dancing around his true question: *will there be magic?*

"Mostly," Tessa said just as carefully. "I wouldn't want anyone watching to think we were fighting in earnest."

There are too many eyes, and I don't wish for them to know I have any magic at all.

"Very well. I accept the challenge of fighting the two toughest opponents in all of Yfirgardr, if not Hjorrfold," he teased as he extricated himself from Reka. "Dagger today?"

"As you like," she said and whistled for Reka to follow her to one end of the training pitch.

It was slow going at first, with Reka too excited at having a friend play with her, but soon they fell into a rhythm of working through attacks, counters, and retreats. Reka followed orders and was both nimble and quick, but too excitable. She required short bursts of practice and frequent breaks to maintain her control so she wouldn't actually bite Stigandr by mistake.

A few times, Tessa found herself so lost in the fight, matching him move for move, trying to find the weak points in his defense to exploit, that she forgot all about Reka. She'd opted for a practice sword today instead of a hammer, and it made them more evenly matched than usual.

"You're good with a knife," she commented, mesmerized by how fluidly his hands moved. If they ever did fight, she'd be glad of her war hammer; she'd never want him to get past her guard or she'd be dead before she could stop him.

Reka jumped in and grabbed a mouthful of his sleeve, stopping his most recent thrust. It was well done if you ignored the way her tail wagged and her growl was more of a pleased yammer.

"You've won, sweet girl." Stigandr shook off Reka so that he could sheath his dagger. "You disapprove of knives?" he asked Tessa, eyebrow raised.

"No, but I find it a curious choice for a—" She went through several words to see if any were suitable to be overheard, and floundered. "It's not common," she said instead.

Stigandr looked amused at her avoidance. "It's not," he agreed. "I only chose daggers and knives because my brother couldn't be bothered with them. I was never meant to be better than him at anything on the battlefield, and he had many years head start. So I'd trained in all the manners expected of me, but I'd only ever put any effort into knives and daggers, because that was the only thing I could hope to best him at."

"And did you best him at it?"

Stigandr chuckled. "Once I disarmed him of his longsword in front of the entire court. Everyone had laughed and cheered, and even Hav—my brother had clapped me on the back and told me I'd done well." His smile faded at the edges, his expression wistful. "It had been a friendly rivalry back then. Out in the open with no stakes. When he could be proud of me instead of suspicious."

"But it seems a dangerous way to fight," she said. Stigandr was quite good and could beat most warriors in a fight. He wouldn't beat Havardr, though. If he came at Havardr with a dagger, he'd end up with a sword through his heart. "Isn't the whole point of magic to fight from a distance?"

Where you'd be safe.

Stigandr's expression was unreadable, as though Ashk's face and Stigandr's were showing different emotions and she couldn't pluck them apart to see either properly. She cursed their weak bond for not yet being strong enough to give her any clues.

"I suppose that's one advantage," he said.

Instead of letting it go, she pressed on. "With the right magic, you need never let an enemy get close. Daggers are such an intimate form of fighting." She stepped forward, well within his reach; he swallowed. "You have to let them get close to do any real damage, and that invites its fair share of danger."

Stigandr smirked, a charming sort of smile that she was sure had every lord and lady at court swooning back when he was a respectable prince worth swooning over. She rather liked that he was her wayward prince, turning his charms on her and her alone. "My lady, I'm not afraid of dange—"

She hooked her leg behind his, sweeping his feet out from under him. As he toppled backward onto the frozen sand, she landed on top of him, her knees pinning him. Before he could even think of retaliating, her left hand was in his hair, pulling his head back, and her right held one of his daggers to his throat.

He looked up at her, at her mercy and his eyes wide with shock. Then, in a show of trust she was unused to, he shifted to expose more of his neck to her. Goosebumps prickled along her arms. She wasn't sure she could ever return the gesture, though. Her mind roiled at the possibility of baring her throat to anyone, even him.

She leaned down and kissed him. He strained up to meet her lips, even as the metal bit into his skin. She pulled away first, jumping to her feet and leaving his knife on his chest. It was well into the night by now, and she hoped the darkness afforded them privacy in that foolish moment of weakness.

"Let's get back to it," she said, voice hoarse. "We've much to do before we retire."

Stigandr sat up slowly, a hand coming to his neck and leaving behind a smear of blood. He held her gaze as he licked his fingers clean. "As you wish, my lady." His voice was as wrecked as hers.

"On second thought," she said. She offered him her hand. "I'm tired and need my rest. Escort me to my room?"

He accepted her arm and together they got him to his feet. He lingered in her space, whispering, "And after I escort you there…?"

She took a step toward the keep, extricating herself from his hold. "Come find out," she called over her shoulder, knowing both he and Reka would fall into step behind her. "The night's young, after all…"

54
Ove

521

Ove wound his way through the streets of Yfirgardr, the low ones closest to the merchant quarter by the city gate, keeping his head down and fixed on the path ahead. He was too well known in these parts, first for how determined he'd been to drink himself into an early grave and now because of his standing among the guards; he didn't want to be recognized for either. It had never bothered him on previous visits to Valdis and the other merchants who traveled to Hundrfeld on Tessa's behalf, but this was more openly treasonous.

There had been no explicit reason Tessa shouldn't be in contact with her uncle, and so Ove had gladly helped. He'd also seen firsthand that her messages and exchanges with Trond had been innocent enough. Helpful, even, and for the betterment of Hjorrfold.

His current task wasn't so innocent.

After much discussion between Dagrun and Stigandr (Stigandr! He still couldn't believe the lost prince had returned, *and* that Ove had all but encouraged Tessa to fall into his bed. Time would tell if that'd been a mistake...), they'd agreed on a course of action. The four of them would each spread rumors of Havardr's misdeeds and hope the flames of discontent caught.

In some cases, it was hardly a rumor but the bitter truth: Havardr had killed Tessa's father despite their years of friendship. The idea made Havardr's blood run cold. A man who could so callously kill his dearest friend was not one to be trusted. Part of him wished there were more to it, some hidden motive or accident that had caused the terrible deed, though it wouldn't exonerate Havardr fully: he'd hidden it and not made the necessary reparations for the death.

There were also the very factual cases of Havardr going to war again and again to conquer neighbors, and by doing so, neglecting his people and his duties in Yfirgardr. They were mere observations, and anyone could draw whatever conclusions they liked from them. If they saw the expanded lands as a boon—as he knew many did—that was their business; if they thought the dangers didn't outweigh the good, well, that was their right, too.

But the other cases, those truly were gossip. That Havardr might have played a hand in his mother's death was the worst, but there were other accusations. That he had coerced his father and brother into leaving. That he planned to kill Stigandr and Ragnhild if they ever returned. That his wars were destroying Hjorrfold with his aggressive ambition. These things could not be proven, and each claim weighed heavily on Ove. He'd sworn his loyalty not to Hjorrfold, but to King Alvis and to Havardr.

Spreading rumors and stirring unrest, it was all so... *underhanded*. Ove was a warrior, a raider, for fuck's sake. He faced his enemies head-on, no trickery or deceit. This scurrying about in dark corners, whispering truths and falsehoods without caring which was which, it was beneath him.

It was beneath Tessa, he thought, though he understood her situation was different from his. She was the one with a father to avenge and scores to settle. While her family had sworn an oath generations ago to Hjorrfold, she had personally sworn none to Alvis or Havardr or anyone: she broke no vows working against Havardr.

Tessa had sensed his reluctance and left the bulk of the work to Stigandr. Instead, she'd asked Ove for one great task that was not much different from the ones she'd given him before, and one that surely couldn't be viewed as treason.

And yet Ove felt sick to his stomach as he pushed into a tavern at the fringes of the market. The thin door shut behind him like he was cattle in a paddock, and his stomach churned at the feeling of being trapped. There was his usual table in the back corner, tucked away behind a pole and just out of reach of the nearest torches. Only a small candle lit the space, and the wobbly table and crooked bench were less than inviting; not once had Ove ever seen another patron sit here unless the whole tavern was full to bursting.

It wasn't full today, though it was rather busy. The influx of soldiers had certainly spent a great deal of their time and gold in the taverns, pubs, and brothels lining the lower levels of the city, and the growing snowdrifts were more invitation to stay inside drinking than wander back home and catch a chill. Even so, none of the patrons paid him any mind as he settled on the bench, and he was glad to turn his back on the room.

A woman stopped by with a mug and a plate of coarse rye bread. He thanked her as he shook off the snow clinging to his cloak. He wouldn't drink the mead, but it was easier to accept it than send it back. No need to draw attention to himself as the only warrior in all of Yfirgardr who didn't have a taste for alcohol. He ate the bread though, nibbling on it in the hopes it would settle his nerves. Even before a raid, his stomach had never felt so twisted in knots as this.

"Do I not travel enough for you and your lady?" Valdis sat across from him and took his mug. Some of the brown liquid splashed onto the table before she stole a long swig of it.

"Is it too much for you?" Ove asked. "I thought you were well compensated for your efforts."

Valdis rolled her eyes before wiping her mouth on the back of her sleeve. She had several beaded bracelets on, a recent addition to the lone necklace she wore. The polished beads glistened even in the low light, a few looking like they were made of bronze or silver. "I am. I'm more than happy with the arrangement, Ove. You needn't worry on that score. I was just hoping that perhaps I would have more than a week to myself before I journey out that way again. The snow makes it slow going."

"I understand." Truly, he did. He wouldn't want to go anywhere in the winter if he could help it. "I need you to deliver a letter."

Her demeanor shifted instantly. She sat up straighter and leaned forward. "A letter? On parchment? From your lady herself?"

When Ove took out the letter, neatly folded and sealed, he could practically taste Valdis' eagerness to get her hands on it. He knew she wouldn't read it, least of all because it would ruin her to break faith with Tessa; her enthusiasm was likely from the novelty of it, and her interest in seeing Trond's reaction.

"This isn't going to Hundrfeld," he said, because he had no wish to lie directly. The outer layer did indeed bear the seal Tessa used on official correspondence—an empty throne with an upside down crown upon it, to represent her role as a regent not of the royal line—but she had not penned the letter hidden inside. Indeed, there was another seal in golden wax next to Stigandr's signature, his appeal to his father with proof of his birth side-by-side. "I need this letter taken to Pegjajord."

Valdis stared blankly at him. "Pegjajord?" she asked, as though she'd never said the word in her life. "The mountain sanctuary? Whatever for?"

"It's a letter for Alvis," he said carefully, and watched as his meaning fully sank in.

"The king!?" she mouthed, nearly silent in her exclamation. The questions seemed to whirl through her head faster than she could voice them, and the one that came out first wasn't the one he'd expected. "Are we in danger?"

"No," he said. Not a lie so much as a wish, and he would do all in his power to make sure it was true with respect to Valdis. "Tessa has information for him, and she trusts few to deliver it safely." He offered her the letter. "Do you accept this responsibility?"

She reached for the letter but hesitated as her finger grazed the edge. "Is this about the disasters?"

"I cannot tell you more than I have," he said sternly. "I chose you for this task because of your discretion. You're trustworthy and talented."

"Talented," she scoffed, but she took the letter. "It's not hard work to travel from one keep to another."

"Take the compliment," he said. "Keep that letter on your person until you deliver it into Alvis' hands. Don't read it."

Valdis looked offended by the very notion as she tucked the paper into her belt. "I'm no amateur."

"No," he agreed. "You'll need to leave as soon as possible. On horseback. No wagon. The weather is not on our side."

"I'll leave in the morning," she said. "Am I awaiting a reply?"

"You needn't," Ove said. "If you can deliver the letter, that'll be enough."

He'd argued with Stigandr on that point. Stigandr had insisted she should stay until she'd gotten a written response from Alvis... or ideally she'd return with the king himself. Ove had insisted that was too much to ask of someone who wasn't privy to the risks she was taking by helping them.

"Right." She nodded. "I can manage that. It shouldn't be more than a week's ride to Pegjajord, I reckon."

"Two, more like," Ove said. He'd thought the same, since the mountains were about a week's worth of travel due north, but Stigandr had said the pass to the sanctuary was farther west and difficult to find. Ove slid over the map Stigandr had drawn for her, more detailed than any she'd have access to. It showed the local farmsteads that provided food to Pegjajord, as the penitents and mourners had little concern for worldly goods and so the sanctuary was of no interest to merchants. With so few visitors, it was rarely added with any care to maps. "There are some settlements along the way that can give you shelter if the storms get bad. They're marked in blue."

"Sounds like a long and arduous journey."

Anticipating her request, he pulled out a bag of coins and discreetly pushed them across the table. "All gold," he said.

"Well then." She took the map, the coins, and his mead. "I'd best get ready." She winked at him over the brim of the mug before disappearing into the back of the tavern. Ove watched her go, worried for her and wondering if he should've offered to escort her. Valdis would've likely refused—she had an independent streak that he was sure her mother found infuriating—but it would've made him feel better to at least try.

"It's not about you," he grumbled to himself and ripped off a large chunk of bread. He chewed it angrily as he thought about the state of things. Squabbling princes and missing royals and an orphaned girl caught between it all. His guilty conscience mattered very little in the grand scheme of things. It was such gloomy thoughts that kept him company until, abruptly, he was no longer alone.

He startled slightly as a plate of cold meats was placed before him and a figure took Valdis' vacated seat. Indeed, he thought it might be Valdis, returned to say she wouldn't help him after all or that she'd counted the gold and wanted more, but instead it was a young man with hair as fair as snow and a crooked nose. Nothing about him looked familiar, not in the long sweep of his eyebrows or the slope of his shoulders or his broad forehead. He didn't have a soldier's look to him either, and he was too clean to be a tradesman.

Ove was about to tell the stranger to fuck off when the man's eyes flashed bright green for a breath, then returned to their muddy brown.

"Nice trick, that," Ove said, embarrassed that he hadn't seen through the disguise. There was no way he could have. Now that he knew, he squinted and tried to see the familiar faces of Ashk or Stigandr beneath this stranger, and couldn't. It was likely a sign of Stigandr's skill as a mage, but it felt like a failing on his part. "You following me?"

Stigandr shook his head. "A happy coincidence." When Ove scoffed, he laughed. "Really! I was in the area looking for someone, but I couldn't find them. Thought I owed myself a break after all my hard work."

"Of not finding someone?" *I think I liked you better when you were Ashk*... "Who was it, anyway?"

"A friend," Stigandr said. He put his hands on the table to reveal the ink-blackened skin. "I was spreading a few choice words on a few walls." Before Ove's eyes, the ink disappeared, sucked into Stigandr's skin as if it'd never been there at all. "You had a brother who was a raider before you came to Yfirgardr."

Ove reeled from the abrupt shift in topic. "I did," he said hesitantly, then felt guilty anew. It was always hard to think of Halle, let alone speak of him, and baring his pain to Stigandr left a sour taste in his mouth.

"He died on a raid, did he not? Around twenty-one years ago?"

"He did." He gulped. "Look, with all due respect, I don't—"

"I remember that raid," Stigandr said. "I was only about five or six years old. Havardr was always going on raids. This one was, in many ways, a completely unremarkable voyage... except that a dozen men left, and only two returned."

Ove's mouth went dry and his throat tight. He dreaded hearing what Stigandr would say next, but in his heart, he felt it coming. The surf pulling out from his feet and a wave on the horizon rushing toward him. Still time to run.

He didn't; he sat there numbly and waited for it to break over him.

"The two were my brother and Sindri. It was considered rather strange at court that such a skilled crew could all be lost, and with no bodies left to give their kin. Havardr claimed it was a storm, and Sindri said nothing at all. He looked ashen, haunted and hollow, so unlike himself." Stigandr's gaze was fixed to the middle distance as he recalled that day years ago, then he shook his head and snapped himself back to the present. "I didn't know it then, but that was the last time I would ever see Sindri."

Stigandr reached into a pocket on his tunic and produced a sheet of parchment. As he spread it onto the table between them, Ove could make out Halle's name among a list of others, with Havardr and Sindri's near the top. He knew records were kept somewhere in the castle, information about each official raid: who went, where they sailed, what they pillaged, if anyone died. There were red Xs next to ten of the names listed, which told him all he needed to. With blurry eyes, he looked away.

"I knew he died in service of the prince," he said, and cursed himself for how weak his voice sounded. "What of it?"

"Based on what's written in Havardr's prophecies, that was the raid where he took Sindri to Spakonaheim. They left a party of twelve and seemed to return a party of two, but I suspect there was a third kept hidden."

"Tessa," Ove breathed, and the single word sucked the air out of him. He wondered at the chances that his little brother should've been there, in her orbit, when she was but a babe. Like their families were fated to connect. He remembered a beach on Fyrrey where he'd wondered that before, but he'd deemed it too much of a coincidence. "But how could a storm kill ten grown men but not an infant?" As soon as he asked, he knew. He understood what Stigandr was trying to tell him.

"My brother thinks of Tessa as a means of conquering the world. We know he killed Sindri, likely because of her. He took great pains to keep her existence hidden from everyone outside of Hundrfeld. It..." Stigandr paused here, appraising Ove like he had a change of heart and didn't want to ruin him with what came next. He must have seen that it was too late to turn back now, because he continued. "It stands to reason that he killed the crew on that raid to maintain that secrecy. If he was willing to kill his best friend over it, ten men who were but names on a ledger would be nothing to him."

Ove flinched, though he knew it was true. Havardr was an outstanding warrior who protected his comrades in battle and who honored the fallen, but Ove had seen the way he threw line after line of soldiers at an enemy in battle. He cared in the detached way most nobles seemed to about the men and women in their care: they were tools as often as they were people. Ask Havardr about a warrior who'd fallen more than two battles ago, and it was clear he didn't remember them. Oh, he could bluster his way through and make them all feel that he did, but it'd happened one too many times for Ove to believe it anymore.

Stigandr might worry that Tessa was some 'great weapon' in Havardr's plan, his war axe, his longsword; all the rest of them were merely daggers and knives, useful in their own way but easily replaced when broken.

"Are you telling me that Havardr killed my brother?" He remembered the chest of gold sent to Rotby with the prince's personal condolences. Blood money. A silent, unacknowledged reparation for the ill he'd done. It was a meager consolation that Havardr would do that small thing for them.

"I can't prove it," Stigandr said, so full of sympathy it was worse than if he'd been cold and unfeeling.

"Then why tell me?" Ove barked. "I was perfectly content not knowing." He wasn't, in truth. Halle's death had always been a hole inside of him, one that had never closed. Over the years, it had changed from a deep agony to a dull ache, sometimes so faint he could almost forget it, and then it would twist itself into fresh pain when he saw how close he'd come to forgetting.

"I thought you had the right to know, because he was your brother. And because I know you're a good man. A loyal man. What we do, it requires you to pick between Tessa and those you've sworn yourself to, and no one can fault you for not wanting to break an oath to your prince. But you should know what kind of man he truly is and know that he would not keep the same faith with you." Stigandr rose from his bench. He reached out as if to place a hand on Ove's shoulder, then seemed to think better of it. "I'll see you back at the keep. I have work to do, and I fear I've given you much to think about."

Ove grumbled something that might pass as a farewell. He knew not how long he sat there, mind twisting and turning over everything that had happened the past few weeks. All the revelations, all the plots and the intrigues. He'd thought Tessa at the center of it all, but suddenly there was Halle too, sucked into the whirlpool of Havardr's ambition.

"You all right here, sir?" a barmaid asked. "You seem rather lonesome, tucked away back here."

"I'm fine," he grumbled. He rubbed a hand over his face. It felt like he hadn't slept in a year, and his head ached. When the barmaid curtsied and turned to leave, he caught her sleeve. "Could you bring me a pint of mead, love?" he asked. "Strong as you can find."

"Of course, sir." She curtsied again and was off to bring Ove the only way to oblivion he'd ever been able to rely on.

55
Stigandr

521

STIGANDR HADN'T WANTED to tell Ove about his brother. He'd put the pieces together by mistake after an errant comment from Dagrun about the prophecies. Spakonaheim was a mythical island that, according to some legends, was the origin of magic. It was a place of pilgrimage for a certain type of mage, but it was also a wandering island that was nearly impossible to find. The prophecies listed years and a direction to sail to the island, the most recent of which was the year Tessa was born. After Dagrun pointed it out, Stigandr's mind had whirled with possibilities. He'd checked the records from that year to confirm his suspicions as best he could. His only interest has been in unraveling the mystery.

When he'd brought his suspicions to Tessa, she'd sagged from the weight of them. She'd been the one to spot Halle's name on the list, and its significance had landed like a blow.

"We need to tell him," Tessa had said with resignation. He could see it hurt her to know the unwilling part she'd played in his brother's death.

"It'll hurt him."

"It's already hurt him. He deserves to know why. It might help."

Stigandr had almost argued the point, but he understood her meaning. The lingering doubts about his own mother plagued him, and he wanted to know the truth. Whether to condemn or to absolve his brother...he hoped for the latter, though he'd never be able to hush his doubts until he knew. Tessa had found something akin to comfort from learning the truth about her father's death. It had at least given her purpose, though he worried that she let that purpose drive her so completely.

But it was done. He'd relented and offered to tell Ove himself, as it was his brother, his discovery, and his attempt to spare Tessa further guilt. Granted, he'd hoped to do it in the castle, but perhaps it was a blessing it hadn't been there. It might give Ove the chance to take it in before having to face the rest of them.

Exiting the tavern, Stigandr retrieved the paint and brushes he'd stashed behind a frozen water trough and got back to work. It was no easy task keeping the paint and walls warm enough as he graffitied slander against his brother. The frigid air at least afforded him ample opportunity to work. Few ventured out of doors, and those who did stubbornly kept their heads bent and walked as briskly as they dared across the frozen streets.

He'd already spent hours at this task. He'd leveled a variety of accusations at his brother. *Who killed the Queen? Havardr abandoned us. Havardr would trade his crown for a sword. Havardr's war kills our soldiers. Havardr Prince of Neglect.* On and on, pointing out that Havardr wasn't here and cared only for his conquests.

He'd also attempted a crude drawing of his brother pissing on Yfirgardr, and another where he stood on the prone forms of their parents. There were enough illiterate among the residents that he would need more than words to reach everyone.

But he admittedly had a poor understanding of the city. Very little of his life had been spent with the common folk who called Yfirgardr home, so he didn't know how best to reach them. The right tact, the most frequented places, the neighborhoods most likely to sympathize with their cause. It had been his hope to find the boy Egil and seek his assistance. He seemed to be a clever lad who knew the city far better for his having lived in its hidden corners than Stigandr ever could.

Despite his best efforts, he hadn't been able to find Egil. He hoped the boy was warm wherever he was.

With the dipping temperatures and the influx of people because of the raids, natural disasters, and wounded soldiers, food was not as plentiful as it had been a month ago. Just the day before, three wagons full of survivors from an avalanche in the mountain region had arrived, starving and desperate. Yfirgardr had never turned its back on those in need, and Tessa especially was too kind-hearted to send anyone away without having somewhere for them to go.

Her good nature was why he secretly hoped he could salvage this mess with Havardr. It needn't end in death.

These were the thoughts that occupied him as he put down his bucket of paint and set to work outside a tavern halfway up the hill to the keep.

He'd started the day farther down the slope, hoping to reach the lower classes, the ones who were the most disrupted by Havardr's war. They were the ones who had lost family to the army, the ones who'd been displaced by raiders or disasters, or were the working class who bore the brunt of making room for the refugees. Their spoils of war would be indirect. If the soldiers and enriched nobles spent their plunder in their establishments, it would be some time yet before they could hope to see any of that gold themselves. The houses higher up the hill were filled with wealthier, more established families who would have no current grievances against the way of things. Their houses weren't over-crowded, their relatives had gone for glory, not out of desperation, so they were already reaping the benefits of prestige. He suspected he would have more sway with that lot as himself, not as anonymous words on walls.

He wiped the wall clean of snow and dirt and began. He wasn't sure what he would write this time, but started with a bold HAVARDR that glistened in the sunlight. It was as if the stone itself was bleeding, and it gave him an idea.

HAVARDR BLEEDS HJORRFOLD DRY

He stepped back to admire his work—uneven, with the last two words at a drooping angle—and was met with something solid behind him. He startled and turned to find a wide-shouldered, barrel-chested man behind him. Half a foot shorter than Stigandr, but with enough muscle to account for the difference. The man wore a sword on his belt, with only a thin deerskin cloak to protect him from the winter weather. A soldier's cloak.

"What are you doing?" the man asked, brow downcast. He spoke with the gruffness of a man used to being answered, placing him higher than a common soldier, but not so high that he could afford a nicer cloak.

"Are you one of the men who returned from Fjarriheimr?" Stigandr asked, making his own manner open and unassuming.

"Yes," he huffed as if this were obvious, though he was proud enough to answer. "I asked you a question."

"You must be happy to return home after so many months of fighting. Yfirgardr welcomes her soldi—"

"What are you *doing*?" he demanded.

"This?" Stigandr hooked a thumb at the wall. "Spreading the word." Hopefully, the man was illiterate, and Stigandr could lie about the message.

"And what word is that? Treachery?"

Ah. Too bad, then.

Stigandr considered his options. The alley had but one way out, which the soldier blocked. The man had shown he was less than sympathetic, so reasoning with him might prove impossible. A soldier, he wouldn't be shy of fighting and after so long away from civilization, he might be more easily moved to violence. If Stigandr attacked first, he'd have the element of surprise. He knew his current disguise looked like a weak wisp of a man, unthreatening as could be.

No, there's no need for that, he thought. With an open smile, he said, "Surely, you have seen how much blood and life have been spent for the sake of the prince's whims. Hjorrfold was prosperous without the need to—"

The man shoved Stigandr. The blow was so quick and hard that Stigandr staggered back and slammed into the still-wet wall.

"Clean it off," the man hissed. "How dare you spread such lies about your prince? After all he's done to protect you."

Stigandr stood and straightened his tunic. "I assure you," he said, "Havardr hasn't protected me in many years."

They drew their weapons at the same time. The soldier had a longer reach with his sword, and his first swing cut across Stigandr's chest. He ignored it, hoping it wasn't too deep, and focused on aiming his dagger. In one smooth motion, he'd brought the dagger right through the soldier's belly. He twisted it, hearing the man's pained gasp right in his ear as he crumpled against Stigandr. He clutched feebly at Stigandr's shoulders. There would be no healers or potions for him: Stigandr's blade was enchanted to draw life out of its victim. The longer he kept the blade buried in him, the faster his life would bleed out of him.

Stigandr eased the man to the ground, careful to keep the dagger deep inside him, if only to put him out of his misery sooner.

Stigandr stood there over the prone form, panting and wondering what he would do. A soldier's body. His own injury. The blood soaking into the snow next to his graffiti.

"What's going on here?"

Stigandr tensed, acutely aware of how things looked—they indeed looked very much like what had actually taken place—and shuddered. There was still the chance of talking himself out of it, claiming he was attacked and merely defending himself. The words were already on his lips when he looked up.

His stomach sank as he recognized the man at the end of the alley: Sten, one of Havardr's old raiding comrades. Stigandr had vague memories of him, mostly from the time they'd killed a whale that had attacked their dreki. They'd tied the dead creature to the ship and dragged it back with them. The poor beast's bones still littered the beach in a small monument to Havardr and the trip. The other raiders and crew who'd accompanied him had earned their own small measure of fame, as well as Havardr's continued favor. But it was, most unfortunately, not the whale that came to mind first.

Stigandr had been equally surprised and unsurprised to see Sten at the head of the injured troops. He was unsuited for such a task (he'd rarely been given leave to command his own raids, and those few had been lackluster), but Havardr wasn't one to care about qualifications as long as the person was suitably loyal to him and reasonably skilled at fighting. Honestly, it was so like Havardr that Stigandr was annoyed at himself for not having guessed it.

The point remained that there was no one in all of Yfirgardr that Stigandr wished to see less than Sten.

"Did you kill Sune?" Sten demanded. He drew his sword, and Stigandr knew that no matter what he said, even if he'd been innocent, he was a dead man in Sten's eyes. Sten stepped forward, blade poised to strike. "Cast aside your weapon, stranger, and we'll take you to the keep for the king's justice."

We?

"There is no king, so I'm not sure whose justice you'll be appealing to."

He wondered what his chances were in a fight, but another figure appeared at Sten's right. This man bore the same buckskin cloak as his dead comrade, the same shabby sword, though he hadn't unsheathed it yet.

Between Stigandr's injury and Sten's superior size and experience, Sten alone would be a challenge. Outnumbered, Stigandr was truly fucked.

"Blasphemy," Sten growled. His misunderstanding of the word told Sten all he needed to know.

In a flash, Stigandr dove for the dead man's discarded sword. He barely got it up in time to block Sten's blow, but the impact sent a jolt through him that rattled his teeth and made his wounded chest ache. His tunic was already soaked through with blood, the warmth of it a reminder of how little time he had. This needed to be quick.

He sucked in his breath and held it, drawing what little energy he could. His reserves were lower than usual, but he reckoned it would do. In all their practices, Tessa was the only one who'd ever used magical shields and barriers; Stigandr emptied both his magic and his lungs, praying he could replicate it this once. It left him like a wave, the air crackling as it expanded outward. Not so powerful as when Tessa had first used it on him in the courtyard, but enough of a push that Sten thumped to the ground and his sword was knocked aside.

"You wretch!" he screamed from the muddy snow, his boots slipping as he tried to right himself but couldn't. It was all Stigandr could do to keep himself upright. In that momentary lapse in control, as he tried not to retch or tumble over, he felt his disguise slip away unbidden. Sten pushed up onto his elbows, and his face went ashen as he stared at Stigandr.

As bad as things had been, they'd just gotten much worse.

"You," Sten choked.

There was no magic left to him, no way to shift his features once more, so he stood as straight as he could. "Me," he agreed. And then, with the little physical strength remaining, he leapt over the dead body, around Sten, and past the dumbstruck soldier watching it all.

As quickly as he could, he ran into the city, ignorant of where he went as he moved from alley to street to alley again, over and over, his only thought of escape. He didn't slow until his legs burned and his lungs ached, and still he stumbled on a few more steps before his body gave out. As he collapsed against a wall, panting, he waited until he was sure he wasn't being followed before he fainted into oblivion.

56
Tessa

521

THE AIR WAS heavy and tepid. At the request of Lady Gunvor, the servants had put too many logs on the fire, though she sat near the hearth bundled in several cloaks despite the oppressive heat. She was well over eighty and the oldest person Tessa had ever met. Normally she was quite amiable and easy-going, requiring only the comforts her age and status entitled her to, but she hated the cold.

"I remember the winter Havardr was born," Gunvor grumbled, hands splayed out to the fire as a servant stoked the flames. "Eighteen months of bitter cold. A third of the city starved or froze to death, to speak nothing of the peasants. Nearly three years with no good harvests." She shuddered. "We ate horse meat and withered potatoes."

"Well," Tessa said, "Havardr's birth saved us from one winter. Perhaps he can save us from another." A perfect symmetry to his life, though no one there knew she meant his death.

After the niceties of small talk, Tessa cleared her throat. They discussed the state of things: supplies, the latest string of disasters at the edges of Hjorrfold, the speculation about Fjarriheimr, and the recent decrease in raiders (the only blessing). Despite the ill tidings, there was a sense of peace in the Council chambers. Sten had inserted himself in their meetings once or twice, feeling the self-importance of being in Havardr's inner circle and having some standing among the warriors. He soon learned the bureaucratic nature of running a kingdom was not much like maintaining an army and held none of the excitement of battle; he stopped attending without being asked, and the Council seemed relieved to be rid of him.

They were a snobbish group, and Sten would always be a boorish provincial in their eyes (especially when he conducted himself without the usual decorum or the slightest show of deference to even the elder Council members). Tessa herself was of an old family who'd had their keep since before the founding of Yfirgardr, her blood more 'noble' than most of the people before her, yet it had taken time for them to warm up to her. After all, she'd never been in the capital, and her family hadn't claimed their seat on the Council in generations. She might as well have been a young upstart as far as they were concerned.

Though that attitude had long softened. They'd always yielded to the authority Havardr had given her, but she'd had to earn their respect all the same.

"We are well stocked thanks to your care and foresight in grain collection," Lord Birger said with a nod to Tessa, "and we have much salted fish and meat, but if Havardr returns soon with the full army…" He trailed off, wringing his hands together.

"Horse meat and potatoes," Dagrun mumbled.

"Sten doesn't believe he will return soon," Tessa soothed. "And we should trust that Havardr wouldn't do so without his own supplies from Fjarriheimr." She had no such faith in Havardr, but if she claimed she did, he would look all the more incompetent before the Council. "They are known for their mild winters, are they not?"

"They are," Birger conceded. "Let's hope they aren't so war-ravaged that they cannot contribute their share."

Their share. A strange idea, as though it was only fair they helped their conquerors survive the winter.

"There are simply too many people," Gunvor said. "Should this winter last longer than usual, we are in grave danger. We mustn't overextend ourselves. We must conserve what we've saved and encourage all to do the same."

This again. It was so easy for them to see the stockpiles of food safeguarded within the city and think of it as theirs, forgetting it had come from the farthest reaches of Hjorrfold. They'd been entrusted with it to take care of everyone, not just those who lived in Yfirgardr.

"We will conserve, but we won't deny anyone. I don't want this to become a situation where we help some but not others. All who need help will find it here, so long as I am regent." Tessa drew in breath to say more, but the air became trapped in her lungs. Her thoughts fell like shattered glass around her. A burst of pain cut through her, slashing right across her sternum. It reminded her vividly of that first fight on Fyrrey when her shoulder had been cut open. It hurt so badly, she clutched at her chest, but the wound eluded her touch. When she looked at her hand, she fully expected to see blood staining her fingers; there was none.

The Council hadn't noticed her momentary distraction, pressing on in their concerns for food and who was worthy of it and who should be burdened with contributing it. She drowned out their words until they faded into nothing, ignoring Reka nosing at her thigh as she turned her attention inward. What was happening?

She locked eyes with Dagrun. She frowned at Tessa, and as she tucked a loose curl behind her ear, Tessa saw her hand bound in cloth from her blood oath; with growing horror, Tessa understood.

"I'm sorry." She stood abruptly, hands spread on the table to steady their trembling. She didn't know if she'd interrupted someone and was beyond caring. "We'll have to end early. I have a sudden headache and am not at my best. Please know I value your input, which is why I feel I must end things if I'm to properly consider your advice."

Startled faces turned from her to one another. She must have looked as bad as she felt, because they muttered in sympathy and took their leave one by one. Only after they were gone did she allow herself to collapse back into her chair. Instantly, Dagrun was by her side with a mug of water, and Reka tried to climb onto her lap to lick her face.

"What is it?" Dagrun asked. "I would've guessed you'd never gotten a headache before in your life."

Tessa accepted the mug automatically, her attention turned inward. The pain in her hand a few weeks ago, it had stung. Sharp but quick, a faint echo of it had lingered but had faded by the time she'd returned to the keep. This was…not that. It wasn't as bad as when she'd first felt it, but it had receded little. The line of it throbbed, a raw wound that was too deep to be accidental.

Too much of a phantom to be her own.

"Is Ove back?" she asked, the words sounding as though they came to her from a great distance. With more concentration, she tried to ground herself in the present. She grabbed fistfuls of Reka's fur and looked into the dog's blue eyes, taking a few breaths in and out before she turned back to Dagrun. "Is Ashk back?"

They never knew when people might be listening, ears pressed against doors or an unlucky echo, so they never uttered his true name in the public parts of the castle.

"I'll check," Dagrun said, though her pinched expression suggested her worries were for Tessa and not the two men. "Can I send for a healer?"

"No, I'm—yes." She swallowed. "I don't know. Not for me, but I fear Ashk is in trouble."

Fear was all but foreign to her, yet it now curdled her blood and made her lightheaded. Never had she needed to fear for someone else. Rarely had she feared for her own safety. Pain and danger were her expected lot in life, and she'd grown numb to them years ago.

"I'll look for Ove and Ashk," Dagrun said. "I'll send up food for you and have the healers prepare a satchel with remedies."

She was gone before Tessa could protest. She didn't need food or drink or anything but Stigandr standing before her in one piece. With one hand, she massaged her chest over her tunic, her fingers trying to shoo away the ache that had settled there; with the other, she absentmindedly pet Reka. What to do, what to do…

She'd have to find Stigandr. There was nothing for it. He'd gone out into the city on some errand after conspiring with Dagrun the day before. Never had she worried for Stigandr's physical wellbeing, because she knew from personal experience he was more than capable of taking care of himself; only discovery could ruin them. Why hadn't she insisted he not go alone?

It was a painfully long time before Dagrun returned, though notably without the food or the satchel.

"Ove and Ashk aren't in the castle," she said in a clipped tone. "Sten is here and demands to see you."

Tessa raised an eyebrow at that. "He demands? Of me?"

"I tried to defer him until later, but he was quite insistent that—"

The door slammed open, and Sten stormed inside, red-faced and hobbling, with a young soldier behind him. "We have an emergency."

Tessa, sighing internally, stood up and walked to meet him before he could bring his storm of unrest through the Council Chambers. "What is it?" she asked sternly. She hoped this inconvenience could be resolved quickly, but his harried expression filled her with dread, and she knew what he was going to say before he said it.

"I was just attacked by Prince Stigandr."

Dagrun went still beside her.

"Prince Stigandr?" Tessa was shocked at how breezily she spoke. She lied so rarely, she didn't think she had a talent for deception for anything but her hatred for Havardr. "Havardr's brother? I thought he hadn't been seen in years, now suddenly he's here in Yfirgardr?" She paused, raising an eyebrow. "Attacking you?"

"You doubt me?" He rose to his not inconsiderable height as though to intimidate Tessa into submission. It didn't have the intended effect: Tessa straightened as well, putting them at eye level with one another, and placed her hands on her hips. She glared at him until he took a step back, only somewhat cowed.

"Well, forgive my skepticism, but this is a rather unlikely story." She offered a condescending laugh, all the while plotting how to get Sten out of here so she could find Stigandr. Any doubts she might have held about him being in danger had been crushed. She could think of no one worse to have found out, no one who could be less sympathetic to Stigandr's arrival.

"I know what I saw!" Sten bellowed so loudly the words echoed around them, without even an ounce of shame at the outburst and who he was directing it toward. Reka bristled where she stood, ears pressed tight against her head as she watched Sten with dangerous focus; the fool didn't notice. "He's here. He killed someone. He attacked me."

"If Stigandr were in the city, why would he—?"

"I don't know!" He clenched his fists in frustration. He looked like a petulant child, about to stamp his foot at not getting his way. "He's here to steal the throne or otherwise undermine Havardr. We must apprehend him as quickly as possible."

"Very well." On that they could agree: Stigandr must be found. "Where is he?" Tessa asked, not quite able to keep the edge from her voice and glad that Sten would willfully misinterpret it.

"The bastard got away," he snarled. "Killed one of my men before he disappeared into the alleys. We'll need to mount a search party immediately and—"

"You're certain it was Prince Stigandr?" Tessa asked. They were on the edge of a cliff, and it was for Sten to decide which way they tipped.

Sten huffed in frustration. "Absolutely certain, yes. It's been years since I've seen him, but I don't forget a face. And those eyes. My lady"—she could tell the title still irked him, now especially—"we must hurry, so he doesn't have time to escape the city."

"And you will swear on your life before the Council that you've seen him?"

"Yes! On my life, I—"

The dagger was out of its sheath and in her hand in the blink of an eye, then deep in Sten's ribs before he finished speaking. His mouth rounded in shock, and it was only when she withdrew the dagger and stabbed him again that his expression crumpled into pain. He staggered forward, only to impale himself further on her blade. A tinge of regret went through her; not that she'd killed him, but that she hadn't given him a faster death. The only thing left was to guide him to the ground before letting him gargle out his last breaths.

Still crouching over him, she pulled the blade out of his gut and looked at the man Sten had brought with him, rigid with shock. Tessa was well aware of how she must look, calmly murderous and splattered with blood with her dagger still dripping wet, and she thought it did him some credit that he didn't cower. He didn't try to run or fight either, and she didn't think that boded well for his future as a soldier.

"And you?" she asked him as she wiped the blood off on Sten's tunic before standing once more. She tried to look relaxed, but she was ready to spring forward in a second if need be. "Did you see the prince?"

He gulped, glancing reflexively from her knife to Sten's body. "I did not, m'lady."

"Are you sure?"

"I swear on my life," he stammered. "I saw nothing."

"Who killed your friend in the alley, then?" Dagrun asked. Tessa didn't dare turn to look at her, not when she had to watch this man so carefully, but to her ear, Dagrun sounded no different from when she read through the cases in the Great Hall.

The man's chin trembled. "I don't know," he said, then offered, "It was a drunken bar fight. It was dark. It happened quickly. I don't know what happened."

Tessa nodded approvingly. "How unfortunate for your friend. And that Sten should try to help him, only to be injured. Dangerous to interfere in such squabbles, even for a man of such strength and prowess in battle. At last, he's earned his chance to retire home to Eirbjod."

Words failed him at last; he clamped his mouth shut and nodded, his whole body slumped in defeat.

"What's your name?" Tessa asked him gently. She stepped around Sten so that the man could focus on her and not the body. He flinched as she approached, so she didn't come too near. "Where are you from?"

"Torsten," he all but whispered. "From Murtrthrope. Out east. A fishing village."

"I've not had the privilege of going there," Tessa said. She spoke the way she did when trying to settle an excitable pup. "Would you like to return?"

He whimpered and nodded fervently.

"Dagrun, let's arrange for Torsten to be returned to his home in Murtrthrope. Such a good soldier deserves to return home, well rewarded for his service to Hjorrfold."

"Of course." Dagrun bowed and led him out, and Tessa was alone with the weight of her actions.

She looked down at Sten. Forced herself to really take him in. She'd never killed anyone until she came to Yfirgardr. Sixten had been an accident, but the men and women on Thrireyna weren't. Each swing of her blade had been deliberate, either to injure or kill. If it was possible to excuse those deaths, then so be it; this had been murder. She could offer no justification other than keeping her own secrets and protecting someone she cared for, though it could easily be painted as more mercenary than that.

Two years gone from home, and so much of who she aspired to be had been whittled away to make room for who she must be instead.

Bjarngrim's teeth, this was a mess.

"Reka, come," she said. The only delay she allowed was to get her elk-skin cloak trimmed with fox fur and her sword. Then, she and Reka were down the hill leading to the city. She knew the city outside the keep so little—a failing that she took full responsibility for, somehow overlooked as she'd settled into the role of regent—and didn't know where to begin. Stigandr hadn't shared much of his plans, and fool that she was, she hadn't pressed for details.

Reka, for all her progress, had never been intended as a hunting dog. She could take down prey no doubt, but tracking and scenting them weren't skills she had. They wandered through the streets and alleyways, searching for blood on the snow and bodies in the shadows.

Not a body, she reminded herself. He was alive. She had to believe that. If an injury could hurt her so, his death would level her. The pain was fading, but—

She stopped dead outside a teahouse high on the hill. Could she…?

Stigandr had said magical bonds were weakened by distance and time, so proximity must strengthen them.

Tessa closed her eyes and took a few experimental steps down the hill. At first, there was nothing but the sense of imbalance from walking along the uneven cobblestones. She felt a fool for taking blind steps and was about to give up when there was a flash of pain, not across her chest but in her lungs, each breath hurting like the chill had settled in deep.

"All right then," she said, opening her eyes and recalculating her path. "Let's find him."

It took ages, a slow process of following the tug of their bond. She often had to stop and close her eyes before taking tentative steps in a new direction. Reka was patient, head cocked in curiosity whenever Tessa did this, but about a third of the way down the winding hill towards the city gates, Reka's ears perked up and she yapped in agitation.

"Go,"Tessa ordered, and Reka bounded down a tight alley between a blacksmith and a crooked stone house. Reka nosed at a lump in the shadows, snow making it impossible to tell it was a person until Tessa had kneeled beside him. Her chest hurt fiercely, and suddenly her joints ached from the cold, and she felt light-headed. The pain ended the moment she touched Stigandr, as though the bond was satisfied because she knew his distress and would handle it.

"Thank the spirits," she mumbled as she felt his pulse, slow but steady. His tunic was matted with blood, but it appeared mostly dry. It was his true face he wore, handsome though gaunt. "How did you get yourself into so much trouble?"

She lifted Stigandr and slung his arm over her shoulder, his limp form unwilling to move. She could've carried him completely, but this seemed less likely to catch anyone's attention: a drunken friend being helped home. There was no way she could bring him safely to the keep, not in broad daylight looking like the lost prince of Hjorrfold for all to see. No, she'd have to be clever about it. But first things first: she needed to get him out of the cold.

"Right." She shifted his weight and started walking. They were hardly out of danger, but the relief of having found him eased the rapid flutter in her chest. She kissed the top of his head, his hair stiff and frozen, and counted her blessings.

It was so inconvenient to learn her heart resided outside her chest.

57
Stigandr

521

Stigandr's chest ached. His head ached. His legs ached. There was no part of him that didn't ache, including parts he hadn't known *could* ache. For a time, he clung to sleep enough that he barely felt it. Whenever he became conscious enough for the tidal wave of pain to overwhelm him, he forced himself back under.

In the few lucid moments he had before he pushed them away, details of the world were forced upon him. He was in a comfortable bed, not on the snow-filled streets. There were people tending to him, for he could hear their voices. Medicine had been applied, the thick minty paste crusted across his chest making it hard to move or even breathe. And sometimes, a hand laced into his, a soft press of lips to his brow, fingers running through his hair.

But eventually, after hours or days or weeks that felt like years, he opened his eyes, and his head was clear. The pain had ebbed to faint echoes of his injuries, though he couldn't quite remember how he'd been hurt. He pushed himself up to lean against the headboard and tried to think.

He was in his own room with the fire low and sunlight trickling in through the windows. A small table had been pulled next to the bed, with an assortment of potions, tonics, and ointments laid across it, as well as, rather curiously, a book of children's stories. He reached out and traced a hand along the spine, the title so worn with age that he could only make out the words *The Dog's Mane and Other Tales* from memory. Too tired to read, he left it alone and hoped it'd still be there when his head and his eyes were up to the task.

Resting his head back, he stared at the tall ceiling and tried to remember what had happened. He followed the cobwebs and the rafters, watched the dust motes dancing through the air, and slowly pieced together what he could.

He'd been in the city painting graffiti. He'd been doing it for hours, only magic keeping the winter chill from settling into him. Ove had been there, though Stigandr couldn't quite pull that thread loose to know why. And then there'd been a fight. His dagger in his hand, magic, his own name hurled at him, and running, running, so much running until he couldn't anymore.

This was where he was when the door opened, standing in an alleyway about to fight for his life. He tensed out of habit but relaxed when he saw Tessa enter with a flagon and tray of cheese and fruit. She hadn't yet noticed he was awake, and he soaked in the sight of her. The dark tangle of braids cascading over her shoulders, the way her belt accentuated the slight curve of her hips, the gentle way she nudged Reka into the room before kicking the door shut.

Reka spotted him first. She jumped into the air and let out an excited bark before rushing forward. She didn't leap on the bed, thankfully (he didn't think he was well enough to bear even a friendly attack), but placed her paws on it and sniffed him enthusiastically.

"I'm well," he promised her. When he moved to pet her, a lightning burst of pain went through his chest, and he flinched. "Almost well," he amended.

Tessa clicked her tongue at Reka and took the dog's place at the side of his bed. She sat there and gave him the flagon, dark eyes watching him intently as he drank. It tasted like every tonic his mother had ever given him when he was ill. He resisted the urge to gag, but his throat was so dry he drank half of it.

"Thank you," he said, passing it back. His voice sounded rough as bark. "How long was I asleep?"

"Only a few days." She brushed a lock of hair from his forehead, and he was too tired to stop himself from leaning into her touch. She smiled ever so slightly and rested her hand against his cheek. He closed his eyes and stayed there for untold minutes before she spoke again. "Do you remember what happened?"

"A little." He blinked his eyes open. "How badly was I hurt?"

"All things considered, not too badly." She pulled her hand away, and he sighed at the loss. "I found you, which is all that matters, though not as soon as I would've liked. I'm also no healer, so it was up to me and Dagrun to do what we could with what the healers gave us. I'm sure more skilled hands could've had you mended much sooner, but given the circumstances"—she gestured at his face, which he took to mean his lost disguise—"secrecy was essential. I wouldn't have risked involving anyone else unless I thought you were at death's door."

"Was I not?" he grumbled. He wore no tunic, and he gingerly pulled at the edges of the cloth binding his chest. There was no dried blood, and it was loosely bound. He hoped that meant his wounds were mostly healed, and he only needed ointments to ward off infection. He couldn't remember ever seeing the wound, only feeling it and the wetness of blood soaking through. Never had he been so injured. It was fortunate that Tessa had found him at all, though he couldn't believe it mere luck. "How did you find me?"

She scraped her teeth over her bottom lip in consideration before saying, "I used our bond." And then, before he could revel in the pleasure such a notion gave him or ask for more details, she plowed right on. "You were unconscious behind a blacksmith shop. I bribed the blacksmith to let me keep you there and sent word to Dagrun. Ove and I had to hide you on a cart to get you into the keep."

He couldn't picture any of this. Tessa searching for him out in Yfirgardr. Ove dragging a cart. Dagrun pestering the healers. It wasn't the absurdity of the situation that baffled him; it was that all three were so willing to help him.

"Please thank them for me. I..." He tried to push up more and instantly collapsed back again, exhausted. "I fear I'll be bedridden a bit longer."

"Hmm," Tessa hummed. She gave him a tonic from the side table, one that smelled sour and tasted of old grain. It was one of the restorative draughts he'd shown her, one that restored energy from heavy magical use. He sipped it under her heavy gaze until she was satisfied and took it away. "I couldn't tell which hurt you more, the cut or how tired you've been since coming here."

"Both equally, I'd expect." Spending time alone with Tessa had given him a brief reprieve from powering his disguise, but he'd been overdoing it for so long that he'd never quite recovered. He remembered now, quite distinctly, that his magic had slipped away after he'd been hurt, failing him at last after months of pushing himself too hard. It would be some time before he could build up the reserves of magic necessary to conceal his face again.

As if she sensed his thoughts (and for a terrified moment, he thought she had somehow, through their bond or some magic she'd learned while he was unconscious), she said, "You can't be Ashk anymore."

"Not for a while," he agreed.

"I don't mean when you've recovered. I mean ever. Ashk has been gone for a week." If she saw him flinch at hearing that, she mercifully didn't mention it. "There are no city guards who can simply disappear for that long without reason or consequences."

"Oh." He hadn't considered that. "So have I been charged with desertion?"

"I've taken care of that, at least. The Council had been concerned about the increased number of residents in Yfirgardr and the difficulties in feeding everyone. I offered to release any soldier or guard from their duty without penalty if they wished to return home for the winter. I've even incentivized them with early pay or their share of the spoils from Fjarriheimr. Many have accepted and have left. Ashk was the first to do so, and Sten the second."

Stigandr felt a twinge of sorrow, as though Ashk were a real person who'd died. He'd never intended to play the part of a city guard for so long, but he'd grown comfortable in the lie. It had allowed him a place in Yfirgardr that was free of the burden of his birth. He could simply *be*, a state he wouldn't be able to occupy much longer. The walls were closing in: he would need to reveal himself soon.

"A pity. I rather liked Ashk. He had a far less complicated life."

Tessa laughed. "Perhaps, but he wasn't nearly so handsome." She took Stigandr's hand in hers. "Are you really all right?"

"I will be," he assured her. "What's next? With no Ashk to hide behind..."

"Rest and recovery first." Tessa's gaze went distant as she stared at their joined hands. "Sten is dead."

"Sten?" And then it hit him, a flash of memory and a jolt of fear. "He... he saw me. He knew me." He frowned as he tried to work free the rest of that day.

His dagger in someone's lungs, angry words flung at him, and dual recognition. "Was he the one I killed?"

"I didn't know the man you killed. One of Sten's friends. I'd seen him in the Great Hall, but never spoken with him. Doubt he was a pleasant sort if he ended up dead by your hand." She paused just long enough for Stigandr to wonder who had killed Sten if not him, or if fate had dealt him some blow, but then put him out of his misery by answering. "I killed Sten."

Having killed many in battle, no one would think another death would weigh on Tessa's conscience; Stigandr saw it did. She hadn't particularly liked Sten or what he represented or who he served, but she wasn't one to kill a man for being unlikable. It had been for Stigandr's sake that she'd done it, and he was more indebted to her than he'd been before.

"I'm sorry." He brought her hand to his lips and kissed her thumb. "You wouldn't have had to if not for me."

"Aye," she agreed. "But there was nothing for it. Once he'd seen you, it was too late. He'd signed his death warrant by pressing the matter so obstinately. Between the two of you, I'd always choose you."

He squeezed her hand almost as hard as his chest tightened around his heart. He was so helplessly smitten with this woman. To know she felt even a small measure of what he did lifted his spirits more than any remedy ever could.

"You shouldn't have to choose," he said. "I was careless. It should've never come to that."Warrior or not, Tessa didn't have the heart for murder. Everyone told him how affected she'd been by Sixten's death, and that had only been an accident.

But Tessa's face hardened; she shook her head. "There was always going to be bloodshed."

He wanted to argue. There didn't *need* to be. All he wanted was peace for Hjorrfold, and for himself and Tessa. But there were too many ghosts in Tessa's past making demands on her future, and now Sten was among them. Stigandr doubted there would be any way to talk her out of killing Havardr, but he hoped so. And if he couldn't, he'd be there to help her pick up the pieces of her conscience and rebuild it.

He sighed so deeply it hurt. Wincing, he withdrew his hand from Tessa's and put it to his chest. If only he'd learned more healing magic as a boy, but he'd never thought it useful. Not for him, anyway. He only went on the half dozen raids he was expected to and then gave it up, and he'd never expected to be much of a fighter. There were actual healers who would do the job for him if need be.

The trajectory of his life hadn't quite followed his expectations, though.

"Sorry I'm so useless," he grumbled, so thoroughly annoyed at himself for his weakness and his misstep. What good was he if he had no disguise and wouldn't be out of bed for another few days?

Her brow creased. "You're more than your utility."

"I don't know about that." He was too weak to hear or offer any confessions of affection, especially when he felt he deserved none at the moment. It was safer to redirect to lighter ground. "You only ever liked me because I was a good training partner."

Gone was the earlier darkness in her countenance; she softened, and her smile returned in full force. "Am I so easily won over?"

"Easy? Sparring with you isn't *easy*. Much harder now that you've some magic." He almost told her how he'd used her shield to defend against Sten, the feeling of it resurfacing with more clarity than the actual image, but stopped himself.

"Come now," she teased, "I was always out of your league. You do very well for a mage, though. Better than the ones on Thrireyna, anyway."

"Thrireyna..." He settled down again in the blankets. He knew he would fall asleep again soon, but he wanted Tessa to stay until he did. "I've never sailed as far as that. Tell me about the journey. Did you enjoy the dreki?"

"The journey was amazing. I'd never seen so much water before in my life. The *creatures* that lurked beneath the surface." Her whole body radiated glee at the recollection of the trip, and for a few moments Stigandr imagined himself there with her, bobbing along the waves and navigating by the stars until he drifted back to sleep.

58
Havardr

521

The march from Fjarriheimr to Yfirgardr was endless. Havardr didn't remember having traveled so far to get to the capital, but even taking the most direct path back, the road stretched out for miles and miles before them. It wasn't merely the worsening weather that slowed the way: his wife's retinue of attendants, the hostile negotiations with villages who hadn't quite yielded to Hjorrfold's control, and the sinking morale of the troops all hindered their progress.

That surprised him, how reluctant the army was to return home. They wanted rest after the arduous campaign and were so desperate for it that they complained about traveling too quickly as if they'd rather have stayed in Fjarriheimr. Such whining did nothing but make Havardr spur them on faster. Once they were back in Yfirgardr, they'd thank him. They'd grown soft and lazy once the fighting had stopped, perhaps because it had ended in surrender and not bloodshed. A pitiable end, admittedly. A fate Hjorrfold could never endure. Should they ever be in that position, Havardr would rather every man, woman, and child sacrifice their own lives for the dignity of their kingdom. And he would be the last of them, the final defense, never yielding an inch until death took him.

An honorable end, if an ending there must be.

Eventually, they were greeted by familiar sights. The smooth beaches with their crashing waves were a welcome sight after the stony shores of Fjarriheimr had hidden them from view. He was tempted to find some dreki to finish the trip—Havardr would never ride a horse more than a mile again if he could help it—but the sea had become too rough to risk the voyage, so on they trudged.

When some people in the villages and farms they passed recognized him as their prince, he felt truly at home again.

"How many days' walk are we from Yfirgardr?" he asked each time as he accepted their gifts of hospitality, and each time he was pleased that the number was smaller than before. When they told him it was less than a hundred miles, but a five day's walk away, he sent a messenger ahead with instructions that a huge feast should be prepared to honor their return and that the people should line the streets and welcome back their triumphant prince.

"Perfect, is it not?" he said to Hakon. "We arrive at the new year. They'll celebrate my victory with the turn and forever link the two. A new beginning for Hjorrfold's glory."

Hakon grunted his agreement, and Havardr lamented having left Kerr in Fjarriheimr and having sent Sten ahead. Hakon was dim-witted as a heifer, and about as interesting company.

His wife took in the news of their impending arrival with the same bland serenity she'd accepted everything since their wedding. She sat quietly on horseback and followed along with the rest of the soldiers. She endured the icy winds and growing snowfall. She offered no rebuke to the soldiers who leered at her or muttered scorn for her father under their breaths. She lay in Havardr's bed each night. All these things she bore as though they were of no consequence.

It hadn't bothered him until she showed no interest in Yfirgardr. Fjarriheimr's capital might be a wonder of polished white stone, but Yfirgardr was a proper city. It had a heart and soul; it could be lived in without fear of staining it.

And she'd dismissed it without ever seeing it.

He was rougher than her with usual, both in body and words, though it soothed him that she wouldn't be able to keep her cold indifference when she saw the keep on the hill. He would watch it thaw and then shift into awe, and she would come to understand the honor he'd done her by marrying her. She would be the mother of the next king or queen of a kingdom far greater than her strange home in the west.

For five days, one after another, the weather was stormy. They could see no more than half a mile in front of them because of the thick fog that greeted them most mornings and the snowstorms that plagued the dwindling daylight hours. He'd hoped to spot Stigandr's tower early on the third day. It was always an impressive reveal from that lone spire as the rest of the city slowly came into view. He'd wanted to watch Idonea's wide-eyed appreciation as the city grew before them.

It was not to be. Perhaps it was better the way it happened: they were only a few miles out when the air cleared and Yfirgardr stood before them in all its glory. Even Idonea, with her refusal to acknowledge anything or anyone with more than a disinterested nod, gasped in awe when she saw it. Snow outlined the keep's wall and the rooftops of the homes winding up the hill, and the rising sun stood directly over Stigandr's tower to cast the castle itself in silhouette.

"A proper seat for a kingdom, isn't it?" he asked her, loudly enough that those riding beside them might hear.

"It's very impressive," she assured him. She said it as if she were being gracious with her praise, casting an annoying kernel of doubt on the words.

Havardr sent her a sharp look, and he was gratified to see her flinch. He always enjoyed those slight breaks in her poise, the only proof that she was more than the royal shell she wore. He was the only one who could get those reactions, and he viewed each as another victory.

"Never been conquered. More than most cities can claim," he said with a stony glare, but she'd already recovered. She lowered her gaze and nodded.

"I can see why, Husband. It is a mighty city."

Better.

The nearer they drew, the less of the castle and city they saw, and the more the tent city drew their attention. Havardr's hackles rose as he saw his wife's wrinkled nose at rows upon rows of tents filled with soldiers. It annoyed him so greatly he had to stop looking at her at all. He fumed at the indignity of having to walk through it to get to the city gate. Had he not left all this behind in Fjarriheimr?

It was unfair of him, he knew. The tent city had been erected when he'd called for warriors before heading to Thrireyna, and it had only grown when he'd announced his plans to travel west. Indeed, there appeared to be more permanent hovels of stone closer to the walls, so ugly they weren't much better than the canvas tents. Yet he couldn't reasonably be upset. He'd sent these very men and women back to Yfirgardr months ago: where else would they be if not here?

He was mollified a little as they walked through the camp itself. The soldiers had spotted their approach and had come out of their shabby tents and huts to stand beside the snowy road and greet their returning fellows. They bowed to Havardr as he passed, and some raised cheers, though they had a sickly edge. If they were to sound so terrible, why shout at all? But he smiled and waved at them all, because he must. Leading a successful raid hinged upon convincing the other raiders of your concern for their well-being, whether or not it was true. It took very little attention from a prince to make peasants believe the lie, so he put in the effort when necessary.

Finally, they reached the city gate. Most of the men and women who followed would make it no farther than here. They'd trickle in throughout the day, walking in a long column and no doubt finding the first available spots to clear out snow and set up their own tents. There was nothing for them in the city, not with winter set in and every open room claimed by those wealthy enough to afford them. They would need to claim the best spots while the sun was up or else face pitching a tent in the dark all the way on the shore.

Just inside the gates was the true welcome he deserved: the Council, dressed in their finest, and an honorary escort from the city guard. Tessa was there as well, standing at the head of them in an elk cloak that was rather drab for a warrior of her standing. Why not wolf skin or a bear? And she wore no jewelry and a thin belt that had no buckle, instead tied upon itself to keep her tunic in place. She certainly looked nothing like a regent, except for her posture and upturned nose.

It irked him, though he wasn't sure why. This was rather fitting. She was a warrior, not a leader, and he was glad she hadn't learned to aspire for more while he was gone. But this was a celebration! Could she not have found a gown or at least a better tunic?

"Havardr," she greeted, and everyone in the crowded square bowed to him. All but her. "We welcome you home, both as our prince and as a conquering hero."

Havardr dismounted, glad to be rid of the damn beast—he hated riding and dreadfully missed the comforts of his dreki—and stepped forward with open arms. "Sister," he said amiably. "It is so good to return to Yfirgardr. We've been lacking civilization for some time now. I look forward to the feast you've prepared for my return."

She was stiff as he embraced her, but she'd always been that way. She reminded him of Ragnhild, coming back from Vaettfangkirk harsh and sullen. He released her and clapped her hard on the shoulder.

"Three nights of it," she said. She didn't step back to make room for him, and he wouldn't yield to her, so he stood there a foot away from her and hoped she'd realize her mistake. She didn't. "With dancing and toasts on the third night, to welcome in the new year. There are nobles riding in from their homes to attend and raise their goblets in your honor."

This was good news. He hadn't thought of having a large celebration and inviting more nobility. It was the perfect opportunity to bribe them into committing more soldiers for his next campaign. He could even announce the plans to move against Andiby at the last feast while everyone was in high spirits and thirsting for more.

"Excellent. We—" Something pushed between him and Tessa, and he took a step back in surprise. He was even more shocked to see a large dog sitting before Tessa and looking at him with blue, unblinking eyes. He took another step back as he recalled dozens of similar dogs trailing after Sindri. Sindri's laughter as they chased him playfully. Sandri's merry chatter as he explained their names and their lineage and their training. Sindri—

"You have a dog," he said stupidly. It looked at him knowingly, seeing through him like that pair he'd told Sindri to leave behind on their hunt, as if it knew what he'd done as surely as those ones had known what he was about to do. They'd howled like mad, only shutting up when he'd put them down like their master.

He squeezed his eyes shut, hoping the blackness would chase away his memories. When he opened them, he made sure to look only at Tessa. Thank the spirits, she looked nothing like Sindri.

"As you see," she said. When he didn't respond, she continued. "I'm training her for battle. With your return, I hope to take her hunting, and when spring comes, I'll take her raiding."

They'd had this discussion before on Midreyna. She thought war dogs would've helped them take a village quicker by incapacitating the natives instead of giving them time to mount a resistance. While the battle had resulted in most of the village dead, Havardr didn't think it worth the inconvenience of training, feeding, and housing dogs. He didn't have his mother's aversion to the animals; it was a matter of practicality.

It was also a matter of keeping the past in the past, and his attention fixed on the present. Tessa was so little like her father that it was easy to forget; with a dog trailing behind her, Havardr would be stuck with this living reminder of the only true friend he'd ever had.

"Tessa," he growled. "We've been over this—"

"Oh, it's one dog," she said dismissively, as if that were the end of discussion. Strange. She'd never argued with him before. When had that started? "If she fails to meet expectations, I'll get rid of her."

"But—"

"I trust your exploits were successful to see you return with such a retinue," she said, and he was so thrown off balance that he allowed the change in subject.

He wanted to put his foot down about the dog, but he couldn't without looking petulant. Not that he cared about the stupid beast, but he did care about Tessa's defiance; if he let it go on such a trivial matter, she might think she had leeway to argue on a more important one. This was too public a place to have such a petty argument, and there were much more serious matters on his mind.

"Indeed. We've taken all of Fjarriheimr. Their king surrendered the entire kingdom, and Kerr remains to oversee things until we can come to a more permanent arrangement. This"—he gestured behind him to Idonea, and her ladies scrambled forward to help her dismount—"is my wife Idonea, the former princess of Fjarriheimr."

Tessa's attention shifted to Idonea, her head tilted in curiosity as she took in the other woman. The Councilors behind her chattered excitedly at the news. He knew they would be pleased at having her royal blood strengthen his, especially with the obvious magic in her. That was the only reason he'd allowed her the splendid clothing and jewelry she'd brought with her: she painted the perfect picture of a graceful princess and future queen. And with her quiet, accommodating disposition, she'd be an easier queen to endure than Ingegerd had been. They would like her very much, he knew, and when she bore him children, it would all but seal his claim on the throne. Wherever Stigandr and Ragnhild were, he doubted they had any such partners that would appeal so universally to the people of Hjorrfold.

But though the crowd watched Idonea's approach with eagerness, Tessa's reaction was muted. Her dark eyes were cold and calculating as they took in the princess, roaming from her silvery hair done in careful braids around a circlet, to her thick wool cloak trimmed in white fox fur, down to her leather boots with the pointed toes. After her inspection, Tessa settled back on Idonea's eyes before blinking in boredom and turning back to Havardr.

Havardr wilted at Tessa's disinterest, but then he reminded himself that Tessa was more warrior than noble. She saw the trappings of wealth and royalty as a weakness, because she herself would never be so ill-prepared for battle. Even safely within the city, she had a sword at her belt and looked ready to spring into action at a moment's notice. It was a fitting reaction, and he decided he preferred it. This proved Tessa was better suited for war than court life, precisely as he needed her to be.

"You've won yourself a lovely wife," Tessa said. "She'll have a place of honor at tonight's feast." Then she stepped aside, and everyone else scattered as well to clear the path up the hill. Havardr led the way, with Idonea on his right and Tessa on his left, followed by Hakon with the city guards, and then the Council behind them. The people within the city were more appropriately vocal and cheerful about their prince's return, and he reveled in their adoration. There were no flower petals raining down on them like when they'd returned from Thrireyna, but he hadn't expected any. They'd be wilted, dried, pathetic things, and the citizens seemed determined to make up for the lack with boisterous applause and whistles.

They'd long needed something to celebrate, and he was all too happy to provide it.

"A glorious day for Hjorrfold!" he bellowed again and again.

"Glory to Yfirgardr!" they shouted back, and Havardr couldn't remember being happier.

59
Stigandr

521

STIGANDR MOVED GINGERLY through the streets. He'd more or less recovered, but whenever he used magic, he felt far weaker, and the lingering pain from his injury was more evident. Today he wore a random face, a mishmash of features from the patrons at the tavern where he was staying. Mostly he'd kept to himself and stayed in the Valdis' room—its temporary use gifted to him when she'd departed the city—but today was Havardr's return. Foolish a risk as it might be, he wanted to see it.

It felt like the whole city was lining the roadway from the city gate to the keep, though he knew they weren't. There'd been plenty of people sulking in the tavern when he'd left, complaining about Havardr coveting the throne and taking too many liberties while the king was away.

"Let's hope Alvis returns soon."

"Or one of his other children. Someone with some sense."

"Lady Tessa's got sense."

"Too bad she's not one of Alvis'. We've been in good hands this last year."

"Here here!"

And they'd all raised their mugs.

He wondered, as he found a place in the tight throng of people, how many were here out of curiosity and boredom versus those who were here to congratulate their prince. As Havardr approached, the cheers suggested it was the latter. Stigandr tried not to read too much into it—it was easy to get caught up in the moment with hundreds of others—but it was disheartening. His brother deserved praise for his abilities in battle, but Stigandr couldn't understand cheering for the subjugation of an entire kingdom because of one man's vanity. What had the Fjarriheimr ever done but be their neighbors?

When he turned away in disgust, his attention snagged on a dark-haired boy lurking in a doorway. Stigandr backed out of the crowd and took a long, circuitous route around a couple of buildings. Doubting anyone outside the keep would know Ashk or that he was supposed to have left Yfirgardr, he shifted back into the familiar face. Havardr must be close, based on the swell of noise from the crowd, and he used that to approach the boy unnoticed.

"Egil!" he called over the uproar. The boy turned to him, black eyes finding him instantly. He offered a shy smile and a wave, but then turned back to the procession. Stigandr followed the boy's gaze and saw that Havardr had indeed come into view. He waited a moment, letting Egil take in his prince uninterrupted.

"I haven't seen you in a while," Stigandr said once their view became Havardr's back instead of his smug face, kneeling a bit to be near eye level with the boy. "I was worried."

Egil's eyes were fixed on the retreating forms of Havardr and Tessa. "I wanted to see him for myself," he said, though there was no curiosity or admiration in his tone. He was devoid of feeling, distant in a way Stigandr had never seen before.

"And?" he asked, hopeful to see Egil once again become the mischievous lad looking for a few gold coins. "Does our noble prince meet your expectations?"

Egil's stony gaze slid from Havardr to Stigandr. "He looks exactly like I thought he would," the boy said, with more contempt than the sentiment seemed to warrant.

"A strong warrior?" Stigandr pressed. That was how Havardr had always been described, and Stigandr couldn't deny he looked the part. Regal, strong, and imposing. Dirty-blond hair left to drape over his broad, muscular shoulders, and a well-trimmed beard to show he was no longer the young boy who'd so delighted them with his successful raids decades ago. Charming, if he wanted to be, which was rare; why charm when he could order or take?

He was charming today, Stigandr was loath to admit. His smiles to the crowd had been quite genuine.

"He's not a good man, is he?" the boy said darkly, attention back to the line of soldiers marching by. Havardr and Tessa were out of sight, around a corner for the next group of well-wishers to cheer them on. "My ma never liked him. You hear whispers of what he's done."

Ah, the rumors were taking root then. Good, if people like Egil were listening and believing them.

"You never saw him before?"

Egil shook his head. "Never had much interest in him before."

"I thought all the young lads dreamed of being a great raider like their prince."

"I'd rather be a mage," Egil said. He finally looked at Stigandr, his eyes flitting over his face in a way that made Stigandr worry he'd misarranged the features. "Were you looking for me?"

"I was, actually." He considered how convenient it would be to have Egil take over the graffiti project and then immediately dismissed the idea. It was one thing to put himself at risk, but Stigandr had seen firsthand how dangerous the task was. He couldn't take advantage of a boy desperate for coins like that, especially not with Havardr back. "I'm glad you're safe. These are dangerous times."

Egil snorted. "It's not so bad. We're safe here in the city, anyway."

I wish I had your confidence, he thought, but instead said, "Are you attending one of the feasts?"

A haggard messenger had arrived with but two days' notice of Havardr's impending return and his grand expectations for feasts and revelry to celebrate his victory. Stigandr had worried that Tessa would contrive to kill Havardr in the midst of his celebration, but she'd gone about the preparations as ordered. Hers was not the traditional revenge most in Hjorrfold demanded, a life for a life, or she would've already denounced and challenged Havardr. No, hers was deeper, wishing to ruin Havardr, because she knew nothing would hurt him worse than to lose the throne and see his name sink into shame. There was time yet before she raised a blade against him, and until then she was willing to play the part of a supplicant.

There would be several days of feasting, with the third day the high point and a day of rest mandated throughout the city. As many noble guests as could reasonably travel on such short notice were invited, and more food than could comfortably be given out was prepared. The Council was against such extravagance, and though Tessa in her heart was as well, the missive sent by Havardr had been clear. The only thing Tessa could do was make sure the common folk were able to attend, giving out invitations to as many of the citizenry as possible for one of the three feast nights in the castle.

"No," Egil said, his eyes twinkling. "I sold my spot for three gold coins."

Stigandr was growing light-headed from his overuse of magic, so he patted Egil on the shoulder and said farewell. He needed rest, and lots of it, tucked safely away in Valdis' room, where he could hide without masking his appearance. Havardr's return and his inability to use Ashk's identity anymore had forced their hands.

Prince Stigandr would return to Yfirgardr in three day's time, and he needed to be ready.

LANTERNS LIT THE path up to the keep, and the road had been shoveled clean that morning. Music rang out from the castle walls, and when Stigandr passed through the gate, the whole courtyard was lined with tables. Snow fell in heavy flakes that melted as soon as they landed, but it in no way hampered the merriment of those inside. It was the eve of the new year, after all. What wasn't there to celebrate?

Stigandr stood there and took it all in. His people, happy despite the ruin in the west. Rejoicing as they forgot their cares for a few nights, with the cold realities waiting to pounce upon them once more tomorrow. He wished this night could be as straightforward as it seemed, with everyone's spirits lighter, but all that was about to go up in flames.

"Sir," a guard said. "Do you have your feast token?"

When Stigandr turned at the sound of his voice, he recognized the young man. They'd been on wall duty together, though he might never know it. When their eyes met, the young man reeled.

Stigandr wore the fine mountain lion coat he'd brought from Bjardleith, the spoils of killing a beast who'd been stalking a tribe for months and killing their gatherers. He'd not worn it at all since leaving the mountains, but he'd taken it and some of his princely clothes with him from the keep. His tunic was a thick wool dyed a deep green and trimmed with leather decorated with embroidery stitched with actual silver. His belt bore not only his two daggers, but a silver belt buckle that bore a crown with a lightning bolt.

He was clean-shaven for the first time in ages, with his hair bound low with a tie made from the same leather and silver thread. His breeches were unremarkable, except that they perfectly matched his tunic. Like his cloak, the boots would have drawn attention for their strange design and craftsmanship, made for navigating the narrow, rocky passes of the mountains and not the open plains of Hjorrfold.

But the true elegance to his appearance came in the jewels: garnet and sapphire rings, a golden chain with his mother's compass resting above his heart, and the bright emerald earrings that matched his royal eyes so perfectly.

It'd been many years since he had dressed so splendidly and with an aim to impress. He'd seen his reflection in the small looking glass in Valdis' room and been satisfied he looked sufficiently regal, and that was just from his face. The full effect would be much better.

The guard gulped as he took this all in. "Sir?" he asked with a pleading note, as if he hoped he was wrong in what he saw before him.

Who he saw.

"My apologies, but I have no feast token, and I arrive unexpected. They'll be able to find a place for me, I'm sure."

Paler than the snow, the guard licked his lips and, with a trembling voice, asked, "Your name, sir?"

"Stigandr." He smiled, hoping to put him at ease. "Would you be so kind as to announce my arrival in the Great Hall?"

There was nothing the poor man would've liked less, but he was too in awe to protest. He moved numbly through the feasters in the courtyard, and at the entrance to the Great Hall, he asked one of the guards at the door for their horn. He visibly collected himself, and then, with his shoulders set, he strode into the hall.

The Great Hall was decorated with lanterns, bouquets of dried flowers, and banners from all the noble houses represented by the Council. Stigandr had eaten with the city guard here many times and was used to the crowded tables pressed together; tonight, the tables were pushed to the far walls, leaving the center of the hall open for dancing. A band of musicians was at the very center, with the revelers moving about them with faces lit with laughter and delight.

And at the far end of the hall, right across from them, stood the dais: Havardr on the king's throne, his new bride to his right in their mother's spot, and Tessa in a seat of honor to his left. A long table was in front of them, with some of the elder council members filling up the rest of it. Havardr's cheeks were flushed from drink, and his poor wife looked like she was counting the seconds until she could politely excuse herself.

Tessa, radiant as ever, didn't look any less bored, though she at least possessed a relaxed air that showed her comfort in the space and with the people. He was shocked by her casual ease, given she knew this pleasant evening was about to be turned on its head. It was only through their bond, stronger now than it'd been in their days apart, that he could sense an undercurrent of anticipation radiating through her.

The guard took a few steps into the room, though few noticed him. When he blew the horn, it started as a low rumble that turned heads, but the sound grew to echo through the hall as the music stopped. All eyes were on the guard. It was only those closest that saw Stigandr behind him, and in none did he see any spark of recognition.

"I present," the guard said, each word carrying in the silence, "Stigandr, Prince of Yfirgardr."

Stigandr watched as his brother's head snapped around. Their gazes locked, and he was a ten year old boy again, about to step onto the training pitch to face his brother. His brother, twice his size and skill, and no longer the boy who'd play with Stigandr when it amused him but the man who'd seen his little brother as a threat.

But this wasn't the training pitch. There would be no bruises, no smug words to endure as he wiped sand off his clothes. This was the first time in his life that Stigandr felt he had the upper hand.

"Brother," Stigandr said with a wide smile. "How good of you to arrange a feast for my return!"

"It's not for you," Havardr growled. Then he seemed to remember the crowd watching them intently, because his anger shifted into something stern but almost benign. "It's to celebrate my victory in Fjarriheimr."

"Victory?" he asked with mock surprise. "Were our neighbors under attack? I hadn't realized you'd gone to defend them."

He saw Havardr's wife—her name still a mystery, since none of the gossip about her was so good as to include her name, instead focusing on her strange appearance and how wonderfully lucky she was to marry into such a prestigious line when her own kingdom was in ruin—stiffen at that, her curious auburn eyes turning keenly upon him.

"You have missed much during your ten-year absence," Havardr said. He stood, his enormous frame blocking out the fact that he'd been seated in their father's chair. "You would do well not to make a fool of yourself in front of our good people."

"I have been gone for a while," he conceded. No need to match Havardr's pettiness and point out it had *not* been a decade. He stepped forward, and the crowd parted before him. "Had our parents not sent me so far on such an important task, I would've been here to honor our late mother."

Stigandr watched to see how Havardr reacted at the mention of their mother, but he was frustratingly impassive.

"And that task?" Havardr asked. "What was it?"

Stigandr had reached the dais and looked at his brother, though he didn't feel any smaller for looking up. "Pray tell, where is our father? I'd very much like to discuss it with him."

The hall, despite bursting with people, was so quiet he could hear his pulse thrumming in his ears. He watched a vein on Havardr's neck bulge as he struggled to wrangle in his temper, knowing he was in a delicate situation. Despite his victories, he was no king. Yet he'd been caught red-handed, taking their father's throne and lording over everyone as if he were. He'd gotten away with such liberties before, but he could hardly do so with Stigandr there.

"Stigandr." Havardr's wife pulled his sleeve, urging him to sit. Her velvety voice was soft, but it carried well, and everyone leaned in, as curious as Stigandr to hear her speak. "You are most welcome. We have ample space, especially for my husband's brother."

"You are most generous." Stigandr gave a low bow. "I'm sorry I was too late to attend your wedding, Lady...?"

"Idonea. Princess of Fjarriheimr." She looked askance at Havardr as she said this, as though she was unsure she still had any claim to the title. "And you needn't apologize. We were married in my father's palace, with few in attendance."

"Ah. Is this then to celebrate the union? Is that what my brother meant when he said victory in Fjarriheimr?"

Havardr's hand was around his goblet, as though he meant to hurl it at Stigandr. Stigandr arched an eyebrow at him, daring him. He'd seen plenty of Havardr's tantrums; let the court see one as well.

This time it was Tessa who intervened, drawing attention away from Stigandr. "Your brother should take my seat. I don't know the customs of court, but shouldn't princes take places of honor over all others?"

It was only then that Stigandr allowed himself to look at Tessa. He'd seen her from the doorway, but as soon as his presence was announced, he'd pretended as though she weren't there. This entire performance required him to feign ignorance about a great many things, but he feared he wouldn't be able to hide his feelings when it came to Tessa. As lovely as she was from a distance, she was beauty incarnate up close, her sharp features coming into clear focus.

Stigandr had only ever seen her wear tunics and breeches. As a warrior, that would always be her preference. Tonight she wore a dress with long sleeves that went to her feet, the neckline low enough to reveal her collarbones. The dress was a dark blue that was almost black, and she wore some small pieces of silver jewelry. No belt, no sword, though he spotted the tips of her usual boots poking out beneath the hem of her dress. Her hair was in two long braids that rested over her shoulders.

And those eyes. He adored much about her appearance, but first and foremost were those dark eyes and the depths of feeling they contained.

He wondered if this had been her idea, or if she'd been forced to look like a noble lady for the feast by Havardr. Perhaps it'd been in solidarity with Idonea, who was wearing a dress with material so stiff it looked uncomfortable. Neither lady looked out of place on the dais, but Tessa certainly was more at ease there.

"I'm sorry, my lady," he said, pushing down everything he truly wanted to say to her. "I fear we haven't been introduced."

Havardr tensed. He looked trapped, sitting there between a wife who disdained him and a secret he'd kept hidden for so long. If the stakes weren't the whole of Hjorrfold, Stigandr might have pitied him.

"I'm Tessa of Hundrfeld, daughter of Sindri and ward of your brother, Havardr."

Stigandr raised his eyebrows. He drew on the actual surprise he'd felt when first learning all of this, then turned to his brother. "Sindri had a daughter? I never knew. Is that why he hasn't come to Yfirgardr in so long?"

"My father hasn't come to Yfirgardr because he died twenty years ago," Tessa said, voice as hard as stone.

"Enough of this," Havardr hissed. He meant not to be overheard, but with all ears trained upon them, it was impossible. "We celebrate tonight. Tomorrow, Stigandr can bore us with recounting the details of all he's missed."

"I didn't realize your best friend's death was a boring matter. Twenty years ago…it seems that news should've broken long before my travels. But as you like, we can discuss all these matters tomorrow." He turned his back to Havardr and faced the crowd. "Come! A new year, a wedding, a victory of some sort, and now a returned prince! This is indeed a celebration, so let's have music and drink worthy of it!"

The musicians, who seemed thoroughly relieved to have an excuse to play again, took up their instruments once more and started a lively song. It would do some good in cheering the room and distracting from his arrival, though plenty of heads ducked together and hands went up to shield their whispers. They had decided not to push the people too far so soon—Stigandr's presence was enough to cause gossip—and Tessa was motioning over some servants to arrange for an extra seat to be placed between herself and Havardr.

Stigandr stepped onto the dais and around the table, standing behind her with his hand outstretched. She frowned at him, thrown off by his break from the script.

"Would you like to dance, Tessa of Hundrfeld, daughter of Sindri?"

She stared at him as if he'd grown a second head. There was a lot of incredulity to be read in her unflinching stare, and he was certain she thought it too risky and would turn him down.

Havardr huffed. "Tessa doesn't dance, she's—"

Tessa's hand was in his before Havardr could finish. "I'd love to," she said and followed him to the dance floor. With their hands linked behind their backs, they joined the crowd as they hopped and paraded and twirled around the musicians. Stigandr was years removed from his days of dancing with the nobles who came for the annual festivals. He'd never much cared for it, but he'd done it at his father's insistence, so he knew the steps fairly well. Tessa seemed to have none of her usual grace, stepping on his foot and poorly anticipating which way the crowd would shift next.

"They don't dance in Hundrfeld?" he teased, loud enough that she could hear him over the music.

"They do, but I don't," she grumbled while shooting him a glare. "Unfortunately, Havardr was right. Sometimes, the warriors would dance when they were drunk on mead and victory, but I never joined."

"We'll manage it." Stigandr twirled her a few times, hands on her waist to keep her balanced, then moved them to join the outer circle. It was easier there, where the men and women held hands and circled side to side, backwards and forwards, while the pairs inside did the more complicated dances. Slowly, he felt Tessa's hand relax in his, and her feet seemed to find the rhythm. They went through two, three dances at this slow, easy pace before one of his favorites began.

"Ready?" he asked and saw a look of horror cross her face before he pulled her out of the circle and into the center.

"What? Stigandr, no!" But she allowed herself to be dragged forward. "This is a bad idea, I can't—"

"You can," he assured her. He found a spot amidst the couples closest to the musicians. "It starts easy, I promise."

"Starts?" she asked suspiciously, but it was too late: he guided her through the first part of the dance. He hadn't been lying when he said it started easy, an almost painfully slow beat unlike all the songs before. It would stay that way for three rounds, enough time for all those unfamiliar with the dance to learn the steps, and then would gradually go faster and faster. Those forming the outermost circle of dancers clapped along, with a trio of stomps signalling when the pattern started over. The whole point was to get everyone dancing, and then to humble even the most experienced when the music became too fast for anyone, musician or dancer, to keep up.

By the time they were really going, Tessa was moving as well as any of them. Her cheeks were rosy as she hooked elbows with Stigandr, then the man next to them, clasped hands and spun with the woman behind them, and back to the start. It was Stigandr who tripped first, nearly colliding with another pair on his way to the ground, all because he'd been too mesmerized watching her.

She lasted a few rounds longer, and Stigandr just barely managed to rush in and catch her before she tumbled into a young girl playing the pipes. She was laughing, her braids loose from so much twirling, and he enjoyed having her in his arms as he guided her away from the circle.

"That was wonderful," she said through giggles. "I should have you as a dance partner more often. I might learn."

"You can claim me as a partner as often as you'd like," he said and meant it. They waited with the other spectators as the dance reached its final crescendo, the music more a single note than a melody, the dancers a blur. Those who'd made it that far—two barefoot ladies and a spry older man—finally fell over to everyone's applause and cheers. Servants rushed in with drinks for the band and the fallen dancers, and Stigandr was sure there was nothing better happening anywhere in all the world.

"Let me return you to your keeper," Stigandr said as he took her hand in the crook of his elbow. "How do you think it's going so far?"

He felt more than heard her chuckle. "He's furious, so it must be going well. Look, he's moved you to the far side of Idonea, away from him."

Stigandr turned and met Havardr's calculating glare. "Oh no," he said. "He moved me away from you."

60
Tessa

522

TESSA DIDN'T LIKE her time to be wasted, so she took pains not to waste other's. She strove to be punctual, and didn't initiate small talk unless it was necessary to grease the wheels of favor among the nobles. Today, she was late for the Council meeting. Not to upset the Councilors, but because she wanted to inconvenience Havardr as much as possible in the little ways allowed her. It was a game she'd perfected years ago on Thrireyna.

When she entered the long corridor that connected the private wing to the Great Hall, she was surprised to see many of the Councilors were gathered outside the Council chambers. As she drew nearer, she could sense their unease. They must dread this meeting as much as she did and didn't want to bear the brunt of Havardr's anger without her to shield them.

That was fine; the more they appreciated her, the better.

"Sorry I'm late," she said, because she was sorry to keep them waiting.

"No Reka today?" Lord Birger asked. "I brought snacks for her."

Tessa smiled. "Thank you, my lord, but no. She seemed content by the fire, so I left her in my room." More accurately, Reka couldn't be trusted not to growl or glare unblinkingly at Havardr. That had left Tessa with few options but to keep Reka restricted to the courtyard and her room, so as not to give Havardr reason to reinstate his mother's edict.

Birger sighed. "Such a sweet pup. You know I had one like her when I was a boy. A gift from your grandfather. I couldn't bring her to Yfirgardr, though. She had too much energy, and I couldn't bring myself to deprive her of running through the fields at home."

"You knew my grandfather?" she asked in surprise. She'd heard little mention of her family since leaving Hundrfeld, and still less of anyone save her father.

"Many years ago."

"Enter!" Havardr called angrily from the Council chambers, cutting off any chance Tessa had of inquiring further. She shared a look with the Councilors, then led the way inside.

"Where's Sten?"

Tessa didn't break her stride. "He returned home over a fortnight ago," she said. "His family needed him."

The words seemed to make no sense to Havardr. "He's a warrior. What could they possibly want him for? *I* need him."

You must not need him so very badly, not to notice his absence until now.

"Perhaps to deal with the increased raiders in the outlands," she said as she took a seat across from him. She wouldn't sit next to him if she could help it. "Should we wait for your brother?"

Again, the words might as well have been in ancient runic for all he seemed to understand them.

"What for?" he asked. "This doesn't concern him."

Tessa shrugged, content to leave the idea among the Council and let them mull it over, but to her surprise, it was addressed immediately.

"Matters of state don't concern him?" Lady Gunvor asked, her face severe, and Tessa wanted to order the servants to put two more logs on the fire in thanks. "I saw two queens before your father sit the throne, and I've yet to see his replacement be lawfully chosen. We cannot by rights exclude any member of the royal family from a Council meeting should they wish to attend. If it concerns Hjorrfold, it concerns him as much as it does you. While we fill you in on all the business of your homeland, remember that you are both in the dark as to the events of the past eighteen months, though you by choice and him by order."

"Indeed. We are quite eager to know where he was and why," Lord Orger said more diplomatically. He was a small, portly man who looked a great deal older than he actually was. "He speaks of a task given to him by your illustrious parents, and your father had hinted at such on several occasions. There is much to be discussed by all parties, as we also wish to hear the details of your glorious victory."

This last bit mollified Havardr. "You are welcome to send for him if you wish, but we'll not put our business on hold. We're all here, ready and—"

"You needn't wait on my account." Stigandr strode into the room and took a seat near his brother. Out of arm's reach, Tessa noted, with two people between them. Not at the head of the table, but not so far away as to be out of sight while others addressed Havardr. "I'm here and more than ready to begin."

Seeing the brothers so near each other, Tessa found the slight similarities in their appearance. The same nose, the same upright posture, the same color eyes, though Havardr's were smaller and Stigandr's a touch farther apart. But the differences were more striking: Havardr's hair looked blonder in contrast to Stigandr's chestnut; Havardr's shoulders broader, his hands larger, and his skin more sun-touched; Stigandr's bore laugh lines where Havardr's brow looked like it had born many scowls. Though they looked enough like brothers, it was the contrasts that stood out.

The meeting was tense, though it would've been with or without Stigandr. Havardr wished to talk of his mighty conquest, but only in broad strokes. The spoils and the land, with no recollection of the casualties or the specific homesteads taken. He wanted praise and no more, as evidenced by his disinterest in the news of raiders or disasters, and even less so in the minutia of running the kingdom. Tribute, grain supply, petitions, these were all so beneath him he couldn't be bothered to feign interest as the Councilors took turns reading reports and bringing up their concerns.

But Stigandr was interested.

He listened and asked questions and offered solutions. That the solutions aligned with hers was no accident: they'd discussed many of these same issues. He'd agreed with most of what she'd done as regent, and as he talked through some concerns with the Council, she in turn agreed with much of what he said. Not that she could outwardly show her support. It had always irked her to perform before Havardr, but it had been a single lie then. Her distaste for him ran deep, a weapon she'd kept sharp for years; her feelings for Stigandr were rawer for their being newer, and she hadn't quite learned how to conceal them. She yearned to look at him, to speak to him, but she couldn't afford to.

"You have your father's knack for this," Birger said, then sheepishly looked at Havardr. Havardr glowered but didn't lash out; he treaded dangerous ground with his brother on one side and the Council on the other. He couldn't very well anger the nobility and send them running to Stigandr.

Tessa had hoped Havardr was so foolhardy he might. Alas, he was proving her wrong.

Blushing, Birger cleared his throat and asked, "What state are the troops in? I'm sure they are happy to be back home. Or near enough to home, after Fjarriheimr."

Tessa answered, speaking up for the first time during the meeting. "Dagrun is consulting with the officers to get numbers for supplies and troops." Havardr's brow furrowed, as though he'd once again forgotten who Dagrun was, but he seemed to think it not worth the effort of asking. "Around one thousand soldiers returned with Havardr. Some two hundred had already returned with Sten, though more than half have returned home already. I suspect more will do so once things settle, as there's some six hundred men and women living outside the city walls."

"Will we have enough supplies to feed such an army?" Lady Gunvor asked. "Our larders must have been substantially depleted after the past few days."

"We are fine for the immediate future, but we'll need to ease the burden on Yfirgardr," Tessa said. "Some of the soldiers will need to leave. Soon," she added with a hint of edge.

"Good," Havardr said. "Once those tallies are done, I know exactly where the army will go next."

The room froze, everyone wondering if they'd misheard but knowing they hadn't. It was Stigandr who spoke first, with a judgemental, "Didn't you just get back?"

"Your point?" he snapped. "You needn't concern yourself with matters of battle craft. If we need to make something glow, you'll be the first we call."

Stigandr ignored the barb and aimed his own. "I may be no warrior, but I've seen enough raiders come and go, and even the best among them waited more than three days before planning their next raid."

"You paint yourself a fool to think I made this decision after a mere three days. I've been planning this next conquest since before we left Fjarriheimr."

"So worried about your next slice of cake before you've finished chewing the first," Stigandr said with no venom. He spoke plainly, as if it were a matter of fact, not an accusation. She wondered if this was how it had been between the brothers before her arrival: Havardr easily provoked and Stigandr unimpressed with his older brother. "I see not much has changed."

"Nor have you gotten any smarter. Our enemies know we—"

"Neighbors," Stigandr corrected. "Hjorrfold has no enemies."

Havardr ground his teeth so hard together it was a wonder he didn't break a tooth. Jaw clenched, he said, "They know we have our sights on expanding our territory. The longer we wait, the more they will fortify their borders and gather their own warriors to repel us."

"It's the beginning of winter." Stigandr looked as calm as ever, making him seem a parent dealing with a petulant child. "It would be foolish to start any campaign when we don't know how long the storms will last. We could lose hundreds of men and women, and for what?"

"Bah!" Havardr said with a dismissive wave of his hand. "Only someone who's never had to fight for honor would ask such a question. And all you do is illustrate why it is the perfect time to strike! No one will expect it, and we will break their defenses before they've even erected them."

"All of that is neither here nor there," Odger said. "We cannot spare you, Prince Havardr. Not with the concerns we've put before you, and not with the added confusion of having two princes and no king in Yfirgardr. We should wait until the king has returned before either of you leave the city."

Havardr grinned, as though this was exactly what he wished to hear. "*I* won't be going." He paused here long enough for several to look at each other in confusion. "Tessa will lead the army. She is a skilled warrior and has shown she has a knack for leadership. She will do well against Andiby."

There was a single second of silence as everyone drew breath, and then the room erupted.

"Andiby? They have been nothing but trusted allies since before the first rocks were laid in Yfirgardr!"

"You would send a girl of scarcely twenty years to lead an entire army?"

"Think of those warriors, just arrived home!"

"Andiby? *Andiby?*"

"Your mother would not approve."

"Do we think his father would, either?"

"This is too far—"

"Enough," Stigandr said. He didn't yell, just spoke firmly. It was enough that everyone settled down, though they looked like a clutch of chickens with their feathers ruffled. He turned to his brother, and with the first show of emotion, he asked, "Why are you doing this?"

"It's what needs to be done. I don't answer to you, Brother. When Father returns from mourning, I will gladly discuss it with him. But as it is, the men and women out in those tents swore an oath to me, and to me alone. It's always been my business where I go raiding, and this is no different. I will send them where I see fit, when I see fit, and am perfectly within my rights to do so. If it is such a tremendous concern, I will pay for this campaign out of my own pocket, so that no one can claim I misuse the treasury or our father's name."

Tessa could tell from Stigandr's reaction that Havardr hadn't lied: this was within his capabilities, with or without the Council's blessing. His eyes were pinched as he considered, and Tessa hoped he would find a way to unravel this fool's errand she was about to be sent on. She didn't want to leave, not like this, with so much work left undone.

Alone. Without Stigandr.

"You risk a great deal," Stigandr said. She could hear the strain in his voice. A final gambit. "This is our mother's home. If you are wrong about Father's acquiescence, it'll cost you a great deal of consideration for the throne."

"I think I've earned a fair amount of leeway in the matter, given my previous success."

The Council's heads turned back and forth to watch this verbal sparring.

"You forget to ask Tessa if she wishes this burden of war against an ally so close to her own ancestral home. Hundrfeld would suffer the consequences should she fail and Andiby retaliates."

Havardr shrugged. "It seems to me she'll have more reason to succeed, and more resources to draw from. I'm sure her uncle would give her assistance if need be." When Stigandr continued to glare at him, Havardr turned to Tessa, his first time acknowledging her presence since he'd announced her departure. "Shut him up, would you? Do you want to go?"

No, she didn't. It was too soon. She couldn't reveal her true feelings yet, not until she was ready to strike. If she were to leave, let it be to Hundrfeld and peace, where she might learn to bury the hate in her heart. There would be no such peace for her in Andiby; it would only harden her resolve.

"I go where I'm bidden," she said. It was the only answer she could afford to give.

She didn't look at Stigandr, but she could feel his hurt and frustration at her answer. Had their bond grown again, or was she imagining his reaction? How far from Yfirgardr would their bond stretch before it snapped?

She couldn't think about that.

"You see, it's settled," Havardr said. He bore his smugness the way a fisherman bore his catch of the day, with experienced ease. "Tessa will go within a week's time. Stigandr and I will stay, awaiting our father's return and managing the kingdom with the Council's aid. Within a few months, we should have another victory to celebrate."

"And another people to strip of their freedom," Stigandr mumbled. "When will be the end?"

"It has always been the right of those stronger to take from those weaker. That's the raider's creed. You question the very foundation of our people—"

"We haven't needed to raid for centuries. We have wealth. We have food. It's only been an excuse to kill others and take more than's our due, all while calling it honor. What honor is there in it?" Stigandr looked and sounded truly disgusted.

"What honor?" Havardr balked at the question, and many of the Council members flinched at his raised voice. "You ask what honor there is in proving your skill? In being king of the largest kingdom the world has ever known? You couldn't have better shown you understand nothing of honor."

"Yes," Stigandr said with a mirthless laugh. "I think we've both illustrated quite well what we find honorable."

Everyone sat there, fidgeting in discomfort as the two princes glared at each other. Tessa felt ill.

"If there are no other pressing concerns," Tessa said, "then I hope you will excuse Havardr and myself while we discuss how best to proceed."

Most of the Council looked relieved to be offered a chance to escape. Again, that feeling of hurt struck her as Stigandr excused himself with the rest, muttering about how he clearly wasn't wanted and had much to do. Tessa used the departure as an excuse to look at Stigandr. She only got a view of his back, but she saw the tension in his shoulders and his clenched fists. Hopefully, he would find a way to come to her soon; she couldn't stand it if she didn't get to see him before she left.

In a week. Bjarngrim's mercy.

"My brother is a pest," Havardr said before the door had closed. "I'm glad he didn't arrive before me. He would've been a nuisance for you and the Council to handle without my help."

Tessa made a noncommittal noise.

"You needn't worry about him," he said. "My father will support my claim. And don't concern yourself with Andiby."

"They know no battle magic?" she asked. She had no intention of attacking Andiby, but Havardr's plans might precede her arrival, so best to know what she was facing.

"Pssh. They're all soothsayers who babble nonsense and don't know how to wield so much as a knife, nevermind a sword."

"Will they not foresee us coming?"

"They're not so good at seeing the future as they think they are," Havardr said, a conspiratorial note to his words.

"Your mother was from Andiby. Were her predictions often wrong?"

"Who knows? She never shared them. But she didn't foresee her sickness or sudden death, so what good were her omens, anyway?"

Fair point, she supposed. Worried she'd shown too much interest in matters beyond her concern, she asked about the campaign itself. He had indeed thought through some details: how many troops he planned to send, the path she should take, how long he expected it all to last. She listened attentively and only asked what he expected to hear.

"Who do you wish to bring?" he asked. "I'm sure you have your favorites among the city guard."

"You may pick for me," she said. "I have no favorites, and they're all competent. Whoever it pleases you to send or keep, I won't interfere. I shouldn't take more than half of the guard, though. They're the most familiar with the city and the keep. For the protection of Yfirgardr, you'll want as many as can be spared."

This answer seemed to please him. He sent for a list of the guards and went through at random to identify those he would send with her. She would gladly have taken them all, having trained many of them herself and knowing they were fond and respectful of her. She had no knowledge of the troops living in the tent city, though; she bore no preferences among them and worried they would hold the same indifference towards her. Even among her own staff and servants, she didn't dare show any favoritism lest it cast herself or them in suspicion.

In the end, she'd been given Dagrun and lost Ove. Ove, as so respected an officer among the guard, was indispensable; Dagrun, a mere steward, was deemed replaceable. Tessa counted it as a blessing that she had one of them by her side.

Yet inside, all she could think was, *Stigandr, Stigandr, Stigandr, I want Stigandr with me.*

"Within a week," he reminded her when it was done. "You'd best start packing."

TESSA FOUND HERSELF removed from all her former duties. After three days of festivities, the city was asleep. Well into the afternoon, few sounds drifted up from the city below, and within the keep, most kept to themselves. There would be no petitioners today, and when the Great Hall was opened again, she wouldn't be the one to hear the requests. It would be Havardr or Stigandr or possibly both of them, given how little they seemed willing to concede ground to the other.

In the courtyard, it was so bitterly cold that she couldn't find the will to work with Reka. There were no distractions for her, no tasks to occupy her, so when she left the Council chambers, she had nowhere to go but her room.

Long hours of inactivity didn't suit her, so once she'd arrived, she did the only task left to her: she packed.

From her years at Vaettfangkirk, she'd learned to travel light. There was little she'd been allowed to have with her but clothing and weapons, and she wasn't nostalgic. She didn't need tokens from home to know the place it held in her heart, so she'd long parted with the dolls and gifts from Trond. They awaited her in Hundrfeld; for the first time in four years, she'd be returning there.

She packed a single chest with what she wanted. The clothing best-suited for the harsh winter, with her father's dagger and her belt hidden at the bottom. Some gold and jewels she could sell if in dire straits. The smallest books on magic she could tuck behind a book on Andiby. Her sword, hammer, bow, and shield laid on top. She'd leave everything else—mostly trinkets gifted to her by thankful peasants and bootlicking nobles—and return the other scrolls and books to Stigandr. She'd leave nothing incriminating behind.

As she locked the chest, Reka awoke from her nap. She yawned, attention fixed on the door, and Tessa dreaded who might be visiting. She'd already exhausted her patience with Havardr and had planned to take dinner in her room to avoid him. There was only the faintest of knocks—she questioned whether she'd heard it at all—before the door slipped open and then shut again. She stared at the empty space next to the door, something wrong about it, like there was a shadow there despite the light or like when there's a smudge on the looking glass.

In the next instant, Stigandr was there, filling that strange emptiness. Without thinking, she rushed over to him and into his arms, Reka at her side yipping happily.

"I didn't know I could miss someone so much after only four days," he whispered into her hair. He breathed her in as she did him, his scent sweeter than usual.

She pulled away and held him at arm's length. It was Reka's turn then, as she wedged between them to sniff and rub against him in satisfaction. Apparently, Tessa wasn't the only one who'd missed Stigandr; it never failed to warm her heart when she saw Reka and Stigandr's affection for each other. Aside from loyalty to their masters, the dogs of Hundrfeld had an uncanny ability to sniff out the unworthy. She watched the pair with a lightness in her chest.

He'd been handsome as Ashk, though that was more how he bore himself. After he'd revealed himself as Stigandr, he'd been more attractive, his features more pleasing and his expressions richer. But now he stood before her dressed as a prince and not a common city guard, and he was absolutely striking. Everything from his tunic to his jewelry to the arrangement of his hair was so purposefully done to highlight his eyes, his cheekbones, his height. She'd never minded his beard, but she liked seeing the outline of his jaw. If they'd first met like this, him as his full self, she might've dismissed his worth, since it would be unfair to make someone so handsome and give them other fine qualities as well.

"How's your chest?" She'd been observing him in the few safe moments she could steal, and he seemed fine. But she knew he was adept at concealing himself, and she worried he wasn't as well as he appeared.

"You can barely see a mark anymore. Luckily, raiders don't care for poisoned or enchanted blades, or I'd be a dead man."

The image struck her then. Not a limp, unconscious Stigandr found exhausted in the streets, but a cold, dead one brought to her feet by Sten.

It would've done very little to change Sten's fate, though she would've made it hurt a lot more.

"Try not to get attacked, then," she said, voice thick. "Why did I spend months training with you if you can't even avoid a sword?"

She'd meant it to be teasing, but her words fell flat. Stigandr eyed her sharply. "I don't think I'm the one who needs to be worried about swords."

"You mean in Andiby?" She didn't plan on raising her hammer against his mother's people if it could be helped. Inevitably, she'd use her hammer on this trip, but she hoped it was against raiders or as a show of force. But of all her concerns, her own safety wasn't among them. "Don't worry, I'll be fine. I'll be safer out east than you'll be here in the keep, I dare say. You'll be careful and have guards, won't you?"

His face reddened, and he drew back from her. "I can handle Havardr. Don't change the subject. You're the one going to war."

"I'm not—"

"You should've told him you didn't want to leave," Stigandr said, pacing back and forth in front of the door with Reka watching him curiously. "Especially with winter set in. It's dangerous, and how can we work together with you gone?"

Tessa crossed her arms across her chest, her earlier pleasure at seeing him washed away by his agitation. "Of course I said I'd go." He stopped abruptly and stared at her. "I could hardly refuse, and this is an opportunity I can't ignore."

"An opportunity to what?" he asked incredulously. "To conquer in his name and further aggrandize him among the people?"

Tessa nearly drew back at his tone, but stopped herself. "You're right. Far better to stay here and taunt him during Council meetings like bickering children."

His shoulders sagged. "I admit that wasn't the best way to go about it. But exposing his pettiness and selfishness is a priority."

"But collecting an army isn't?" she shot back. "You wish to take the throne from him, but he'll never give it willingly. You'll have to pry it from his grip, and there's no way to do so with words. We need force, and short of storming his room and killing him right now…"

She paused to gauge Stigandr's reaction. They were on the same page with everything except Havardr's fate. Havardr needed to die, preferably by her hand, or else he would never yield. It was easy for her, who held no fond memories of Havardr to dissuade her. But this was Stigandr's brother, and Stigandr was no warrior, despite how capable he was. When Stigandr didn't speak up, she took it as confirmation of what she already suspected: he didn't want Havardr dead.

"I will go east," Tessa said. "I will take the warriors your brother gives me. I will win them over to our cause, and I will gather as many allies as I can. When I have enough, I'll return."

"I'll go with you—"

She took his hands in hers and held them to her chest. "You can't. No one in Yfirgardr can know we're aligned. If you and I left together, you know your brother would assume the worst, and he'd be right. Besides, you heard the Council. They don't want either of you to leave until the succession is settled. Valdis has already left the city. Hopefully, word will arrive from your father within the month, and it can all be sorted out without me needing to do anything."

"I know, I know." Stigandr pulled their joined hands to his lips and kissed her knuckles. "Even if my father comes... you'll still want to kill Havardr, won't you?"

She pulled her hands away. "He deserves it," she snapped, and she could feel how the words hurt him.

He didn't argue, which was a relief. He might hate her for killing Havardr, but he wouldn't stop her. She would bear his hate, if need be, but she didn't want to go through him to get to his brother. She hoped he wouldn't make her choose between them.

"So it's done," he said, face downcast in resignation. "In a few days, you'll be gone, and I'll be alone."

She pulled him close, so they were chest to chest, their noses knocking together. "You're not alone now, and when I'm gone, know that my heart will still be here with you." She closed the small gap left between them and kissed him. She worried he'd remain stiff and unyielding, his anger getting the better of him, but he sighed and melted into the kiss, an arm at her waist and one tangling in her hair.

"When I'm back..." she said when they broke apart, but he shushed her.

"No more of that. You're right. I'm not alone now. Let's enjoy the time together that we have left." There was a moment when it seemed he might say more; too scared to hear it, she pulled him back for another kiss, and then another.

Epilogue
Stigandr

522

Stigandr stood at the window in his room, watching the army disappear toward the horizon. There'd been a huge send-off in the courtyard, with most of the city guard following Tessa down to the city gate. He hadn't attended. He'd hidden away in the keep and watched from afar, refusing to show his interest to Havardr and hoping his absence would speak to how strongly he opposed this campaign.

Ignoring the chill, he opened the window and leaned out to see the long column of soldiers trudging through the snow. They'd had to wait for a break in the storms, and still they'd needed to send a dozen horses ahead, pushing plows to clear the roadway enough for the soldiers on foot and all the supply wagons. It was ill-advised to depart in winter, but Havardr couldn't be reasoned with.

It hadn't helped that Tessa had seemed eager to go. He knew it wasn't him she fled; rather, she was running toward a plan of action and not away from anything or anyone, but he couldn't help the hurt that coursed through him. He'd had but two nights alone with her since his and Havardr's grand returns, and two nights would never be enough when he wanted them all.

That last night had been so bittersweet. He'd given her the only things he could to help her: a satchel of magical stones and ingredients; his emerald ring with his initials inscribed on the inside; the snowflake from Drusilla; and what little of his mother's ashes the servants had returned to him. They at least had known how much his mother would've hated her funeral pyre and how desperately she'd have wanted to be placed somewhere fixed. They'd also known better than to give the ashes to Havardr: an older servant had approached him with the urn and told him what it held.

"She would've wanted to be laid to rest in Andiby," Stigandr had told Tessa. "It's incredibly important that you take her there."

Tessa hadn't argued, though he could feel her skepticism so much it made his skin itch. Their bond had grown remarkably in such a short time, and he was already mourning it crumbling apart. Its destruction was as inevitable as her departure; he could only hope to reforge it upon her return.

He wasn't the only one with gifts. She had nothing to offer him against Havardr, so she'd given him a lock of her hair, a sentimental gesture that had marred her cheeks with a rare blush. He'd bound it with an ebony ribbon and put it in a locket he wore by his heart under his tunic.

He clutched the locket now, a plain silver circle with no ornamentation and sealed by magic. "Don't die before I see you again," he said when he caught sight of her checking the line of soldiers. Despite the vast distance, he recognized her helmet and her silhouette on horseback.

It was impossible that she'd heard him, bond or not, but he swore she turned his way. He imagined their eyes met, that she knew he was watching; she turned away and continued to ride.

"Luck is made," he whispered, face so frozen he could barely form the words. He didn't shut the window until the very last soldier was out of sight. He smoothed his tunic, wiped tears from the icy wind away, then strode to the door. He had work to do.

Characters & Name Meanings

Alvis *(all wise)*: the King of Hjorrfold

Ase *(goddess)*: Alvis' grandmother, the great-grandmother of Havardr and Stigandr

Ashk *(ash tree)*: a member of the city guard, a disguise of Stigandr

Bergunn *(protection)*: one of the skjaldmaer teachers in Vaettfangkirk

Birger *(keeper)*: a member of the Council

Bjarngrim *(bear shadow)*: the legendary founder of Yfirgardr and Hjorrfold, Havardr and Stigandr's ancestor

Bodil *(penance and fight)*: a dog breeder from Hundrfeld, Valdis' lover

Dagrun *(secret knowledge)*: Tessa's steward in Yfirgardr

dreki *(dragon)*: the warships used by raiders, named for the dragon shape at the prow of a ship

Egil *(awe, terror)*: a young boy living in Yfirgardr

Flekkr *(speck, spot)*: one of Tessa's dogs as a child

Gorm *(he who worships God)*: Alvis' father, Havardr and Stigandr's grandfather

Gunvor *(cautious in war)*: a member of the Council

Halle *(rock)*: Ove's younger brother, he dies on a raid

Hakon *(high sea)*: a raider and friend of Havardr, one of Havardr's generals

Havardr *(high guardian)*: eldest son of Prince Alvis, a warrior and raider

Idonea *(suitable)*: princess and heir of Fjarriheimr

Ingegerd *(enclosure)*: Queen of Hjorrfold and Alvis' wife, a seer originally from Andiby

Ingolf *(wolf)*: Tessa's grandfather

Gudridr *(beautiful god)*: Tessa's grandmother

Jotunn *(giant)*: one of Tessa's dogs as a child

Kerr *(rough ground)*: a raider and friend of Havardr, one of his generals

Knud *(knot)*: Alvis' brother, Havardr and Stigandr's uncle

Odger *(wealth and spear)*: a member of the Council

Ondljosbod *(spirit light festival)*: a festival celebrated in the northeast of Hjorrfold to honor the dead

Ormrdreyri *(snake blood)*: the seer who wrote Havardr's mysterious book of prophecy

Ove *(edge of a sword)*: a raider and member of the city guard in Yfirgardr, his younger brother died on a raid

Ragnhild *(battle, advice, counsel)*: the third child of King Alvis and Queen Ingegerd, a skjaldmaer and warrior

Randel *(high son)*: the fourth and youngest child of King Alvis and Queen Ingegerd, a mage

Reidun *(nest, home)*: Trond's wife

Reka *(wreck; drive, herd)*: a dog from Hundrfeld, Tessa's dog

Sindri *(sparkling)*: Havardr's best friend, father of Tessa and Trond's younger brother

Sixten *(victory stone)*: a noble son training at Yfirgardr, from an island off the coast

skjaldmaer *(shield maiden)*: women trained in Vaettfangkirk, a school for warriors that only accepts women

Sten *(stone)*: a raider and friend of Havardr, one of his generals

Stigandr *(wanderer)*: second oldest child of King Alvis and Queen Ingegerd, a mage

Sune *(son)*: a soldier and Sten's friend

Tessa *(to gather, harvest, reap)*: future Lady of Hundrfeld, daughter of Sindri, a warrior

Thrya *(helpful)*: Alvis' mother, Havardr and Stigandr's grandmother

Torsten *(Thor's stone)*: a soldier and Sten's friend

Trond *(to grow, prosper)*: Lord of Hundrfeld and Tessa's uncle

Valdis *(goddess of the dead)*: a merchant in Yfirgardr who sometimes works for Ove

Viggo *(war)*: a member of the city guard

Locations in Nordastr Herath

Andiby *(spirit village)*: a kingdom that shares Hjorrfold's eastern border, home of Queen Ingegerd

Bjardleith *(mountain path)*: the mountains that line Hjorrfold's northern border, filled with many unconnected tribes and clans

Draugrheimr *(ghost land)*: the land of the dead, where spirits go after someone has died

Eirbjod *(bronze field)*: a keep in the northwestern part of Hjorrfold

Fjarriheimr *(far land)*: the kingdom that shares Hjorrfold's western border

Fyrrey *(first island)*: the most eastern of a trio of islands southwest of Yfirgardr

Hjaeyna *(near island)*: the closest island to Yfirgardr and one of a handful that belong to Hjorrfold

Havareyna *(Havardr island)*: the first island conquered by Havardr

Hjorrfold *(sword fields)*: the largest kingdom in the known world

Hvalreyna *(whale island)*: a keep on an island southeast of Yfirgardr

Hundrfeld *(hound spring)*: a keep in the eastern part of Hjorrfold, known for breeding war dogs, home of Tessa

Leidby *(road village)*: a small homestead to the northwest of Yfirgardr

Lengraey *(farther island)*: the farthest, most western of a trio of islands southwest of Yfirgardr

Marrtoft *(mare town)*: a small homestead to the northwest of Yfirgardr

Midreyna *(middle island)*: the middle of a trio of islands southwest of Yfirgardr

Murthrthorpe *(small fish settlement)*: a village on Hjorrfold's eastern coast

Nordaster Herath *(farthest north country)*: all the lands on the northern coast of the sea

Obygdvollr *(wilderness field)*: a keep in the eastern part of Hjorrfold

Pegjajord *(silent world)*: a mountain sanctuary northwest of Yfirgardr, mourners can pay hefty sums to stay here in silent meditation
Rotby *(root village)*: a small homestead to the northwest of Yfirgardr
Spakonaheim *(witch home)*: an island in the sea with no fixed position, a place of pilgrimage for some mages though few can ever find it
Thrireyna *(three island)*: a trio of large islands southwest of Yfirgardr
Vaettfangkirk *(battlefield church)*: a school for training skjaldmaer
Vittagardr *(enchanted dwelling)*: a keep in the southeast of Hjorrfold
Yfirgardr *(above dwelling)*: the capital of Hjorrfold

About the Author

A. L. Heard is a Pittsburgh-area writer. Her first novel, Hockey Bois, was published in 2021 and she's published several short stories through the indie press Duck Prints Press, where she also contributes as an editor. In between writing projects, she's a teacher, hockey-player, and hockey mom, and spends her weekends visiting local breweries.

Social Media:

Website: http://ashheardwrites.com
Bluesky: @ashheardwrites.bsky.social
Instagram: @ashheardfantasy

Other Titles by A.L. Heard

Hockey Bois: A Beer League Romance
The Trade Deadline
Drop the Gloves
Vampires Don't Play Hockey
The Lady or the Duke? A Victorian Era Decide Your Fate Story

www.ingramcontent.com/pod-product-compliance
Lightning Source LLC
Chambersburg PA
CBHW051934020726
47501CB00001B/117
* 9 7 9 8 9 9 1 1 8 8 1 5 9 *